NEW WRITING 13

Toby Litt is the author of various novels and collections of short stories including *Adventures in Capitalism, Beatniks, Corpsing, deadkidsongs, Exhibitionism, Finding Myself* and, most recently, *Ghost Story*. He is one of the *Granta* twenty Best of Young British Novelists. He lives in London.

Ali Smith was born in Inverness. Her novels are *Like* and *Hotel World*; a new novel, *The Accidental*, was published by Hamish Hamilton in 2005. She has also published three short-story collections, *The Whole Story and Other Stories, Other Stories and Other Stories*, and *Free Love and Other Stories*. She currently lives in Cambridge.

Also available from Picador

New Writing 10

New Writing 11

New Writing 12

NEW WRITING

edited by **Toby Litt** and **Ali Smith**

PICADOR

In association with

First published 2005 by Picador
an imprint of Pan Macmillan Ltd
Pan Macmillan, 20 New Wharf Road, London N1 9RR
Basingstoke and Oxford
Associated companies throughout the world
www.panmacmillan.com

Published in association with the British Council and Arts Council England
http://newwriting.britishcouncil.org

ISBN 0 330 48599 7

Collection copyright © The British Council 2005
Introduction copyright © Toby Litt and Ali Smith 2005

Edited by Toby Litt and Ali Smith
For copyright of contributors see pages 355

9 8 7 6 5 4 3 2

A CIP catalogue record for this book is available from
the British Library.

Typeset by SetSystems Ltd, Saffron Walden, Essex
Printed and bound in Great Britain by
Mackays of Chatham plc, Chatham, Kent

Contents

INTRODUCTION

So, what's new?

The common assumption is that the realm of the new is the playground of the young – or, at least, that it is the young who monopolize all the really fun stuff. There they are, shouting from the very top of the climbing frame, building radical cities in the sandpit. The truth is that the young may equally well be stuck on the accelerating roundabout or hitting repetitive highs and lows on the swings.

Meanwhile, newness is quite a venerable category. There's not much that's new about it. In the 1930s, when a magazine called *New Writing* was first published, it had to compete with *New Signatures*, *New Country*, *New Verse*, the *New Statesman* and *Nation* and *New Theatre*, and what with the *New Woman* of the 1890s and new everything else, even then, new wasn't the new new.

So, here's new writing from Muriel Spark and John Berger and Edwin Morgan, as well as a story by Heloise Shepherd, eighteen and not yet done with university.

If we've achieved diversity, it's because our submissions were themselves diverse; and the final selection is representative of the proportion of short stories to novel extracts, poems and essays that were submitted.

We read our way through the unsolicited submissions alphabetically, by surname. Our first reaction, in each case, was given (via email) without knowing the other editor's reaction. Our only criterion with each and every piece was whether it worked for both of us. It was surprising – though reassuring – that we agreed 95 per cent of the time, and were able to compromise within seconds on much of the remainder.

The most popular form by far was the short story. This is

probably explained by there being, at the moment, so few outlets for shorter prose fiction. In the end though, as we read through the large stack of manuscripts, we began to believe that somewhere out there is a strange, pseudo-English country called Short-Story-Land where all day long, peculiarly short-story-like things happen. We began to dread starting a story only to find we were once again in Short-Story-Land.

It's worth pointing out: a lot of what was submitted was dauntingly undaring. On the whole the submissions from women were disappointingly domestic, the opposite of risk-taking – as if too many women writers have been injected with a special drug that keeps them dulled, good, saying the right thing, aping the right shape, and melancholy at doing it, depressed as hell. Thank god for the writers here, then, who refute this strange trend; to name just a few – Nicola Barker's understanding of the strangeness of social structure, Frances Gapper's pier-end eccentricity, Kamila Shamsie's visceral force, Susan Irvine's good aggressiveness of form, Monique Roffey's theatrical panache.

We have opted, throughout, for writing that renews language itself, or battles with the old shapes of things. What this book reveals, most interestingly, is a generation of, yes, young male writers who have gleefully ignored Short-Story-Land and all its dutifulness: Peter Hobbs, Martin Ouvry, James Hopkin, Steven Hall, Tim Jarvis. Writers not so in love with realism; writers keen to ditch the -ism.

With novel extracts, we have tried to choose the sections that work in and of themselves – though it is hard to imagine the reader that wouldn't want immediately to keep reading the new novels of Shyam Selvadurai, Kate Atkinson and Nicola Barker, all briefly excerpted here.

Essays and other non-fictional writing were the rarest submissions, but the two we've included, from Lawrence Norfolk and Paul Bailey, have themes remarkably in common.

Much contemporary poetry, judging from our submissions, seems insecure about its validity as poetry. In order to justify its existence, it will build upon non-fictional information: histories, biographies, secondary sources of all sorts. Many poems have the tone of 'and here's another interesting and little known fact'. The madly visionary, the harshly satirical, the straightforwardly funny – all these modes seem out of use.

One of the most interesting poets we read is Ismail B. Garba, who undermines notions of poetic originality by taking originals as templates (Sylvia Plath's 'Poppies in October', for example) and grafting different words onto their recognisable syntaxes and rhythmic structures. Being unoriginal, in his case, leads to something more inventive and innovative than the 'sincere' emotions of many other people who submitted work to us.

Originality is only proven over time, paradoxically. We are confident that some of the names here you've never heard before will become very familiar. They may even disgrace themselves by winning prizes, becoming established, etc. But they'll be the kinds of writer, like the known names published here, for whom everything they write is a renewal – of language, of place, of the senses and of the contemporary.

Toby Litt
Ali Smith

Muriel Spark

Authors' Ghosts

I think that authors' ghosts creep back
Nightly to haunt the sleeping shelves
And find the books they wrote.
Those authors put final, semi-final touches,
Sometimes whole paragraphs.

Whole pages are added, rewritten, revised,
So deeply by night those authors employ
Themselves with those old books of theirs.

How otherwise
Explain the fact that maybe after years
Have passed, the reader
Picks up the book – But was it like that?
I don't remember this . . . Where
Did this ending come from?
I recall quite another.

Oh yes, it has been tampered with
No doubt about it –
The author's very touch is here, there and there,
Where it wasn't before, and
What's more, something's missing –
I could have sworn . . .

Niall Griffiths

Adrenalin

At first I don't recognize him cos he looks so bloody *healthy* and it's only when he grins and comes over to my table and starts talking that I'm convinced it's him. Andy, old Andy the Nurse. He looks so *well*. I'm amazed. This is the man who usually causes you pain just to look at him, all his protruding bones and compost skin and dental pandemonium and nicotine-orange eyes, but here he is, head held high, muscle on his bones, his voice projected and confident and not his usual death-rattle croak. I'm shocked.

Jesus, Andy, I interrupt him. What's happened to *you*?

He looks down at himself and smiles. Aye, I look all right, don't I?

I nod. How come?

He leans closer, over the table: I've found it, man.

Found what?

The wonder drug, he whispers. The friggin elixir of existence.

Yeh? And what's that, well?

I'll tell you. Just let me get a drink. You having one?

Nah. I point at my nearly full pint of Guinness. I'm OK for the mo.

I watch him go to the bar, which is rammed, three-deep, but he just kind of elbows his way through the crush without actually touching anybody. The huddle just kind of parts for him, as if he has a forcefield, or even just some kind of charisma which, to tell the truth, he's never had before. I can hardly believe this. I'm shocked at the transformation. Flabbergasted. From zombie junkie to *this* in less than two weeks. Last time I saw him he was begging for spare change outside Boots dressed in rags with a stink coming off him in visible wavy lines and it's difficult to reconcile that vision of wretchedness with the filled-out, cleaned-up, smart-shirt-wearing *glowing* figure returning from the bar with a beaming smile and a pineapple juice. Something's going on here. What is it?

That pure juice, Andy?

Yep. He sits and sips.

No vodka? Just pineapple juice?

He nods and grins and I take a sip and sure enough there's no alcohol burn at the back of my throat, none at all.

I *told* you.

How did this happen, Andy? This is weird, it's friggin Arthur C. Clarke stuff. Can't get me head round this. Tell me what this wonder drug is quick cos I could do with some meself.

A shout goes up from the bar. A goal must've been scored or something. I'm not particularly interested today.

I'm aware of my belly hanging over my belt. I'm aware of my boy boobs beneath the baggy fleece I wear to conceal them. Andy looks so *healthy*.

You gunner tell me, well?

I'm trying to think of a way to explain it . . .

I light a Lambert and offer him the pack and he shakes his head.

You're not gunner tell me you've given up smoking as well, are you?

He smiles again and nods. Even his usually snaggled teeth seem to have straightened themselves out, whitened too. His eyes sparkle. The skin on his face is zit free and without the maroon lace of broken veins that used to make it look like raw sausage. His lips aren't dry and cracked. He just radiates health and clean living, but Christ, this is Andy here, Andy the Nurse who got sacked for raiding the pharmaceuticals cupboard in the hospital and who treated his body like a bin for years, so much so that once when he went for an AIDS test the doctor said that he was virus free but that he had toxic blood. That his blood in any other lifeform would kill it as quickly and surely as battery acid. But look at him now, though; he *hums* with health. The air around him seems to throb with his well-being. I ask again, How did this happen, Andy?

He shrugs and crunches ice. Just cleaned meself up, that's all. Sorted meself out.

What, in two weeks?

Another shrug.

Bollox. You were a walking corpse, man. Last time I saw you you were more dead than alive. And what's this fuckin wonder drug, eh? What's that?

Again a collective yell from the bar. There's a TV screen facing me high up on the wall but I can't take my eyes off Andy. He *shines*. He is in peak condition.

Remember that girl I was seeing? Michelle?

The one with the blonde hair?

He nods. I remember Michelle; a half-rotted corpse in a Marilyn Monroe wig.

Yeh, well, she OD'd. A too-pure batch came in straight off the docks and that was it. She jacked up, carked it in seconds. I was in the kitchen cooking up, like, and when I went back in the room there she was on the bed all blue. Stiff as a board as well. I slapped her a few times, threw some water on her, like, but there was nowt I could do, really. She was too far gone, *well* over the other side. Plus I was enjoying my own high too much to let anything spoil it like so. . . . He catches my eye. Aye, I know what you're thinking. But that's heroin, eh? Bad, bad drug, man. No good for anything. I *know* that now.

So that's it, then; this wonder drug of Andy's is death. Someone else's death. A brush with the blackness can prompt you into sorting yourself out in no time at all. I'm about to ask him what he did with the body but he goes on.

One time years ago, when I was a med student like, I used to attend autopsies as part of the course. And one time there was this lad, a young lad, who'd OD'd. It was explained to us that the panic and terror of his death had caused his body to pump out huge amounts of adrenalin and that this could be seen in his swollen glands, the suprarenal capsules, situated just above the kidneys.

A collective groan from the bar. I can feel acids leaking between my inner organs, hear them gurgle; too much stout and not enough solid food in the past two days, probably. Andy isn't looking at me now, he's staring down into his juice. There is moisture on his lower lip. His healthy sheen is all of a sudden looking a bit plasticky. Too white. His voice drops.

And there they were, his endocrine glands. Stuffed full, man. Enough adrenin and epiphrenin to keep this entire city high for weeks. Pure biological adrenalin; best, most powerful drug known to man. And it's right *here*.

He looks at my face now and points at my belly, just below my ribcage. I suck my paunch in.

It's in *you*. It's in all of us. Every day your body produces bottles of this stuff and you don't even know it. Makes heroin seem like a sherbet dib-dab. Most powerful psychoactive substance *ever* and each and every one of us can manufacture it, every hour, even when we're asleep. Incredible, innit?

I nod, but I'm somewhat disappointed; I thought Andy was going to outline some amazing discovery, some blinding revelation, but all it is is the usual clichéd crap of the recently cleaned-up; 'oh, yeh, adrenalin, man, best drug in the world'. In a minute he'll start advising me to climb a mountain and 'get high on *life*, man'. What a let-down. No wonder he's beginning to look *too* shiny, *too* healthy; he's like one of those fake-tan bleached-blonde sillycone-tit things you see on stuff like *Buywatch*. It's all false. It's fake.

Time I was somewhere else, I think.

Well I'm glad you've cleaned up and all that Andy but I—

I watched her for ages, he says. Michelle, like. Just sat on the edge of the bed with me brain in the clouds, like, and just watched her being dead.

His voice has gone all low again, low and small. Dropped gaze, too. His body may have sorted itself out, like, but it's clear that his head hasn't followed suit. It's cracked a bit. Which is what staring at the carcass of your dead missis will do for you, eh? That, and several years of prolonged drug abuse.

Match over and the bar's emptying out now, streams of half-pissed people heading for the doors. I'll join them. I stand and start putting on my coat.

She had a bayonet in the flat. One of her junkie mates, ex-squaddie, he gave it to her as a present. For her own protection, like. Said if anyone ever came through her window at night then she had something to stick 'em with. She kept it under the bed.

My coat's hanging off one arm. I'm sitting down again. Andy's voice is quiet but so is the pub now and I can hear every word he's saying with perfect clarity.

I came down, like. Off the drug. Nowt in the flat, no money, nothing. Didn't quite know what I was doing . . .

What?

Just kind of on automatic pilot, like, I was . . .

What did you do, Andy?

He delves with his fingers in his glass and extracts the orange slice and puts it in his mouth and swallows it, peel and pith and all. The sheen of his face . . . how false it looks now. Like make-up. Like if you rubbed it with your finger powder would come off and the decayed state of his face would be revealed.

God, you should've seen them. Gorgeous, they were. Like tennis balls, man, so full . . . swollen, like, cos of the fear. The panic and terror as she died. Thought it might pop as I stuck me spike in like but it didn't, it was fine. So I sucked up a barrel full. Looked like weak tea it did, kind of orangey coloured. And the *hit*, man, Jesus Christ . . . like hanging off a mountain top by my fingernails for twenty minutes. Thought I was gunner cark it myself. But *now*, tho . . .

He looks up at me with a great big grin. His teeth are so *white*. So *long*. His eyes are so *blue*. He spreads his arms and says, Look at me. I'm *buzzing*.

Sick, sick bastard. He's lost it. He's flipped out. I'm getting miles away from him.

Where you going?

Away.

Why? I was just about to get a round in. What you having?

Nothing from you.

Why? What have I done?

You're a fucking murderer.

She OD'd!

An accessory, well.

Rubbish.

You cut her open! You chopped her up! You butchered her

body just so's you could get another hit! Sick bastard! You're a fucking—

He's leering. With them sparkling eyes and that white, white grin he's leaning over the table and leering at me.

Oh yeh, that's right . . . go on . . . get yourself worked up . . . get yourself *excited* for me . . .

Fuck off, Andy. You're ill. You're twisted.

I stand and he stands with me, then starts laughing. Laughing loud.

What's so funny?

It's a *joke*, lad! I made it up! It's all a big joke! Got you going 'n' all, didn't it?

He's really laughing. He's finding something genuinely amusing here.

So Michelle's not dead?

He shakes his head.

Where is she then?

He shrugs. Dunno. Dumped her two weeks ago. Dragging me down, she was. Becoming a liability.

He's smiling, beaming. He looks so *good*.

So what about this? This . . . change, like? How come you look so healthy?

The adrenalin, man, the adrenalin in *me*. The stuff that my body produces. The adrenalin *inside* me from my own glands. Just had my first shag in ages, y'see. Works wonders.

He stands there smiling at me across the table. I can see his chest rise and fall. See his eyes all skittery. There is something inside him. Definitely; he has *something* at work inside him.

So what are you drinking, then? Same again, yeh?

Stale inch of warm Guinness in the bottom of my glass. Too heavy, that stuff. It's got me all bloated.

Martini, I say. Dry, loads of ice. Splash of lemonade.

Andy tweaks my nose and laughs again and goes to the bar. His hand smells of honeysuckle soap. No *way* he can look that good in such short time . . . no *way* just getting laid can have that effect. It's not possible. There's something going on here. He has something inside him.

He walks, no, *struts* to the now empty bar, back straight,

chest out, proud, almost graceful. He leans against the bar with one hip cocked and that position creates a bulge at his left side, between pelvis and ribcage, a large bulge clearly visible beneath the clean fabric of his new shirt. It is shaped like a small loaf. I wonder if it would taste like one. I haven't eaten in some time.

Nicola Barker

Darkmans

[novel extract]

To all intents and purposes, Daniel Beede was a model citizen. So much so, in fact, that in 1983 he had been awarded the Freedom of the Borough as a direct consequence of his tireless work in charitable and community projects during the previous two decades.

He was Ashford born and bred; a true denizen of a town which had always – but especially in recent years – been a landmark in social and physical reinvention. Ashford was a through town, an ancient turnpike (to Maidstone, to Hythe, to Faversham, to Romney, to Canterbury), a geographical plug hole, a place of passing and fording (Ash-*ford*, formerly *Essetesford*, the Eshe being a tributary of the river Stour).

Yet in recent years Beede had been in the unenviable position of finding his own home increasingly unrecognizable to him (*Change*; My *God*! He woke up, deep in the night, and could no longer locate himself. Even the blankets felt different – the quality of light through his window – the *air*). Worse still, Beede currently considered himself to be one of the few individuals in this now flourishing 'Borough of Opportunity' (current population c.102 000) to have been washed up and spat out by the recent boom.

Prior to his time (why not call it a life sentence?) in the hospital laundry, Beede had worked – initially at ground level (exploiting his naval training), then later, in a much loftier capacity – for *Sealink* (the ferry people), and had subsequently become a significant figure at *Mid Kent Water plc*; suppliers of over 36 million gallons of H_2O, daily, to an area of almost 800 square miles.

If you wanted to get specific about it (and Beede always got specific) his life and his career had been irreparably blighted by the arrival of the Channel Tunnel; more specifically, by the eleventh hour re-routing of the new Folkestone terminal's access road from the north to the south of the tiny, nondescript Kentish village of Newington (where Beede's maternal grandmother had once lived) in 1986.

Rather surprisingly, the Chunnel hadn't initially been what you might call Beede's political *bête noire*. He'd always been studiously phlegmatic about its imminence. The prospect of its arrival had informed (and seasoned) his own childhood in the same way that it had informed both his parents' and his grandparents' before them (as early as the brief *Peace of Amiens*, Napoleon was approached by Albert Mathieu-Favier – a mining engineer from northern France – who planned to dig out two paved and vaulted passages between Folkestone and Cap Gris Nez; one, a road tunnel, lit by oil lamps and ventilated by iron chimneys, the second, to run underneath it, for drainage. This was way back in 1802. The subsequent story of the tunnel had been a long and emotionally exhausting tale spanning two centuries and several generations; an epic narrative with countless dead ends, low points, disasters and casualties. Daniel Beede – and he himself was the first to admit this – was merely one of these).

Politically, *ideologically*, Beede had generally been of a moderate bent, but at heart he was still basically progressive. And he'd always believed in the philosophy of 'a little and often', which – by and large – had worked well for him.

Yes, of course – on the environmental brief – he'd been passingly concerned about the loss of the rare spider orchid (the site of the proposed Folkestone terminal was one of the few places it flourished, nationally), and not forgetting the currently endangered great crested newt, which Beede remembered catching as a boy in local cuts and streams with his simple but robust combination of a small mesh net and marmalade jar.

And yes, he was well aware – more, perhaps, than anybody – of what the true (and potentially devastating) implications of a channel link would be on the Kentish shipping industry (a loss of around 20,000 jobs was, at that time, the popular estimate).

And yes, *yes*, he had even harboured serious fears – and quite correctly, as it later transpired – that many of the employment opportunities on the project would pass over local people (at that point Ashford had one of the highest unemployment rates in the country) to benefit non-indigenes, foreign investors and foreign businesses.

It went without saying that the Chunnel (now a source of such unalloyed national complacency and pride) had caused huge headaches – and terrible heartache – in east Kent, but Beede's greatest betrayal had been on a much smaller, more informal, more *abstract* level.

Beede's maternal grandmother's home had been a neat, quaint, unpretentious little cottage (pottery sink, tile floors, outside lavvy) in the middle of a symmetrical facade of five known as Church Cottages. They were located at the conjunction of the old School Road and Newington's main, central thoroughfare the Street (no shop, no pub, twenty-five houses, at a push). Much as their name implies, Church Cottages enjoyed a close physical proximity with Newington's twelfth-century church and its similarly ancient – and much-feted – graveyard Yew.

Beede's paternal grandparents (to whom he was slightly less close) also lived locally; several hundred yards north up the aforementioned Street, in the neighbouring village of Peene. Just so long as any inhabitant of either of these two tiny Kentish villages could remember, they had considered themselves a single community.

When the developers' plans for the new Folkestone terminal were initially proposed, however, it quickly became apparent that all this was soon about to change. Several farms and properties (not least, the many charming, if ramshackle homes in the idiosyncratic Kentish hamlet of Danton Pinch) were to be sacrificed to the terminal approach and concourse, not to mention over 500 acres of prime farmland and woodland, as well as all remaining evidence of the old Elham Valley Railway (built in 1884, disused since 1947). But worse still, the access road from the terminal to the M20 was due to cut a wide path straight between Newington and Peene, thereby cruelly separating them, forever.

Beede's maternal grandmother and paternal grandparents

were now long gone. Beede's mother had died of breast cancer in 1982. His part-senile father now lived with Beede's older brother further west along the south coast, just outside Hastings.

Beede's parents had moved to the heart of Ashford (fourteen miles away) two years before he was even conceived, but Beede maintained a lively interest in their old stamping ground; still visited it regularly, had many contacts among the local rotary and cricket clubs (the cricket grounds were yet another Chunnel casualty), friends and relatives in both of the affected villages, and a strong sense – however fallacious – that the union of these two places (like the union of his two parents) was a critical – almost a *physical* – part of his own identity.

They could not be divided.

It was early in the spring of 1984 when he first became aware of *Eurotunnel*'s plans. Beede was a well-seasoned campaigner and local prime mover. His involvement was significant. His opinions mattered. And he was by no means the only dynamic party with a keen interest in this affair. There were countless others who felt equally strongly, not least (it soon transpired) Shepway District Council. On closer inspection of the proposed scheme, the council had become alarmed by the idea that this divisive 'northern access route' might actively discourage disembarking Chunnel traffic from travelling to Dover, Folkestone or Hythe (Shepway's business heartland) by feeding it straight on to the M20 (and subsequently straight on to London). The ramifications of this decision were perceived as being potentially catastrophic for the local business and tourist trades.

A complaint was duly lodged. The relevant government committee (where the buck ultimately stopped) weighed up the various options on offer and then quietly turned a blind eye to them. But the fight was by no means over. In response, the council, Beede, and many residents of Newington and Peene got together and threatened a concerted policy of non-cooperation with *Eurotunnel* if a newly posited scheme known as 'The Shepway Alternative' (a scheme still very much in its infancy) wasn't to be considered as a serious contender.

In the face of such widespread opposition the committee reassessed the facts and – in a glorious blaze of publicity – backed down. The decision was overturned, and the new southern access route became a reality.

This small but hard-won victory might've been an end to the Newington story. But it wasn't. Because now (it suddenly transpired) there were to be *other* casualties, as a direct consequence of this hard-won alternative. And they would be rather more severe and destructive than had been initially apprehended.

To keep their villages unified, Newington and Peene had sacrificed a clutch of beautiful, ancient properties (hitherto unaffected by the terminal scheme) which stood directly in the path of the newly proposed southern link with the A20 and the terminal. One of these was the grand Victorian vicarage, known as the Grange, with its adjacent coach house (now an independent dwelling). Another, the magnificent, mid-sixteenth-century farmhouse known as Stone Farm. Yet another, the historic water mill (now non-functioning, but recently renovated and lovingly inhabited, with its own stable block) known as Mill House.

Beede wasn't naive. He knew only too well how the end of one drama could sometimes feed directly into the start of another. And so it was with the advent of what soon became known as 'The Newington Hit List'. Oh the uproar! The sense of local betrayal! The media posturing and ranting! The archaeological *chaos* engendered by this eleventh-hour re routing! And Beede (who hadn't, quite frankly, really considered all of these lesser implications – *Mid Kent Water plc* didn't run itself, after all) found himself involved (didn't he owe the condemned properties that much, at least?) in a crazy miasma of high-level negotiations, conservation plans, archaeological investigations and restoration schemes in a last-ditch attempt to rectify the environmental devastation which (let's face it) he himself had partially engendered.

Eurotunnel had promised to dismantle and re-erect any property (or part of a property) that was considered to be of real historical significance. The old Grange and its coach house were not 'historical' enough for inclusion in this scheme and were duly bulldozed. Thankfully some of the other properties did meet

Eurotunnel's high specifications. Beede's particular involvement was with Mill House, which – it soon transpired – had been mentioned in the Doomsday Book and had a precious, eighteenth-century timber frame.

The time for talking was over. Beede put his money where his mouth was. He shut up and pulled on his overalls. And it was hard graft: dirty, heavy, time-consuming work (every tile numbered and categorized, every brick, every beam), but this didn't weaken Beede's resolve (his resolve was legendary. Beede gave definition to the phrase 'a stickler').

He was committed. And he was not a quitter. Early mornings, evenings, weekends, he toiled tirelessly alongside a group of other volunteers (many of them from Canterbury's *Archaeological Trust*), slowly, painstakingly, stripping away the mill's modern exterior and (like a deathly coven of master pathologists) uncovering its ancient skeleton below.

It wasn't all plain sailing. At some point (and who could remember when, exactly?) it became distressingly apparent that recent 'improvements' to the newer parts of Mill House had seriously endangered the older structure's integrity.

Now hang on –
Just . . . just back up a second –
What are you saying here, exactly?

The worst-case scenario? That the old mill might never be able to function independently in its eighteenth-century guise; like a conjoined twin, it might only really be able to exist as a small part of its former whole.

But the life support on the newer part had already been switched off (they'd turned it off themselves, hadn't they? And with such care, such tenderness), so gradually – as the weeks passed, the months – the team found themselves in the unenviable position of standing helplessly by and watching – with a mounting sense of desolation – as the older part's heartbeat grew steadily weaker and weaker. Until one day, finally, it just stopped.

They had all worked so hard, and with such pride and enthusiasm. But for what? An exhausted Beede staggered back from the dirt and the rubble (a little later than the others, perhaps; his legendary resolve still inappropriately firm) shaking his head, barely comprehending, wiping a red-dust-engrained hand across a moist, over-exerted face. Marking himself. But there was no point in his warpainting. He was alone. The fight was over. It was lost.

And the worst part? He now knew the internal mechanisms of that old mill as well as he knew the undulations of his own ribcage. He had crushed his face into its dirty crevices. He had filled his nails with its sawdust. He had pushed his ear up against the past and had sensed the ancient breath held within it. He had gripped the liver of history and had felt it squelching in his hand –

Expanding –
Struggling –

So what now? What now? What to tell the others? How to make sense of it all? How to rationalize? Worse still, how to face the reams of encroaching construction workers in their bright yellow TML uniforms, with their big schemes and tons of concrete, with their impatient cranes and their diggers?

Beede had given plenty in his forty-odd years. But now (he pinched himself. *Shit.* He felt *nothing*) he had given too much. He had found his limit. He had reached it and he had overstepped it. He was engulfed by disappointment. Slam-dunked by it. He could hardly *breathe*, he felt it so strongly. His whole body ached with the pain of it. He was so stressed – felt it so *invested* in his thwarted physicality – that he actually thought he might be developing some kind of fatal disease. Pieces of him stopped functioning. He was *broken*.

And then, just when things seemed like they couldn't get any worse –

Oh God! The day the bulldozers came! He'd skipped work. They'd tried to keep him offsite. There was an ugly scuffle. But he saw it! He stood and watched – three men struggling to restrain him – he stood and he watched – jaw slack, mouth wide, gasping – as History was unceremoniously gutted and then steam-rollered. He saw History die! He saw it die!

– just when things seemed like they were hitting rock bottom –

You need a holiday. A good rest. You aren't dying, but you are absolutely exhausted. Dangerously exhausted; mentally, physically . . .

– things took one further, inexorable, downward spiral.

The salvageable parts of the mill had been taken into storage by *Eurotunnel*. One of the most valuable parts being its ancient Kent peg tiles –

That, at least, was something.

Then one day they simply disappeared.

They had been preserved. They had been maintained. They had been entrusted. They had been *lost*.

BUT WHERE THE FUCK ARE THEY? WHERE DID THEY GO? WHERE? WHERE?!

It had all been in vain. And nobody really cared (it later transpired, or if they did, they stopped caring, eventually – they *had* to, to survive it) except for Beede – who hadn't really cared that much in the first place – but who had done something bold, something decisive, something out of the ordinary; *Beede*; who had committed himself, had become embroiled, then engrossed, then utterly preoccupied, then thoroughly –

Irredeemably

– fucked up and casually (like the past itself) discarded.

And no, in the great scheme of things, it didn't amount to very much. Just some old beams, some rotten masonry, some traditional tiles. But Beede suddenly found that he'd lost not only those tiles, but his own rudimentary supports. His *faith*. The roof of Beede's confidence had been lifted and had blown clean away. His optimism. He had lost it. It just *went*.

And nothing – *nothing* – had felt the same, afterwards. Nothing had felt comfortable. Nothing fitted. A full fifteen years had passed, and yet – and at complete variance with the cliché – for Beede, time had been anything but a great healer.

Progress, *modernity* (all now dirty words in Beede's vocabulary) had kicked him squarely in the balls. I mean he hadn't asked for much, had he? He'd sacrificed the spider orchid, hadn't he? A familiar geography? He'd only wanted, out of *respect*, to salvage . . . to salvage . . .

What?

A semblance of what had been? Or was it just a question of . . . was it just *form*? Something as silly, something as apparently marginal as . . . as *good manners*?

There had been one too many compromises. He knew that much for certain. The buck had needed to stop and it never had. It'd never stopped. So Beede had put on his own brakes and he had stopped. The compromise culture became his anathema. He had shed his former skin (*Mr Moderate, Mr Handy, Mr Reasonable*) and had blossomed into an absolutist. But on his own terms. And in the daintiest of ways. And very quietly –

Ssshhh!

Oh no, no, *no*, the war wasn't over –

Ssshhh!

Beede was still fighting (mainly in whispers), it was just that – by and large – they were battles that nobody else knew about. Only Beede. Only he knew. But it was a hard campaign; a fierce, long, difficult campaign. And as with all major military strategies, there were gains and there were losses.

Beede was now sixty-one years of age, and he was his own

walking wounded. He was a shadow of his former self. His past idealism had deserted him. And somehow – along the way – he had lost interest in almost everything (in work, in family), but he had maintained an interest in one thing: he had maintained an interest in that old mill.

He had become a detective. A bloodhound. He had sniffed out clues. He had discovered things; stories, alibis, weaknesses, inconsistencies. He had weighed up the facts and drawn his conclusions. But he had bided his time (time was the one thing he had plenty of – no rush; that was the modern disease – no *need* to rush).

Then finally (at last) he had apportioned blame. With no apparent emotion, he had put names to faces (hunting, finding, assessing, gauging). And like Death he had lifted his scythe, and had kept it lifted; waiting for his own judgement to fall; holding his breath – like an ancient yogi or a Pacific pearl diver; like the still before the storm, like a suspended wave: freeze-framed, *poised*. He held and he held. He even (and this was the wonderful, the crazy, the hideous part) found a terrible *equilibrium* in holding.

Beede was the vengeful tsunami of history.

But even the venerable could not hold indefinitely.

Ciaran Carson

Two Eugenio Montale translations

The Lemon Trees

Listen: the poets laureate
walk only among plants
with precious names, like box, acanthus, privet.
Me, I love the streets that fade
to grassy ditches, where from arid puddles
young lads scoop
a few emaciated eels:
tracks that wind along the slopes
and slither downwards through the tufted canes
to lose themselves among the lemon groves.

Better if the yakking of the birds
be suffocated, swallowed by the blue:
it's easier to hear the whispering
of friendly branches in the almost breathless air,
to breathe this odour
grounded in the earth, that drills
its sweet disturbing rain into our breasts.
Here, by a miracle, the war
of thwarted passions is assuaged,
here even we poor folk are dealt our share of riches,
which is the fragrance of the lemon trees.

See, in these silences where things
resign themselves and seem
about to yield their final secret,
sometimes we feel we're on the verge
of stumbling on a fault in Nature,
the still pivot of the world, the untenable link,

the thread which, disentangled, might at last
direct us to a central truth.
The eye delves,
the mind investigates aligns divorces
in this perfume that contrives to bloom
when day is most lethargic.
Silences where one can see
in every fleeting human shade
some wandering Divinity.

But the illusion wanes and time returns us
to an urban hubbub where the blue
appears in patches only, high among the rooftops.
Rain falls bleakly on the earth then;
winter tedium weighs on the house,
the light grows miserly, the soul embittered.
Till one day through an ill-shut gateway
from a tree-filled close
the lemons burst out in a blaze of yellow
and the ice in the heart melts
and we are smitten to the core
by arias pelted forth
from golden horns of elemental sun.

Ballad Written in a Hospital

For Neil Belton

In the slough of the emergency:

when beyond the mountains
August fired its deranged comet
through the still tranquil air—

but darkness, for us, and terror,
bridges and pavilions raining
down on us, ensepulchred like Jonah
in the belly of the whale –

and when I turned, my mirror
told me I was not the same, since you
from chest to throat had been
encased with one fell swoop
in a plaster bust.

Deep in your eyes
the tears shone lenses
thicker than your oversized
tortoiseshell glasses
I remove at night and place beside
the vials of morphine.

Not ours the bull-god, but
the God who sparks
the lilies of the ditch:
I summoned Aries, and
the horned beast's spoor
engulfed whatever pride I'd left, this heart
racked by your cough.

I wait for a sign that the hour
of final rapture is upon us:
I am ready, now that penance
is initiated in this sullen wailing
from the hills and vales
of the *other* Emergency.

You kept on your bedside table
the wooden bulldog by the clock
whose little phosphorescent lances
cast a dim illumination
on your half-sleep,

the nothingness that will suffice
for those who want to force the narrow gate;
and, outside, being hoisted high,
a cross unfurls its red on white.

With you I turn to face the voice
that breaks into the dawn, the enormous
presence of the dead; and the howl

of the wooden dog is my own, unutterable.

Lawrence Norfolk

The Words on the Page and the Noise in My Head

Part One

Making coffee and smoking are good ways to waste time. Reconfiguring the computer, sharpening pencils and answering emails are better. Phone calls to one's agent rate high but best of all is *deciding what to put on the stereo . . .*

One can write to certain kinds of music; others not. But which? And why? These are troublesome questions for writers. Noisy rock music and avant-garde contemporary classical music seem to share the necessary quality, which is a certain structurelessness: a 'looseness' which lets the listening writer drift in and out of full attention, or to snap in and out of it as the slower internal mental dialogue that produces words comes up with something worth recording, or abandons that process and relapses into some less conscious mode of production. You tune in and out, not listening and then listening again, or seeming to (seeming to yourself, that is). Music is the thing that allows you to fool yourself that you are working, that you are not 'failing to come up with something'. Something has to fill those dustbowl moments (and minutes, and hours). Against the sterility of over-focused concentration, music maintains a certain level of attention, functioning as a sump into which unproductive brain power can be drained off. You switch on, and you switch off, and you find similarly stable states at all points between these two. You're fooling yourself, but happily. Music pulls you out of your own dead ends.

There are kinds of music which are good for this and there are kinds of music which are no good. Beethoven is no good. The

Hammerklavier Sonata will not take you anywhere other than where it itself wants to go. You can take it or you can leave it, but nothing in between. Its claims on your attention are absolute and to tune out during, say, the theme's first stretto in the largo means that by the time you are ready to rejoin the music, a dozen or so fugues later, it has inexplicably turned into an unlistenable noise. (Nietzsche is unhelpful but succinct: 'Beethoven's music is about music'.)

This claim on your attention can take other forms. Melodiousness can be quite as coercive. Lennon and McCartney were the masters of making quite long melodic lines sound very simple, which is the trick at the heart of 'catchiness'. I don't think anyone has ever constructed a good sentence while listening to 'Norwegian Wood' because while there may be little to think about in 'Norwegian Wood', you do have to listen to it. A song you can't get out of your head is a liability and an impediment, if you write books. Of course, if you write songs, it's a big house in Surrey.

This is not an argument for bad music being the midwife of good novels. Music which offers a flexible claim on one's attention is not weak; on the contrary it's all the more resilient for still functioning as music whether you've clamped a pair of speakers to your head or are half-listening from the kitchen where you are primarily engaged in making coffee. Brian Eno's *Music for Airports* is not the model I have in mind.

The trouble with this operation is its location: the inside of one's head. That implies that you can confer this resilient quality on any piece of music, that there's a dial you can twist. That's not true. Some kinds of music can do this and others cannot. This quality – or its lack – is intrinsic to the music.

Part Two

Timbre is why a middle C blown on a trumpet is not the same as a middle C struck on a piano. It's why instruments sound different. If you express a note as a wave, its length determines pitch, its height determines volume, and its shape determines timbre. A perfect sine wave will be heard as a pure note, a pure sound. An electronic oscillator can produce that timbre, but all other instruments produce mixed sounds, made up of the note plus its overtones.

As an example, middle C, or any other note, will produce the same note one octave higher, then the fifth, then the same note again but two octaves higher, then the third, the next octave, and then the minor seventh. The minor seventh is actually flattened very slightly (by a sixth of a note) for reasons which are not well understood. And the series continues, sub-dividing the preceding note's frequency by one half, into those frequencies which only dogs can hear. So middle C actually produces a higher C, the G of that octave, a higher C again, the E of that octave, a higher C again, the B flat of that octave (slightly flattened), and so on. If you strike a bell you can hear some of these overtones quite clearly, but most are almost inaudible, and those which can be heard usually (but not always) become quieter as the progression moves higher in pitch. Several notes played in the lower register of the flute cannot be distinguished from the same notes played on a violin because the harmonics produced by both coincide almost exactly but this is rare. Instruments sound different because they produce their harmonics at relatively different volumes. Their sound profiles are different. The colloquial term for this is 'colour'.

In addition, every instrument also has its peculiar attack transients (the kind of sound made by the particular way in which the note and its harmonics are generated: a string being bowed, a trumpet tongued, a piano string struck) and decay transients (the sounds made as the note and its harmonics die away). Lastly, there are 'edge tones', which are the sounds produced by the initial stream of air striking a sharp edge, such as the reed, which then go on to propagate a steady-state oscillation in the air column (of an oboe, for example). The time it takes for this steady-state oscillation to establish itself and thus for a 'true' note to be played is called the 'transient time'. Each instrument has a different time and human listeners are very sensitive to their relative speeds. There are also important inharmonicities (produced for example by the bass strings of a piano) and some rather raucous dissonances are produced by that part of the bell of a trumpet, tuba, or horn of any kind whose 'flare' exceeds in angle a regular cone (the applied physics of this is quite complicated). Open tubes, or air columns, will produce all the harmonics (i.e. nearly all wind instruments) whereas effectively closed ones (the clarinet) will only produce the odd-numbered harmonics. The same dynamic means that, looked at a certain way, a clarinet actually plays its clarinettist rather than the other way around.

The point of all this is that acoustic instruments do not just sound *different*. They sound *very different*, and the wide variations between their different timbres means that the sound (not necessarily the music) is complex. This complex sound is constantly surprising and disruptive of itself. It does not admit of an easy mode of listening and so, for the purposes of novel writing, orchestral music is out. Whenever Mahler's Ninth Symphony is happening, it is the *only* thing happening.

There are composers, of course, who organize their work so intricately (Ligeti) or so loosely (Takemitsu) that the uneducated ear (mine e.g.) hears it only as a particular kind of noise. One can work to this. This mis-listening is productive but hard to apply to rock music. Each rock band has a 'sound', a set of tropes which function rather like the distinguishing harmonics among the orchestral instruments, and, in each case, it is by and large always the same sound.

The instruments in a guitar band have very similar timbres. There is a marked difference between the sound of a Fender guitar and a Gibson guitar, but it's nothing to the difference between a trombone and a triangle. This makes it quite hard to produce a sound which is obviously 'wrong' (the most original-sounding bands are those which approach 'wrongness' the closest, but without reaching it). Most other instruments used by rock bands, or R 'n' B bands, are reduced to the role of percussion (the brass in James Brown's arrangements) or emphasizing the melody. They have no independent voice: the vocals supply that. It could be argued that the instruments in a rock band exist as a life-support machine for the singer.

It could also be argued, with reference to historical examples (Clapton, Hendrix), that the lead guitar can take the singer's role. But, finally, most electric guitars sound quite similar, there is a definite limit to the number of twenty-minute solos you can listen to, and it takes a very high level of technique to play the electric guitar well enough to rival the human voice. Very few rock musicians come anywhere near the technical standard of a classical musician. Also, Hendrix and Clapton didn't just play. They sang as well. Eddie Van Halen was probably the last musician to attempt guitar-heroism seriously.

So we're back with the voice, or with different voices, and so with different kinds of singers: shouters, droners, screamers, talkers, growlers, mumblers, and Bjørk. Bjørk is classically trained, like Nina Simone, but most rock singers are not trained and have quite a limited range of pitch. Robert Plant can sing a few octaves but Bob Dylan has been losing a note a year since the mid-sixties and Lou Reed has only ever had two. The narrow range of the singer's voice corresponds to the narrow timbre of the instruments and once put together these two make the kind of sound that one can work to. The fact that nearly all rock music is both rhythmic and repetitive makes it easier still, but I think the characteristic sound of certain kinds of rock music is the crucial factor. All the action happens in a narrow band of sound. That is a provisional answer to the question 'What?'

Part Three

The question 'Why?' takes one into less comfortable territory. Why listen to anything when you're writing?

I outlined an image of the writer as see-sawing between the text in front of him – the text he is supposed to be writing – and the music around him, which absorbs any attention not focused on the writing. One oscillates between these two, but one's total absorption, be it in the music or the text, or any one of their admixtures, remains constant.

The question 'Why music?' remains. Why not have the TV on? Or the radio?

The answer depends, I believe, on the fact that writers have a peculiarly vexed relationship with music in general, and with rock music in particular. The *person* who happens to be a writer probably likes, or loves, rock music, but the *part of that person* which does the writing hears rock music as a kind of taunt, because rock music is everything that writing is not. Rock music is ecstatic and spontaneous in style, self-generative in elaboration, and communal in performance. Writing is laboured and cramped, eked out word by word, and consumed in private. Rock musicians play their keyboards: writers type on theirs. Rock musicians – some of them – move, which makes it harder to play the instruments but easier to make music because rock music is made with the whole body. There have been surprisingly long periods in the history of rock music when it was possible to refer (unironically) to an electric guitar as an 'axe'.

I don't think writers envy rock musicians their face-to-face engagement with the audience, nor even the series of mutual confirmations which pass from stage to arena and back again ('Hello Boston!' Boston cheers, etc.), the anticipatory applause (always louder at the beginning of a well-known track than at the end), nor the fake ritual of the encore.

What writers envy is the facility of rock musicians, how they seem to simply become the music that they play and how their excitements and excesses seem to enrich their music in an unproblematic way. If you can just become the right person and reach a high enough pitch of energy, so it seems, then the music will follow. Hendrix was a musician not only to his fingertips but even his teeth.

It's an illusion, of course. Part of the act. The songs have been composed, the performance rehearsed. But writers cannot even manage a semblance of such artistic nonchalance. You're always the wrong person and in the wrong frame of mind. Writing is always difficult. Jack Kerouac fed a roll of wallpaper into his typewriter, hammered keys for forty-eight hours, and the result (iconically enough) was *On the Road*. No one mentions the two-year-long writer's block which preceded that outpouring. Writing is not physical, hence the macho over-compensations of Hemingway and Mailer, of Saint-Exupéry and Hugo.

But sometimes – very rarely – the writing goes right. It flows. It stops and starts, but those halts and resumptions have a rhythm which accords with the sentences unfolding on the page in front of you. It comes out right first time and one's fingers have trouble getting the words down fast enough. For a few brief beats, you the writer can believe in 'You the Writer Reimagined as Rock Musician'. Sometimes life is easy. But very rarely.

Nearly always, good writing is the product of self-restraint, narrow concentration and obsessiveness. The act of composition is delicate; it cannot survive in the environment in which rock music is made. A writer letting it all hang out is, usually, unreadable. A reader (or more often a critic) sensing 'joy' in a piece of prose is reading his own emotions, not those of the writer. The production of good writing is never a good experience, never 'fun'.

But rock music looks like 'fun'. The full identification between the music, its performance, and its reception – the thing that happens between rock musicians and their audience. That's in stark contrast to the ceaseless and neurotic monitoring of the writer's distance from his characters and story, the writer's pernicketiness and basic dissatisfaction. I'm not arguing that writers want to have fun. If they did, then they would not have chosen to become writers. But they – we – sense something lacking. This.

Trace rock music back to its roots, through white American rock and roll and black American blues, from Chicago to the spirituals of the Mississippi Delta, back through the songs carried over on the slave ships from the west African coast, and what one finds is gangs of people gathered together for the purpose of making an enjoyable rhythmic noise.

Now trace literature back, through the novel and the romance, through the epic and dramatic traditions to fifth-century Athens and earlier when the chorus was led by a man with a stick which he would thump on the ground to keep time for those chanting the lines of the comedy or the tragedy, and what one finds is . . . gangs of people gathered together for the purpose of making an enjoyable rhythmic noise.

The first ever stadium gig took place in Greece more than two and a half millennia ago. In our own century the Russian poet Yevgeny Yevtushenko and the children's author J. K. Rowling have pulled crowds of 20,000 or more . . . But no one else has. The *performance* of literature, which is to say the continuance of its ancient link to the practice of song, is all but dead. How many now would rather go to a Günther Grass reading than a U2 concert?

The preference marks a split. Rock music still stirs the same emotions that Aristotle wrote about when analysing the feelings stirred by Greek tragedy. People still gather for the purpose of making an enjoyable rhythmic noise. Instead of a man banging the ground with a stick there is a man banging a very expensive drum kit with two sticks. Instead of Yoruba cult masks and Athenian dramatic masks, one has Bob Dylan circa 1968 in white face paint, or John Cale in an ice hockey face guard, or Gene Simmons. And beyond that is the full panoply of a rock musician's 'image'.

On the other side of this split, I think literature is better than rock music. It is more penetrating in its critiques and more fitted for the world in which we find ourselves. There is almost no limit to the kinds of things you can say in a novel. That is not true of a three-minute pop song. But literature has lost its music and with it that immediate appeal to the senses which music – all music – retains. Those who practise literature, those who write, feel that loss keenly. Its pathology is convoluted and its symptoms contradictory. I listen to rock music because I like it . . . I only wish it was as simple as that. I've put Jimi Hendrix and David Byrne of the Talking Heads in my novels. Have they ever invited me on stage, d'you suppose?

Jackie Kay

Husky

The voice of the husky in the snow
was hoarse, packed with loss
like snow that never melts.

Paw prints that the wind blew
over, an old love letter,
fierce, ice-tight, blast.

If you'd never started out
wishing in the white, white snow,
you'd never be here now, howling, lost.

Martin Ouvry

Narcissus

Loping down Venus Hill in the direction of the city, stylish and late, and stirring with my rhythms the blood of a new idea, I was disturbed to find, standing at a bus stop, a girl I'd shared a house with the previous year. Not that I disliked her, but I didn't want to get sucked in when I'd only just set out. So I stopped (of course) and we said our How's-it-goings, and I explained that I was late, and she said 'Thought you might be somehow;' then we said our See-you-arounds, and without inquiring whether the house was still as bad, or had she found a better one, I headed off – I had to – kicking myself for being such a White Rabbit when the girl's dissolving face said *Stay*.

The thing was this: Zelda, with impeccable timing, had rung me twenty minutes before the film was going to start. I'll never make it in less than twenty-five, I told her – ten to get my shit together and fifteen to get down there. What I didn't say was that I had just had a vision, a glistening statue of a poem, a thing I wanted to catch and hone before it slipped back into the ether, which would probably take me all night.

'But we *have* to go tonight,' Zel said. 'I've just turned down a dinner invitation – *in fact that's their taxi leaving now.*'

Despite my doubts about Zel's taxi story, I gave in and made it with time to spare. Easing my way into the crowded foyer, I spied her in the ticket queue scanning the heads with her dark, damaged eyes, and I hung back, re-reading her, enjoying how she was outside of me. She was total, like East meeting West, in that home-made skirt of printed cloth cleverly wrapped and pinned, her hair still damp and falling straight, and long, and black, like an epic, the *Rubaiyat* or an Iliad.

Thinking made me want her, so I went to her in the queue, and when she saw me she smiled, and we kissed. 'Hi, babe,' she said. 'You made it then.' She knew I'd got there as quickly as I could, and she wasn't complaining – not now, not even as a joke.

Into the café-bar then, a vaulted hall between the theatre and a church, for a last-minute cigarette and Coke; but the bar was three-deep, and we looked at each other like 'Fuck that for a laugh, let's hit the circle while we can still get decent seats.' So up we went, and I handed our tickets to the usher, who said her Anywhere-you-like, and I slipped the torn halves in my pocket.

'It's nice to have a real date instead of being together the whole time, isn't it?' Zel whispered as the lights went down and the stars came out. I turned to her and smiled, and said 'Yes, very nice,' and we held hands in the constellated dark.

The film was scary, funny, sad. It was about cities, and people growing up in them skint and on the dole; it was about friendship and love and violence, and drinking and doing drugs to forget that you have nothing and can't see any future; it was about turning to crime because that might give you one. We clung to each other in the darkness, and squeezed each other's hand through the tragic bits, like when the four of them are fixing in the bombed-out flat while the baby crawls around them, and like when its mother's screaming hysterically, and you know why she's gone crazy but knowing isn't enough, they're going to show you her baby anyway, dead in its cot, dead from the smoke maybe. And when you see that, the fear and pity rise up inside and hit you on their way out, and Zel and I squeezed each other white, the way a baby bites your knuckle to communicate the pain and to make it go away.

Winding downstairs afterwards, the whole theatre was subdued, and there was as much thinking as talking, singly and as one. Zel suggested a drink in that artless way she has, which humbles me and brings me down to earth. 'Yes,' I said, 'I could do with one,' so we went back into the bar. I queued for a while and bought the drinks while Zel sat at a table watching me order and looking at the people in the busy room and getting looks from most of them.

'You know the last time we were here?'

I put the pint and a half on the table.

'Valentine's Day, *Breakfast at Tiffany's*,' I said, pulling a face. Pleased with that, Zel swapped her frown for a smile that said our fight in the restaurant afterwards was just another memory now, and time had done its work.

We lit cigarettes and sipped our drinks, face to face across the planks. While Zel talked about her cousins, parents, sisters and brother, and Leeds and India and job hunting in London, I glanced across the room, amused at the way these boys were checking her out. They would eye her up, then look away, ashamed whenever I caught them; you could tell they were desperate not to look again, but Zelda's irresistible and they were drawn to her like dogs.

'—can't wait to see her,' she was saying.

She was talking about her cousin, whose parents had emigrated to Canada. They were back in her home town on holiday.

'You do know I'm going home, Ed? I'm going to put it to my aunt that I stay with them in Vancouver, maybe get a job out there. Even something voluntary in a good museum or gallery would stand me in good stead for later on. And even if it turns out to be just a holiday, I need to do something, I've been feeling so down lately. You do think it's a good idea? Ed?'

Sitting there with Zel, I felt male and proud and a little bit cruel watching those lads check her out; but I was also beginning to get uptight. Not because of them: it was me. I was only half there with that beautiful girl; the thing from before had stolen back my head, the statue, my creation, invisible to all but me, among yet not among us, uncurling in the cradle of its infancy . . .

Pause in the lane at the gate before the house. Tall, silent, stranger-dark, the place lowers down. And up there in the roof, in my lonely attic room, in the mind, the soul of the house, there it will be, supple and beautiful, the muscular form of a new beginning, turning in its sleep in the lap of Venus, waiting for me – and me alone – like a promise and a betrayal.

*

Disturbed by my silence, Zelda looked down and lit up.

'—Yes; I think going to Canada would be good for you, Zel. But I think if you were out there for any length of time you probably wouldn't come back. The standard of living is higher, the people are more laid back. You'd find a job, move out of your aunt's—'

'Of course I'll come back. Hey.'

She reached across the table and put a hand on my arm. 'Don't worry, babe. But I need some time away from my parents, that's all, put some space between us – like a few thousand miles! You know what they're like: my job at the gallery isn't a *real* job, I'm too thin, my clothes are ratty, too tight, too short, too young. They think they're getting me ready to be *looked at*, that's why I'd be going.'

'You'd still be with family, Zel. Your parents would know exactly what you were up to.'

'But they'd have to ping to the fact that I've got a life. I'm sure it would be good for me, aren't you?'

The beer was tasting better and better. I drank the rest quickly and stared down through the crusts. How vulnerable she seemed to me then, when she needed me. The question in her face sought words of encouragement, signs of reassurance, but her need snagged my higher thoughts and staunched their natural flow.

'Yes, it would be exciting,' I managed. 'And a definite confidence boost. Try and suss it out this week. —How's the cider going down? Fancy another?'

'Um . . . OK.' A flutter of disquiet above her dark, damaged eyes. 'But let's go for dinner after that? Pizza's only a fiver each.'

'Sure.'

I felt poor and wanted to drink. I pushed back my chair along the boards, stood up and went to the bar.

How will it go? Pass a hand through the gate and lift the latch. Before me, the house. And under the eaves, up in the gods, the athlete, my creation, paragon of euphony and rhythm, wrestling the shadow of its unborn brother in the flood of lamp and smoke.

I mount the steps and face the door. The key. The bolt. I step into the hall.

'You really don't want to go for dinner, do you, Ed?' Zelda looked disconsolate as I slid her cider across. I forced a bright note. 'There's the rest of that bolognese at mine. Shall we do that instead? Needs eating.'

'OK,' she smiled. So sweet, she would always defer to a louder voice, a stronger conviction than her own. 'Go back via mine? I'll need to pick up some things if we're going to stay at yours.'

But of course she'd agreed. Hadn't dinner been a feint, a ruse, to stay with me that night and break our resolution to spend more time apart? We'd had it with living together out of sheer lack of funds; both of us needed more space. Then why had I not told her that all I wanted to do that night was climb the ladder to my attic room, where the Velux tilts and the smoke whips up, then rushes away down the surface of the glass, deep into the lung-pools of the night? That all I craved was to witness with my lead that golden form emerging from the flood?

Then I would feast. Then I would truly eat.

'To be honest, Zel, I'm really not hungry. If you want to go out let's go to the Hyperbowl: have a dance, couple of drinks, maybe score some dope?'

If I couldn't eat then I would drink. The good beer in that café-bar was filling me up with song, and if I couldn't be alone in the ballads of a gypsy soul then maybe I never could. I craved performance now, to be back in that room with those shabby old duffers crashing around on the landlord's mouldy sofas among beer bottles, sweet sherry, harps and guitars, strung out and howling of loss.

'Oh, Ed, not the Hyperbowl. What's on anyway? It's gay night, isn't it?'

'Well, mixed – you know: girls who like boys who like boys who meet girls . . .'

'I've got to be at work really early tomorrow, clear my desk before I leave for Leeds. And anyway we can't afford it. I'm *hungry*. If you don't want to go back to yours then I'll have a sandwich at mine.'

The barmaid called time. As Zel put on her cardigan, I looked to give those dog-boys one more stare. But they had gone.

'Sorry, Zel?'

'Don't worry. I'll have a sandwich. Walk me home?'

As the sky's frayed hem belled out above the city, we wound our way through narrow lanes below the market square, hand in hand in silence, slacking neither for pub nor church, and climbed the footbridge above the ring road where the houses have been stripped away and the city starts to fade to the skirts of Nowheresville.

'So what did you think of the film?' I tried.

'The film? I liked it. I'm sorry Ed, I'm feeling a bit brain-dead tonight. I've had a shit day at work and I'm not up to anatomizing.'

Down past the cathedral now, our footsteps ringing from the walls, those white stones heaped towards an unstarred sky a rhetoric of Dominion. Above us the moon, full and huge. By the time we reached Zel's it would be dark.

'Ed?' she began, a faint reed in the open. 'You don't mind me talking about my family, do you?'

The door clicks shut. I move down the hall enfolded in the night, towards the staircase, towards my brilliant idea. One hand on the newel post, one foot on the stair.

'No, of course not. I should know about your family.'

But why, when she wasn't coming back?

'What made them choose Canada?'

'Oh, various things. My uncle wasn't working and a job came up out there.'

'Mm. And what made your parents leave India, d'you know?'

'Yeah. Same sort of reasons: good cheap schools, the NHS. They were planning a big family, four or five kids.'

Hand on the stair rail polished by a century of touch. One . . . two . . .

'You see, that's what gets me about their attitude towards you and your sisters—'

. . . three . . . four . . .

'—They come here 'cause it's an easier option in terms of raising a family, then they want you lot to conform to the ways of the old country—'

. . . five . . . six . . . seven . . .

'—What you and your sister are doing, the English life you have, is kind of like a payback maybe—'

. . . eight . . . nine . . .

'—A moral whatdyoucallit—'

. . . ten . . . eleven . . . twelve . . .

'—An oblique fulfilment of the fairy-tale wish.'

. . . thirteen. Thirteen stairs.

Eyes bright with street lamps and resentment, Zelda glared. Tearing her hand from mine, she stamped off down the pavement, tossing her head as though to shake the insult from her face. All evening she'd been fine, and I had made her angry.

'Why must everything always look like an easy option to you! Nothing's been easy! They've been paying from the start! And look at the English when they live abroad, hoarding their relics of Little England!'

'I agree a hundred per cent. But face it, Zel, that's how your parents are thinking when they plan to have you looked at.'

'Yeah. And how you're thinking when you go on about poetry.'

That was an ignorant phrase, 'easier option'; and to read Zel's parents' emigration as a story of illusory goals and inevitable disappointment had been mean; but the thought had formed and the words slipped out, 'cause while I climbed the ladder to my lonely attic room, lured by the imminence of solitude, I'd left some laddish quarter of my brain unpoliced, and its joyriders had lost no time in driving the decent citizens of Zelda's thoughts out of their peaceful home.

Head down and walking fast she crossed the road, putting a stream of cars between us.

I caught her on the next corner. Touched her shoulder. 'Zel?'

'Don't talk to me. You don't know how my parents think.'

'It was just an idea.'

'I'm sick of your ideas. Get away from me.'

'I'm walking you home.'

'Leave me alone. I don't want to see you any more. I don't want you anywhere near me.'

We'd been here or hereabouts before: as far as her parents' Sikhism went, we could both make a case for the old ways and the new. Surely that wasn't it. No; it wasn't what I'd said to Zel that was the issue so much as what I had not: in my mind was the promise of another love, and soon I would betray her.

Even before I rounded the yard wall, I heard her, banging around the cupboards in the narrow kitchen. I sidled past her turned back and went into the sitting room. I'd forgotten she was hungry. I fixed my eyes on the dark TV – my TV – knowing Zel was watching me and knew what I meant by it, the threat it was. I began to roll a cigarette ready for the blast, but still her words shocked me when they came.

'OK you can go now.'

So parched they held no sustenance.

'I'm going,' I said, not moving but watching Zel's flatmate emerge from her bedroom wearing only a long T-shirt. Yawning and stretching, the way some people do when they walk in on an atmosphere (you cough, maybe, or hum some hook, to get the place breathing), the girl braved our silence and went to the kitchen. She said hi to Zel, got no response, and came back with three gin and tonics. She sat in the armchair and we tasted our drinks, and the taste in our mouths got us talking. Zel got jealous: she came in from the kitchen, picked up the *Guardian* and read with all her might, and seethed, and didn't drink.

In every lull in the conversation we shrank at the force of Zel's reading, and soon her flatmate got the message and went back to her room and shut the door. I looked at my hands and concentrated on rolling one to tide me home. Smoothing the licked edge down, I raised my eyes to tell Zel I was going, but the words stuck in my amazement at what she had become. She was standing back-lighted in the connecting doorway, hands on hips, her head angled somewhere between seduction and reproach. Her smile was saying, 'OK, you can stay – I do want you here and I know you know it.' But I knew something more, had for hours and maybe longer: I was going home.

'I'm going now.'

'No,' she said, the magic gone, the mask transformed again. 'Don't go. Please stay. I need you. Just tonight. Stay. Please.'

She came to me across the room, took my hands, pulled me down onto the sofa (the rug slid off the back as we crash-landed), and she fixed me with her dark, damaged eyes. 'Just tonight, Ed. Please.'

'No. I'm not staying.' I was tired of all this flying to extremes and determined to stick to our resolution, even if it was that, and not what I'd said about her parents, which had made her angry in the first place.

'I'm going home. Tomorrow. Tomorrow we'll stay together. Don't worry, Zel, I'm only round the corner. It's not as if I'm leaving you.' And seeing that nothing she could do would change my mind, she said, 'Go then. I'm going to bed. I don't want to see you any more.'

'I'll let myself out,' I said quietly as she went upstairs. Then I picked up her untouched glass, sat in the armchair, and drank.

A sadness came over me. Zel had tried to compromise and still had come off worst. Maybe we'd blown it 'cause our timing was out. I thought of our fight in our favourite restaurant, and the torn half-tickets in my pocket, and the girl I'd found at the bus stop, her bad house and dissolving face; and rising from the chair I wondered if what we had, Zel and I, was not a bad house too. And those feelings came back up and hit me; but this time, since there was no theatre, no hand to squeeze, this time they couldn't get out; they just kept hitting me, harder and harder. And then I almost knew that quite soon the thing we'd had those past two years was going to be over.

I put down the glass on the unfitted carpet and went out by the back door, closing it carefully to give Zel the choice of telling her flatmate what had gone down or keeping it to herself. As I walked the passage from the backyards to the street, I was glad to be on my own at last, to have stuck to our resolution, but sad too because I felt that that, the thing we'd designed to make us more alive, was killing us. And the mixture of feelings, like something in a glass, brought a song which I cried as I walked down the hill: *Laying about, lying in bed, / Maybe it was something that I thought I said. / With the tempo of today and the temptation of tomorrow, / I don't know if I could give you anything but sorrow.*

And coming to the chorus I felt a surge of elation, like triumph in defeat, as the singer who spies his ex-lover in the audience tries to hit them with all a voice can project, to make them feel once more the sad ecstasy of bodies, so they see past your irony, remember who you are, smile that smile, and you know you have them but for the last time; and then they go, never to return, and you cast your voice on the empty winds, never to reach them again, 'cause your stage is still that deserted street corner or the back of some smoky dive, and they, in the throes of a new seduction by wine and candlelight and someone rich, have forgotten the piper's sweet sorrow; and you know then as surely as your body is your instrument, that your loneliness is of its own making, that your song has driven your lover away.

With notes of that colour I sang the chorus, the third syllable of each line soaring on the warm night air, then shot down, spun to earth, the way the black church singers do it, with a dying fall: *Losing you is just a memory. / Memories don't mean that much to me. / Losing you is just a memory. / Memories don't mean that much to me.*

Past the dark pub, a single lighted window above, net curtain flapping and a television on, the roar of an Olympic crowd and a hoarse voice witnessing a record-breaking run: 'Can. He. Do. It? . . . Oh . . . Yes! . . . THE TIME HAS GONE! . . .;' past a room where silhouettes shift behind students' makeshift curtains, where music and laughter feed into the street, I headed west and instantly was back on Venus Hill.

Here was the house, so familiar yet so changed. Was it mine? All seemed overgrown, untenanted, as though many years had fallen between my leaving and return.

I went in directly, looking neither left nor right, went straight upstairs and climbed at last the ladder to my room, taut with expectation, and spurred by my adjacence to – what *was* it? I opened the window in the slanting roof, sat at my trestle, in the plain wooden chair, began to watch the smoke, in the light of a single lamp, coil up and rush away into the lungs of the breathing night – and fell asleep.

The following evening I went round to Zel's with a copy of *The English Patient*, which she wanted to give her sister for her birthday and which I'd dug up by chance in my favourite second-hand bookshop. When I got there she was cooking, and I went into the sitting room and rolled a cigarette; and for a while I held my breath, counting the seconds, waiting for thunder, but none came. The storm was driving fast into the east, the sun piercing the clouds. 'Are you hungry?' she said, and we talked and ate and said what we couldn't say the night before. I admitted to my failure, and Zel confessed that on top of everything she'd been late, later than she'd ever been, but it was OK now, don't worry; so we faked grim looks and laughed about an oblique fulfilment of a fairy-tale wish. We went across the road for last orders and sat talking about people we knew and the people in the bar we didn't, and wondered whether the magnums and jeroboams were full or empty. Then we felt good, and we decided that as well as people sometimes being the best kind of poetry, real food on real plates was often better than other kinds too; and we almost knew, if we ate together, talked together, got our rhythms right and kept control, that what we had was a good house after all, and might well stay that way. So we headed back to Zel's and went to bed, and we got that right as well; and in the morning she went away to Leeds and I felt bad, 'cause I knew there was no way I could call her – not there, not where Zel had gone.

Now I was sad to be alone, but happy that we'd decided things and got all that stuff into the open, and I carried those feelings around with me all day and most of that night. And at first I thought it was the mist that sometimes calls on these parts in the early hours, but as I sat at my trestle, in the plain wooden chair, watching the sky pinken in the east, a presence seemed to pass between the window frame and sill – a shape, an almost human shape, to move across from that to this – a new beginning, stirring in its crucible, starting to uncurl, then rising, gaining strength and weight, substantiating the breakthrough I had sought: dark, damaged, beautiful, on the new ground of my day – and there it was.

Ramona Herdman

Eight poems

I should write you a love poem, Ghost –
lay you to rest.

But you cling, half-dead thing,
like the wren in the frost
with its white claws stuck in my glove.
I shook it sharp off, laid it in bramble,
hoped as I walked it would mean
a warm mouthful – used to the point,
if not meaningful.

I left it to cool in the weeds like a star
and when I walk past I look for the scar
of ribcage and claw, the pointing skull.
I expect it to soar, skeletal, screech
needle-winged down my throat:
'Hypocrite, ingrate, idiot, dolt –
turned your nose up at a teaspoon of flesh.
The world's blood beats in your step
and you retch.'

But it has not.
All that remains
is my shaking right wrist.

And when I cross the footbridge, Ghost,
you float –
impossible, as lovely as you were,
against the city light
snow a diadem in your hair.

There are noises round the house I can't explain.
The audacity of leaving you in the heavy wet ground.
I keep watching at the window for your corpse
to roll up like a root in the five-foot rain
and bang its sodden mass against the glass.
I'm waiting for the reckoning to start.

A boy and a girl on a moped, she shrieking
and all along the grass hump other girls watching.
The first leaves astretch in the high evening –
fingers wide out for the word past exquisite.

Every time at the end of a phone call
you slip in 'I love you' and sound stoop-shouldered,
slack-mouthed in the dizzy buzz after
and I am weary and I can't say 'Goodbye' and leave it
    at that any longer.
So I say 'I love you' and my seal mother
laughs seaweed-green, seaweed-lumped lungfuls of
    water
storm deep under and I shiver for my silkie-skin
left split and drying on the moonlit rocks
and my heart bobs like the gobbet of blubber it is, in
    my gullet.
I always think That's done it.
As if saying anything could sew up gills
and grow me eyebrows.

It is good to see a snail reach a grand age.
Good to see one going on sanguine in the rain.
To know there are some nuisances yet to the borders.
To change your step and nod, 'Pass, friend.'

It is hard, too, to be the beloved,
to kindly lie and to suspect
that you would know if this were what you wanted.

I have swallowed another man's cum since then
and I have kissed past counting –
you won't take me back to your castle, o king –
I won't go back under the mountain.

Mother's gone out in the mist again.
Mother's gone out to the sea.
She can't stop believing that something will,
that something must come to be.

The something is almost hatched out of her eyes,
the something is clawing in.
She is breaking out in scales and boils.
She is fighting inside her skin.

She has discussed this long enough
and found no one to hold her spear.
She has gone slippered into the mist
for there's nothing will hold her here.

Tim Jarvis

Beyond the Pale

In the farming community of Steerford a freakish child, with a
forked tongue and reddish, scaly skin, was born to the young
daughter of a cattle herder, Julia, and her husband, wealthy
industrialist Thomas Compton. For fear of Compton's reaction,
Julia's recently widowed mother, Jeanette, who had acted as
midwife, procured a stillborn child from the village and persuaded
her daughter, who was still disorientated by the pain of the
breach, to pretend that her child had come into the world dead.
Jeanette need not have concerned herself, however, for Compton,
who had been called away on urgent business, was a kind and
gentle man with a boundless affection for his pretty, young wife.
But, despite Julia's reservations, the plan was carried out. On his
return, when the dead infant was presented to him, Compton was
distraught, but phlegmatic, and attempting to comfort his wife,
said, 'There will be other children.'

Jeanette took the hideous baby back to the family farm and,
suckled on goat's milk, it grew to be a healthy, if unsightly, child.
Though forbidden by her mother from seeing her son, Julia visited
the farm often, hoping to glimpse the boy, but he was always
hidden away in one of the many outbuildings as soon as she was
sighted approaching the house. The frustration of her maternal
urges cruelly tormented her. Compton was shocked by the change
that came over his formerly happy and affectionate wife during
this period. She became melancholy, took to drink and refused to
sleep with him, or even to suffer his hand upon her person; within
two years her former beauty had been ravaged by alcohol and her
relationship with the industrialist had been permanently soured.
Drowning in a welter of despair, Compton became solipsistic and
spent much of his time reading in his vast library. But Jeanette
insisted that her daughter continue the deception, in spite of the

suffering it was causing, and the young mother, deranged by whisky, agreed.

Over time the child's deformities did not heal as had been hoped. His skin retained its reptilian aspect, despite the frequent application of unguents and lotions, and his tongue remained bifurcated, retarding his ability to pick up speech. By the time he uttered his first, clumsy sentences, the lives of those connected with his unfortunate birth had been laid waste; his grandmother, burdened with his care as well as the running of the farm, was deathly tired, his mother was a drunk and his father, who did not even know of his existence, had become a recluse.

On the fifth anniversary of the child's birth, Julia, driven to madness, committed suicide by drinking a draught of hemlock stirred into a half-pint of whisky. When her handmaid discovered her she was insensible and, though a doctor was called for immediately, she died without once regaining consciousness. In death she looked like a woman thirty years older than her twenty-four summers.

On the day of the funeral the sky was overcast and a light rain fell. The crape weeds, quickly saturated, began to unravel and hung from the mourner's arms like the blood-blackened bandages of soldiers returning from war. The funeral was poorly attended and, though a few of Julia's childhood friends watched the ceremony from a distance, only her mother and her husband stood at the graveside. When it was Jeanette's turn to throw dirt down onto the coffin, she began silently to cry, but her tears were lost quickly in the rain running down her face. Dragged from his books into the daylight, to which he was unaccustomed, Compton stood pale and blinking and displayed no emotion at all.

When Jeanette returned home she discovered the child torturing one of the farm cats. She locked him in an outhouse for two days without food or water and when he emerged his lizard's hide was blanched and his forked tongue was dry and cracked in his mouth.

The boy's fits of evil temper became more violent and outlandish during the following year, until Jeanette was no longer able to control her grandson. It was as if his devilish appearance was a sign of the depravity of his soul. He killed sheep at night, larding himself in their gore and running, raving, on the moors. The local farmers began to tell tales of a monster loose in the countryside and when the widow took tea with her friends the topic often turned to this beast. She sat politely as it was discussed, then returned home to cry with shame. So when a circus passed through Steerford, a few days after the child's sixth birthday, she went to the ringmaster, taking her charge in a hand-drawn cart, hidden under a tarpaulin. Impressed by the lizard boy's wildness and his appalling appearance, the ringmaster immediately agreed to take him in and make him the central exhibit in his freak show. He paid Jeanette a fistful of silver in exchange for the child.

*

Many years passed. Jeanette, tormented by guilt, aged rapidly and became a frail old woman, bitter and alone. From travellers passing through Steerford she heard rumours about her grandson, and, always careful to appear uninterested, she learnt that soon after his sixteenth birthday, the young man had taken control of the circus following a bloody coup, in which the ringmaster was murdered. Apparently, one of his first edicts upon gaining power was that no one should again call him lizard boy, the only name he had known his entire life, but that from that moment forward he was to be referred to as the August Lizard of the Bleachers. Under his leadership the carnival became popular and infamous on the Continent, known as Beyond the Pale, the circus run by freaks. Jeanette was told that he ruled his domain cruelly, meting out brutal beatings to his terrified subjects.

Thomas Compton's health had deteriorated following his wife's suicide and he had confined himself to his library, only leaving to wander his mansion during the night, his laborious gait like that of a puppet in the hands of a drunk. Then, one moonlit witching hour, twenty-six years after the August Lizard's birth, he was staggering through the corridors of the east wing when he suffered a stroke. A doctor arrived quickly and offered what succour he could, but his prognosis was dire; he thought it unlikely that Compton would live more than another two months.

Relatives, most of whom Compton had had no contact with for years, were summoned by letter, letters that the dying man insisted on writing himself, terse, partially illegible notes on heavy vellum. Among those sent for was Compton's mother-in-law, Jeanette, and, on the day on which she had been asked to attend, which was a bright and clear spring day, she wrapped herself up in a warm coat before beginning the short walk from Steerford to the grand house. When she arrived she was ushered into the industrialist's bed chamber, where he lay under a mound of blankets, his mottled skull propped up against the headboard. He spoke to her about his beautiful young wife's descent into depression, following the stillbirth of their child, and her eventual suicide, describing these events as if Jeanette was a stranger who had no connection with them. Raising himself on his elbows, he told her that his greatest regret was that he had no offspring to bequeath his vast empire to. Her resolve weakened by the guilt and the horror she felt at the sight of her gravely ill son-in-law, and badly in need of a drink, Jeanette confessed everything, unburdening herself of her dark secret. Compton wept bitterly and, galvanized by his fury, insisted that the old woman tell him how he could locate his son.

'I've followed the course of his career,' she replied. 'He runs a famous circus, Beyond the Pale, and goes by the name of the August Lizard of the Bleachers.'

Compton violently rang a handbell to attract the attention of his household, and, once they were assembled, told them of Jeanette's revelation. Then he instructed several of his most trustworthy staff to ride out in search of his son to persuade him to return to Steerford, stressing the urgency of haste and promising a substantial reward to the man who found the August Lizard. On hearing Compton's instructions Jeanette fell to her knees at his bedside imploring him not to carry out his plan.

'He is an evil man,' she pleaded, 'cold and callous with a black heart. Should he return here he will certainly have us both killed. Please reconsider.'

But Compton, wrathful, refused to listen, cursing Jeanette for destroying his and his wife's happiness. He had the old woman dragged from the room by two of his servants.

One of Compton's footmen, who had ridden westward, arrived, early one afternoon, into a frontier town called Meadowbank and discovered a flier for Beyond the Pale posted in the window of a brothel, which invited the people of the settlement to an 'evening of grotesquery' that very day. He went into the saloon bar on the main street to ask for directions to the circus. Inside the air was choked with smoke and raucous music, and violent men played acrimonious games of poker in the penumbral margins. The barman told the servant that Beyond the Pale had pitched their tents to the south of the town, out on the prairie, in a natural depression known locally as the Devil's Kettle. Setting out immediately, the servant rode through a landscape more barren than any he had encountered before, marvelling at the herds of stately buffalo that he saw in the distance, their deep, ruminative voices carried to him by the wind, and at the occasional eagle that soared far overhead, stationary in the rising currents of warm air, as if hung from the roof of the world. The hollow concealed the circus from an observer on the plain and it was not until the footman reached the rim of the crater that he saw the tents laid out before him like the incursion of some gaudy bedlam into the bright daylight, with, at their centre, the vast big top, its dark red canvas scrawled over with crude, bestial sketches and obscene phrases.

Reeling at the scene, the servant dismounted and led his horse down among the outlying caravans. Approaching nearer, he saw the circus folk wandering to and fro, practising their routines, or sitting, indolent, gnawing at food, playing cards and drinking. He walked past a man covered in coarse reddish hair who was cuddled up to a female cyclops, and then a small boy, with two good arms, approached him, offering, in greeting, a third, which protruded, shrivelled and useless, from the centre of a pocked chest. Allaying his fear and revulsion Compton's servant asked the boy where he might find the August Lizard. The child responded by pointing with one of his healthy limbs to the big top.

Inside the tent the sunlight filtering through the red cloth gave to everything a hellish cast. A troupe of dwarfs, heaped chaotically, towered over the figure of the August Lizard. His scaly hide was the same colour as the sandstone escarpments that rise sheer from the western deserts and which are said to mark the resting places of gods and devils who walked the earth in the ages before man. He wore the traditional morning jacket and top hat of the circus ringmaster and had a red carnation in his buttonhole. Upon sighting the approaching footman, the dwarf at the summit of the tower leapt forward, somersaulted in the air, landed, then ran off, the sawdust underfoot scattered by his passing. The other acrobats swiftly followed their comrade, leaping and tumbling in the gloom. Compton's servant approached the ringmaster, his hand held out in greeting.

*

By the time the footman's telegram reached Steerford, Compton had suffered a massive cranial haemorrhage, dying without uncovering the secrets of the hermetic texts that he had studied, or ever seeing his son. The communication was brief, stating simply that the Lizard was to travel alone, eager to make haste, with his entourage following on behind, whilst the footman, exhausted by the long distances he had covered in his search, was to rest in Meadowbank for a few days before heading home. Compton's advisors, a council of wise, grey-bearded elders, who had run the industrialist's affairs ever since depression had forced his retreat from the world, were gravely concerned by the news. Compton had never made a will and, as a result, the management of the tannery, and with it the running of the town's affairs, would pass into the hands of the August Lizard. Aware of his violent reputation and terrified that he would instigate an immoral reign of terror in Steerford they convened an emergency meeting.

The government feared and despised the Lizard, but had been unable to prosecute him for his crimes as no witness would testify against him in court. The elders knew that if they were to have the monster killed the country's rulers would grant them immunity. However, they could not take such action alone and, as the inhabitants of Steerford were by nature peaceful, the council realized that they would have to seek out persuasive evidence of the Lizard's iniquities before consulting with the townsfolk. The very next morning they rode to nearby Seven Spires to take a train to the capital city.

During a week spent researching the Lizard's past in libraries and archives, the elders disinterred a number of manuscripts that documented a repugnant life. They returned home, their brief-cases full of copies of newspaper articles, legal files and government dossiers, and, upon their arrival into Steerford, immediately called for a community gathering.

The town hall was a large building which had statues of great men from Steerford's past adorning its exterior. Legend claims that the timber used in the construction of its high, vaulted roof had been salvaged from the remains of a large ship found buried under the vast mound of earth which stood guard over the river crossing for which the town was named. This barrow is also said to have contained a casket which held precious stones and archaic scientific instruments. However, if it ever existed, this reliquary had long since disappeared. Apart from children and the infirm, almost the entire population of Steerford gathered under the ancient beams to hear the elders present their case. Ashamed, Jeanette did not attend.

At the allotted time, Simon Haller, the head of the council, made a gesture for the door to be closed. He sat, with the other aldermen, at a long table on the raised dais that was situated at one end of the hall. Standing, he approached a lectern and addressed the room.

'I will move, without preamble, to the issue that has moved us to call this meeting today. Some of you may be aware of the concerns I am about to express, but I would beg your forbearance. I would also request the undivided attention of everyone present, for the matter I am about to discuss is one of grave importance to us all. It is not widely known that Compton's wife, Julia, gave birth to a son, some years before her unfortunate suicide. That son is the legitimate heir to the Compton estate.'

At this revelation there was general shock and some in the crowd began whispering to their neighbours. Haller called for silence and rapped his fist on the podium.

'As I speak, this son is returning to Steerford to take up his inheritance. His name will be familiar to you all. Compton's estranged child is none other than that infamous abomination, the August Lizard of the Bleachers.'

There followed an awe-struck silence. After a moment's pause, Haller continued his speech.

'I am sure that you are all aware of the hideous crimes of which this evil man has been accused, but lest you think them mere rumour, my fellow council members and I have collected a number of documents which, taken together, tell a horrifying tale of depravity. It is my belief that the evidence contained within will convince you that drastic action is required if we are to save our town.'

Haller went on to explain that the first section he would read out was taken from an account which had been published anonymously in a popular newspaper. Its author claimed to have been a former member of Beyond the Pale and it described the brutal regime change that had allowed the August Lizard to take power. Haller waited until there was silence in the hall then began.

'During the chaos someone had tied the ringmaster to the central pole of the big top, using his ceremonial whip to bind him. When the uproar had died down the Lizard trained one of the spotlights upon our deposed leader then crossed over to join him in the circle of illumination. Turning to address the crowd gathered on the bleacher seats the Lizard asked them, "How shall we deal with this man? How shall we vent our grievances?" The circus folk jeered and stamped their feet. "We know well what he deserves, do we not," the Lizard continued, "he shall receive no pity from us."

' "Throw him out, throw him out," the carnies cried in chorus. "No," the Lizard replied, "that is altogether too merciful." Then, drawing a wicked curved dagger, the Lizard fell upon the ringmaster and disembowelled him at a stroke. The fettered man's head fell onto his chest and his viscera were spilled, blossoming in the sawdust. There was a moment of shocked silence, then a cautious cheer rose from the stands.'

When Haller had finished reading he placed the sheet of paper on the lectern in front of him and raised his eyes to the wormy, age-tarred beams, his stare seeming to pierce through the roof and the low cloud cover and the glassy firmament and look accusingly upon heaven. There was silence in the great hall, all attention fixed morbidly upon the dais. Haller then read aloud further documentary accounts of the Lizard's malice, stories of brutal punishments suffered at his hands by performers in the circus and of the rapes, drunken brawls and thefts committed or instigated by him that lay in Beyond the Pale's bloody wake. It was a mounting howl of infamy eloquently delivered by a calm and pious old man and when it was concluded all present sat benumbed. After some minutes the elder spoke again.

'At this very moment the August Lizard approaches our town and his army of freaks will not be far behind. Sadly we may be required to forsake, for a short time, our pacific natures. This creature will not submit to human rationality and must be met with the kind of rough justice he himself metes out.'

Haller blinked then looked around the room. All met his scrutiny with a nod of acquiescence.

*

On a cold, still morning the August Lizard sighted Steerford in the distance, striations of smoke rising unwavering from its chimneys. Singing as if keenly in love with the knife-edge scent of apple blossom and the verdant robes which cloaked the trees, the birds draped the forest in a dulcet chorus. A small boy who had been dozing by the path leapt to his feet at the sound of hooves drumming on the packed earth and ran ahead, the apple that he had been eating, forgotten, falling from his hand.

Passing under the West Gate, the Lizard looked up at the arch of crumbling masonry and saw an iron ring set into the keystone, a frayed length of hemp tied to it. Entering Steerford he discovered that it was silent and deserted. Wary, his mount tried to turn back, but the Lizard dug in his heels and pushed the animal on, emerging from the narrow streets into the small square at the centre of the town, which was surrounded by timber-framed buildings crowded together like paupers seeking alms outside the House of Our Lady in the city. Many displayed signs advertising commercial enterprises, but there were no signs of life within. At the centre of the square a scaffold had been raised to support a gibbet, a noose turning slowly in the rising breeze.

In an instant the Lizard understood that his father was already dead and that the people of Steerford, aware of his dire reputation, meant to lynch him. Tugging hard on the reins, he turned his horse about and galloped back towards the gate, hooves striking fire from the stones. It was hopeless. Two wagons had been used to barricade the breach and the mob waited for him there, milling about, armed with billhooks, pitchforks and cudgels. They surrounded his horse and dragged him from the saddle, clubbing him to the ground, before dragging his insensate body to the gallows. At the heart of the baying crowd Jeanette screamed louder than any other voice, fear turned to bloodlust. Trying to get closer to her hated grandson's helpless frame she was hit by a stray blow, knocked down and trampled underfoot. Old and frail, she died, broken, in the dirt.

The appointed executioner tied the August Lizard's hands behind his back, slipped the noose over his head and poured a bucket of cold water over him to revive him. The run off from his dirt-heavy travelling clothes stained the fresh pine of the gallows. Shaking his head to clear it, the Lizard opened his eyes, and, sore thirsty, stuck out his forked tongue to taste the droplets which clung to his two-week-old beard. The townsfolk gathered in the square shrank back in revulsion. Haller climbed up onto the scaffold.

'We cannot allow your evil to taint our peaceful community,' he said. 'So, for your past crimes and to prevent any future iniquities, we are putting you to death. Have you anything you wish to say?'

Looking up at the man who condemned him, the Lizard blinked before turning to address the crowd.

'I had hoped to be reconciled with my father and my birthplace, but . . . I curse this inhospitable town. May your wells become stagnant and foetid, your soil barren and your marriages childless.'

Then, at a signal from Haller, the hangman hauled upon the rope and hoisted the Lizard into the air, his feet kicking beneath him. His last harsh and ragged breaths faded, then a spasm went through him and he fell still. The townspeople were silent, then, as one, they turned and filed out of the square. Later in the day some of the menfolk came and cut the body down, placing it in a woven wicker basket which they hung from the iron ring set into the West Gate. Carried by word of mouth, the news of the August Lizard's death spread like a fever through the land.

*

Five days later Steerford was roused from its slumbers by the tolling of a watchman's bell and shouts running through the streets. Still hindered by the fetters of sleep, the townsfolk gathered at the West Gate in their night attire. In the distance a procession, lit by flickering torchlight, approached. It was the circus folk, come to claim their dead leader, and, riding alongside, Compton's footman, who had caught up with them on the road. The town militia drew arms, but as the cavalcade drew nearer it was clear that there would be no violence; the freaks, dressed in mourning, were solemn and peaceable. Their brands drove outlandish shadows before them and lit the foliage that flanked the road where, like diamonds laid out on a jeweller's black cloth, the eyes of curious nocturnal animals gleamed in the dark.

The inhabitants of Steerford looked on in silence as a troupe of dwarfish acrobats, in sombre apparel, climbed upon each others' shoulders and cut down the cage containing their former ringmaster's body. They lowered it reverentially to the ground, then, tearing the wicker framework open, laid the August Lizard upon a pallet draped with finely embroidered fabric. Filing past the body where it lay in state, their torches held aloft, the freaks of Beyond the Pale scattered rose petals upon the catafalque. Whilst these obsequies were observed, a beautiful giantess sang a wordless requiem in a sweet and pure voice. Then the dwarfs shouldered the bier and the procession began to return the way it had come. The footman sat astride his horse shaking his head as if in the grip of some great sorrow. One of the young men of Steerford stepped forward. He stood with his fists clenched by his side and his face drawn, the tendons standing out on his neck.

'Aren't you pleased that that evil man, who treated you so rough, is dead,' he called after the departing circus people, 'and will not trouble you again?'

A wolfman, covered head to foot in matted chestnut hair,

turned back and addressed the speaker, a look of bitter incomprehension in his eyes.

'A kinder, more generous man could not be found. It is true that some spoke ill of the Lizard, prejudiced by his appearance, and that he, to generate interest in Beyond the Pale, for fear is our livelihood, encouraged these insinuations, but that is all they were, lies and insinuations.'

Then the wolfman, without waiting for a response, rejoined the ranks of carnival folk as they filed away down the road, carrying their terrible burden. The young man turned to the footman, who shuffled uncomfortably in his saddle.

'Jonathan, is this true?'

'It is,' the servant replied. 'I talked to the Lizard for some time and was struck by how gentle and amiable he seemed. He was no monster and you have all made a grave mistake.'

When he had finished speaking the footman spurred his horse forward and caught up with the cortege, falling into line behind it. The people of Steerford stared after the departing freaks until the forest had swallowed up the last vestige of their torchlight.

*

Though the Lizard's terrible childhood should have left him with no capacity for empathy, in the nurturing hands of the kind circus folk he had grown up to be a compassionate adult. He was determined that he would never be guilty of treating anyone in the appalling way that he himself had been treated and to that end always behaved with kindness. The story of the coup had been fabricated, as a ruse to draw the crowds, at the suggestion of the ringmaster the Lizard was rumoured to have killed, who had actually retired to a small farm to live out his days in peace with his wife. The Lizard hated playing the villain, but knew his evil persona to be crucial to the continued success of the circus and, therefore, selflessly encouraged a belief in his depravity. He had inherited, from his father, who had been, before his decline, one of the most astute businessmen in the country, an aptitude for commerce and, in his gentle care, Steerford, through its leather industry, could have become a very wealthy town. Instead, in accordance with his prediction, within three years the town was impoverished, its finances mismanaged by the council of elders who, following the death of Haller in an accident at the tannery, grew increasingly rapacious. After the true story of the Lizard's life and death became known Steerford was increasingly shunned by travellers and the people of neighbouring settlements. Within two generations it was deserted, a ghost town, filled only with shadows and the ticking of death-watch beetles burrowing through its rotting beams.

Gerard Woodward

Ecopoesis

Now it is time that gods emerge
from things by which we dwell . . .

— Rilke

1. Mirrors

The sky had nested itself in the rocks,
The regolith, the frozen poles.
They had digested its curled-up weather,
Its soufflé sunsets and pavlova hurricanes
Locked in sub-surface cupboards of ice
Well beyond the nip of our tools.

Being vain men ourselves, our first
Thoughts were of mirrors, fleets
Of them hanging in the sky
To redirect and concentrate the sunshine,
And when they were built – a vast
Necklace of reflecting pearls in orbit,
Made from the scraps of sails,
Shafts of holy light appeared,
The sort that might bring simple
Shepherds to their knees
But which failed to convert
A single pebble of that
Endless beach. After fifty years
We took the mirrors
Out of their echelons
And sewed them together to make
Just two huge patchwork quilts

Of silver, each the size of the state
Of Michigan, focusing all
Their vicarious light on the poles.

At certain times, if the incline
Was right, a telescope would reveal
A planet multiplied by double reflection –
Trailing off like beads on a string into the curved
Darkness of space. A good sign, we thought,
The first step to an infinite universe
Of habitable worlds.

2. The Factories

Having done our violence,
Within sight of the tear-drop shaped
River Islands south of the Elysium
Volcanoes, out beyond the sulphur
Scablands and the potassium forests
We built our first factories.
They sat like any factories
Though fashioned out of native materials,
With silica and quartz-encrusted
Fumeroles they looked like colossal,
Empty evening gowns
Standing alone in the desert,
And had no product,
Only by-product, the halocarbons
We longed for, the CFCs,
The cocktails of halogens,
Fluorine, chlorine, bromine, iodine,
The redeeming pollution. It took
So much work to produce
The necessary filth, our complex grew
To the size of Maryland, trainloads
Of matter every day, trainloads
Of refined waste leaving, a workcrew

Of thousands, as if bred for the sole
Purpose, and yet looking at those
Sequined chimneys you couldn't swear
That anything was happening
Until one day we noticed how the air
Began to weigh heavily on us,
How we each began to feel that we
Were carrying a small child on our shoulders,
A little, grey-haired girl called
Barometric Pressure who told us
We had at last fastened the atmosphere
To the planet and that we could go
Naked for the first time in centuries.

3. The Bombardment

When the mirrors failed to fill
With more than a puddle
The depressions of the minor deserts,
Our third plan was put into action.
We found the hypothesized asteroids
Out beyond the orbit of Saturn
Wandering lamely like demented
Children in trouble with their guardians
And dressed in torn frocks of ice,
Rich in ammonia, which gave them
A lemony blush, as though a crop
Of daffodils had appeared in this
Little quarter of the infinite.
We strapped our nuclear rockets
To their backsides and let them
Fart across the parsecs until
They crashed on Mars – thump
Thump. They sprinkled the arid
Plains with their valuable, volatile
Salts and compounds, disturbing
The sleep of the sky as it lay still.

The proto-colonies had long since left
And we witnessed a landscape shift,
Dusty weather clearing to reveal
The impacted prospects,
The new lowlands where ranges
Had been, and a shock of orange
Liquid brimming in the remembered
Courses. The rivers went where rivers
Had been, redefining the estuaries
And islands with sharp, golden shores.
We'd refilled the drained cup
Of the oceans, a trillion tons of water
Converged on a bed the size of Connecticut,
And we cast our nets in a sea of piss.
So much, we thought, for ecopoesis.

4. New Forms of Architecture

From poor Mars to rich Mars,
But the only enduring thing we had
Was our language. We pitched tents
Of it. We shepherded information,
Penned and stalled ideas, farmed
Conversation, planted orchards
Of discussion which fruited,
Ripened then fell, spawning
New lines of thought, of argument.
And sometimes our talk
Was a shed of crumpled tin
And sometimes a limestone
Cathedral, until by the time
We had the chance to build
Something permanent, we felt
Almost afraid for the demolition
Of our own history, word by word.
And this made us shy from the question –
How should our cities look?

Until then our habitats had been
Mere attachments, things pegged,
Clipped, riveted or bolted
To the surface, memos on a planetary
Noticeboard, but when we had
The chance to work with stone,
To embed ourselves with foundations
And cellarage, we found ourselves
Reverting to classical forms, the old
Orders – columns, pediments,
Entablatures, scrolled finials,
Pilasters, though we lacked
The essential tools and skills
To make our parthenons anything
But rough-hewn, wonky
Approximations of venerable
Geometries – like Cornish mansions
Our schemes had all the ambition
But none of the craft.
Some of us planned to build
Venice from an old book,
As an island city it seemed
Strangely appropriate, palaces
Teetering on a brink, but it was enough
To have the idea only, its execution
Seemed neither necessary nor possible.

And we sided in the end with those
Who wanted to shake the habit
Of being human and take the chance
To start afresh and let our buildings
Somehow grow like the green corn
That had taken so well, that we should
Farm our houses and let their form
Be determined by their time and place.
And so the ancient cities of Earth
Made their reappearance.
We still had our bodies, that
Was the problem. Houses are somatic,

Born from our dimensions and habits,
Ur, Nineveh, Babylon, their dumpy
Ziggurats, trailing plantlife, floods . . .
It took our cities to remind us
We were human.

5. We Were Pedestrians

We called them the Icarus Years
Because nearly every day
A boy would fall out of the sky,
And girls, their parents,
Uncles, grand uncles, whole
Families, sometimes several
In one day, sometimes the sky
Was a weeping mosaic of silver
Parachutes falling slowly,
Seriously, the airbags bouncing
Unpredictably in market squares,
Scattering geese and goats, landing
Sometimes in a fountain or fish pond,
To then hatch with a sound of zips
And Velcro unfastening (how touching
Those sounds), and out they'd step,
Carrying a sack of photos and keepsakes,
A chair, the odd statue, and always
A packet of seeds.

It took the average factory worker
A thousand years to earn enough money
To emigrate to Mars, so that it was
Only the rich who fell from the sky.
Money travels just one way through space.
Perhaps that accounted for the looks
Of horror on their faces when they
Discovered how we lived, as goat herds,
Burlap-wearing scratchers of livings,

Bearded, Biblical, folksy. They were shocked
To find we were pedestrians. Mars
Was to have been a gateway to an infinite
Universe of habitable worlds, they
Told us, and look what you've done.
Where there could have been space ports,
Universities, bridgeheads to miracles
Exploiting low gravity and untold
Mineral wealth, there were chickens,
Cathedrals on crutches, mucky
Compounds. They lectured us
On economics, reminded us
That the ecopoesis of Mars consumed more
Of Earth's energy than was used
From the founding of the Roman
Republic to the birth of the Beatles.
Of course, that was before
They'd seen the maize we'd cultivated
In green swathes all across
The Basin of Hellas, or the vineyards
That thrived on the tongue-shaped
Lava flows of the Tharsis volcanoes,
Or the lupin fields that dressed
With pink and purple skirts
The giant Olympus Mons.
They remembered the old pictures,
The bouldery tracts, courtyards
Of nothing, Empires of Emptiness.
They knew they would never
Want to go back.

6. Flora, Fauna, Geography

It was good to have new geography,
New shapes on the maps
To have so much to name
On the small, local scale of things.

We soon knew our way round.
The yellow lake (called *Yellow Lake*)
With its crystallized shores, almost
Named itself, as did the hill
In the shape of Brian's nose
(Called *Brian's Nose*). All this was new
And varied, and meaningful,
But when it came to animal
And plant life, we have to admit
We lack variety. So far, our ways
Are birdless. Try carrying an egg
From Earth to Mars without
Breaking it and you'll see how
Difficult it is. And fledged birds
Cannot cope with zero gravity,
I've heard how they beat
Their wings to no effect, to fall
And drift regardless was something
Neither hawks nor nightingales
Could cope with. Insects were easier,
They came in boxes freeze dried,
Like gravel, though one had to remember
To pack a packet of the seeds of their
Feeding matter. So we planted nettle groves
For the butterflies, dock, rock rose, gorse,
But it is an edited evolution we enjoy,
The minimum needed to sustain
An ecosystem, we make up for
The absence by a burgeoning of fairy tales.
And we tell our own histories
Over and over. My father, and my
Grandfather, dealt in horses – shoed them,
Broke them, sold them at fairs
In the fields beneath Neil Armstrong.
My mother sold milk and butter.
Her people were pig breeders
In Nixon where the pink rills bubble
And the downfall glitters on the plateau.

7. Looking Back

The last millionaires fell from the sky
A century ago. They brought with them
Sad stories of the lives they had left,
How a belief in unicorns and mermaids
Had revived, how the cities had been
Consumed by privet and laurel,
Of sickness, reforestation, wars of religion.

Our children listened entranced
And filled with longing to be
In the world of islands with all
Its rich, rewarding dangers.

Our atmosphere factories have begun
To take on something of the mystery
And charm of pyramids, though
They remind me more of coffee pots,
Or cafetières, and the pillowy mountains
Behind them with the croissant-shaped
Pebbles that strew their slopes always
Remind me that what we have made here
Is one vast room, world-sized,
Near whose ceiling two acorn
Moons float. Sofa hills. Lamp-stand mountain.
You have to keep a sense of proportion.

Last week the mirrors were ripped
To shreds as they re-entered the atmosphere,
And poured their mirrory rain over a field
The size of the state of Missouri.

Peter Hobbs

Deep Blue Sea

I Could Ride All Day In My Cool Blue Train

I live in a town full of rain, a liquid city. We've got water up to our gills and I'm having trouble breathing. The bilge pumps are struggling and the overflows are overflowing, hell, even the *air* is wet. Before today it rained for thirty-three consecutive days and the water level went up eight inches. The Stilt was cramped enough already, and now the water's pushing up and we're pushing out. The Fixers are getting ready to build another level and move us all upstairs again.

All this water, and we can't drink any of it. We're down to two cups of clean a day. It's probably a good thing. Sal joked the other day that one misplaced piss and we might all be swimming. The clean pipe which runs from the purifiers up to the kitchen is beginning to taste no different to the rest of it. The water in the showers is thick and coloured and you feel cleaner without it. After the rain, everything stinks. The purifiers can only do so much. The food situation though is just about stable. There are seaweed crops. Some days we eat fish and some days we eat *fish substitute*.

As of last week, downstairs became submarine. It's like someone drowned my youth, because we were brought up down there. That was back when there were still children allowed on the Stilt, before all of that was taken over to the Dries. I was eleven then. A big transport arrived and mothers and children made a mass exodus. Except for me, because my mother was dead and I was sick and didn't qualify. They left me to see if I'd make it. I tell myself that maybe now that I have, someone will come back. They never do, though. Soon after that the travel permits came in, and no one goes now who isn't taken. People arrive, and are put to work. But they never leave, no one gets permits now.

Once when the water was lower, before the Overboards were even built, I sat on a step and watched the last swan anyone here ever saw, floating in the water like a long-necked lily, an opening fist of a flower. Then the thunderous snap of its wings in take-off. The immense clean span of its flight. Maybe it's gotten bigger as I remember it, but it was *huge*. Even then it looked like a creature from myth. No one dared kill it, not for food.

But now the Overboards are built, everyone else I knew then is gone, no one's seen any kind of a bird except seagulls for years, and even they've finally learnt to stay away from the rigged netting we set. From time to time a helicopter flies over, going this way or that. Out to the west the line that looks like the horizon is actually the start of the Dries – a great levee keeping the water at bay. Though with the weather lately, I don't want to think about the kind of trouble they're having over there.

There is Upstream and Downstream. The main currents run right past town, and lately there's something dark in the Wide Channel, like a slip of oil spooned into the river and threading along it. They've cut off the inflow for a couple days while someone works out who's dumping what, but in the meantime everything is progressively stagnating, and after all the rain there are traces of black even in the water downstairs. There are rumours it's infiltrated the seaweed crop, though I haven't been to see. Can't stand the smell there, is the thing. And no one knows what the dark stuff is. A couple of people have grown sick.

But I've been sick a long time, since the beginning. Since I remember, which is always. I get chills which come and go and I natter my teeth with nausea for a day. All I can do is give the doctor a call, then curl up and wait for someone to bring pills. They bring pills.

Those days I stay in my bunk. We're berthed in a raised railway carriage, the insides torn out and the bunks built in, just the blue of the upholstery remaining. Most days I'm the only person in. Everyone else works. It sways on stilts in the wind.

And with the noise of the bilge pumps churning away on the lower decks below you might just think you're moving, if you take your pills and close your eyes.

I could ride all day in my cool blue train
if my cool blue train would just stay in lane

I've been writing lately but it hasn't been going well. No one likes the stories I've finished, and I can't seem to get them out. For a few days now I've been trying to write a story I've called 'Trash'. It's about a world ruined by a Major Climate Event so that everyone who can has left the world. The firefighters and geriatrics have gone off to live on the sun. Anyone who can afford it has relocated to cooler planets out in the solar system. There's just an underclass left on the world living in these tiny cells which are part of one great machine, which gives energy and cools the temperature to bearable by recycling waste. Air and water are strictly rationed. Nothing is thrown away. There's terrible overcrowding, but strict individual segregation has been established by some unknown controlling body to quell trouble and prevent breeding. So there are these tiny cells full of the inhabitants' own waste and rubbish, and in one of these cells there's a desperate man who feels he does not belong there, who is forming a plan to get up out of the cells, and thinks that he could survive it all if only this one girl was there with him. *If you were with me*, he thinks, *I could survive it all*. But she's not, and I can't work out how to end it. I'm really not good at science fiction. But I think it's a pretty funny story, considering. One they'll appreciate.

But even with the pills I can't get it done. I just curl up and get as warm as I can, and still I keep shaking. Then before everyone else gets back, I fall asleep, riding all night in my cool blue train. You can get travel sick staying in the bunks too long.

One Day I Grow a Horse's Head

Today I take my pills and grow a horse's head. It's something I've been meaning to do for a long while. When everyone else is out of the bunks I take my pills and my forehead splits and lengthens.

I look for a reflection in the murky glass window, and I'm a horse, I'm a horse. I stay that way all day and by the evening I've got a big old headache in my big old head. Still, the thing about horses is that they're honest above all, and some days you need to be that way.

I get dressed and go deck to deck until I reach the bar. The rain's holding off and it's a dry walk over. Heavy tarpaulins hang over the bar entrance and you have to slide in through them. The air inside is close and thick. Everyone's there, everyone who can be. They can't drink water so they come to drink the whisky.

By the entrance on the inside there's the Idol. The Idol's made from an old diving suit stuffed with plastic straw, the suit itself too ripped and the rubber too spoiled to be any use. The head is a round mask with black stone eyes, like an insect's, and has two old flippers for oversized ears. The Idol blesses the bar, and if you baptize it with whisky it'll bless you too. But there's always the weighing up to do – precious whisky or unlikely luck? I always choose the whisky. After all, how lucky can anyone get?

Sal's waiting behind the bar, a worn look on his worn old face. He's standing beneath a fading drawing of an alligator someone did once, charcoaling it onto the wood wall at the front. The alligator grins, and I grin back.

Whisky, Sal? I say.

You're late, he says. Maybe when you're done. If you're good.

He bangs the bar and things quiet down, a little. Sometimes they want to listen and sometimes they don't. Tonight they don't seem too sure either way.

I stand up on the bar and read out a story. It's an old one but they haven't heard it, and I couldn't write anything new. It's about a boy and a girl who meet and fall in love and generally cause each other completely inexplicable amounts of happiness. They get engaged and exchange vows of *undying love* one perfect day. They live Happily Ever After, until one day when she tells him she's leaving him. She takes her bags and starts to walk out on him and he can't believe it, he's in tears, I mean he's being completely *torn apart* here because very real pieces of him are going out the door with her and the horrible bitterness on his tongue is a foretaste of his own death, but he gets himself together enough to say, *but you said you'd love me forever*. And this at least causes her to pause at the door, and she turns round, and he's waiting for her to Come Back In and Realize She Made A Mistake, and to Make It All Alright Again. Or at least *explain*. But in fact all that happens is that she slips a puzzled look on her face and she says, *well gee honey, it sure* felt *like forever*. And off she goes.

They don't like this one at all. Some of the Fishers and Fooders who have been struggling all day to gauge and gain resources don't want to hear this kind of thing. They do not like it one bit, and for a minute I'm in danger of being lynched by a couple of the larger thugs. There is a distribution of discontent, which can always get nasty. Then one of the Lazy Sunbathers stands up from where he's been sitting, holding up his bag of stones, and things calm down. Grateful, I'm merely kicked out of the bar. Forbidden from reading stories for a week, and told in whispered threats that whatever it is, it had better be better next time, or I'll be looking for a new career.

As I'm being dragged out the crowd disperse, dousing the Idol with whisky on their way out to purify the place after my disturbing of the peace. Bad stories will do that. I go back to skulk in the bunks for a while. Then the chills come over me and I get a heat beating at the thin skull around my temples and my teeth begin to natter.

I could sleep all night in my cool blue train
if my cool blue train would just kill the pain

Getting Back Together Was One Long Negotiation

At the end of the week a helicopter flies over and hovers a while. I was with the chills up in the bunks and didn't see it, but Sal did, and he comes by to tell me about the hovering. He says he saw ropes flung from the inside of the helicopter, and four men in black leap out and slide down, landing on the decks where the canoes are usually moored. Not that we have any canoes any more. He laughs and tells me that one of the men took one step and fell straight in, and the others dragged him out. They waved to the helicopter, which then flew off. With a lot of slipping they got off the decks onto the ladders and clambered like lizards up to the Overboards, heading, for sure, for powwow with the Lazy Sunbathers. They'll be out in their deckchairs wrapped in thick towels against the cold.

I feel a lot better after he tells me that. Men don't come from helicopters just to stay. They come with reasons. Something important. Contact with the others is always good for the Stilt. You can go for months otherwise and think that you're all there is in the world. And then they might just have come for you. You never know. I think to go over to the main deck to see what's going on, but I know I'll never get close.

By then my ban from the bar is over so I spend the rest of the day writing a story which I read out that night. The bar is full, as it's always full. Everyone's in. There's something strange about the atmosphere. They're waiting for news from the Lazy Sunbathers apart from everything else. We like to be kept informed. But the Lazy Sunbathers aren't here, which means they're still in counsel. All the same I sense there's something I'm missing.

They're expecting better, warns Sal when he sees me. Don't disappoint, will ya?

He gives me some whisky and I take a bitter sip to loosen my lips. Then I climb on the bar and begin to tell them a story. It's a story set over in the Dries. It's about a terrible earthquake which consumes a city, and how all these wonderful buildings with people in them turn into mass graves of rubble. I know they'll listen. They like to imagine the Dries, or have it imagined for them. They like to hear words like *concrete* and *skyscraper*.

It's about how after the tremors died down and nearly everyone's dead and buried, the rescuers are making a futile and endless effort to search for survivors. And how constantly hanging around them is this one little girl who's just in floods of tears because she's lost her mummy, and she's lost her dog as well, and no one has any time to pick her up and comfort her.

It's an affecting story, seriously.

So this girl is wandering around crying and eventually one of the rescuers, an exhausted fireman, stops from lifting rubble and bends down to face her, and in his weary way is about to tell her that *everyone's dead* but that they will keep looking for her mummy, even though he knows in secret that her mummy is certainly and painlessly pancake-flat, but meanwhile she should follow the other people back to the gathering point where she can get some food, because isn't she really hungry? He's just gathering these words together when there's a bark, and he's back and focused in an instant because he thinks it's one of the rescue dogs that's found someone – probably a piece of someone rather than the whole of someone – but then he realizes that the bark was muted and suppressed like it came from beneath the rubble, from where nothing's been heard for many an hour. A dozen rescuers converge on the spot and start shifting wreckage, just to get to this possibly trapped animal, because frankly any sign of life is going to feel like redemption on a day like that. Behind the fireman, though he can't see, the little girl's face has just lifted because she knows she just heard *her* dog bark, no way in heaven she'd fail to recognize it. And she quietens down and sits, waiting for the rescuers to fetch her dog.

Then there are no more barks and I play with my audience a little. You know – maybe they've dug in the wrong place, maybe the dog's going to be dead by the time they get there, maybe it's not really the girl's dog after all, that kind of thing. Keep them rapt. Then there's a huge block lifted and in an impossible crawl-space beneath it is the little girl's beautiful dog, looking up anxiously at the sudden light and all the people. And the rescuers are completely stopped in their tracks, because what is more, the dog is being held in a woman's arms, and the woman, though covered in dust and suffering some obvious distress and a trapped foot is not only alive but *awake*, and when they pull her out the little girl stands up and in the happiest tired voice you can imagine, says: *Mummy.* And her mummy reaches out a hand for the little girl and when their hands meet she says, *oh sweetheart, it's alright sweetheart, I've got you.*

I hear Sal sob just behind me. The regulars are in tears. I swear there's rainfall from eye level down. Like I've precipitated a micro-climate localized in the bar. With absolutely no exceptions, except for these four guys dressed in black who I only just notice at the table at the back, just round the curve of the wall. Who have apparently finished consultation with the Lazy Sunbathers and have come to sample from our whisky still. And who are not crying. Though they appear to be listening.

These, though, are distractions I can't deal with now. I haven't finished my story, even though they think I have. I regain their attention. I speak with scorn. I go on to say that because they're crying, they haven't understood a word of what I've been saying, that they didn't seem to understand that it was a terrible story, that *thousands of people died,* that the ending was not a happy ending but a false one, a jarring one, an ironic one. That their reaction is sentimental and naive and disappointing, that despite everything here they're still pumped full of illusions, that they still have illusions practically *flowing* out of them.

That what they think I meant to say was: there's so much crap in the world, and then all of a sudden there's honesty and humanity and hope.

Whereas what I actually meant to say was: it's *all* just crap.

The silence continues just a bit longer, while they weigh this up. Then there is uproar. *You little fucking shit. You little fucking cunt.* This time there are none of the Lazy Sunbathers here to calm it down. Something glass is thrown hard at me, a whisky glass heavy in the air as it whisks past my ear and shatters against the alligator drawing. They do not like being mocked. They do not like being made to feel stupid. I jump down quick behind the bar, but Sal steps away from me. I had him, too. One of the big Fooders from the kitchen leans over the bar and makes a grab for me. He has tears still smudged in the dirt of his cheeks, but he's looking ugly, murderous. He's balled his fist. It goes back to his shoulder and I curl up down on the floor waiting for the pummelling. One blow hits my back but it's soft, he's in an awkward position leaning over and I sense him readjusting for better purchase. But nothing comes except air, and the noise is no longer all around, but becoming isolated. Everyone was shouting and now there's just one person shouting. I get up to see who it is.

It is one of the men in black. A ripple of silence emanates

from him, goes along with his voice. He *shouts* and they *quieten*. I can see it crossing the room, and it looks like fear to me. They are afraid of this man. Who does not even bother to reveal his gun. Everyone already *knows* he has it. Even if no one knows who or what he is. No one has ever explained. Some things we just accept.

Quiet, he says finally, when he no longer needs to shout, and the whole bar is already quiet, more than it's ever been before. He looks round to catch the eyes of the room, and none of them seem inclined to meet him. Then he looks at me, and I look at him and I can't look away. He's younger than I thought. Just about my own age. Then he smiles, so quick it makes me doubt I saw it.

Just *pipe down*, alright? he says as he looks at me.

Then he sits down with the others and they resume their drinking, all in silence. And so does everyone else, but only in fear, not because they mean it. They don't dare look at the men in black, but they look at me, and they haven't forgotten.

I want to go over to the table where the men in black have settled back down. They are not looking at me. I want to see if I recognize the others, if one of the men is perhaps a woman. If they have new friends now. Not that it matters. But Sal has grabbed my arm and pulled me back behind the bar.

You'd better go, he says. You might not be reading any more, but you'll live, if you're lucky. There's always a job in the kitchens, right?

He pushes me into the back room, the one with the still. A yellow liquid bleeds through thin tubes where Sal turns water into whisky. I think to go back into the bar but then Sal would probably kill me himself, so I lift the trapdoor and go down the ladder into the dank lower decks, the rank smell of salt and rotting seaweed, the foetid warmth.

Deep Blue Sea

It's all very well feeling safe when there are protective men with guns around, but outside the bar there's no certainty that a Fisher or a Fooder won't be hanging around, waiting for me with a meat hook. And seeing as dumping bodies is an A-list crime at the moment (it pollutes the water Downstream, causing diplomatic issues) there would only really be the kitchen to drag me to, and *fish substitute.*

So I hang out for a while, not below decks where it's dark and shadows and I can't see anyone coming, but up on a small disused fishing deck far from the bar, near the carriage. It's cold, but I can live with that. There's a moon, off-round, but big and white and silvering the water so I can almost see the black in it. The clouds are thin grey ghosts speeding by on the ethers. I sit and shiver, and it's not the chills for once, just the cold. No one comes.

I get to thinking I might have been a bit hard on them with the story. After all, everyone here lost their mother once. Maybe I was wrong to mock their illusions. I get quite miserable, thinking about it. It makes me think I should write another story for them, to make up for it. But they'll never let me read again now. Which gets me further down. So I try and work out whether I'm going to be able to get out or not. I give the men in black time to leave the bar. I stay crouched on my deck and then when I think it's safe I just shin straight up a stilt and over to the carriage.

Back to my bunk room, but there's no sign of anyone, which I'd half been hoping. Maybe they haven't come after all. Maybe I misunderstood. But then I see my bunk. There, wrapped with an outrageously inappropriate blue ribbon and topped with an enormous matching stick-on bow, is an aqualung. It's a little battered, with a dent in the tank, but there is a gauge and a tap and a mouthpiece and I know it will work.

Beside the aqualung is a lattice of dry sticks tied together with twine. It looks like a cat's cradle of string, except there's a nagging familiarity to the design of it. A larger stick down the centre with a tiny white shell glued beside it, another shell at the edge of the criss-cross structure. I turn it both ways, circle it round, and looking down on it eventually work it out. It's a map of currents. The large stick is the Wide Channel. The shell beside it is a big arrow saying You Are Here. The other shell represents

Something Else. And for a while I'd thought all the clues were going to be in code, and I'd be always wondering if they were even there.

I take the last silver strip of pills from my stuff, and make to pop a couple through. So I can do it. But then I stop. Perhaps the pills are a bad idea, the last thing I need. It's not the time to be confused. No pills today, then. My cool blue train will have to stay away. I'll be going under my own steam.

I sort my stuff and listen for sounds. About the time I feel the bunks will start filling up I gather my stuff together then leave by the Overboards. No one takes the Overboards at night because they're not that safe. Even if I hit the water when I fall, I can't swim. The water's not clean, so who learns to swim? If you fall in and don't get pulled out, you drown, the way my mother did. If you fall in and get pulled out, the way I did, you get sick.

This time though I don't fall. I thought I'd have trouble lugging the aqualung but its weight balances me. I take the high boards all the way until I'm above the bar, and then I wait up there till it empties and I see Sal come out. And then I wait some more. The misshapen moon circles round for a better look and the wispy ghosts go by.

I slide down a stilt and push through the tarpaulins. Inside it's pitch but I find the bar with outstretched arms and make my way round it. I reach up to the shelf with my hands, careful not to knock anything glass. I take the waterproof torch from the tin over the bar and switch it on, so I can operate quicker. I put the tin back. I dismantle, as quietly as I can, the idol by the door, ripping its flipper-ears off and pulling free too some strands of plastic straw I can use, to tie them to my feet. I tear patches off the rubber suit for warmth.

And then I drag everything back up the stilts, tie the flippers to my feet and the rubber patches round my arms and legs. I belt up the aqualung, and suck hard on the mouthpiece. The needle on the dial flickers, but doesn't drop down from the FULL indicator. I pick up the torch and the map. Then I lean backwards, knowing I should probably have tried to get down the ladders so I was closer to the water when I fell, but knowing too that the best way of persuading myself to get into the water at all was to take myself by surprise, a pre-emptive strike. With the heavy lung on my back I rocket downwards, over head and headfirst, and penetrate the water. There's an immense splash that consumes me before I leave it behind. I'm so shocked I forget to go to the surface, then as I start to sink I begin to panic, until I realize I can breathe just fine. I appear to be all there. Just the map disintegrated in my hand – I think I crushed it myself in the fall, or perhaps it wasn't meant to be used underwater. But I don't need it. I am by the little shell. I am heading for the other shell. I give my flippers a kick and I'm propelled pretty effectively through the murky water. Somehow through all of that I managed to keep hold of the torch in my other hand, and even luckier, the torch works.

I never thought I'd be submarine again, not after the first time. There are two things about the underwater that overwhelm me, only one of which I was expecting and that's the cold. It's not like air cold. Wrapping up doesn't help. The rubber doesn't seem to help. There are cold currents and warmer currents, but basically it's cold like death. It presses in. My eyes are wide with it. All I can do is keep moving.

The other thing is the possibilities. A world in three dimensions of a scope bigger than I imagined. Directly beneath the boards it's not so deep – I can see the muddy bottom where most of the stilts are buried, and where the bar's anchor is half buried. The torch can sort of pick them out. But where the Wide Channel is, the water floor just drops sharp away into a trench and it opens out all oceanic and limitless, the water cleaner and the visibility, too, improved. Then you feel like you're floating above a great space, rather than thinking about how deep beneath the surface you are.

I know I have to cut first across the Wide Channel. I can see the stain of black running thicker than ever above me but I glide right beneath it through clearer waters. Just little kicks of my legs, flicking the flippers, and I move right along. I've never felt so free. I go kick kick kick slide.

I could ride all day in my cool blue train
In my cool blue train I'll shelter from the rain

I've a head full of shells and shelters. I get out far beyond the Wide Channel. It's difficult now to keep my bearings, to be sure I'm still going away from the Stilt. Sometimes I have to stop kicking, to see if I'm being moved by a current, to see if it's taking me left or right or forwards or back. I check my air and it's still in the upper half. I slip into one of the current streams and slide along with it. I start to keep an eye out for the pipe, if it's there, if I don't miss it. If I go too far, how do I get back?

Keep quiet there. Pipe down. There is a pipe, and I will follow it down. Those were the instructions. It's good for once to have instructions. After you decide to follow them everything is easy, you don't need to make anything up.

The dial is registering almost empty, less than a quarter left, when I find the pipe. It is large and iron and runs along the sea bed, then turns a corner and plunges over a cliff, going straight down to where the moonlight doesn't reach. I shoot down along it, kicking all the way. I keep my torch on the iron side of the pipe and soon that's all I can see. The pressure hugs me, squeezes me till I start to feel dizzy. I can see cold and black and just a tiny patch of light and this pipe still going down. I could surface, but I'd never get back so deep again. And there's nothing up above me anyway. The surface seems a lonely place to be.

Just before the pipe runs straight into the mud floor there's an oval opening. My torch shines into it, but it's just the inside of a pipe. A small compartment. I swim in. With one hand and the torch looking I feel round the edge of the opening and find a door. Some kind of airlock. A door on the outside and somewhere, then, a door on the inside too. The first door shuts infinitely slowly. The dial on my air reads empty. I pull a breath and it still comes out so I hold it for as long as I can. I look for the switch or the sign or the way out. The second door. I scan the insides of the pipe section, trying to orient which way is up, which way is out.

Then the torch goes out.

Then I take a breath which cuts out half way through.

The tank is empty. My arms and legs spasm in a panic which takes hold of me, I'm squirming and kicking out, thrashing and trapped, until I bash my arm and feel the pain from it, a numbness heavier than the one already overtaking me.

There is something on the wall. Some kind of a handle on the wall. A circular handle on a shaft. I grasp it in my left hand and pull myself to it, holding what's left of my breath. Too late now to surface. Too late for most everything. Not too late to decide which way the handle turns, if it even turns. Clockwise. I turn but can't move it. Too late to try the other way? Or should I just keep forcing it? It might not have been moved for generations. Too late for any of this?

I bring my legs up past me and plant my feet on the wall. I grip tighter, apply torque. The last of the breath bubbles out of me with the effort. I suck but nothing else comes and my chest leaps like a mad heartbeat.

And then there is a give, a definite slight give. And then a further turn. But there is no air, and my arms and head are rebelling, threatening to convulse.

Everything is already black, but the black is coming further inside now, into my blind eyes and my empty lungs. I force the handle one last time and there is a silent roaring which takes everything away in a long dark falling, save the blackness.

*

It's the shivering that wakes me. My body shaking like a Fooder has gotten hold and is rattling me like a bag of stones. But my lungs are going, clattering in and out. The air is awful, and I make to reject every breath, but I stutter and cough and carry on. I pull off the heavy aqualung, which was lying awkward beneath me, keeping my face out of the water I'm in. I stand up and choke, and kick something with my foot, which turns out to be the torch. I can hardly get my hand to close on it, it seems to take minutes to get my grip. Irritatingly enough, the torch seems to be working again.

I have a look around. I'm in a pipe, but not the one I was just in, because this one seems to go horizontally. My hands can't untie the flippers and in the end I just rip them off. Some of the twine digs in my foot and cuts through the skin. My feet are too cold to feel it. The skin is blue and no blood runs. I choose a direction and start to slosh along through the water.

The pipe tilts upwards, fractionally. The water is definitely getting shallower. The inside of the pipe is thick with slime. It is dark and cold and heavy and where I am I don't know. I walk for ages, until the torch dims and the water's down to my ankles.

There is another door blocking my way but it has a handle which twists it open to a shrieking of rust and metal. The tunnel beyond it is cleaner. Less muck, less slime, hardly any water on the floor. And then I realize I don't need the torch any more. It was dark and then it isn't. There's a light at the end of the tunnel, a faint light, but it reflects off the wet of the pipe and I can see where I'm going. I turn the torch off to save the batteries, and stumble on.

At the end of the tunnel there's a sealed door with a thick window in it. And through the window I can see someone standing there with his back to the door, apparently guarding it. He's dressed in black like his own shadow and is carrying a large gun. Beyond him I can't quite make things out. Things seem to be green. Things seem to open out a bit.

I bang on the glass with the butt of my torch and the guard physically leaps about a foot in the air. He pulls his face up to the window and peers through, blind in the darkness. His face looks weird pressed up to the glass, I can see every flattened pore, and the panic in his eyes. Then a shift of the light or his eye and I know he can see me. We stare at each other a moment, and I watch his mouth drop open in slow motion. Then he is gone. The seal cracks, the hatch opens inwards and I tumble in, and for a second time black falls all over me, but this time I'm grateful for the body heat.

There is shouting in a language I don't understand. Pinned on the soft floor I can smell something. Not just the shock of outside air after the aqualung's rarefied mix and the stagnant air of the pipe, not just that. Something else. Something too beautiful for words, something that needed to be shared. Something you'd smell that would remind you of your youth, maybe even something that would cause you to go back. I'm too crushed to start laughing, but the shivering starts, and makes me feel warm.

David Mitchell

Hangman

Dark-light, dark-light, dark-light: the windscreen wipers couldn't keep up with the streaming rain, not even at the fastest speed. Juggernauts slapped up spumes from the pools flooding the road. 16:05, said the dashboard clock. My public hanging was just fifteen hours away. Mum dropped me at the Malvern Link traffic lights outside the health centre (nearly forgot my diary in the glove compartment) before driving off to choose new bathroom tiles in Lorenzo Hobson's. ('Jason' isn't great but anyone called Lorenzo'd get bunsen-burnered on their first day.) Last year's leaves'd blocked up the drains so the car park was half flooded. I leapt from dry bit to dry bit like James Bond escaping from the crocodile pit. Two kids from the Chase Comprehensive saw my enemy uniform (our fourth years meet in a field every summer for a mass scrap and if you don't go you're a puff, and if you tell a teacher, you're *dead*) but today it was raining too hard for them to bother hassling me.

The pretty receptionist in the health centre said, 'I'll buzz Mrs Warwick to tell her you're here, Jason. You take a seat.' The people waiting didn't seem like they had anything wrong with them, but then I don't, not to look at. Waiting rooms're awkward. You all sit so close to each other, twiddling thumbs, but what can you say 'cept for, 'Why are *you* here?' Best just to pretend you're alone in an empty space. One old biddy crocheting; a hobbity kid with watery eyes rocking to and fro; a coat-hanger man reading *Watership Down*. There's a cage for babies and a hill of sucked toys. The tables've got women's magazines that tell you how to shed those excess pounds with a calorie-controlled diet. I read a tatty *National Geographic* about a lady who taught chimpanzees sign language. A stern clock tocked, *to-mor-row's – coming – soon – oh – yes – to-mor-row's – coming – soon.*

Most people think stammering and stuttering are the same but they're not. Stuttering is when you say the first bit of a word but then can't stop saying it – *st-st-st-stutter*, like diarrhoea. Stammering is when you get stuck after the first bit – st – . . . – . . . – . . . – am*mer*. Constipation. My stammer's why I go to Mrs Warwick and ask myself questions that don't have answers, like these: What did I do wrong when I learnt to speak? Don't know, but most cursed people don't deserve their curse. When did it start? Don't know, but I remember one hot afternoon in my first year at St Michael's, Mrs Jackle was playing hangman just before lunch. We'd got to N E   E R. I saw the word was obviously 'NEVER' so I put my hand up and Mrs Jackle said, 'Yes, Jason?'

The word 'never' kaboomed round my skull, but it just wouldn't come out. A noose'd strangled the root of my tongue. The 'N' got out OK, but not the '-ever.' The harder I forced it, the tighter the noose got. Avril Copson whispered, Simon Preedy sniggered. Maybe I'd've laughed too if I hadn't been me. Stammerers' eyeballs swell up, our gobs gupper, we go hot red. It's not funny when it's you, though. Mrs Jackle, every kid in that room, that school, in England; every bird, roundabout, spider, cloud . . . they all froze, listening, waiting for Jason Taylor to say 'never'.

But I *couldn't*. Shocked, scared, breathless, ashamed, yeah, most of all ashamed as if I'd wet myself, I said, 'No, I'm not sure, Miss.' Mrs Jackle said, 'I see,' and she did too, she phoned my parents and one week later I went to see Mrs Warwick for the first time. Five years ago.

So anyway, if I sketched my stammer, it'd be a hangman. A masked, lipless, hangman (nothing cartoony mind, more a man who turns round in a dream and looks at you and suddenly you're in a nightmare) in the baby room at the hospital and tapping my koochy lips, murmuring . . . *Mine*. It's his hands more than his face I know him by though. Slippery fingers strong as boa constrictors but as inside me as veins and the roots of my tongue. These hands clench my tongue and seize my windpipe on 'N' words, tighter so my throat aches. Where these fingers touch, it cramps up and nothing works. Nothing'll come out. When I was nine, I dreaded people asking, 'How old are you?' 'cause answering was like an arm-wrestling match. I used to have to hold up nine fingers. Hangman used to attack on 'Y' words, too, but lately it's changed to 'S's. Twenty million words begin with 'N' or 'S'. My biggest fear, bigger than anything, 'cept nuclear war, is that the Hangman'll start picking on 'J's 'cause then I won't be able to say my name unless I change it by deed-poll but Dad'd never let me. The only way to outfox Hangman is to think one sentence ahead, and if you see a stammer word coming up, switch your phrases so you won't need to use it. Without the person you're talking to catching on, of course. Reading dictionaries helps you get better at these ducks and dives. Saying 'er . . .' buys you time though you sound like a right dimmer if you do it too much. If a teacher asks you a question in class and the answer's a stammer word, best play dumb. These strategies mean speaking's like one-legged hopscotching, through a minefield, in a maze, but what choice do we have? Not speak? The world won't let you. There's no braille, no deaf-aids. Get the label 'Stammerer' plastered on your face and back? That'd mean getting picked on, massively, till either the end of the world or the end of you. So I struggle on.

Now, I've always *just* survived OK, *just* managed to hide Hangman in public, but tomorrow morning at form assembly this is what'll happen. I'll stand up in front of everyone, Gaz Kane, Dawn Madden, *everyone*, and do a reading from Mr Berkshire's form assembly book, *Plain Prayers for a Complicated World*. There'll be dozens of stammer words there I *can't* replace and I *can't* pretend to not know, because they're printed there. Hangman'll skip ahead, underline his favourite 'N' and 'S' words and whisper, *Here, Taylor, here, try and spit* this *one out!* My blood'll heat and expand and the Hangman won't just tighten my throat he'll *crush* it and I'll stammer worse than I've ever done in my *life*. My face'll scrunch up like Joey Deacon and by the end of first break I'll be the one, the only, official school stammerer. Fatsoes, creeps and sport billies have company, at least, but I'll be alone.

Here's just about the horriblest thing I ever heard. One time, this kid in my sister's sixth form was doing a chemistry A level, but he hadn't revised enough. He stared at this impossible exam paper, took two Bic biros from his case, held the pointy ends against his eyes and *WHAM!* Headbutted the desk. Right in the exam hall. The biros skewered his eyeballs and sank so deep into this kid's brain, only an inch stuck out of the punctured sockets. He died pretty quick, but it must've been dead sloppy. The headmaster hushed everything up so it didn't get on the *Nine O'Clock News*. Right now, swear on my mother's grave, I'd rather kill my stammer that way than let the Hangman put his noose round my neck and hang me in the morning.

I mean that.

Mrs Warwick's shoes clop so you know it's her. She's forty or even older, with fat silver brooches and wispy bronze hair. This afternoon she smiled at the pretty receptionist, tutted at the rain and said to me, 'My word! A subtropical rainy season in Worcestershire!'

I said, 'Yes, it's chucking it down,' and left with her quick (in case I stammered and the other patients guessed why I was there) down the Dettol-smelling corridor past the signpost with PAEDIATRICS and ULTRASCANS and arrows. (No ultrascan'd read *my* brain. I'd beat it by remembering every natural satellite in the solar system.) 'February's so *gloomy* in England,' Mrs Warwick said. 'You leave home before light and go home in the dark. On wet days like these, it's like living in a cave, behind a waterfall.' I told Mrs Warwick that eskimo kids sit under artificial sun lamps during winter, otherwise they'd get scurvy, cause winter lasts six months up there. Maybe she ought to get a sunbed? 'I shall think on,' replied Mrs Warwick. We passed a room where a howling baby'd just had an injection. We passed a room where a freckly girl Julia's age was in a wheelchair with one leg not there. I thought, Yeah, she'd swap her missing leg for my stammer. Is being happy about finding someone more miserable than you? Cuts both ways though. Who looks at me and thinks, Well, at least I'm not Jason Taylor?

After tomorrow morning they will.

Mrs Warwick's right about February. It's not a month, it's one twenty-eight-day long Monday morning and it's Hangman's favourite month. He gets dozy in late spring and hibernates over summer, so after my first run of visits to Mrs Warwick's (five years ago I mean) I stopped stammering by the time my hayfever started up and everyone thought I was cured. But come November he stirs again, then gets stronger over Christmas and January. This year's the worst, worst, worst, ever. Aunt Alice stayed two weekends ago and when I was crossing the landing in my pyjamas I heard her saying to Mum, 'Honestly, Helen, when are you going to do something about his stutter? It's social suicide. I never know whether to finish the word for him or just leave the poor child dangling on his rope . . .' (Eavesdropping saves time 'cause you learn what people really think, but eavesdropping makes you miserable for the same reason.) When Aunt Alice'd gone back to London, Mum said it mightn't do any harm to visit Mrs Warwick again, and I said OK, 'cause I'd actually wanted to go back, but I hadn't asked to because even mentioning my stammer makes it realler.

Mrs Warwick's office smells of Nescafé. Two ratty sofas, one yolky rug, a dragon's egg paperweight, a Fisher-Price car park, and a giant Zulu mask. Zulus live in huts in South Africa where Mrs Warwick was born but she was told by the government to leave the country in twenty-four hours. Not cause she'd done anything wrong, but because they shoot you in South Africa if you don't agree black people should be kept herded off in to mud huts. She and her husband escaped in a jeep over the border to Rhodesia but left all their belongings behind. (*The Malvern Gazetteer* interviewed her once, that's how I know all this.) Their summer is our winter. Mrs Warwick's still got a slightly funny accent and her 'Yes' is 'Yis'.

'So, Jason.' She sat on one sofa, me the other. 'How are things?'

Most people only want a 'Fine, thanks' when they ask that but Mrs Warwick actually means it so I told her about tomorrow's form assembly. Talking 'bout my stammer's usually as embarrassing as stammering itself, but it's OK with her. Hangman knows Mrs Warwick's dangerous, so he hides away. Which is good, 'cause it proves I *can* speak like a normal person, but bad, 'cause how can she get rid of Hangman if she never even sees him properly?

When I finished, Mrs Warwick asked, 'Have you asked your form teacher if you can be excused for a few weeks?' I already had done, I told her, but Mr Berkshire'd replied, 'We must all face one's demons one day, Taylor, and for you, that day is nigh.' Form assemblies're read by students in alphabetical order, we'd got to 'T' for 'Taylor', and for Mr Berkshire that was that.

Mrs Warwick made an 'I see' noise.

We said nothing for a moment.

'Any headway with your diary?'

The diary's a brand new idea, prompted by Dad. Before I went back to Mrs Warwick this time, he phoned her to tell her homework'd fix my stammer sooner so Mrs Warwick suggested a diary, just a line or two per day, to record when, where and what word I stammered and how I felt. This is Week One:

TIME	PLACE	WORD	HOW I FELT
12th Feb	Dining Room	Normal	Bad
13th Feb	Gym	Simon le Bon	Stupid
14th Feb	School Bus	Synchronised swimming	Bad & stupid
15th Feb	On telephone	Nottingham	Awful
16th Feb	Village Shop	Newspaper	Awful & bad
Yesterday	French Lesson	Nous Allons	Stupid & awful & bad

'More of a chart, then,' Mrs Warwick commented, 'than a diary in the classical mode?' (Actually I wrote it last night. It's not lies, just truths I made up.) 'Most informative. Very neatly ruled, too.' I asked if I should do it next week too. Mrs Warwick thought my father'd be disappointed if I didn't. Then we did some reading with the metro-gnome. Metro-gnomes're machines that music students normally use, a pendulum without the clock, but small, maybe that's why they're called gnomes. Speech therapists use them too. You read aloud with its ticks, like this: O – ran – ges – and – le – mons – say – the – bells – of – Saint – Cle – ments, like that. Today we read a stack of 'N' words from the dictionary. Hangman hides from metro-gnomes too, though I think he wets his pants laughing. Non – ent – it – y – Non – fic – tion – Non – sense – Noo – dles – Noon – Noose. Easy as singing. Problem is, I can't carry the metro-gnome round school all day.

Kids like Wilcox'd snap off its pointer. Afterwards, I read from *Z for Zachariah* without the metro-gnome. (*Z for Zachariah*'s about a girl who lives in a valley after a nuclear war's poisoned the planet and she might be the only person left. Right now I wish I was right there with her.) I got stuck on 'niggling' and 'knotted', but you'd hardly've noticed if you'd not been looking for it, not really. What Mrs Warwick was showing me was, *See, you* can *read aloud without stammering*, but there's stuff about stammering that Mrs Warwick doesn't know. These are the Four Laws of Hangman:

1st Law: If Taylor's with a speech therapist: Hide.
2nd Law: If Taylor's nervy and stressed about stammering: Attack.
3rd Law: If Taylor's relaxed and his guard is down: Ambush.
4th Law: When you get the chance to label Taylor 'stammerer' in public: Execute! Destroy Taylor's dignity and he's yours forever.

First law kicks in with Mrs Warwick. Fourth law kicks in tomorrow. Just before we finished, Mrs Warwick asked if I felt more confident about the morning. I could've said 'Sure!' but Mrs Warwick's one of those women with a built-in lie detector. 'Not a lot,' I answered, and asked if stammers are like zits you grow out of, or if kids with stammers are like toys wired wrong at the factory and stay busted all their lives. (You get stammering adults too, on TV comedies like that *Open All Hours* about a stammering shopkeeper. The audience think they're hilarious but God they make me shrivel up like a plastic wrapper on a fire.)

'My honest answer,' Mrs Warwick answered, 'is "It depends". Speech therapy is a very imperfect science. Did you know, Jason, there are thirty-four separate muscles involved in producing human speech, and millions of electrical switches in the brain? It's no wonder that not everyone can speak perfectly. Yis, I've worked with some youngsters who are speaking like cricket commentators after only a year, but miracle cures are very rare. In the majority of cases, it's a question of coming to a working accommodation with the impediment. In a way – and this sounds nutty – it's a question of *respecting* your stammer. Of learning how it operates; of not fearing it; then letting it subside, gradually. It'll flare up from time to time, yis, but if you understand why, you'll know how to let it flare down. Some people get dispirited, quit therapy and have difficulties all their lives. Attitude plays a big role, Jason. Attitude.'

Mrs Warwick's no idiot but she's no match for Hangman.

Five o'clock. Mum was in the waiting room reading *Fear of Flying* (which hasn't got a single aeroplane) and the pretty receptionist was telling someone (her boyfriend?) on the phone about how to heat up the casserole. I get jealous. Not 'bout him, 'bout *anyone* who's free just to say what they want, at the same time as they think it, without testing it for stammer words, they're *so* lucky and they don't even know it. Is being miserable about finding someone luckier than you?

Dinner was steak and kidney pie, boiled spuds, frozen peas and sweetcorn. Less than great. The gravy and steak bits were OK, but kidney makes me reach for the vomit bucket. I try to drop bits onto my lap when no one's looking. (Mum and Dad never force each other to eat things *they* hate. So unfair. Mum never says, 'No one in *this* house is going to use the dining table as a battlefield for teenage rebellion, young man!' to Dad. Me? Rebellious? The *idea* makes my guts go cold.) Dad was talking about a new trainee salesman at Greenland in Oxford called Duncan. 'Only two years in college and he's as Irish as Hurricane Higgins, but that lad's kissed that Blarney Stone a dozen times if he's kissed it once! Talk about the gift of the gab! He's got the makings of a top-flight salesman. When Craig Salt puts me in charge of general sales, young Duncan Lawlor's coming with me.'

'The Irish've always had to live by their wits,' said Mum.

Dad didn't remember it was my speech therapist day till Mum said she'd written a 'plump' cheque for Lorenzo Hobson. Dad asked what Mrs Warwick'd thought about his diary idea. 'Most informative' put him in a better mood. 'Informative? Indispensable. I told Duncan, any operator is only as good as his data! Without *data*, you're the Titanic, crossing an Atlantic of icebergs without radar.'

Julia asked, 'Wasn't radar invented in World War Two?'

'The *management* principle, O daughter of mine, is a universal constant. No records: no progress assessment. One day in your brilliant future career at the Old Bailey you'll learn this the hard way and think, "If *only* I'd listened to my wise father! How right he was!"'

Julia snorted horsily which she gets away with 'cause she's Julia. I can *never* tell Dad what I really think, not if it's against what he thinks. Stuff you don't say stays rotting inside you like mildewy potatoes. Stammerers can't win arguments, no matter how right we are, 'cause once you stammer, hey p-p-presto, you've l-l-lost. When I stammer with Dad, his expression goes to how he looked when he got his Black and Decker Workmate home and found it was minus a crucial packet of screws. Hangman just loved that expression.

Later my parents watched *Blankety Blank*, a glittery new quiz show with Terry Wogan where contestants (no stammerers on quiz shows ever, thank you) guess a missing word in a sentence, but it was too stupid to take my mind off tomorrow's hanging. (Wogan makes crap jokes with crap celebrities – except for Kenny Everett – but the prizes are crappest crap specially imported from Planet Crap. Mugs on a mug tree or a weekend for two in Snowdonia.) So I came to my room to do homework on the feudal system but a burning poem (about an iced-over pond) sucked me in so I lay here on my bed and wrote most of it in one go, then suddenly it was gone nine o'clock. The rain drummed my bedroom window. Metro-gnomes're in rain and poems, not just clocks, they're in breathing too.

Across the landing Julia's door opened and Dire Straits came out, it was 'Romeo and Juliet' off *Private Investigations*. She went downstairs to ask if she could phone Kate about their economics and world affairs homework. (She had to half-shout to be heard over the nine o'clock news.) Dad said OK, but when Julia picked up the phone in the hallway her voice wasn't her normal Kate voice so I hid my poem, slid out of my room and lay by the banisters.

'. . . no, it's *tipping* it down,' Julia sort of purred. 'I'm not going out to the phone box in this.' (A pause while the other person spoke.) 'Uh-huh, they think I'm phoning Kate. But listen, you *know* why I'm calling! Your driving test! Did you pass? Did you pass?' (Pause.) '*Stop* horsing around! Did you *pass*, Ewan?' (Who's Ewan?) '*Ex*cellent! *Brill*iant! Fan*tas*tic! I knew you would!' (Pause.) 'No! No! He's *never*! That sky-blue sports car?' (Pause.) 'Yeah, but even so!' She made an *oh!* moany noise I've never heard her do before. 'You're *so* lucky! God, why can't I have a filthy-rich uncle too? Lend me one, go on, your family's got plenty to spare!' I didn't know she had this laugh. 'Saturday's fine. Oh, you've got classes all morning, haven't you?' (Cathedral School kid? Posh.) 'Kate'll drive me in, she's got a piano lesson.' (Pause.) 'Russell and Dorrell's. That flowery cafe. I know it. One thirty.' (Pause.) 'I certainly will *not*!' *Thing* spends his Saturdays skulking up trees or hiding down holes.'

Blankety Blank music and living room lights flooded the hallway, and Julia switched to her Kate voice. 'Got that bit, yeah, but I still can't get my head round part two. I'd better check your answers before the test. OK, Kate, and thanks. Yeah, thanks a lot. G'night.'

Julia's an ace liar, got to admit it. She's applied to do law at university and she's got offers already. (Liar, lawyer, lawyer, liar, never noticed that.) She came back upstairs (I'd already sneaked back to my room, I'm an expert) and put on *Ninety-Nine Red Balloons* and sang along which she only does when she's happy. The idea of any boy snogging my sister makes me go *yeurrgh* but quite a few Black Swan Green kids fancy her. Bet Ewan's a posh super-confident sixth former who wears Blue Stratos. Bet he speaks in well-trained sentences which march by in perfect order. Speaking well is the same as commanding men.

Julia takes the piss out of me non-stop (it's her main hobby) but she's never mentioned my stammer because she knows I couldn't retaliate. I s'pose I should be grateful for this No Go Zone but her mercy's just as humiliating. One time Goofy Morris (this rocker from Winnington Gardens with a massive *Highway to Hell* patch sewn on his denim jacket) came into Mr Friend's shop just as I was going out and he said in this Woody Woodpecker voice, *S-s-s-say, s-s-s-sonny, where'd'ya get the s-s-s-speech imp-p-p-pediment* like it was a line from a film or sketch or something. I just carried on walking but just remembering that time makes me feel sick. Then last sports day, Andrew Reeves just came out and said, 'Why *can't* you speak properly, Taylor?' Luckily no one else was there, and it wasn't nasty how he said it, it was just curious. Stammering doesn't get talked about, not like blindness or deafness, 'cause even friendly people like Aunt Alice know it'll flush you with shame so they leave it alone. Other people *can* leave it alone, but Hangman never wanders far. I worry about when I leave school. What job'll he let me do? Not a lawyer. You can't stammer in court. Not a teacher. The kids'd crucify me. Monks don't speak, but God, church's more boring than Open University TV. Lighthouse keeper? All those storms, sunsets and Dairylea sandwiches'd get lonely. But lonely is something I'd better get used to. What girl'd kiss a stammerer at the end of a disco? The last song'd be over before I could spit out, 'Would you like to d-d-d-d-dance?' Or how about at my wedding, 'I d-d-d-do?' Can't, can't, can't.

Julia's put on 'Songbird' by Fleetwood Mac.

Dad gets up at 6 a.m. on Wednesdays 'cause he's got to drive to Greenland HQ for his midweek meeting. The garage is below my bedroom, so I heard the Rover's engine growl, then its tyres make a *shissshhhh*ing noise in the wet and its wipers squidge. My clock radio warned, 06:35. I prayed to God to make each minute last three months so I'd be middle-aged by breakfast and dead before 9:05. The columns and rows of faces at form assembly, smirking, pitying, greedy, I imagined them. Does Hangman enjoy his work? Or does he just do it, like a virus, 'cause he's Hangman and that's what he does? I gave up trying to sleep and imagined my ceiling was a lunar landscape I'd crash-landed on, but fell asleep before my moon buggy reached the lampshade.

'Quarter to eight, Jason!' Mum yelled up the stairs. (I'd been dreaming of waking in a thorny blue wood. I've never dreamt of stammering. Maybe it's enough of a nightmare already. You can't stammer when you sing, either. (Or when you try to stammer.) But I can hardly *sing* my *Plain Prayers for a Complicated World* reading.) 'Up time!' yelled Mum, like this morning was any other muddy February morning. I obeyed, of course, you have to obey when you're thirteen. (If Julia's anything to go by, ages should be counted like this: ten years old, eleven, twelve, obey years old, obey some more years old, obey even more years old, obey when you have to years old, then seventeen years old, eighteen, nineteen . . .) The bathroom mirror showed no signs of leprosy. My lucky red underpants were in the wash so I settled for my banana yellow ones. (Not a PE day today so it won't matter.) Downstairs, Mum was watching the breakfast TV on BBC (it only started recently) on the sofa (we're not allowed to eat there 'cause of crumbs) and Julia was just finishing her bowl of Kellogg's Country Store, sliced banana and yoghurt. I said, 'Hi.' She warned me keep my grubby fingers off her *Face* magazine. Any other day I'd've asked, all innocent, 'Is *Ewan* allowed to put *his* fingers on your *Face*?' but doom'd dulled me this morning and turned my Weetabix to balsa shavings. Julia left for Kate's. (Kate's mum teaches domestic science at Julia's school so she drives them in in her violet Vauxhall Chevette. It's the same school, but the fourth and fifth years have a new site across the road and the sixth formers are in a building from Cavaliers-and-Roundheads time.) I cleaned my teeth, packed my Adidas school bag and checked I had biros in my pencil case. This is how a kitten in a sack being taken to the river feels. When I left, Mum was talking to Aunt Alice with the Lorenzo Hobson catalogue on her lap. She gestured at me, cupped the phone, and asked had I picked up my lunch money? Now was my last chance to . . . do what? I just nodded and left. Outside was blowy, like a rain machine aimed over Black Swan Green. Rain-stained houses, dripping feeders, swilling ponds, shiny rockeries. A smoky cat watched me from a dry porch. I passed the bridleway gate, and thought about climbing over the stile and following the track to wherever it went. But kids like me just don't do that. If I wasn't in my classroom for form assembly Mr Berkshire'd notice straight off, he'd know why, Dixon the headmaster'd phone Mum at home, she'd phone Dad at Greenland, there'd be searches, interrogations and I'd be labelled a truant *and* stammerer *and* skinned alive then Moulinexed, so I just carried on walking out of Kingfisher Meadows and to the bus stop. Once you stop and think about consequences, you've had it.

*

Girls were clustered under rainbow umbrellas outside the Black Swan but boys can't use umbrellas cause umbrellas are gay. I wore my navy duffel, which keeps your top half warm but your shins get soaked when cars splash you. My socks were gritty and wet. The boys were having a puddle fight but just as I got there the ancient, Noddy-eyed school bus lumbered up. Psycho Spike was driving. I got on board, the door hissed shut and turning back was impossible. Hangman checked my watch and chuckled and I felt my shit liquidize. Thirty-three minutes to go. Wished I'd brought some tacks from Dad's DIY cupboard and scattered them on the road so the bus'd get a puncture. That'd've earned me an extra seven days and the Russians might launch an attack in that time and save me. (But I shouldn't joke about that or they might really and then how'd I feel?)

On rainy days like today the bus stinks of boys, burps and ashtrays. The best front seats (where you're like Monkey on his magic cloud zooming along the road) get bagsed by kids who get on at the Rhydd. Sitting at the very front of buses is ace, it's like flying. The next three or four rows are filled up by girls who talk about homework. The hardest kids go to the back, and sometimes open the emergency exit for a laugh, but today Psycho Spike was driving. (Psycho Spike's never been known to speak 'cept one time when he threw Goofy Morris off his bus straight into a ditch for flobbing. 'Oy! You busted me arm!' Goofy Morris wailed up from his ditch. 'You gob on my bus,' Psycho Spike roared back (hearing him speaking amazed us as much as what'd he'd done), 'and I'll bloody bust every last bastard bone in your buggering body you bony-arsed baboon-shat bollock-brain!' and drove off. And to this day nobody's ever flobbed on Psycho Spike's bus.)

So anyway, there's about six rows in the middle for middle-rank kids like me. (If you've got homework to do, sit on your own 'cause otherwise you'll never get it done.) Moran got on at the Gilbert's End stop and I said, 'Hey, Stu, sit here,' and he was so pleased I'd used his real name in front of everyone he plumped right down. I wasn't just being nice for his benefit. Later, on the way back, I'd be lucky if the invisible man'd sit by J-j-jason T-t-taylor the S-s-s-school St-st-st-stammerer. Moran and I played Connect Four on the steamed-up windows. The heater was so hot it melted your trousers. Moran'd won before we got to Welland Cross. (He's in the bottom class but he's no duffer, it's just all his family'd give him a hard time if he did too well at school.) Someone dropped an eggy fart and Upwater yelled *'Squelch's dropped a gas bomb!'* and Squelch grinned with his brown teeth, proud, then blew his nose on an empty bag of Monster Munches and chucked it at the girls but crisp bags don't fly and it landed on Robin South. A black horse stood in a rainy field, looking miserable but nowhere near as miserable as me in twenty-three minutes and counting. The bus stopped in front of school and we piled out and ran inside 'cause on wet days we wait for the registration bell in the main hall instead of the playground. School was skiddy floors, cagouls and anoraks, hurrying kids, shouts, girls walking along with linked arms. My heart thumped mad like an animal desperate to get out but can't, but I couldn't let it show. Eight minutes to go before the entire school knows.

'Taylor.' Mr Berkshire appeared from nowhere and pinched my ear. 'I have some utterances to make into your auditory organ.' He led me towards the cloakroom (where rainstained PE bags hang like sacks of drowned puppies) towards the staff room where no living kid's ever been and, sure enough, we stopped half inside the store cupboard. I was wondering what I'd done. 'Five minutes ago,' Mr Berkshire said, 'I received a call on the telephone, concerning yourself.'

You just have to wait with Mr Berkshire.

'From a well-wisher. Petitioning me to grant you clemency.'

I still didn't know what he was on about.

Mr Berkshire sighed at what he wanted me to think was my stupidity. 'I understand you anticipate this morning's assembly reading with a level of trepidation one might accurately moniker "dread".'

Mrs Warwick's white magic? I didn't dare hope it'd be powerful enough to save me, not yet.

'Your dedicated speech therapist is of the opinion' (Mr Dixon rushed by just then smelling of anger and tweed) 'that a postponement of this morning's "trial by ordeal" may be conducive to a longer-term confidence vis-à-vis public speaking. Do you second this motion, Taylor?'

Mr Berkshire wanted me to act confused. 'Sir?'

'Do you wish to be excused your assembly reading?'

'*Yes*, sir.'

Mr Berkshire squished up his mouth. People think not stammering is about courage, of jumping in at deep ends, of baptisms of fire. Crap. Forcing a stammerer to read out loud is like forcing a blind man to walk down the M1 to cure his blindness. Deep ends are where you drown. Baptisms of fire give you third-degree burns. People who don't stammer don't understand, can't maybe. Not stammering is about *not* trying not to stammer. Like how you can chuck a scrunched-up paper into a bin across the room when it doesn't matter 'cause no one's watching, but when you try, when it matters, you miss by a mile. (I don't know why this is true but it's true.)

'You'll have to vanquish your speech defect sooner or later, you know, Taylor.' (Hangman loves hearing one of his names.) 'You can't go through life turning tail at the prospect of public speaking.'

You reckon? But I nodded, all serious. 'Yes, sir, that's why I'm trying my best to master it now, sir, with Mrs Warwick's help.' (Mr Berkshire was thinking of TV stammerers who, one magic day, are forced onto a stage in front of a thousand people and lo and behold this perfect voice flows out. *Look!* Everyone smiles. *He had it in him all along! All he needed was a bit of confidence! Now he's cured!* Crap, Crap, Crap, Crap, Crap, Crap, *Crap*. If that ever happened in real life, it'd just be the Hangman obeying the first law. Lie in wait. Go back and check up on that 'cured' stammerer next week, you'll see.)

'Nothing seems to be wrong with your speech *now*, does it? You're communicating perfectly well with me *now*, aren't you?' (Play dumb. They *never* understand.) Mr Berkshire sighed again. 'Very well. We'll opt for later rather than sooner, I suppose. But I'm disappointed, Taylor. Had you down as having more pluck than this. I must conclude that I had you down wrongly.'

I watched him go. Relief never stays long but it's beautiful.

At form assembly Mr Berkshire read from *Plain Prayers for a Complicated World* himself, about how in life it rains for forty days and forty nights but a rainbow always appears in the end no matter what, because God has promised that he'd never let it rain forever. I thought that was that, but afterwards, Gaz Kane put his hand up and said, 'Excuse me, sir, but isn't it Jason Taylor's turn to read today?' He knows. Everyone watched me. All those eyes. Do they all know? I stared at the chalk clouds swirling on the blackboard. I sprung sweat in fifty places. About five hours passed by, sweated drop by oozed drop, but it couldn't've been more than five seconds. Mr Berkshire finally thanked Gaz Kane for his spirited defence of protocol, and that he himself had felt disappointment at the change of plan, but that he'd received reliable intelligence to the effect that poor Jason Taylor's vocal chords were in an injurious condition, so I'd been excused on quasi-medical grounds. 'Next week is T-for-Tomlin's turn. Alphabets march on, regardless of the Glorious Fallen.' I didn't care if everyone guessed why I'd been let off. That's not really true. I mean I was so relieved I couldn't think of much else. If I'd been the Pope I'd've made Mrs Warwick a saint right there, right then.

*

First and second period on Wednesday is double maths, just about the worst lesson of the week. It was now raining so hard the fields and houses outside were dissolving. Upton-on-Severn'll be flooded again. Mr Manning starts each lesson by asking arithmetic questions to kids at random. He caught me trying to avoid his eye. 'Jason Taylor. The square root of eighty-one, *is*?'

I tested the word 'nine' but Hangman was already plucking my tongue, blocking my throat with his fist. 'Er . . . is it . . . er . . . eight, sir?'

Mr Manning took off his owlish glasses. ' "Er . . . is it . . . er . . . eight, sir?" Tell me this follow-up question.' He huffed on the lenses and began polishing them with the fat end of his tie. 'Why do we get up in the morning, Jason Taylor? Why, oh *why*, do we flipping bother?'

Stones E.J, Likes rain on the sea 61993

Stones G, A dreamer 57889

Stones G&W, Expensive TV, old kitchen 58000

Stones H.S, 'Take a deep breath and tell me' 54063

Stones Ian, Is just a pawn in their sick game 57620

Stones J, Would, for free 64427

Stones J, One eye 57332

Stones J&D, 'It's best with John at the back' 56011

Stones J.M, Is not her real name 60861

Stones J.R, Draws around puddles with chalk 67550

Stones K, 'I love you' 53350

Stones L, Dull 63938

Stones M.A, One of Elvis P's hairs behind sink 55044

Stones P,

Has fantastic dreams, doesn't remember them 58022

Stones P.A, Put up to it by his friends 59884

Stones P.F, Looks like Steve Davis 67679

Stones R, ' – If you get my meaning' 69937

Stones R.A, 1 out of 10 for effort 57445

Stones S.F, Around the world at 19 61946

Stones T.D, Loves pineapple 53449

Stones T.R, 'I guess I'm not a nice person' 67231

Stones V, Thinks too much 56564

Stones Y, And gentlemen in London, still a-bed 63951

Stoney A.D, Very thin hair 54810

Stoney M, Shot video of Nessy, fears ridicule 69992

Stoney R,

Draws maps of imaginary places 58810

Stonham S, Doesn't fancy yours much 65018

Stonham W&D, Comedy double act 61554

Stopford B, She loves the way his body smells 64925

Stopford K, White hair, was a Royal Marine 62451

Storer A, Has smiled at a crocodile 60023

Storer G.D, Hears voices 61843

Storey A.C, Could have, but didn't want to 69486

Storey A.J, Made bow and arrows as a child 63688

Storey A&P, Christian swingers 54404

Storey A.R, MBE 66676

Storey A.T, Have you seen this man? 61113

Storey Bridget, Professional freediver 51997

Storey C, Lonely 69944

Storey D, Played Macbeth 55066

Storey D.N, 'No, that's exactly what I expected' 52222

Storey Eric, He talks to the animals 61444

Storey E.D, Ex punk 65911

Storey F, Interrupts saying 'no' & waving hands 50724

Storey G.L, An identical twin 59006

Storey G.W, Is a cad and a knave 65711

Storey H, Closet Nazi 62966

Storey H.A, 'Whatever you want, hon, seriously' 57524

Storey I, Has a star named after her 56710

Storey I.M, 'No way, baby' 60026

Storey J, Very bad taste in men 56696

Storey J.T, An identical twin 60198

Storey K,

'What do you mean "Merry Christmas"? Come

here and say that. I know where you live' 59822

Storey K, 'No, that was the other guy.' 60993

Storey K.S, Gets depressed 61354

Storey K.V, To touch it is to die 68879

Storey L, Grandfather was a mercenary 63955

Storey L.B, A disaster waiting to happen 68734

Storey L.J, Scratch card addict 57765

Storey M, Semi Pro – Tennis 1983–87 56061

Storey M.E, Spiritualist 64722

Storey M.T, 'All around the world, same song' 65565

Storey N.S, 'Stop it.' 64751

Storey P.P, Worries about lycanthropy 57132

Storey Q, Blows on lost eyelashes & wishes 58203

Storey Robert, 354 clocks in the house 66998

Storey S&I, A body under the floorboards 54309

Storey S.B, The sleeping monsters of childhood 57884

Storey S.K, Just once, to see what it was like 56433

Storey S.V, Is going slightly mad 65440

Storey T.S, 132 sexual partners and counting 58872

Storey V, Fears sharks, esp. the great white 58874

Storey W, Inspector 63813

Storey W, 'I'm sorry. It'll never happen again' 59234

Storie H.H.D, Dreams of one big win 57771

Stories for a Phone Book Steven Hall 56751

Stork A.P, I am reborn through football 57777

Stork C, 'This is not what I signed up for' 56140

Stork C.E, I dreamed I was a golden fish 56009

Stork D, 'I did it, I did it!' 57320

Stork D.A, Brown trousers, black shoes 58843

Stork F, Midwife 57830

Stork G.S, Made prank calls to Paul Auster 57092

Stork H.D, Collects found objects, esp. letters 56654

Stork I, Inflatable penis 58739

Stork K, Messy 58392

Stork Kevin, Favourite number – 12 56007

Stork N, 'During the great war ...' 58801

Storm D, Actually, he doubts it 91916

Storm G, Flash photography & big stereos 67330

Storm M&H, 'He'd have chips every day ...' 68675

Storr A, Makes grown men cry 55766

Storr A, Gold filling 55876

Storr A.L, Good listener 69741

Storr A.R, Makes films in his head 51515

Storr A.T, Of course, this is only temporary 61009

Storr Carl, 12 pints of lager and a kebab 55693

Storr D, Blood doesn't clot 51153

Storr D, Fool 64329

Storr Daniel, Valuable things unseen in loft 51001

Storr D.S, Dreams of going into space 67635

Storr Dr.D, Really cares 68354

Storr Edmund, Has nightmares 51862

Storr F.M, Wonders what went wrong 50734

Storr G, Has a four-leaf clover, it's unlucky 65846

Storr G&H.J,

'It's not working, I don't love you.' 69786

Storr H, 'You lookin at me?' 56952

Storr J, Left foot slightly larger. Trouble w. shoes ... 57705

Storr J, A lack of vision 61324

Storr J.E, Descendant of Cromwell 67883

Storr J.K, 'Is there anybody there?' 69867

Storr J.W, Wishes for something better 63687

Storr Kevin, Worships his Susan 63222

Storr L, Inherited madness 57292

Storr L.O, 'It's all in the past' 52927

Storr M, Wants it constantly 69836

Storr M, Loves the old movies 61229

Storr M.R, The looks but not the lifestyle 63449

Storr N, The looks and the lifestyle 63445

Storr O, Collects UFO photos 57221

Storr Philip, Lazy eye 66550

Storr P.T, Winner – Miss Wales 1977 60999

Storr R, Dotdotdot, dashdashdash, dotdotdot 64556

Storr S, 'I can and I will' 53820

Storr S, Hacker alias 'BlairCow' 56603

Storr W, Wouldn't if you paid her 68332

Storr W, Owns crystals of power 64420

Storr W.B, Tends to leave the taps on 69187

Storr W.C,

And if you believe that, you'll believe anything 61002

Storr W.R, Met John Lennon 66136

Storrer A.A, Collects comics & old toys 65042

Storrer B, Lucid Dreamer 57665

Storrer Jack, Says 'aluminium' American style 59184

Storrer L, Plays wheelchair basketball 60005

Storrer N, Is an enemy of the Daleks 63861

Storrer S, Calls pawns prawns 56205

Storrs B, Fire alarm – no batteries 51886

Storrs C, Works out regularly 67309

Storrs G,

Has concrete imprint of dead pet cat's paw 56096

Storrs Paul H, 'Now, the thing about me, right' 57743

Storrs R, Loves evening light on leaves 69447

Storry Barry, Writes under an alias 58111

Storry E.F, 'But I'm worth two of him any day' 59331

Storry F.G, Has a three legged cat called Easel 68934

Storry I.P, Is in denial 61586

Storry L, Instinctive understanding of evolution 54009

Storry M, 'The Lord giveth and the Lord . . .' 54956

Storry Philip, Was mugged on holiday 60224

Storry R.F&L, 'We're trying for another' 63741

Storry R.M, Crabs 60166

Storton E.K, Kickboxer 66857

Story B, Has met God but didn't realize 52887

Story B.C, Dances the night away 68719

Story C, Waits in for her to call 60507

Story D.M, Drinks on duty 63667

Story J.W, 'You don't mean that, you're angry' 57533

Story S.R, Has cause to wonder 63306

Stothard A, Works on platform/platform of art 51111

Stothard Alan, Keeps a scrapbook 53753

Stothard P.H, 'You shouldn't laugh though.' 51391

Stothard R, Works in a call centre 6/6/3

Stott A.A,

Loves the smell of napalm in the morning 51185

Stott D&M.E, 'Friends, we are gathered here' 59493

Stott K, Reads the tea leaves 68442

Stott M, 'If I looked like that, would you?' 60927

Stott Robert, AKA – Stott Rachel 69836

Stott R.B, Undiscovered 'green thumb' 63769

Stott S,

Is a complicated man/ and no one understands

him but his woman/ Stott S/ Right on 64916

Stouph M.F, Distrusts déjà vu 68194

Stout Ben, Loves trashy Westerns 50764

Stout D, Cheers for the underdog 58270

Stout L, Is bankrupt .... [disconnected]

Stout M.J, Remembers the old 78s 6/142

Stovin A, Dead on the sofa 65036

Stovin A, Owns a 12-inch dildo 62534

Stovin J, Submarine captain (retired) 64330

Stovin J.F, Records sound poetry 52851

Stovin K, He can't handle the truth 50361

Stovin M,

And Claire are always under the same sky 60406

Stovin M&T, 'Will you be quiet' 69353

Stovin P.A, Attracts strangeness 43961

Stovin R, Just couldn't resist 50064

Stovin T, Doesn't dance for no one 53300

Stovin T, Secret cupboard 54763

Stovinn S, 'So be it.' 87378

Azmeena Ladha

Twenty Gods and the
Pomegranate Seeds

Ma never said whether the rose petals scattered on my matrimonial bed were for sitting on. I picked some up and sat on the bare candlewick, waiting for Hassanali. He bolted the door quietly, leant back against it, smiled, and then, tiptoeing towards me, began, 'I always knew you would be mine one day. I want to share something with you now.' He sat on the pile of petals I had gathered. 'You might not understand this because you haven't been to England, but I have something in my mouth, something my father says I was born with. Don't look so frightened, it is something that brings me luck. It is a spoon, it doesn't get in the way, you can't see it, it's a silver spoon actually, a lucky spoon.' He took my hennaed palms to his lips and kissed my fingertips, once, maybe twice. 'I want to call you darling, like they do in Barnet. I'll take you there one day, you'll see. The leaves on the trees turn golden there once a year, then they drop off and you can walk on them.'

I closed my eyes. I wanted the dark of my own bedroom where I often lay with my headaches, wanting nothing more than the soothing breeze which blew through our mango tree. It was forever green, its leaves would never change colour and drop off to be walked upon.

Hassanali was always the first to land on Mayfair and Piccadilly. Before my brothers and I had a chance to pass Go and collect our £200 or serve our time in jail, he was swapping his four little green houses for a red hotel which he would place on the precise spot that one of us was about to land on. As he waited for his rent, Hassanali would play with his bow tie as though it were the steering wheel of a car he was about to run us over in.

Hassanali had walked down Mayfair and Piccadilly many times with his father who studied there. One year he had returned in a bow tie and that became his trademark. He would not drink tea again in case it darkened his skin. He started bowing his head slightly when he shook hands with anyone in the bazaar. He said please and thank you with every sentence and called his parents Mummy and Daddy. Just sixteen, and he behaved as though he had just stepped down from the Regal Cinema screen. Ma and Bapa liked him. They said he had evolved.

We always had to play with Hassanali, not just when we were young and they lived by the Lighthouse in Mombasa. His father had moved the family to the cooler climate of Nairobi where the roots of their precious roses were no longer eaten by white ants. They travelled down to Mombasa twice, sometimes thrice a year and the long and frequent visits to our house continued. Our grandfathers had played together as boys in the same village in Gujarat and later had both sailed to East Africa in search of better fortunes. 'The Visram family and us, we're from the same gully, the same village, and the same dhow,' Bapa warned us to remember.

'I'd rather not, if it's all the same to you,' is what Hassanali would say whenever my brothers Mohamed and Sadru suggested climbing down the creek at the Old Port or trespassing through the orchards behind the soda factory in search of ripe fruit. Outdoor activities were out of the question. Caram on our veranda was equally unbearable for him: flicking wooden counters across the board hurt his nails. Up-country nails were more delicate than our sun-dried Mombasa nails. That's what Hassanali said. He even said snakes were unlucky. According to Hassanali, if you landed on a snake's head you had to slide all the way down to its tail, which was generally back towards the start, thereby scuppering your chances to win. We didn't like that game. We knew that landing on a snake's head was virtually a sign of victory, that's how Krishna had defeated the serpent king Kaliya, by landing on one of his five heads and then trapping and squeezing each head under his arms. 'You lot don't know anything except ancient Hindu stories,' Hassanali always said. He was the only child Ma put the ceiling fan on for when she gave us permission to play at the dining table.

'Don't you mock that bow tie, how else will people know the boy has been to England?' was how Ma scolded us for mimicking Hassanali when we were young. As we approached our teens, Ma grew more anxious for us to appreciate the Visram family. 'Do you realise how many donations they make? And the hospital corridor, you haven't noticed? His grandfather's photograph has been coloured in, put in a new frame. Your grandfather's photo is still in black and white.' Turning to me, Ma would ask, 'Have you seen the size of the diamonds weighing down his mother's earlobes? Who will wear those next? Think, beta, one brother and all those younger sisters, who is the obvious one for those diamonds?' I never wanted to think about any of the things Ma wanted me to think about. I held up an open book in front of my face. My book was my purdah, my purdah from Ma's voice and her plans for me.

I never told Ma that Mohamed and I mocked Hassanali's name. Hassanali had taken to pronouncing his surname as two separate words, and stressing both equally. He would raise his eyebrows and say Vis Ram. Vis, as though he meant the number twenty, and Ram as though he meant the god, as though that's what there were twenty of: twenty gods. Hassanali had refused to believe that our ancestors were Hindus once. Despite his surname, he liked to think that we had always been Muslims, even all those years ago in Gujarat. That was why his pronunciation of Visram gave us so much pleasure.

I had never wept such joyful tears as I did on the morning my Senior Cambridge results were out. I got eight As. I was not the only girl either, the entire class got outstanding results, and we all wept such sweet tears. The Sisters were so proud of us they gathered in the hall to congratulate us. Mother Superior smiled at us all, even at the three gum-chewing girls who hated school and whom Sister St Viro had recited several additional Hail Marys for and who had managed to scrape Cs. They chewed their gum with pride that day. We were all clapping and singing:

A B C
At the Star of the Sea
It was A B C
In 1943
Not a single D
At the Star of the Sea
Just A B C
In 1943.

I began instantly to dream about the book I hoped Bapa would buy me. Bapa didn't like me reading too many books. The *Reader's Digest* was acceptable, he read that himself, regularly, but not books. 'They give you headaches and we can't have you wearing spectacles all your life, can we?' he would say. 'It's bad enough those nuns allowing you to read Pride and Prejudice books instead of teaching you something useful.' But today, with my eight As Bapa might just let me have another book. If by chance he frowned, I would tell him that *Middlemarch* was written by someone called George. Bapa liked the name George. He had a huge photograph of King George in our shop. As huge as King George himself, Ma always said. I could try telling Bapa that King George wrote *Middlemarch*. Anything with my eight As. We all ran home from school that day, eating raw mangoes and roasted sweetcorn and we didn't even realize it was raining.

Ma called it holy rain, approval from above. She wasn't referring to approval for my Senior Cambridge results. The sherbet and the chicken biriyani were not in honour of my Senior Cambridge results. That was 1943, it was the year people in the bazaar said we had had a third monsoon, the year Hassanali's father made an additional journey home from England to bring us the marriage proposal.

Everyone else in the house seemed to be going along with Ma and Bapa's plans. They were all so happy, so dressed up. Sadru, yes, ever the baby, ever prone to changing sides, but Mohamed too. They both had their top buttons done up as though a bow tie were imminent. They had acquired Parker pens and wore them clipped to their shirts. Their shoes shone like Hassanali's.

Mohamed, my dearest ally, my eleven-months-apart sworn-in twin whom I had made a chilli powder pact with and mocked Hassanali's name with – Mohamed was turning into our father. 'At least they are a top class family, sis. We are lucky to be asked, sis. And think of it this way, sis, Hassanali will probably buy you all the books you want. And after a year or two you could put in a good word for me to have that middle sister of his but I won't get anywhere if you don't clear the path first.'

Bapa came into my room. 'I am the proudest man in Kenya Colony today, giving my princess to a Visram boy, a lawyer's son who is practically a lawyer himself.'

'Bapa,' I tried, but those tears kept letting me down.

'Areh, you are happy with this match?'

'Bapa, can I study some more? Please, Bapa, please can I . . .'

'Study? You want to study? Study and let this match slip out of our hands? Then who will marry you when you have finished studying? Where will I find a professor for a girl who has studied?'

I was summoned to my grandmother's room. Sitting cross-legged on her string bed, snuffbox in one hand, prayer beads in the other and with a permanent frown across her face despite her joy, she asked, 'How many years has it been since you started menstruating?'

'Five years, Dadima.'

'That would have been five years too long in your mother's day. She came to this house immediately after her first bleed. Now wipe those tears, you are lucky to have had five bonus years.' She put the snuffbox down and began fidgeting for something inside her bra. 'Come and take these.' I sat on the edge of her bed and unwrapped several little pieces of purple tissue paper until I saw the contents: earrings, six large diamonds, arranged in the shape of a flower.

'Let nobody in Africa say that only Visram women wear diamonds the size of pomegranate seeds. Ours are just as large, and without a single crack. As you are your father's firstborn, you will wear them now, and make us proud. When your firstborn marries, you must pass them on. Understand?'

Ma took to wiping my face with her fingers. 'All girls cry

when it's time to leave their parents, I did too, beta. You wait till you see the pile of saris you are about to be draped in, raw silk, brocade, badla, you wait.' She took me to Whiteway Laidlow, the European department store that the Visram family frequented. 'Come on,' she said, 'we can spend a few shillings there too!' I had never been upstairs. On Ma's instruction, delivered in her best English, a silver-bunned English lady equipped with a measuring tape ushered me into a little cubicle with a long mirror, and, like our PT teacher, made me stand with my arms outstretched. '32A,' she told Ma as we stepped out again.

'No, no, can't be, that's not enough, make it 34B size, and give me a full dozen, all with circle-stitched cups.'

On the way home we called at the three Hajee Aunties, they were experts at applying bridal henna. The youngest, Farial Auntie, was the most popular. She had graduated from using hairgrips and sharpened matchsticks to applying her henna with sewing needles. It was supposed not to hurt. Ma booked her for my hands and feet.

The Visram family never mentioned Hassanali had a serious heart condition. That was why he walked slowly through the bazaar and refused to climb down the cliff at the Old Port. That was why his father took him to England so often, to consult the specialists along Harley Street. And that was why he always umpired the volleyball at the sports club – nothing to do with fair play, as Mohamad and Sadru had believed.

We did live in Barnet, and we had roses in the front garden, healthy roses, free from white ants and scorched buds. And Hassanali did qualify as a lawyer. His father set him up in a lavishly equipped office in Kensington, it had deep-buttoned leather armchairs around the waiting room and *The Times* newspaper on a coffee table. They hardly attracted any clients, though. They had not accounted for the aftermath of the war. Within two years the Visram family filed for bankruptcy.

We spent the next two years writing and replying to letters, waiting in other solicitors' waiting rooms, borrowing money from close family, Bapa included, and, for Hassanali's ailing heart, seeking several second opinions along Harley Street. We had a newborn baby too, born just when Hassanali had to be admitted into a heart clinic. Within days the doctors suggested moving Hassanali to a large teaching hospital. His father refused, he kept refusing. 'We don't need help from their new National Health Service, we still have our own funds.' When Hassanali's kidneys failed, the heart clinic could do nothing.

I have made a chicken biriyani for our Sunday lunch, and some sherbet. Najma is my reason for this celebratory meal, my celebration itself. She is the girl we were not expected to have. I look at her now, my Barnet baby, and wonder if she will always live alone, always be uninterested in those tissue-wrapped pomegranate seeds from my wardrobe. She spends most of her hours inside a partitioned-off cubicle, advising citizens on their legal rights, eats mostly pasta and ready dinners, and hurriedly. She has lived longer than her father did. She too winds then unwinds a strand of hair round her finger when she is agitated. I wonder if Hassanali would have encouraged her to marry, encouraged her to dress up more, to wear make-up. 'Thank you,' he had said before he closed his eyes, 'thank you for giving me this baby.' She is so Anglicised, my Najma. Well, obviously. Mombasa is merely the place where her parents were born, the resort she chose for a beach holiday with friends after their cheetah safari. Nothing that special.

'Mum,' she says, 'you look pensive today, what are you thinking?'

'Oh do I, beta? Nothing, really . . .'

She puts an arm round me. 'Are you missing Dad, or Mombasa or something?'

I kiss her forehead and say, 'I don't think I've put enough salt in this biriyani today.'

John Burnside

Annunciation with Unknown Bird

As if a cock crowed past the edge of the world,
As if the bird or I were in a dream.

                    Edward Thomas

No telling what there is: blood-warmth or current
plugged into the thornwork of the hedge,

yet something here is on the point of song,
open but not quite singing, hatchling voice

and plumage slick with rain
from somewhere else;

the life I know beyond the life I hold
from others: hatchling and totem

stripped from the wind and only the thinnest flame
sealed in the knot of the throat
                    half-bird, half-god:

though when the song begins, will it not seem
continuous, not one bird in a dream

but thousands, dead and living, nuthatch and swift,
blackbird and wheatear, oriole and pipit

– the voice with which they measure out the days
finding a sound for hazel, or morning snow,

a blood-spill at the far edge of a field,
a thread of smoke unfurling in the wind?

Imagine the hunger they felt, in the world's first dawn,
when nothing knew itself enough to sing,

how, even now, this nothing-as-it-seems
reveals a form that will remain unnamed

till some new shape arrives, fresh from the dew,
to mark it out: impossible and true,

the gap between one sound wave and the next
where love appears and calls us into question.

Annunciation with a Garland
of Self-Heal

Of course we escape:
               the first snow
                          the flight of a bird
anything single or clean
                    anything white
even the sound of rain
                  on a flat tin roof
is loophole enough –
               loophole
                    or faultline
                          or snare
for all the given versions of the self
that each of us leaves behind
turning aside forever
               or just for the moment
crossing a lawn and slipping away through a hedge
gathering windfalls
             or bringing the laundry in.

Of course we escape
               one moment at a time
in every phantom stealing through the dark
to find its elsewhere
               (loophole
                  faultline
                    snare)
the half-life that a lover carries home
surrendered to a gust of summer wind

crossing an empty street: a caul of touch
and blood-warmth
                    held a moment
                                    held
then given up
              a half-life that decays
unnoticed
          on the fingers
                          or the lips
a gradual and unintended thing
leaching away in a fabric of linen and sleep.

Of course we escape
                      and of course we will always return
tracing a path through these backyards of fence wire and nettles
and finding the place
                      like a stain on the morning air
where something has killed a pigeon
                                    the circle of feathers
cool as a smatter of ash
in the summer grass.

Of course we return
                    to touch
                              and to be recovered
though nothing is ever healed
till the world is whole
which is all of the story we know
                                  or can still remember
standing in the gap between two yards
where bonfires are lit
                        or a pool of these wildflowers grows
the common form
                (*vulgaris*
                          not *lacinata*)
the tongue-like florets violet or
                                  (rarely)
                                            pink
                                                  the name

a mystery
          as healing is

                         though standing in the gap
between the world we're born to and the world
we almost but don't quite invent
                                   what we know in our bones
is how much mystery we need to make a world
moment by moment
                    escaping
                              and bound to return
to lose what is given
                  to lose
and to stand our ground.

Annunciation with impending rainstorm: *pasó un ángel*

That moment when the conversation dims
– a beaker of wine on the table
                                       a loaf of bread
the angel not quite here but not quite

passing through unseen –
                           the conversation
pausing while his breath forms on our lips
and fingers
                                   – forms

as cloud-light and a blown track through the grass
where something we've barely imagined

hurries away.

                 But this is the first mistake
                                 to call it lost

given the unfinished sentence that hangs on the air
the bird at the edge of the lawn and the glimmer of bees
that gathers and shifts like a veil in the neighbour's yard.

This is the first mistake:
                       our miracle
– a beaker of wine in the rain
                             a bowl of plums
the angel not quite present in the hush
we think of as an end
                   like memory –

where nothing is ever an end
                          and the new beginning
is never quite the miracle it seems

– rain on a pine wood table
                          a gust of wind
the moment we share

                 and the moment that slips through our hands.

Romesh Gunesekera

Goat

Byron told me to meet him at the New Beacon bookshop on Stroud Green Road, Finsbury Park, at two o'clock. 'Don't be late. Please.'

It took me a while because I had to skirt the crowd outside our newly world-famous mosque to get to the bookshop. When I reached it, I saw him near the window leafing through a massive tome on ideology and land rights. He noticed me. Putting the book down, he quickly slipped out. He looked nervous, but that was not unusual; he was often jumpy.

It was June. The sun was trying hard to give us glitter. Dirty rain, or perhaps cat spray, had laced our London air and made it peculiarly pungent.

'Hey.' Byron hopped forward and grabbed at my arm. 'Let's go.'

'So, what's happening?'

'Let's go, let's go.' He pushed me towards the road.

We waited for the W3 bus to manoeuvre past an abandoned rust bucket and an illegally parked BMW, and then crossed the road to the butcher's shop. Byron stared at the halal counter heaped with meat, bones and flayed goat heads. Next to it was a cooler full of chicken feet, wings, necks and thawing drumsticks. 'I need help, man, I need some real help.' His face seemed to lose colour.

I had first met Byron at a Bhundu Boys concert at the Town and County Club back in the mid-eighties. He claimed to have been a freedom fighter in Rhodesia, pre-Zimbabwe, before getting a British Council scholarship to come to England. I never quite believed him; he didn't seem to have the physique of a fighter. But then, maybe that's why he got a scholarship. What did I know about ZAPU and ZANU? Even Mugabe always looked pretty narrow-chested to me. I had lost touch with Byron for years until a few months ago when I bumped into him at the New Beacon. He had turned into a librarian and said he worked for the London borough of Haringey. He wore gold-rimmed, tinted spectacles and a tweed jacket. 'No longer the good terrorist,' he'd grin. From time to time after that we'd meet for a beer, but we never talked again about his past, or politics, only the minor problems of the day: library hours, reserve stock, the virtues of Black History Month, the dubious effect of overdue fines.

'You know how to make goat curry?' he asked this time, squinting through his lenses.

I indicated, with a little nod, the pile of chopped neck and scrag ends. 'You need goat.'

'I know. But what then? You know what to do?'

'Why curry, Byron?' I had always thought of him as more of a sausage and chips kind of guy, if not actually bangers and mash.

A smile curled out of the corner of his mouth. 'I met this amazing girl.' His head seemed to shrink down as an elderly bearded gentleman in a white kurta squeezed by for a hunk of meat.

'So, you want goat curry now?' I hadn't thought of it as an aphrodisiac – halal or not.

'She's from your hometown.'

'Mine?'

A small storm clouded his face. 'Colombo, Sri Lanka, right?'

I waited. I could see he needed time. His lips had turned dark again. He tugged at the neck of his shirt as though his heart was in trouble. Then he blurted out. 'I told her I can make curry and rice.'

Passion, or perhaps just anxiety at the sight of so many carcasses, had made the sweat break out on his face. He pulled out a crumpled, brown handkerchief and mopped his cheeks, his upper lip. I could see haloes of heat rising off him.

'She's coming to your place to eat already? A Colombo girl?'

He recoiled as though I had slapped him. He shook his head vigorously. 'Not yet. Not yet. I haven't asked her yet.' He steered me towards the Caribbean greengrocer next door. I stepped past a crate of yellow pumpkins and a punnet of bitter gourd. 'You think they have curry powder here? What else do I need?' He frowned at the stacks of plantains, cassava and yams.

I told him he was going too fast for me. I didn't understand what he was trying to do. I suggested we go for a beer and talk things over.

'A beer?' It was as though the thought had never crossed his mind before. He brightened up again. 'Good idea. Let's go have a beer.'

*

We took one of the tables on the pavement, outside the pub. I bought two bottles of Red Stripe and passed one over. Byron poured his out into a glass and took a long sip. He smacked his lips afterwards like a kid. 'Good. That's really good.'

'OK,' I said. 'So, tell me.'

He pushed his spectacles up on his forehead and leant back. He had calmed down. He waited for another bus to trundle past and take the corner before speaking. The buses were coming thick and fast that day.

'I met her only last week. I can't get her out of my mind.' He half closed his eyes as though he was watching her move inside his head. 'She came into the library and wanted to look at all the issues of the *Observer* for the last three months.'

'Why?'

'Exactly what I asked her. We are not meant to ask why, you know. Our job is to provide, not to question. But I couldn't help it.' He pulled off his spectacles and wiped his steaming forehead. 'I felt something, you know. From the moment I saw her. An . . . affinity. I wanted to do anything and everything for her.'

'And?' I had to coax him, bit by bit, out of a reverie.

'Land reform. She's doing a PhD on land reform. She wanted to read up about what's happening in Zimbabwe.' Byron grinned, relieved at how perfectly their interest coincided, viewed even in retrospect. 'Imagine that.'

I knew then it had to be Rehana, but I wasn't sure whether I should tell him. Rehana was a woman whose interest in property had wrecked more than one life. Several families in both Asia and Europe had been ruined by her antics; now it seemed it was Africa's turn. I tried not to sound worried. 'What's her name?'

Byron's face swelled with a kind of smug pride. 'Her name, my friend, is Rehana.'

I cleared my throat.

'Re-hana,' he repeated, waving an arm at an invisible orchestra.

'I know.'

'Good name?'

'Very good name,' I agreed. 'Rehana Jayasinghe, from Middlesex, formerly of Borella, I believe.'

'You know her?' Byron's eyes widened.

'Of her. I know a little bit about her. An expert, I believe, in this land-ownership business.'

'Reform.'

'Yes.' I took a sip of beer. And then another.

*

I had heard about Rehana at the De Silva christening in Wimbledon. I was there, professionally, to do the pictures, but I was drawn by the gossip outside. After tea had been served in the church hall, a group of older ladies – the aunties – had gathered together on the lawn to chat. I was dismantling my tripod nearby when Mrs Amarasekara exploded. 'That girl is a menace. A wretched menace.' The tea from her cup showered several of her huddled companions. More teacups rattled on their saucers as various ladies made exclamations of agreement while others protested, defending the absent girl. A peculiar excitement seemed to spread. I put down the tripod and quietly loaded another film into my Leica. I went for a 400, a touch of speed. I thought something might happen. A skirmish. Some old-fashioned ritualistic cursing. Perhaps even some elderly fisticuffs – Mrs Amarasekara was known to be exceedingly pugnacious. The object of her vilification turned out to be Rehana: the siren who had destroyed the emotional balance and equity holdings of Mrs Amarasekara's favourite nephew – Kaiser. 'She led him on, you know. She just led him on until she got her hands on the house in Borella and then everything went phut.'

'Phut?' Mrs De Silva, the presiding grandmother who had just joined the party, echoed looking puzzled.

'Within eighteen months of the marriage she'd sold the front garden, then the back garden, and then the *house* – just because *she* wanted to come and pussyfoot in England. Kaiser went to pieces.'

'Pussyfoot? Kaiser?' Mrs De Silva echoed again, now thoroughly confused.

'She left the poor boy and came here, pretending to study, and got involved with some German professor and stripped him of all his possessions.'

The lady next to Mrs Amarasekara pulled her pashmina tight around her shoulders. 'You mean in front of everyone? Shamelessly?'

'Took him to the cleaners. The professor lost all his money. House, land, a fortune in Bavaria. Now she's gone to Middlesex.'

One of the other ladies then explained to the gathering that the trouble all stemmed from Rehana's father. He had been in Mrs Bandaranaike's first administration, back in 1961, and was fanatical about the government's land-reform policy. 'They called it redistribution, but all that fellow wanted was to get his hands on everyone else's backside. That's where this girl got all her odd ideas from . . .'

'Backyard,' Mrs Amarasekara corrected. I noted this Rehana's predilection for Bs: Borella, Bavaria, backsides . . .

Sitting in the sun with a Red Stripe in my hand, I weighed the whole scene in my mind. How much of it could I reveal to Byron? I looked up from my beer. Byron's face had lost its tension. His eyes had gone a bit bleary.

'So, what d'you know?' He smiled indulgently. 'Come on. Tell me, man.'

'You've talked to this girl some more?' I asked, playing not just for time but for some sense of where he was really heading. 'Or is this still just a book thing?'

'Newspapers. She was after newspapers. Periodicals. Current affairs. But we've talked. I've seen her outside.'

'Where?'

'Outside, man. Just outside.'

'You mean just outside the library. Like at the entrance?'

'No.' Byron was indignant. 'No. We walked to the bus stop together. We talked a lot, man. Like about Colombo. Harare. Finsbury Park. A lot.'

'So, she told you she likes goat curry?'

'No, but she was on her way to the Crouch Hall Curry Club. I figured she must do. You are always on about goat . . .'

'Mutton,' I said. 'Mutton curry.'

'Yeah, but you told me that for you mutton means goat. Right?'

I conceded. 'Anyhow what does it matter? This Rehana is one who prefers bratwurst and sauerkraut.'

'What are you talking about? What are you saying, man?' Byron was getting annoyed. He didn't like it when I played games with him.

I told him what I'd heard about her marriage to Kaiser and the affair with the Bavarian professor. Both, I said, were left bereft and distraught.

Byron laughed. 'But I have nothing, my friend, and I've been bereft and distraught all my life. Can't you see? It's a perfect match. Everything to pull us together, nothing to pull us apart.'

I was not convinced. Although I'd never met her, I felt I knew her better than Byron. I could imagine the charming smile, the political fug that was her natural habitat, the sly moves of her tight buttocks in pursuit of private gain, as she slipped from plot to perch, continent to continent. 'You should be careful.'

Byron leant across the table. 'Listen, my friend. I can feel it in my bones. Our chromosomes are meant to entwine. We fit like a jigsaw: Africa and Asia. It is in our tectonic whatchamacallit. Our children will inherit the whole earth. I didn't end up in that library for nothing, you know. She didn't come there just for the newspapers. Your Kaiser was her stepping stone to reach me, like your goat – or mutton whatever – will be mine to reach her . . . Destiny.'

'Don't be ridiculous.'

'Come and meet her then. *Kismet*. You'll see. I'll ask her for a drink. I'll tell her you are from Colombo too. Tomorrow evening.'

'At the Goat's Head?'

He laughed and banged my knuckles with his.

*

I went to the pub early. I wanted to figure out a good line to tease him with when he turned up alone. Maybe offer him something sweet like . . . *Liebfraumilch*.

While I waited, I took out my favourite camera: the old Leica that had belonged to my uncle Stanley. Made in 1954, the year he got married. He gave it to me when I first set off to come to London. His wife had died and he had no children. When he also finally died, a couple of years ago, he left me a plot of land in the hills for when I got married and wanted to settle down somewhere quiet and beautiful. Up there I'd be able to take perfect pictures, and make a new life. The Leica was my connection to what had gone before, and what lies ahead. The metal body always feels good and heavy as though it preserves the past in itself with every shot. Through it I feel I can see what is to be. In its frame lies all of life. The lens I usually have on it is a fabulous Elmar Leitz: pin sharp and a dream to use. When I turn the focus ring on the lens with the camera to my eye, I discover things I've never dreamed before. I find it is always with me at the most crucial moments. In the semi-darkness of the pub, I cleaned the filter and checked the winder. The camera has no built-in light meter, but my hands are able to set it by instinct. The Leica never fails. I turned the shutter dial and fixed the aperture. Then I pointed the camera at the doorway and looked through the viewfinder.

Rehana was taller than I had expected and wore an expression that seemed to obliterate everything else in the frame. I had never seen her before, but I recognized her. I saw her move, nothing else, and felt a burn as though something inside me had been clarified by the most astonishing light. There was nothing I could do but wait for her to come closer and closer.

Frances Gapper

Teeth and Hair

The teeth sat on Mr Hitchcock's upturned palm like a joke, as if they might start talking by themselves. But Mr H is a funeral director, not a ventriloquist.

'This won't do, Miss Pilgrim. Stealing or purloining or otherwise abstracting a client's property.' Mr H always calls the dead people our clients. I asked him once, aren't their living relatives really our real clients? Them! he said, no. They just pay the bills.

'What d'you want with these? Eh?' He'd caught me popping them in my bag, just as I was going for lunch. 'Plastic teeth, Miss Pilgrim. That's all they are, you know. Acrylic. Cheap stuff. Worthless. Fetch nothing.'

'I wasn't going to . . .' I wanted to explain, it was the rat man. Because of him; I didn't want him stealing people's teeth. We're sort of related, though I hope not by blood, he's a third cousin at most. But I didn't want to tell Mr H this, or any of it. Privacy is so important, he's always saying, even in death, Miss Pilgrim. Especially in death. Hence the expression, silent as the grave.

He's like that himself, I mean private. For instance, after he went to Torquay. Did you enjoy your holiday? I asked. He replied, it was sunny for at least half the week. And here? The same, I said. It was the same here. Torquay often gets better weather than Margate, he said. More sun, it being on the south coast proper.

From Mr H I learned that talking about the weather isn't shallow or pointless. It's a way of reassuring the other person, while keeping yourself separate.

Hitchcock and Dwell, it says in faded gold letters over our shop – what Mr H calls the establishment. Mr Dwell is dead. His name was really Dowell, the signwriter made a mistake and so they only paid half. But now he's Mr Dwell, for ever and ever.

129

Or until we get a new sign. Maybe Hitchcock and Pilgrim, one day. I think Mr Hitchcock likes my name and wouldn't object to see it painted alongside his own.

After the teeth incident I was so upset, I sat crying on the promenade, on a bench next to the telescope. A man came and put 20p in for a go. What did he expect to see? The horizon. Mr Hitchcock's wife left him years ago, he refers to her as the first Mrs Hitchcock, although there's not been a second. Once he asked me, had I ever 'entertained thoughts of marriage?' Oh Mr Hitchcock, I said, I'm too young for all that. I'm only seventeen. He told me, in some countries and in historical times that would be old. You'd be on the shelf, at seventeen.

The rat man said, 'She done a runner. She ran off.' I don't want to know, I said, that's a private matter, between them. Anyway, it's all in the past. But I imagine her sometimes, in running shorts and trainers. I see her dashing along the promenade, then across the sand – making it spurt up – and leaping over the groynes. On and on she runs, around the coast of England, then Wales and Scotland.

Nothing is truly over and done with except when people die and not always then.

Between the funeral parlour and the sea are a lot of hotels, most are just family houses converted into B&Bs, with strings of fairy lights outside. Old people come in coaches down here from Yorkshire. They waltz very slowly around the ballroom of the Alhambra hotel. Some never go home again. They are delivered to us wrapped in nasty nylon sheets.

I would have to tell Mr H the truth, in order to exonerate myself. The rat man – he was a ratcatcher, then he got taken on by Thanet Council, as a superior kind of dustman, paid extra to be discreet. 'No money in rats,' he said. While Mr H was in Torquay, he tried to corrupt me. 'The bags are round the back,' I said – he'd come in at reception.

Then he started to talk in such a peculiar way, I thought he might be having a stroke or gone a bit loony. 'What?' I said.

'Rings.' As if I was stupid. 'It's rings I'm after.'

'There's a jeweller's in the shopping centre. On the ground floor, just past . . .'

'Off the corpses.'

My fingertips left sweat marks on our pictorial brochure of luxury headstones. Eventually I managed to tell him, quite calmly, we give all personal effects back to the clients' relatives.

Dusty white blind, empty metal flower holder. While Mr H was on hols, I was thinking how I could smarten up our window display. Hitchcock and Pilgrim. I'd got some ideas.

Mr Butt was there when I got back. He and Mr H were drinking the whisky that we keep for the clients' relatives. And from the cut-crystal glasses. Mr H fixed me with a mournful stare, I wondered what it meant. Mr Butt was talking about the atrocious state of the property market, how he ought to have kept on being an air traffic controller, for the salary. He had a breakdown, Mr H told me. Houses don't zoom around like planes, they're not coming at you from all directions, little lights filled with people. But now, often, he complains to Mr H, 'They're not moving.' But that's Margate for you. People around here don't have money. He chose the wrong area to be an estate agent.

I said hello and walked past into the chapel of rest. One of our clients was there, a lady who used to live nearby. It was her teeth I'd taken, Mr H having arranged the face to look natural, using cotton wool and cardboard. He removes the teeth, because of shrinkage.

She was quite old, maybe in her seventies, but not decrepit. I'd done her make-up. And since she'd lived locally, I wondered if my friend Marianne ever washed her hair. She works at Roots & Tips, where they mainly get old ladies. She combs back their wet hair from their naked faces. One old girl, she always comes to find Marianne at the back of the shop, after she's tipped the hairdresser, to give her £1. She's nice, Marianne says, they all are really, even Mrs 'The water's too hot, the water's too cold'. Giving them rinses – 'Mind you don't get soap in my eyes.' Marianne says, 'I like sweeping up the mixed hair, it's dreamy. I love white hair.'

Mr H beckoned to me from the door, saying my name. He closed it behind me, as if the client might be listening. 'That earlier incident,' he said, 'was out of character, for one usually so trustworthy. I shouldn't have left you here alone, Miss Pilgrim, while I was on holiday. It was putting too much responsibility on young shoulders.'

'Oh Mr Hitchcock, please let me explain—' But he held up his hand. 'No need. We've both been under stress, Miss Pilgrim, owing to pressure of work. Our business is growing rapidly in the current recession and I need a partner to replace Mr Dowell.'

The air fluttered in my throat like a dove. I could only manage to say, 'Yes?'

'And so I have asked Mr Butt to join me.'

'Mr Butt?'

Oh!

'He has accepted my proposal.'

If I'd told him – if he'd given me the chance – how I'd been approached by the rat man and not succumbed to temptation – but no, that wouldn't have made any difference.

'One needs capital to enter a partnership, Miss Pilgrim,' he said – guessing the truth, to my shame. 'And you're not quite mature enough. But one day, perhaps . . .'

I'd been deceiving myself and now everybody could mock me. Even the teeth of the nice old ladies would laugh – ha ha ha! Like I saw the rat man laughing in the public bar of the White Hart, making a show of the teeth he'd stolen. 'I say I say I say . . .' His mate pointed at me over his shoulder. So then I knew, I knew I had to do something. It felt like my responsibility. I decided not to tell Mr H. That was my mistake, perhaps.

Hitchcock and Butt!

Teeth are intimate. Since around the time of Mr Hitchcock's big disappointment, his holiday before last on the Solway coast, I've been trying to protect them. Remains of mouths, of kind smiles and loving kisses. The suitcase under my bed won't close now.

A man is standing outside Roots & Tips, in the lamplight and the falling rain. A chancer, a deceiver, a bit of a bully, I can tell, just from the way a person stands. Waiting for whoever-she-is. But the shine of the lamp, in the rain, says she don't want him, it's like she's refusing. I almost frighten myself sometimes. Caring for the dead, see, that's what does it.

Out comes Jen the salon manager, used to be a Goth with

exploding hair, now it's purple. The old ladies don't mind exper-
imental, only not on themselves.

Jen tells him to f— off. He slams the car door.

Inside the salon it's warm and light-hazy. One of them is
complaining about how her scissors aren't sharp enough. A
woman's head is wrapped in silver. Now Jen takes off her coat, I
see she's pregnant. It must be nice when it's not shameful. That
whole secret world inside of you, a new creature being formed in
the living fluid and protected while it grows, you needn't say
anything, people know just from the shape of you.

They know.

But do they know anything, really? They can see you're
pregnant, but not what it means to you. That's a secret you can
never tell.

Men keep secrets too, nasty ones often. For instance, Marianne says that chap's her cousin and she was round visiting her
aunt's house, she'd gone upstairs, then he called her from his
room to just come in here a moment. I've got something to show
you. He's a policeman, still living at home. And he said try this
on you for size, like he was joking. It was a pair of handcuffs. I
didn't know how to refuse politely, Marianne says. That's what
she's like. Brought up to be nice to people and a bit stupid, only
in the way she can't protect herself.

The air smells of mint, Jen is spraying her feet through her
black tights. Hairdressers are like nurses, having to stand all day.
I'm lucky. Marianne says, I just pulled my hand through and
escaped – making a circle of her other hand to show. Otherwise
– well. He was trying to lock me to the bedpost. But then I'd have
screamed, so Auntie Mary would come upstairs. But I'd be so
embarrassed.

My hand slipped through like a fish and I laughed. Can't
catch me!

'You ought to tell someone.'

The old ladies are all gazing at themselves in the mirrors.
Hoping they'll be turned young again. Would I sacrifice myself
for one of them, like if she offered me a lot of money and her
house in exchange for her being young and me being old? I think
yes, I would. So long as I could go on living to enjoy the money,

for at least sixty years. On an old-age pension. But that's not much. Anyway, for sixty years I'd be paying into a funeral insurance fund, so then I could have a mausoleum, black marble and stained-glass windows. And six black horses to pull my hearse, with tall nodding feathers on their heads.

In between the pop songs comes the news. Millions of gallons of oil are escaping from a shipwrecked tanker off the coast of Spain, it's the world's biggest ever environmental disaster. Michael Jackson dangled his baby over a balcony. A man blew up his wife's car with a home-made bomb. A woman's dismembered limbs have been found in a canal and on allotments. The firefighters are going on strike.

One of the girls holds a little bit of dark red liquid in a bottle. Turned upside down, it's a bottle of blood. I feel sick and we go outside. It's not raining. Marianne smokes a cigarette and she offers me one. It stops you vomiting. 'That's why I started,' Marianne says. 'When I was fourteen. I used to be so nervous. But I thought you must be made of iron. I could never touch a corpse or do its hair. Oh Janie, hair is weird, it's like a living creature. I heard of a woman who died when she was quite young and she had red hair down to her shoulders. But by the time they dug her up, there was enough to stuff a sofa.'

Why did they do that – open up her coffin?

To see if she'd been murdered.

I might do that, I said. I'm getting bored with my job. There's always openings. I might train to be a specialist. That word made me think of the rat man. I dismissed him from my mind. I thought of me organizing the priest, the gravediggers, the lights so they could work at night, the refreshments et cetera and the van for transferring the remains to forensics. I'd have my own vans, I'd be a company, Pilgrim & Pilgrim. With my daughter. I'd get her back.

Meanwhile, I should rid myself of those teeth. They'd frighten her. I should let them go, maybe in the sea. I thought they'd look just like the skeletons of sea creatures. Could be embarrassing, though, if the tide washed them all up. I should bury them down deep. In the dark, I walked along the promenade. I saw a bunch of sacking, no, it was a person on the sand. Dead? But by the time I got down there, he'd roused himself. A fringe of beard around his pale face. He'd been looking in the sky for the bright dust of meteors, the lions. Except unfortunately it was too cloudy. Sit down with me. He pulled the band from my hair. Do you mind, I said, not really angry. He said, it's like a waterfall of honey. Sticky, I thought and said out loud, I never meant it to grow. I'm having it cut soon. But it's lovely, he said. I didn't mind when he touched me, I thought, I'm loosening my bonds. He put a ring on my finger, of bone, of shell. Now you're married to the sea. I'll stay on dry land, thank you.

A jogger ran past and funnily enough she looked a bit like my idea of the first Mrs Hitchcock. When would she ever stop running? Maybe she was addicted to the amphetamines or the hormones, or whatever it gives you. Then I remembered my bag and slipped my hand inside, to check for the teeth. Mr H had given them back to me, like a kind of consolation prize. I know, I know, Miss Pilgrim. We'll say no more about it.

'What d'you think I've got in here?'

'Pearls.'

Paul Bailey

The Stricken Nightingale

Some Reflections on the Life and Writings of Panait Istrati

In the 1920s and throughout the 1930s, Panait Istrati was one of the most celebrated writers in the world. His early work was lauded by none other than Georg Brandes, the revolutionary critic whose severe judgments made even Thomas Mann quail. His novels were translated into twenty-five languages. They are still in print in France, and there is a Panait Istrati Society in Paris, which publishes occasional newsletters. He now has few readers in Britain, apart from those like myself, who are fascinated by the history of the Balkans. Unlike Stefan Zweig, who was just as famous in the years before the Second World War, Istrati won't survive as a writer of consequence. Zweig's novellas are at last being recognized as the timeless masterpieces they undoubtedly are, but Istrati's tales of the daily adventures of *haiduks* (brigands) in late nineteenth-century Romania seem destined to be regarded as literary curiosities. There is something almost too exotic about them, something that smacks of operetta, the art form in which thieves and murderers are deemed heroic because they rob and kill the rich and despotic in order to elevate the poor honest peasantry to a better way of life. Istrati isn't as crude as the average librettist of the average Ruritanian musical farrago, if only for the reason that his brigands, male and female, don't miraculously discover that they are really heirs to the throne. What is admirable in him as a man – his constant, unwavering concern for the oppressed – often diminishes his art. And he *is* an artist, in brilliant fits and starts, as I intend to demonstrate.

'He writes as a nightingale sings' – this sentiment became common parlance in regard to Istrati when he was rapidly producing book after book. The nightingale's melody can still be heard intermittently, whenever Istrati's alter ego Adrien Zograffi is simply recording an event or a happy circumstance with what reads like complete naturalness. It's that quality that caused the sceptical Brandes to declare that he 'loved Istrati more than any other contemporary novelist in the whole of Europe'. Brandes was beguiled by Istati's naive style, by a *naiveté* that doesn't register as *faux*. Istrati always appears to be writing from the heart. That was the reason for his huge success, and it's also the reason why so many of the scenes in his fiction are an embarrassment to read today.

Panait Istrati was born in 1884 in Braila, a port in the Danube 'over which float the shining mirages of freedom and infinite space', to use the words of the exiled Romanian novelist and essayist Norman Manea. His mother, Joitza Istrati, was a peasant and his father a Greek smuggler, Gherasim Valsamis, who died of tuberculosis in 1885. He studied at a primary school until he was twelve, and then from 1902 to 1912 he lived the life of a vagabond in the company of his great friend Mikhail Kasanski. He travelled to Egypt, Turkey, Syria and South Africa. He worked as a *valet de chambre*, as a waiter, a sign painter and as an itinerant photographer. The youths became expert stowaways on ships, to judge by the ease with which they contrived to visit one country after another. Their method was to leave each ship at its first port of call.

He wrote to his anxious mother, sending her money when he could and reassuring her that he enjoyed being a vagabond. On his return to Braila, he befriended a militant socialist, Stefan Gheorgiu. He was appointed secretary to the newly formed ship workers union and contributed many articles, in Romanian, to the left-wing press. Romania was still very much in the grip of feudalism, with boyars in possession of large estates and the peasantry eking out a living by working on the land for risibly low wages. Istrati's polemic was considered inflammatory, and it was certainly his intention to make the wealthy feel guilty. In 1913, in Paris, he made the acquaintance of a shoemaker, Georges

Ionesco, another Romanian anxious to end what he saw to be a feudal tyranny. It is a grim irony that at this time Romania was more secure than it had been for centuries, on good political terms with the rest of Europe, especially with Britain. Istrati's socialist dream was not to become reality, and when he died in 1935 his country had no less than two ultra right-wing parties jockeying for power. Which one hated the Jews most? That was the terrible question that had to be answered.

In 1916, Istrati left Romania and went to Switzerland, where he received treatment for his tubercular condition at the sanatorium in Leysin. He decided to learn French, reading the classics with the aid of a dictionary. He published his first article in French in 1919, with the title *Tolstoïsme ou bolchevisme*. A new acquaintance, Josué Jéhouda, introduced him to the work of Romain Rolland, whose novel *Jean-Christophe*, about the growth of a musical genius, led to his being awarded the Nobel Prize in 1915. This turgidly worthy book is now unreadable, its characters lifeless, its prose sermonizing.

Rolland was a genuinely kind and decent man. Stefan Zweig, in his autobiography *The World of Yesterday*, praises his generosity to other artists and his humane understanding of the problems of those less fortunate than himself. Panait Istrati was to be the recipient of his kindness in a startling fashion. On 3 January 1921 he was in Nice, without a job and in poor health. It was on that day that he attempted suicide, by slitting his throat. He was taken to hospital, where he was tended to with care and sympathy. He had on his person a letter addressed to Romain Rolland, to whom it was duly dispatched. The letter ran to some fifty pages, with detailed accounts of his vagabond years and of his peasant life in the countryside beyond Braila and the nearby port Galaţi. (Readers of Bram Stoker's *Dracula* will recall that the undead count returns to Romania in his earth-filled box via Galaţi.) Rolland's response to this eccentric communication, or cry for help, was immediate and enthusiastic. He detected a 'divine fire' in the unknown's writing and declared him the 'Gorky of the Balkans'. With Rolland's encouragement, Istrati set to work on *Kyra Kyralina*, finding employment again as an itinerant photographer along the Promenade in Nice. In August 1923, the novel appeared in the magazine *Europe*, with a preface by Rolland. The next year *Kyra* and the book of novellas *Oncle Anghel* were published to instant acclaim. Bold and beautiful Romanian brigands, fighting for a just cause, were suddenly in vogue. Several instalments of the Romantic saga soon followed, with stronger women breaking the hearts and spirits of otherwise strong men, with cutlasses flashing in the dark, with primitive scores being settled in an appropriately primitive manner, with songs sung round the camp fire while lambs are roasted on a spit and a vast amount of red wine is consumed. 'Freedom' is the word that occurs most frequently – the limitless freedom of the outdoors, of communing with nature and the freedom from Turkish or Greek or, worse, Romanian oppressors. No wonder the books appealed to so many liberal-minded people, particularly in that 'low, dishonest decade', the 1930s. The words are by W.H. Auden, who was not to be made a Nobel laureate.

Istrati wrote in French, as did two greater Romanian writers – the playwright Eugène Ionesco and the mischievously pessimistic philosopher Emil Cioran. He lacks their elegance and conciseness. Indeed, he once remarked that he had little patience with literature and loathed being called a professional author. It was Istrati who summoned up the nightingale, saying that he wanted to write as the nightingale sings. The conceit retains its charm, even as one realizes that his decision to tell his stories in a language infinitely more available to a large audience than Romanian makes commercial sense. Yet the thought persists that the nightingale Istrati might have sounded sweeter in his mother tongue.

In 1928, Istrati accompanied Nikos Kazantzakis – the author of *Zorba the Greek* and *Christ Recrucified* – on a trip to Russia. The passionately left-wing couple were impressed by the prevailing regime to begin with and Istrati even had plans to live in Moscow with a young woman he had fallen in love with. (His marriage to Anna Munsh, with whom he is photographed in 1925, was presumably at an end.) But the naively uncritical Istrati soon found much to criticize, not least the fact that ordinary Russians were granted no opportunities to speak out against the Communist party. He was appalled by this lack of a basic freedom. The truth is that he displayed more political acumen than André Gide, Bernard Shaw and Beatrice and Sidney Webb, who all came back from the Soviet Union bearing the glad tidings that Communism was responsible for an earthly paradise, in which everyone is equal. On leaving Russia, Istrati penned two essays in which he expressed his disillusion with the paradisal state and was instantly chastized for doing so by such Communist stalwarts as Victor Serge, Henri Barbusse (who wrote the superb *Under Fire*, one of the very best novels concerned with life in the trenches during the First World War) and by Romain Rolland. Istrati was dismissed as a *petit bourgeois*, a much-used term of abuse for anyone who dared to express doubts about what was going on in Russia in those days. The high-minded Rolland terminated their friendship, though there was a reconciliation of sorts not long before Istrati's death. The 'Gorky of the Balkans' has the distinction of being one of the first artists who saw through the elaborate facade the Soviets set up to delude liberal intellectuals in the 1920s and 30s and beyond.

The *vagabond du monde*, as he liked to call himself, returned to Romania in his final years. Despite ill health, he continued to help the poor. His last known piece of writing is the preface to the French edition of George Orwell's *Down and Out in Paris and London*. It was published in May 1935, just weeks after his death on 16 April. Like the father he never knew, he died of tuberculosis.

*

'Oncle Anghel', the long story that gives his second book its title – it appeared in Britain as *Balkan Tavern* – contains some of Istrati's finest writing, alongside some of his worst. That's the trouble with his fiction and it is caused by his inattention to the niceties of style and content. He throws everything onto the page – both the dross and the gold – with no compunction to rewrite or reconsider what he has set down in his haste. There are passages that convince the discerning reader that Georg Brandes was correct in his assessment of Istrati's literary status and there are others that lead one to think that his formidable intelligence must have been atrophied. Fate, always capitalized, makes too many interventions, when a simple exposition of a tragic circumstance would suffice to indicate that life for some is hellish. Anghel's story is similar to that of Job in the Old Testament, or to that of Lear, with Adrien Zograffi acting as his Cordelia.

Anghel is a grand creation and at his grandest in the second part of the tale, which deals with his death-in-life. The young Anghel toiled for ten years in the vineyard of a wine merchant before setting up his own business when the war of 1877 against the Turks was won by Romania. Anghel is an innkeeper when we meet him, with a vineyard near the tavern. He is rich, in a community that is mostly impoverished. Then the sad facts of his past are revealed. He has married a physically beautiful woman and discovered that she is a deceitful slut. She bears him three children, whom he sends to school in Galaţi when they are each five years old. His inn is set on fire by envious neighbours, and his wife – who was on the premises – survives the blaze. She dies of pneumonia and despite her serious inadequacies as a mother Anghel feels remorse at her passing. His two little girls drown in the Danube and his son Alexander is killed during a cavalry charge, He is left with nothing but his tavern and the love he has for his nephew Adrien.

Anghel is not drawn to suicide. He drinks instead. His philosophical relationship with the bottle is movingly recorded. Brandy is a substitute for his lost son and daughters, for his bleak loss of faith. He is stoical in his wretchedness. As he lies dying, he reminds Adrien of a Romanian proverb *vermii cei nea dormiţi*: the worms that sleep not – or perhaps more elegantly – the worms that keep eternal vigil. As Romanian proverbs go, this one is very Romanian indeed. Cioran, the author of *The Temptation to Exist*, could have written it.

In the closing pages of 'Oncle Anghel', a marvellous character appears, as poignant as any of Dickens's abandoned sprites. A boy, whose every movement is uncoordinated, makes himself Anghel's servant, pouring his brandy and alerting him to the arrival of strangers. For once, Istrati doesn't explain him away, but affords him the dignity of being mysterious. Bathos and mawkishness are avoided. How did Istrati summon up the tact to free this unloved child from sentimentality? I have no idea, but I do understand his presence in the narrative is believably miraculous.

'Oncle Anghel' continues to haunt me, for all its patent imperfections. It saddens me that Istrati is not substantial enough as a novelist to justify his lapses of judgment, his bursts of well-intentioned editorializing. I despair over his lack of discipline, his misplaced trust in inspiration.

*

Panait Istrati is an enchanting figure, from a culture largely occupied by demons. He writes of a peasant life he was born into, which has still not vanished from Romania. This son of the Romanian soil became a snazzy dresser once he achieved success, wearing spats and plus fours and the smartest tweeds. There he is in photographs at the height of his brief international fame, looking as if he could mingle with Fred Astaire or Scott Fitzgerald.

Istrati was hailed as a genius, as many unformed talents are hailed to this day and will be in the future. Hyperbole can murder talent, by giving it a confidence it hasn't earned or merits. There are writers of the present who will share his fate, though with more justification. He actually was possessed of a kernel of greatness and a voice that soars sometimes into regions other writers haven't visited. I see him as a nightingale with a sore throat, a stricken songbird, a human being of immense sweetness who just might have been a major novelist.

Donald Paterson

The Chain

His mobile phone was in the cottage, two hundred yards away, and he felt that he didn't like to leave the body lying here by itself. He looked along the single row of cottages on the front, to see if anyone was looking out of a window, but there was nobody. It was beginning to get dark and the curtains were all closed. He turned back to the body and forced himself to notice things.

The yellow jumper was torn at the neck, as if it had been caught on the black rocks and pulled apart by the sea. There was a gold chain tangled in the wool. He could see the metal glint in what light was left. A few flakes of snow began to fall, and he shivered.

He looked behind him again then reached forward, clenching his mouth shut, and tugged at the chain. It came loose easily, because it was broken, and it threaded out of the yellow jumper without any problem. He wondered if he had broken it pulling the body from the water, or if it had got broken while the woman was still in the sea, and it was just luck and a fragment of wool that had stopped it from disappearing altogether, forever. It was quite a fine chain, the links too small to see properly in the failing light. He put it in his pocket for safe keeping and stood up beside the body.

The cliff behind the cottages was dark and towering, and the snow was picking up. He could not see up to the car park at the top of the cliff. A wave hit the rocks by the jetty and foam splashed his boots. It was a funny feeling, him all alone with this dead woman, and everyone else safely inside their own homes. He left the body and went back along the front to his cottage.

It was warm inside and he picked up the phone and called the police. While he spoke to them he edged the curtain open a little. She was lying there on the jetty by herself and the snow was already beginning to settle on her even though she would still be wet.

Nothing like this had ever happened to him before. He didn't like it very much.

*

A policeman came, and then an ambulance, and the woman was taken away and he never saw her again.

The policeman was young, about half his age, and he understood right away that Chris was upset about what had happened. He told Chris to sit down, and then went through to make coffee for them. He used the cafetière that Chris had got as a Christmas present from his brother and that he had only used once before, about a year ago.

The policeman sat down and said, 'Now, Mr Neill, just relax a bit and tell me all about what happened.'

Chris told the story and the policeman made a note of it.

'I have to ask you, did you recognize the body at all?'

'No,' said Chris. 'But she was . . .'

'I understand,' said the policeman. 'There's no reason why you should. I just have to ask that sort of thing. You didn't recognize the clothes at all?'

Chris shook his head and the policeman wrote something down.

'There was no sign of a jacket?'

'No.'

After a while they sat and spoke about the weather and the policeman said he'd have to be getting back to the station at Fraserburgh, and that it was possible that there might be another officer coming to see him, but then again maybe not.

After the policeman had gone, Chris locked the door of his cottage against the wind, and went round the house putting out the lights. As he was undressing he found the gold chain in his pocket and swore at himself for not having remembered to mention it to the policeman. He decided he'd go into Fraserburgh the next day to hand it in.

He lay in bed that night and saw the flesh hanging onto the bone, and the chain, shiny in the yellow wool.

*

Chris had never thought of himself as a thief, but as the next day and then another one passed and he didn't go into the police station with the chain, he had to think that maybe he was. He didn't know why he didn't go in. He liked the chain, the way it sat comfortably in his pocket, a woman's possession. It made him feel that there was another part of his life, a part he had never looked at closely but that must have been there all the time.

When he went out of his cottage, after two days inside, Jean Peters was there at her door, as if she'd been waiting for him.

'How are you, Mr Neill?' she asked.

The stone wall of his cottage was to his left, the sea was pounding out its rhythm on his right and Jean Peters was between him and the path up to the car park.

'I'm all right,' he said to her. 'How are you?'

'It must have been awful. If I'd known, I'd have been out to help you. We all would,' she said, indicating the twelve cottages that made up Drailie. 'We'd have been able to help you.'

'I just went out for a walk for a few minutes,' he said. 'And there she was. If I'd turned back a few yards earlier I'd not have seen her. And who knows where she'd have been now?' He'd thought about that in the last day or so, and it frightened him, the idea of being all alone in the waves, having been near a kind of rescue, and missing the chance. He said, 'I tried to help her. At first I thought she'd just fallen in, slipped on the seaweed and fallen, you know?' His intention had been to do good. He wanted to communicate that.

'Well,' she said. 'If there's anything you need.'

He drove the long road to Elgin and wandered around. He bought milk and bread and some biscuits. He didn't feel like buying anything for cooking a proper meal, and anyway there were still things in the freezer. He'd just wanted to get away. He thought everyone was looking at him, but they weren't.

*

For some reason it wasn't until the third day that the story appeared on the television news. The police had called a press conference and they'd got a tailor's dummy and dressed it either in the clothes the body had been in or else in ones very similar.

There was a brown wig on the manikin and the face was blank. They were asking if the clothes rang a bell with anybody. They said that the woman had been found by a resident of the coastal village of Drailie, but it was thought that the woman had come from elsewhere.

Later that day there was a knock at the door and when Chris went to answer it, there was a young man there in a grey donkey jacket. His hair was untidy, blown about by the wind.

'John Phillips,' he said. He was from the *Press and Journal*.

They went in and Chris sat down, and John Phillips took a good look round before he started to speak. Chris felt that the room looked dirty, and he wished he'd had the hoover out in the last three weeks, or that he'd dusted the ornaments that still reminded him of his Aunt Susan.

Like the policeman, John Phillips had a notebook, held closed by an elastic band. He snapped the elastic band off and put it in his pocket. They chatted for a while about what had happened.

'Maybe,' said the journalist, 'if we run a story it'll jog someone's memory. Help the police that way.'

'How old are you?' asked Chris.

'Twenty-six, why?'

'No reason.'

'How old are you, Mr Neill?'

'Forty-eight.'

'You lived here all your life?'

'More or less.'

'Must be a very tight little community. Never actually been down here before. Probably gets a bit spooky in the winter, eh?'

Chris shook his head. 'No, not that tight. Everyone else here has moved into the village. Two of the cottages are holiday homes now. They're standing empty just now. I don't really know anybody that well, when it comes down to it.' He hoped the journalist wouldn't write that part in the newspaper.

'I see. You ever find anything like this before? I mean a body washed up like that?' His pencil was ready.

'No,' said Chris. 'I've found lots of things. The usual stuff – bottles, shoes, you know. Things get washed into the bay, but then they get washed back out again. If I hadn't gone out when I did, she might have drifted off again, away into the North Sea.'

John Phillips took a little digital camera out of his pocket. 'Mind if I take your photo?'

The next day, there he was on page seven of the *Press and Journal*, alongside an artist's impression of what the woman might have looked like, if she hadn't had her flesh scraped away by the salt and the stone. The sketch showed her face and her hair and the top of her yellow jumper, but the chain was still in his pocket.

He wanted to tell someone about it, but he couldn't think who. Everyone he had ever known had retreated into the past, without even a glance over their shoulders. It was too late to call them back.

*

It was on the news for a few nights, and then it drifted away. The appeal for anyone who thought they might know the woman to come forward hadn't worked. Chris took the chain and put it inside a vase that sat on his mantelpiece, and every now and then he would take it out and look at it. The first time he tipped the vase so that the chain slid out, it came with a little cloud of dust and a dead fly. He washed out the vase so that it was the cleanest thing in the room before he put the chain back in.

One day Mr Pettigrew from three doors along, who came from Derby, stopped him as he walked back to his house from the path down from the car park.

'Mr Neill,' said Mr Pettigrew. 'How's the writing going?'

'Fine, thank you,' replied Chris, who hadn't written anything since that snowy night, and not much in the years leading up to it.

'I hear they've found out who she was. Did you hear that on the news this lunchtime?'

It was cold standing there, and Chris could see the water in old Mr Pettigrew's eyes. 'No,' he said. 'I didn't hear that.'

Mr Pettigrew continued, 'It seems she came from Easter Ross. Tarbat. Near where that lighthouse is. She walked out on her husband at Christmas time and said she was going to her sister's.

So her husband goes off to *his* sister's in Munich, so he didn't see the thing on the news about her. Because he was in Germany, you see. But when he came back he phoned the woman's sister, or something, and they realized she was missing. And so on. That's how it came out. Or Berlin, maybe, I can't remember. But that's it.'

'Well, well,' said Chris. 'Really?'

It was on the news later, and he watched it rather than sitting in front of his typewriter again. He thought about the man, a bit jealous of him for having had so much, then losing it, then losing it more permanently.

The man had not wanted to be interviewed, had told the journalist he wanted to guard his privacy, so when he turned up at Chris's front door three days later, it was a surprise. For some reason, Chris had imagined him as quite a big man, strong and tall. But he was a few inches shorter than Chris himself. His hair was receding and he had a little thin moustache.

They walked along in front of the cottages, and Chris was aware of them being watched from the windows.

'I hope you don't mind,' the man said for the third time. 'The policeman said you seemed like a decent kind of man. That you wouldn't mind.'

'I don't mind.'

'So where was it you found her?' asked the man, who had introduced himself as Ronnie, not mentioning his second name, assuming Chris would know it. Chris showed him the place and they stood for a minute, looking down at the sea breathing in and out and the seaweed hanging on to the rock under the water, trying to touch the surface. The man said, 'I haven't seen her. It was . . . too late. I . . . her watch, and her clothes. They showed them to me. That's how I knew her.'

He didn't say anything about how his wife had left him. They walked out to the end of the jetty and watched a big supply boat inch along the horizon. The wind made their eyes sting.

'I wanted to ask,' the man said. 'There was one thing they never had in that metal box. They said it wasn't there. You didn't notice, did you, if she was wearing a gold chain?'

'Round her neck?' asked Chris.

'Yes. It was one I gave her. I was wondering if someone . . . you know . . . maybe someone at the hospital . . .'

'No,' Chris said firmly. 'There wasn't a chain. A gold chain? No, I'm certain there wasn't. I would have remembered.'

'Oh well,' said the man. 'Just a thought. Never mind.'

Chris stood at the bottom of the path, watching, and when the man reached the top he turned and looked back down at Drailie, his shoulders hunched up, his hands in his pocket.

To have all that, thought Chris, as he went back home. And then to lose it all. He discovered the feeling inside was something like anger.

There was paper in his typewriter when he sat down in front of it, but he couldn't think what to type. He worried about himself. He slowly typed the words THE CHAIN in the middle at the top of the sheet, then he pressed the back space button nine times and typed a capital X over each letter. He took the sheet of paper out and went and put it in the fire.

He crouched there, balanced, one hand on the mantelpiece, watching the paper blacken, then burn, then glow red, then disintegrate, then disappear. His hand was close to the vase but he made himself not take the chain out to look at, to let the fine links slip through his fingers, to make a pool of gold in his palm. He didn't even look in at it, although he wanted to.

In his dream that night he saw her fine hair float on the water and it reminded him of smoke, as if something inside him was burning, as if his empty life was being consumed. He woke up asking himself why he'd taken the chain, why he'd pulled the body out and not gone for help, why he'd gone for a walk to the jetty that night. One question led to another.

In the late afternoon of the following day he stood at the end of the jetty for a long time, then he climbed the path and turned away from the little car park along the cliff tops until he came to a place that he knew. There was frost on the grass and he sat on a cold rock and looked out to sea. Away to the west he could see the lighthouse at Tarbat spark with light, then disappear, on and off, again and again. He thought of her body coming from there. The cold that came down with the dark settled on him and he sat there.

He could see Drailie down below him to the left. The roofs were dark shapes and a little light spilled onto the street from the front windows. There was darkness in front of his cottage. He could see no movement down there apart from the inescapable heaving of the ocean.

When it got too cold to sit here, he thought, he'd go down the path again and go in and pick up the vase and look at the glint of gold in the shadows. Then he'd see.

Fay Weldon

A Little Nest of Pedagogues

Some women want to be everything to men and children, and are very dangerous. It is their delight to destroy other women's families. They do it by stealing affection. The thief may come in therapist form – six months later and you find yourself replaced in the affections of spouse, lover, or child, and your once-beloved quoting passages from *Cutting the Ties That Bind* as they pack for pastures new. Or sometimes she turns up in the form of a sex siren, who will use her womanly powers – that is, sheer efficacy of blow job – to oust the wife from the marital bed – but at least this version generally lets you know she is coming. The once-up-and-down look, the 'Well, you're no rival, you poor thing' air, puts you on your guard: the cute leopard-print neck scarves, the little high heels, announce to everyone the would-be robber's on her way. But I have never known one until now who came in so innocent a form, that of a tennis player.

Such a healthy, smiling, friendly soul, was Norma! She had good leg muscles, a pleasant but not over-pretty face, short reddish hair, was a regular church-goer (Catholic) and coached school children at tennis for a living. She was apparently happily married, to Desmond, a primary school teacher, was in her early thirties, and had no children. There was certainly no reason to suspect Norma in advance of any kind of bad behaviour – except, I suppose, that one expects Catholics in their thirties to have children: they disobey the Pope and their God's commands if they do not.

Norma did not seem to have expensive tastes or seductress habits: she wore trainers with her mini-skirts, quite often white ankle socks, not too much make-up, and did not drink. I must confess I sometimes drink more wine than I should. It is the failing of the solitary female who has spent too many years looking for

Mr Right and not found him. Which was not surprising. I could not be happy with anyone who did not share my interest in the classics and that cut down my field of choice considerably.

Norma and Desmond had come to live in the flat next to me, above Roger and Carol, our local antique dealers; *Bric-a-Brac, dealers in objet d'art.* (In vain did I tell them it should be *objets d'art.* They refused to believe me. A French friend had told them the singular was right and nothing would move them.) *Bric-a-Brac's* empire now stretched the length of three shops in the Cathedral Arcade, and of the three flats above, Desmond and Norma had one; I, who scraped a living – but one that I loved – tutoring children in classics, had another; and Marlene, a single woman of a certain age who taught maths full-time, lived in the other. They were cosy flats but no one could pretend they were grand.

Marlene and I used our second bedrooms for tutoring: Norma spent a good six hours a day at the tennis club just around the corner and Desmond supplemented his teaching income with work for the Boy Scout movement. Our three small households shared an entrance – through *Bric-a-Brac's* side door. Roger and Carol believed in letting accommodation to the teaching profession – as tenants we deserved much, demanded little, and behaved well, they said. A little nest of pedagogues, we described ourselves.

Saffron Dellacox was nine and came to me for Latin coaching twice a week. Her parents had already decided on her behalf that she would go to Oxford. Even to me it seemed a possibility: she was an exceptionally bright little girl, and charming with it. Her siblings – Wallace, aged six, and Emily, aged five – were also part of the new coaching culture; that is to say Wallace and Emily both went to Marlene for extra maths lessons, and Emily, whose hand–eye co-ordination was a source of worry, also went to Norma for physiotherapy. It seemed to me that little Emily was just something of a daydreamer and was so impetuous she banged into things, but the adult Dellacoxes left nothing to chance. I cannot really complain about the coaching culture – it is how I and many like me earn our living these days – but sometimes I wonder where childhood has gone? But the little Dellacoxes were avid for learning and seemed happy enough and were in and out of our flats all the time and I would see their noses pressed against *Bric a Brac*'s window, which featured one of the most beautiful and elaborate Victorian dolls' houses you have ever seen; its tiny pieces of furniture bought and sold and forever changing.

All three children were small boned and pixy-like, with large eyes, clear skins and pointy chins. They took after their mother Sheila, who came, as we used to say, from a good family, was slim and attractive, always polite and charming, busy about her domestic business, organizing her large house and her children's social and academic lives, spending her husband's money, going to art classes – she once had an exhibition at the local bookshop and sold every painting. Her life was very different from mine: I suppose many people would see it as much better, that she had everything and I had nothing, but I didn't see it as such. I was happy as I was. I liked to live a tranquil life and was well aware that if you have a great deal you also have a great deal to lose.

I could see the local tennis courts from my back window and every Saturday morning all the Dellacoxes would be down there, improving their strokes; Emily showing off her new dexterity, Wallace forever nearly beating Saffron, Mother happy and laughing, Father patiently instructing. And Norma, who seemed on friendly terms with all of them, would often go off for cold drinks arm in arm with Sheila. The father, Tommy Dellacox, was of a different physical type to the rest of the family – slow moving, big boned, blond, powerful. He had a faraway look in his eye, like some Viking surveying the horizon in search of lost treasure. His serve was devastating, though, nothing laid back or distant about it. Very much here and now. And Saffron said her father played a lot of golf and had a wicked drive. She was really proud of him.

Marlene and I would get asked to the house for their twice-a-year parties. The Dellacoxes lived well – a BMW in the drive, a swimming pool, a tennis court, flowing champagne. He made his money, Desmond told me, importing and distributing Thai furniture. Desmond didn't seem to approve, but then Desmond disapproved of anything that smelt of privilege or unnecessary consumerism. He drank the champagne they offered him, but he never could forgive. (My reference is to the Victorian ballad about the poor but honest parents and the fallen girl – they drink the champagne she brings them, but they never can forgive? I fear you won't recognize the allusion; so many of the resonances of language have gone.) Norma

Sheila would wear some designer dress the likes of us could never afford, and look fabulous, and Tommy would regard his wife with pride and evident affection and pat her shapely bottom, and she would giggle. (Desmond found that excruciating.) Norma would put on a string of beads in honour of the occasion, if we were lucky, and would run round in her no-nonsense chatty way on her stocky legs hanging coats and generally helping out. Norma was not exactly an ideas person. She talked Wimbledon and Tescos, just as Tommy talked St Andrews and Black and Decker, but that was about it. Whereas I could have a good conversation with Sheila about some minor point in Roman history, but that was not Norma's style at all, or indeed Tommy's. Nevertheless I once heard Sheila refer to Norma as her best friend: energy and humour could make up for a lot. Everyone liked Norma – except sometimes, I thought, her husband.

I had been teaching Saffron for nearly a year when I first saw signs of trouble. Saffron came in with her homework not done, and suddenly unable to tell a past pluperfect from a future perfect. I asked her if anything was the matter and she shook her head and clammed up, so I left it alone. Then I realized I hadn't seen Sheila at the tennis club for some time: the family was coming down without her on Saturday mornings. Well, perhaps she had sprained an ankle, or was pregnant, or just had too much to do. People can change their habits without interference or comment from me.

I asked Saffron how her mother was, and she said 'fine'; she'd been to the theatre in London with Norma, so I thought well, that's OK. I was glad for Norma too. Norma and Desmond hadn't been getting on too well – I'd heard the rows through the wall – and Desmond had got a secondment in Delhi for the Scout movement, so he was to be away for a whole year, with only occasional home furlough. At least Norma was getting out to the bright lights with Sheila every now and then.

Then one day I found Saffron staring hard at her hand when

she should have been writing out her vocabulary. She turned to me and asked, 'Is my hand trembling? I thought I saw it trembling.'

I said I didn't think it was, I hadn't noticed, but perhaps she'd been clutching the pen too tight; that could make a hand tremble ever so. She relaxed her hand and the trembling stopped. But she began to cry.

'My mother's got Parkinson's,' she said. 'I'm not meant to know but I do.'

'Don't be silly,' I said automatically, shocked. 'She can't have. She's much too young.' But even as I spoke I remembered the cousin I'd been to school with who developed it when she was in her mid twenties, and I knew well enough that you could never be too young, and what's more, the younger you are when it starts the more aggressively it advances. The illness has all the strength and determination of youth. I supposed Sheila Dellacox to be in her early to mid thirties. I did not want to believe this. If it was true, what she was telling me was terrible in its implications; tragic.

'You can get it at any age,' said Saffron, 'I'm surprised you don't know that. It's all on the Internet. She has the symptoms. I saw a note she wrote to Norma and the writing was, like, so small?'

'I'm sorry,' I said, helplessly.

'You descend it, too,' she said, as if it were my fault. Today's children are in the habit of blaming everyone: their teachers when they don't pass their exams, their parents when they're not happy. They simply cannot accept that neither they nor the world are perfect. The doctrine of original sin, which I learned at my mother's knee, is unknown to them.

'Inherit it,' I corrected. 'Not descend it. You are right, there is a hereditary element involved in Parkinson's, but it's far from inevitable. And has anyone actually told you this? It's not just all in your head, Saffron?' But I realized that for some time now Tommy, not Sheila, had been delivering Emily to Norma and Wallace to Marlene. Saffron was considered old enough to cycle over by herself.

'I know all right,' she said. 'I heard the doctor talking. They thought I was in the pool. I haven't told Wallace and Emily. I think they ought to know. They get cross because Mummy doesn't seem to do anything except sit about. She's no fun any more.'

'What did the note say?' I asked Saffron, I was not quite sure why. It seemed important. I was in a state of shock. No one wants a tragedy unfolding under their noses. That poor woman, that poor family. Whom the Gods love, they love to destroy.

'Just that she didn't think she could get to the tournament next week. Would Norma go in her place. Norma comes over a lot now to help Mummy out. That's OK, I like Norma. So does Mummy.'

It didn't seem to me that Norma was much of a threat to family happiness, not compared with Parkinson's. Norma was too healthy; she had too high a colour and blunt a manner to be a source of illicit eroticism in anyone's life, even though Desmond was away. She was not just an *affaire* kind of person.

I said to Saffron, 'Then that's good, isn't it. But I think you ought to be sharing your worries with your parents, not with me. Shall we get on with the lesson?'

You do have to be careful if you're a tutor not to overstep the mark: the tendency, if left unchecked, is for the teachers to enter into a state of rivalry with the parents: to show themselves as more concerned, more helpful, more loving, more even-tempered than the parents. Just plain better, in fact. I was there to teach verbs and tenses, not to be part of the Dellacoxes life, and had to remember it.

'OK,' said Saffron. 'I get the picture. You don't want to know. Big deal.' And she took up Kennedy's *Latin Primer* – I am a very old-fashioned teacher, I daresay, to be still using the book I myself learned from as a child, but nothing printed nowadays can better it – and she started quarrelling with me about irregular verbs, to which she seemed to take moral exception. She was eleven by now and growing up, and bright children like to defy their text books.

But I did tell her as she left that whatever happened at home, the way out was always going to be through the life of the mind. If something terrible happened there was always that to fall back upon, there was something else to think about other than your own woes, and you could earn yourself a respite from time to time, even from tragedy. Because I knew with a terrible clarity that it was true: that Saffron's mother was ill and was not going to get better. I remember the shock of seeing the signature on my cousin's will, cramped and tiny, when I'd remembered it from school as being large, strong and expansive. When Saffron left I cried for the broken promises the world makes to us when we are young.

That night I knocked on Norma's door and found her sitting on her stairs rubbing athlete's foot ointment between her toes. I don't know why this detail struck me so forcibly – I think it was just that Norma was so monumentally practical, and if I started talking about the broken promises the world makes she wouldn't have a clue what I was talking about, and would suggest I tried a course of antidepressants. Suddenly, I almost disliked her. I asked her about Sheila Dellacox and Norma said yes, it was all a dreadful tragedy, Sheila had been diagnosed with a particularly nasty form of Parkinson's. The doctors gave her two years. The Dellacoxes were keeping it quiet as long as possible and leaving it to the last moment to tell the children. Poor Tommy was devastated.

I was driven to say I expected Sheila was quite upset too.

Norma said Sheila was being completely wonderful about it all. Sheila had asked Norma to be a kind of stand-in for her at the normal events: school sports days, horse trials, concerts, tournaments and so forth, knowing that she, Sheila, would grow progressively weaker and shakier and less and less able to live a normal life. Norma was to go places with Tommy and keep him cheerful and not thinking dismal thoughts, making everything as normal as possible for the children.

I said but it wasn't in the least normal, how could it ever be, and Norma just frowned as if I'd said something puzzling, and finished doing her feet and put on socks and made me a cup of tea and a little ham sandwich. She knew a hungry woman when she saw one. I said she was a good friend to Sheila, and Norma said she hoped so, Sheila was her best friend, and you did what you could for your friends, however inconvenient. I was ashamed of myself. How could you not like Norma? I'd been blaming the messenger for the news.

The children most evidently liked Norma. When she dropped Wallace and Emily round at Marlene's, they'd be giggly and noisy and playing games. Tommy had taken to dropping Saffron at my place by car. He had the strained, almost childish look a man gets when he is afflicted by loss and sorrow, a certain narrowing of the eyes, as if the light is always too bright for him. But you can imagine that kind of thing. If I had not known I might not have noticed.

Saffron did not refer again to her mother. I'd blown that one, apparently. She was to take an early GCSE, at thirteen, and get it out of the way. I said to Tommy that I was sorry to hear of his wife's illness, and he thanked me for my consideration, said that new treatments were making for a positive outlook, and obviously did not want to talk more. While Norma said it was hopeless: it was just a matter of time. Sheila was more or less bed-bound and had taken up residence in the garden room, where it was easier for her to be nursed.

Then Saffron started not turning up to lessons. Her enthusiasm had gone. She said she wanted to give up Latin, she would rather play tennis if she had any spare time. Whatever was the point of an old dead language that no one had spoken for two thousand years? Her friends were beginning to say she was weird. Then Emily and Wallace dropped out of extra maths. I asked Norma what the matter with everyone was, and she said lightly it was probably better for the children to stop extra coaching until the worst was over and done with. That sent chills up my spine. The kids were better out in the healthy fresh air, Norma reported Tommy and Sheila as saying, not poring over books all the time, and brooding.

But Marlene said she thought it was all Norma's doing, nothing to do with Tommy and Sheila. Norma was just sick of the ferrying around. Norma was spending most of her time over at the Dellacoxes'. Had I noticed, asked Marlene, how Norma's dress sense had changed?

I wondered why Marlene had it in for Norma, all of a sudden. It was more than that Marlene now had a couple of inconvenient tutoring vacancies to fill, in the absence of Wallace and Emily – no, there was a real edge to her voice. It's terrible when something so pleasant – like the whole cosy, together world of *Bric a Brac*, its little nest of helpful pedagogues, the doll's house in the window – turns sour and becomes a source of unease. I still did not want to believe it was happening.

'Well, yes,' I said. 'She's lost weight and glammed up.'

'I heard Desmond has taken a permanent job in Delhi,' said Marlene. 'And Roger and Carol are reletting the flat. Norma says she doesn't need it any more. You and I are decidedly out of the loop.'

And the next Saturday, when the Dellacox family, which now consisted of Tommy and Norma, Saffron, Wallace and Emily, instead of Tommy and Sheila, Saffron, Wallace and Emily, put in their cheerful, carefree appearance at the tennis courts, I realized just how popular the new version of the family was. Everyone loved Norma. Quite a few had found Sheila a little too grand, inclined to put on airs, and too ambitious for her children. Oxford, indeed! And all of a sudden Tommy had lost the narrow-eyed, persecuted look he'd had of late, and seemed relaxed and happy.

Then a surprising thing happened. I got a phone call from Sheila asking me to come over and talk about Saffron's Latin. Her voice was weak and thin, but I felt a surge of hope. Perhaps Sheila was in remission? Perhaps they'd changed their minds about the importance of the outdoor life? Perhaps Saffron was going to start again with classics? I hoped so. Anyone can hit a ball but it's a rare child who is prepared to argue about the difference between a gerund and a gerundive. I said as much to Sheila but she didn't seem interested: she just wanted me over there between three and four that afternoon. Saffron would let me in.

So I went. The house was in good order, the pool sparkling and the grounds well manicured. There was no BMW in the drive. I rang the bell and Saffron answered. She seemed surprised and a little embarrassed to see me. She had grown in the four months or so since I'd seen her: tightly waisted skirt and a pert little bosom. She was watching TV and wanted to get back to it.

'I'm Mummy-sitting,' she said. 'She's in the back room. Down the corridor and last room on the left. Daddy and Norma are at Wimbledon. I stayed home: tennis is boring.'

She didn't offer to show me to her mother's room. She went back into the living room. For some reason the backs of her legs put me in mind of Norma's. They were thick and stompy: broad for their length. That's what comes of playing too much tennis when young – or perhaps she'd just decided to grow into Norma, not Sheila.

I tapped on Sheila's door and went in. There was a disagreeable sick-room smell: disinfectant and urine mixed, the kind of smell you get in a badly run home for the very old. I could see why Saffron didn't go in if she could help it. Probably nobody did. It occurred to me that by virtue of a little judicious neglect, Norma could organize that well enough. I put the thought from my mind. Sheila was stick-thin, sparse haired and trembly, sitting in an armchair beside the bed. I sat beside her. She tried to smile but it didn't really work.

'I worry about Saffron,' she said, straight to the point. She didn't have much strength to waste. 'I didn't want her to give up Latin.'

'It happens like that sometimes,' I said. 'It's nobody's fault. Girls used to take longer to grow up. There was more time to get the grammar into their bones before they lost interest.'

'But it *is* somebody's fault,' she said. 'It's Norma's fault. She's sleeping with my husband, you know. They deny it but it's true. I moved out of the bedroom. I came back from hospital and found three red hairs in our bed. Pubic hairs, I think. What do you think?'

She made me open the little leather-bound book of poetry by the bed. It was a copy of the *Rubaiyat of Omar Khayyam*. My favourite book when I was fifteen. This was a nightmare.

'*The moving finger writes*' Sheila quoted,

'*And having writ moves on,*
Nor all thy piety and wit
Can move it on to cancel half a line
Nor all thy tears wash out a line of it.'

And there, yes, between the pages, three short red hairs, curly, and I could see they were quite probably Norma's. I closed the book quickly.

'I love him but he didn't have the stamina to see it through to the end,' Sheila said. 'A sick wife is hard to take and Norma is very good with the children. It's a practical solution.'

'It's appalling,' I said.

'I do worry about Saffron, though,' she said. 'Everything seems to bore her now.'

'They go through that stage,' I said. 'When she's fifteen she may come back to Latin. They do sometimes.'

'Will you try and be around to see?' she asked. 'I won't. And I'm afraid Tommy's lost interest in their education.'

'Reverted to Wimbledon,' I said, and won a glimmer of a smile.

'Strange,' she said, 'how if there are sides to be taken everyone goes with the man. Where the power and the money and the good cheer is. I get very few visitors. The children hate coming in here.'

'I'm sure they love you very much,' I said.

'They love Norma,' she said. 'Why wouldn't they? She made sure they did. She always liked this house. I just want to get out of it, but how can I? I hear him and her in the bedroom upstairs and I think the children do too. That worries me.'

The conversation all but exhausted her. When I suggested that she sue for divorce, left the house and moved in to the flat Norma had abandoned, above *Bric a Brac*, where Marlene and I could visit, and we could get social services in to provide proper nursing, she could only manage a minuscule nod. But nod she did, and that's what happened, and neither Norma nor Tommy nor Saffron nor Wallace nor Emily made any objection.

Six months later the family came to the funeral contrite and subdued but handsome in picturesque black, and they were all there at the wedding three months later, Norma in white, and noticeably pregnant, the children in red velvet with flowers in their hair, and Tommy looking very cheerful. Roger and Carol reported back. Marlene and I had been invited but we refused to go. Let them find their tutors elsewhere.

Ismail B. Garba

1. Metaphors

from *The English Sequence*

Missiles
After whose strike the forest quakes,
And the shocks!
Shocks speeding
Off from the target like tsunamis.

The tap
Collects like ponds, like the
Sea attempting
To reposition its face
Over the steep

That falls and twists,
A brown branch,
Coloured by slimy germs.
Months later I
Meet them on the way –

Metaphors wet and colourless,
The indubitable footprints.
While
From the bottom of the earth, still clouds
Fix a stare.

2. Song

Sometimes, though we cannot sing, a song
plays itself. So, a man will rise
his eyes from the veils of his palms and glare
at the canvas hung by a rainbow, a greeting card.

Some other times, though we are wordless, the rhythms
pierce our silences, that little-known agony;
then a woman will stay stump-still, seeing her past
in the close by Greek tumbling of a plane.

Sing for us now. Level one guitar strings
comfort the gambler grumbling out across
a mid-Atlantic ship. Then dawn, and somebody pronounces
an adult's alias as though they remembered their gain.

Light inside. Outside, the Biblical song –
Beethoven. Wagner. Bach. Stravinsky.

3. Batteries in April

And even the leave-shade this dawn cannot afford such robes.
Nor the man in the carriage
Whose grey hair grows through his cap so astonishingly –

A peck, a friendly peck
Completely uncalled for
By a moon

Boldly and playfully
Removing its burka veil, by faces
Lulled to a slumber under whips.

O, my muse, what am I
That these last days should rise up
In a jungle of jinn, in a morning of cornflakes?

4. Places

I. Exotic Place

I see you strip off by the skyheld moonlight.
We're experiencing a late night. On the radio
happenings from other places sort of attract me.

Each slight shuffle makes a larger image
on the mirror. I remain here silently as clothes fly about.
A foreign station talks of hurricane somewhere else.

But we're there and here now, believing nothing uncritically,
where there are no happenings or hurricanes. Kisses, afterwards
I will feel estranged in this exotic place.

II. Quiet Place

I hear you unfold by the ceiling-high electric bulb.
We're having an early time. On the horizon
light from other stars half-brightens me.

Each silent stir makes blight shadow
on the face. I daze here slowly as words fall.
A hush heart sings of love somewhere else.

But we're there and now, seeing nothing uncompromisingly,
where there is no light or love. Lies, later
I will feel heartbroken for this quiet place.

Tony Peake

A Portrait

As she took up her pencil to begin drawing, it was her eyes that commanded my attention, not – as might have been expected – the glittering flex of her ring-encrusted fingers, the ostentatious elegance encapsulated at that extremity of her restless body.

'Don't move!' she commanded. 'You were at the perfect angle.'

It wasn't the sadness in them – that could have been my imagination; or rather, the paucity of it: after all, sadness was to be expected. It was the – how to put this? – the baffled acceptance. Think of an animal at bay, finally cornered by its frenzied pursuers, and you'll have a sense of what I saw in my friend Vanessa's eyes. Or thought to see.

Head to one side, she was considering my profile.

'I'll swear your nose is longer,' she said. 'Since last time. Leading a dishonest life, Pinocchio, dear?'

Then silence as, with a series of deft pencil strokes, she started to sketch my likeness.

'How long,' she said next, 'has it been?'

This time a reply was forthcoming.

'Twelve years.'

'Really?'

'Really.'

Further silence, in which – without movement on my part (no darting hands, no frowning, no rubbing out) – I copied what she was attempting: a likeness. Beginning with her grey hair (shocking, that: twelve years ago it had still been hazel), I traced with my eyes the way her combs held untidiness at bay, the tilt of her nose, the length and strength of her jaw, wideness of mouth, precision of teeth, erectness of carriage. Then her hands, in many ways her defining characteristic, fingers a team of iron-clad acrobats going minutely through their paces.

'Not just the nose,' she said. 'You've become . . .'

A pause.

'Yes?'

'Less well defined. Facially, I mean. Fewer sharp corners.'

I laughed at that.

'Turned so many. Then haven't we all?'

'Not entirely.'

In contrast to how I saw her now – that dramatic swirl of grey hair, the skittering fingers – came another, earlier image of a young girl on a deserted beach, moonlight accentuating the apprehension and excitement in her eyes. The hunger for experience, the matching dread of it. At her side, an equally young man. Also hungry. Also scared.

'Sorry,' I murmured. 'Wasn't thinking . . .'

Five evenly matched fingers broke into a run for their trainer's cigarettes.

'Old friends,' she proclaimed, once the fingers had attained their goal, 'shouldn't censor their thoughts. What's the point otherwise?' A plume of smoke spiralled ceilingwards. 'Registration. Remember? In the queue on our first morning.'

Once again I had the number of years to hand.

'Three decades ago.'

'Flares!'

'Those dreadful collars!'

'The make-up!'

'The hair!'

I was braced for a further round or two – the music? the shoes? – but she'd returned her attention to her sketch pad, was frowning at what she saw there.

'Tell me,' she said. 'You and Sally. I never understood. Not properly.'

'Splitting up, you mean?'

'She was so much older than the rest of us.'

Again I glimpsed that young man; or – to be accurate – the suggestion of him, for that's all he had been then: a hint of himself, of what he might one day become. Depending on circumstance.

'Twenty-five,' I corrected. 'She was only twenty-five.'

'When you're in your teens,' responded Vanessa, 'twenty-five seems prehistoric. God! She had lines on her hands. You must remember! Lines!'

'Her destiny perhaps?' A not very coherent joke to defend (why?) Sally against Vanessa's remarks.

'Not her palms, idiot. The *back* of her hands. I'm a painter. I notice these things!'

She'd started to draw again: quick stabs of the pencil, as if only by speed, speed and cunning, could she outwit the paper's blankness.

'Well?' she challenged. 'Will you tell me or won't you?'

Sally and me. Where to begin? For it was, I knew, the beginning Vanessa wanted explained as much as the end.

Also at registration, I supposed, but in a different queue, later in the day. The queue for how we might pass the time when lectures were done, learning over.

Hi! My name's Sally. Are you for drama too?

Where Vanessa had been large and tremulous – yes, that was exactly the word: tremulous! Veiling herself in quick, nervous laughter, those fingers of hers running rings around her every utterance – Sally had been a pinprick, expertly aimed. Though by thinking that, far from attempting a defence of her, I was confirming Vanessa's expectations.

'Flattery,' I said, deflecting the attack onto myself. 'I guess Sally flattered me. I liked what I saw in that mirror.'

'Which was?'

'Normality? Children. Marriage. Being accepted. Acceptable.'

'As simple as that?'

Now the fingers were racing for a rubber, which in turn raced across the surface of the sketch with a scouring sound, like that of wind.

'You said yourself: I was in my teens. What did I know? What could I know?'

'What I remember,' she said, 'was how desperate you were. In such a hurry. Like life might be snatched away before you had a chance to experience it.'

'Then,' I added, 'there was you.'

The way in which she reacted to this observation – with a

sumptuous laugh, as rich in delight as in astonishment – put me in mind of that beach again.

'I come into the picture?' she queried archly.

'You said no. Remember? By implication, anyway.'

A young woman, unadorned but for a pair of white panties, races across a moonlit beach. To one side: a young man at the foot of the dunes, eyes fixed on his receding quarry. Except that with the passage of time, I was become the quarry, she the one who observed, for she'd picked up her pencil again, was staring at me assessively.

'Too easy,' I said – in my own defence now, as well as Sally's, 'too easy to say that because Sally was older than me, and then pregnant, of course, she called the shots. I know that's what everyone thought, but it's not the whole story.'

Mirage-like, the milky outline of the young woman shimmies at the water's edge. No matter how he runs, he knows the distance between them will always remain the same. If there's one moment when it happens – his future, that is – it's then, in accepting there are some distances not his to cover.

'I did also love her,' I heard myself saying. 'Sally, I mean. It wasn't just that she was pregnant. And I always wanted children. The good thing is the children.'

Even as I uttered the words, I made an attempt to choke them back – and in the process, did precisely that: choked, coughed, spluttered, risked further disapproval by shaking my head violently, thereby ruining the perfect angle.

The good thing. How could I have been so crass? Despite what Vanessa had earlier said, censorship of thought, especially between old friends, was sometimes essential.

Vanessa, however, appeared not to have registered my gaffe – unless, of course, she was more effective at censorship than I. Censorship of her own reactions.

'Did I really reject you?' she was asking. 'Is that how you saw it?'

Her hand, as she posed the question, swept across her sketch pad. The lines she was now laying down were vigorous and simple: lacking in hesitancy. I tried to follow suit.

A nineteen-year-old boy arrives at university where, on his

first day, he meets two women. The first is called Vanessa. There is about her a tremulousness – that word again; but it is exact – a breathless, elegant tremulousness which, if translated into neon, would read, in letters that blaze: THE FUTURE BECKONS. No wonder she dazzles him. Against which stands Sally, who frowns where Vanessa laughs, questions where Vanessa pronounces. Cautious might be the word – though interestingly, despite her precision of character, Sally precludes exactitude of description, discourages dissection. And so? So he lays gentle siege to Vanessa, they go around together, take in films, exhibitions, talks, go for intense walks in the municipal gardens, visit the seaside, where Vanessa has a friend with a cottage they can borrow. And on the beach, as they strip for a moonlit swim, he thinks he'll tell her how he feels. But doesn't quite manage it, can't find the words, never mind the exact ones, because before he can open his mouth, she is racing away from him towards the water's edge and he knows without having to articulate it, without her having to articulate it, that the answer is no. Sodality is not their destiny.

From here the line is as simple and as vigorous as one of Vanessa's own, leading as it does directly from that beach to Sally's digs and a consoling cup of coffee.

I have to say I've never seen what all the fuss is about, intones Sally. *OK, she's clever, I'm sure she has a glittering career ahead of her, but all that flash. Don't you mistrust it?*

No, he wants to cry. *That's what draws me to her. She's so alive.* But that's something else he doesn't manage to articulate. Instead, he nods numbly, as if in agreement. And doesn't demur when Sally elaborates her point: *I don't call that being friendly, not when she's so obviously hurt you.* Or takes his hands in hers: *Poor baby.* Or was it he who felt for her?

I think the line simple, but it isn't, of course. Can I truly say I turned so fluidly from one to the other? Used Vanessa to gain entrance to Sally? Allowed Sally to use Vanessa? Can I really explain a marriage of three decades and its three resultant children by means of a single mark on the page?

'How do you see it?' I asked.

'See what?'

'You must remember. That weekend we went to the beach. That cottage we borrowed?'

'Of course I remember.'

'Well?'

'With great affection,' she replied, 'if you must know. Though as I've said, you were in a hurry. So eager, bless you, it was . . . Young, I suppose, we were both very young. You, at any rate. Eager.'

She'd laid aside her pencil, turned towards the window and, without warning, begun to cry. Or rather, since she was no longer facing me, that is how I read the rise and fall of her shoulders: to mean that she was crying. An uncomfortable silence fell upon the room, broken first by the snap of her lighter, then the hesitancy of my own voice.

'If you can bear it,' I said, 'I'd really like to know how it happened. You and Henry have been so in my thoughts. Why d'you think I got in touch again, after all these years?'

'Is it really twelve?'

By virtue of her frayed outline against the square of light that was the window – frayed because of the tendrils of hair that had escaped her combs and were curled about the nape of her neck – she'd become a magnified version of one of those miniature silhouettes you see in museums. Except that this silhouette moved – her hand as it lifted her cigarette to and from her mouth – and was wreathed in a consequent haze of smoke.

'That's as long,' she continued, 'as he was ill. Almost to the day. That's why I've not been in touch. I wasn't in touch with anyone.' Still she didn't turn to face me. 'Adolescence was the trigger. He stopped being himself. Of course, we pretended, tried to pretend it might go away, played the normality game, but it, he, was stronger than we were. The lie won out.'

'Did they give it name?'

Her voice remained steady. 'I think of it as a kind of emotional autism. He said to me once, this would have been when he was still in his teens, he said it was like being behind glass. Or in a tunnel, where the light was out of reach. Everyone else, he said, was in the light. Except for him.' Her voice faltered. 'Remember him as a little boy? How bright he was? Sharp? Well, that didn't change, he was still . . . What's the word? Dazzling, I suppose. On the outside. But inside – inside was another matter.'

Finally she turned to regard me, her voice seeming to switch off as she did so. Words continued to issue from her lips, but I was no longer aware of hearing them. Instead, it was as though she spoke to me with her eyes. And it was her eyes – her wounded, baffled, eloquent eyes – that carried the story to its conclusion, spelling out for me how her only son had sunk into such despair that, unable to fight his demons any longer, he'd procured himself a gun and driven to a nearby shooting range where, secure in the knowledge that here at least someone other than his parents would discover his body, he'd slipped the gun into his mouth.

Just as the shot that ended her son's life must have caused, for a moment, the world to stand still, or seem to stand still, for Vanessa and her husband Henry, so too the end of her story. Movement became temporarily impossible. Even to hold her gaze was an effort.

'Mind you,' she said eventually, 'I was glad when I heard. Relieved. It meant he couldn't go on hurting himself. Or Henry, come to that. Or me.'

I found I could speak again.

'I can't imagine,' I murmured, 'what it must be like, losing a child. If one of ours . . .'

'They won't,' she said. 'These things are hardly commonplace. Philip was ill. Very ill. That's what we have to remember.'

'And guilt?'

'Of course. Not a day goes by when I don't wonder if, by acting otherwise, we mightn't . . . if things might have been different. Same goes for Henry, even if he isn't noted for his articulacy. Outside of the boardroom, that is.'

'How is Henry?'

The question raised a smile.

'Oh,' she said, suddenly sounding as if we'd been enjoying the most innocuous of exchanges, 'Henry, bless him, goes from strength to strength. The partnership is one of the largest in the country. Certainly the most powerful. And of course . . .' She stubbed out her cigarette. 'Philip's death has brought us closer. That we didn't foresee.'

She stood up, extending a hand towards me as she did so. The arc of her arm (that and the unusualness of the gesture: when last had she done this?) recalled another such arc, one that paralleled the link I liked to make between our weekend at the beach and my cup of coffee with Sally: the arc that led by contrast to Henry, laconic but dependable Henry (clever Henry, rich Henry), as unsuited in his way to Vanessa as Sally had been to me. Or so I'd always imagined.

'Come,' she said. 'There's something I must show you.'

I took the proffered hand and was led by it towards a cabinet in the corner of the room on which stood a cluster of photographs, all of a smiling young man, a confident, happy young man, the future at his disposal: Philip, before his suicide.

'Dazzling,' she said after a while. 'Utterly, utterly dazzling. No?'

'Indeed,' I assented. 'The only word.'

The fact that my hand was still in hers (the warmth of it, its unexpected roughness, attendant delicacy) rendered the ensuing silence strangely comforting. Companionable, you could say.

'Our one joint effort,' she said. 'Henry's and mine.' Then, 'You haven't told me: why did you want me to draw you again?'

The question called forth as many aspects of our past as I'd the memory to enumerate. Our final evening at the beach, when she'd asked if she could draw me. The fact that Sally and I had not invited her to our wedding. That as a present, she'd nonetheless sent me the sketch, which I'd then had framed. That on her surprise engagement to Henry, Sally had relented (it was Sally who'd not wanted Vanessa at our wedding: *I know she doesn't like me. You can see it in her eyes. She'll only spoil it*). That we had then, albeit stiffly, attended the engagement party, the wedding, had continued on occasion to see each other as careers were started, houses bought, children born, adulthood undertaken. Until our eventual move to another town. My solo return.

'They're so inconsequential,' I muttered, 'my paltry affairs . . .'

Her reply was crisp. 'One of the lessons Philip taught us – by us I mean Henry, Henry and me – is that we are survivors. He wasn't. We are. Survivors go on. That's what survivors do. Go on. They can't help it.'

Still she held my hand in hers.

'Well?' she prompted.

I cleared my throat. 'What it comes down to,' I said, 'is this. The day before I walked out we had a row, the worst ever, and at the end of it – we were in my study at the time – Sally took down your sketch of me and . . .' I saw from Vanessa's expression that I didn't need to continue, not for her sake, which would indicate that what I said next, I said mainly for myself. 'She looked me straight in the eye and then smashed the frame and tore the portrait up. Into as many pieces as she could. A bloody blizzard of them.'

A prolonged silence greeted this revelation. Then:

'She never saw you,' breathed Vanessa, 'for what you were. Only what she wanted you to be. Was that the problem?'

I shrugged. 'In a way. But me as well as her, we both wanted . . .' I paused. 'Something we weren't. An idea, a concept – never the reality. Until in the end, all we could do was hurt each other. That, we were marvellous at. Fucking brilliant. After almost thirty years. A means, I suppose, of establishing that we did still exist.'

'I'm sorry,' she whispered.

Again I shrugged. 'It had to happen. Sooner or later.'

'So you moved back here?'

'Moved back and read in the paper about Philip and gave you a ring.'

What I didn't add was that in the months between leaving Sally and ringing Vanessa, months spent largely alone in a rented flat, I'd come to realize that whereas, as Vanessa said, Sally had never seen me for what I was, Vanessa, by contrast, had always grasped me only too well. So well, in fact, that she'd known not to risk getting too close to someone who, because he didn't properly know himself, could never hope properly to know another. Vanessa withdrew her hand from mine to reach for a photo of Philip as triumphant climber, standing smilingly astride the summit of a mountain. 'You won't remember this, I'm sure,' she said, handing me the photo, 'but that weekend you mentioned, when we went to the beach and I drew your portrait, we went for a swim, a midnight swim, at least I did, and there was actually a moment when I wondered . . .'

'What?'

'If perhaps we weren't—' She gave vent to a surprised laugh, 'Meant for each other.'

'You did?'

'I did.'

'And then?'

'The moment passed, of course. As moments do.'

Taking care not to upset the cabinet's overall arrangement, I replaced Philip's photo among its fellows and felt again for Vanessa's hand.

'So can I see it?' I asked. 'What you've drawn so far?'

'Of course. If you'd like to.'

Moments earlier, she had led me towards the cabinet. Now I led her towards the sketch. As we got there, she released my hand and stood aside to let me absorb her handiwork alone.

What had I been expecting? Something obvious, I suppose, cut and dried: the tired and hesitant fifty-year-old I knew myself to be. Yet that wasn't at all what she'd drawn. Instead, although the fifty-year-old was clearly there, tired and hesitant, each line of the sketch equally told a complementary story. That of an earlier, more confident and hopeful self: a younger me still miraculously present in my present self, part and parcel of the current picture. Not only that, but a hint too of youth in general, of Philip even, before he'd blown his brains out. In Vanessa's hands, her sitter was both young and old, himself and not himself, the might have been as well as the missed opportunity. First Sally had torn up my portrait. Now Vanessa, with her questing pencil, had in *her* way done much the same.

'Well,' I managed. 'You've certainly not lost your touch.'

'You like?'

'Put it this way – it's a challenge.'

'Is that how you see it?'

'Don't you?'

'I see an old friend. That's all. A dear, sometimes troubled old friend.'

Her voice seemed abruptly to recede. I swung round to find her at the door.

'Where are you going?' I asked, half in alarm.

'Coffee.' She smiled. 'We've earned a coffee, don't you think? I won't be a moment. Promise.'

As she turned to leave the room, I noticed that those eyes of hers went briefly to the photographs on the cabinet. They didn't linger – the look was fleeting – but its instinctiveness nevertheless suggested that, much as an habitual worshipper might always genuflect towards the altar in a church, Vanessa couldn't be in that room without confronting Philip's legacy. Then she was gone and I was staring at her surprising sketch again and remembering what her son had so cruelly taught her, about being a survivor. At the same time, I was searching for the right word. Finally it came. The future. Not, of course, the exact word, though for once this didn't seem to matter. Exactness would have been too limiting.

Paul Ewen

Two Pub Reviews

Sun Tavern, Covent Garden

Try and arrive early at the Sun Tavern so you can get a chance to sit at what must surely be known as the Special Table. It's special because it is tall and round with a large golden ring that runs around the outside, and it commands the prime drinking spot at the front of the bar by the window. All the other tables in the bar are much lower to the ground and they come in your usual sizes, shapes and materials. The Special Table, however, is quite clearly *the* place upon which to rest your elbows and glass. It's something else, the Special Table. I noticed it when I first walked through the door and, more importantly, I noticed it wasn't occupied. As I stood at the bar waiting for my drink to be poured, I couldn't help feeling that someone could walk through the door at any minute and slide up to the Special Table before me. Realizing that I was sweating and twitching and attracting strange glances from the staff and patrons, I tried to ease the tension by pulling some funny faces, as I looked around at the other features of this small cosy pub. At the back of the bar I noticed a Wurlitzer-shaped oval archway which led to the toilets and a roped-off staircase. A large red neon sign read, 1ST FLOOR BAR, but the OPEN sign was switched off and I simply wasn't interested. My darting eyes flicked back to the bar, but my pint still hadn't settled. Biting white knuckles, I glanced across to the four large mirrors on the right-hand side of the bar and noted the small framed pictures on the wooden wall partitions between them. How cute they were. How very cute. And I smiled slightly just as the mirror reflection revealed the barmaid placing my full glass onto the bar behind me, and I turned as if in spasm, and snatched it away from the bar top before running at pace to the Special Table laughing, 'Ha!

Ha! Ha! Ha!' I sat atop one of the towering green vinyl cushioned chairs and placed my bag on another, my coat on another and my handkerchief and socks on yet another, just in case anyone tried to muscle in. I had secured the Special Table and it felt great. I sat there applauding my success and raised my glass to the other patrons and to everyone walking past the window outside. The golden ring around the Special Table really was something else, and as I sat there I thought I'd try my hand at steering it. So I took hold of the polished gold rail and manoeuvred it in an anticlockwise direction, and as the table moved slowly around, all of the streetlights outside suddenly dimmed. I didn't think much of this at first, but when I turned it back the other way, the lights all became bright again. I laughed out loud. Then I moved it back the other way again and all the parked cars outside suddenly moved backwards really quickly by themselves and the streetlights dimmed once more! I kept turning it faster and faster and cars came whizzing back past the bar and people also, all running backwards. The hands on my watch were flying around anticlockwise, and my pint glass started emptying and refilling itself. The fancy new building over the road disappeared into the ground and an old-style building from the nineteenth century replaced it, and the cars flying backwards past the window began to look like old vintage cars and the people weren't dressed very fashionably. Meanwhile I kept turning and turning the gold rail on the Special Table and then dinosaurs started flying backwards outside and the barmaid tapped me on the shoulder and said, 'I think you should leave now.' I went outside and everything had returned to normal again, but my arms really hurt.

Prince of Wales, Covent Garden

This well-established pub sits on the bottom corner of an imposing white-stone building on a street known for its theatres and tourist spots. It's a building with a long and varied history, and a plaque on the wall outside declares that the bar area has even served as a potato warehouse in times gone by. Nowadays the large square structure has pretty flower arrangements draping its many windows, and you can store potatoes in yourself when you eat them cooked with your delicious pub meal. There can be no doubting the illustrious past of the grand Prince of Wales, and if you're in the area you should most definitely drop by for a drink. It's funny though, but I have to admit when I first sat down at my table inside, I was actually a bit taken aback by the curtains. Goodness! I thought. They're a bit over the top for a sturdy old drinking establishment aren't they? You see, the curtains inside the Prince of Wales are all flowery and puffed up and frilly at the top. They're tied like a young girl may tie her hair in pigtails, and when you happen to have tattoos like I do, you tend to sit and rub your stubbly chin for a minute or two and ponder all those pub fights that you were never involved with but had heard about from someone. In fact, I even remember thinking to myself, This is not a pub; it's a bleeding doll's house. But then that was when it clicked. Of course, that was the theme! It's supposed to be one of those antique Victorian doll's houses, but with a bar. The curtains, the plants in the window sill, the flowery seat covers and the flowery carpet design. Suddenly it all made sense. It was still as hard as the next place, but the proprietors were clearly just being a bit smarter and a bit more innovative by catching those lucrative tourist dollars while still continuing to dish out good old-fashioned booze to us rough boys. I had a belly laugh and decided that you had to admire their ingeniousness. I also decided that since I was there I should get into the theme of things as well, and I'd start by walking to the toilet like a doll and see if any of the staff picked up on the fact that I knew exactly what was going on. Now as you may have observed yourself, when a child walks a doll along, they kind of jump it along in small hops rather than actually walking it because the doll's legs don't tend to bend much. It's actually harder than it sounds, but I'm sure if I'd had more chances to practise, I would have won favour with the bar staff and maybe got my photo on the wall or something. Anyway, I stood up from my table and hop-walked off along the raised carpeted area of the bar towards the polished floorboards and in the general direction of the toilets. I should mention also that I had a massive big smile on my face, like really big, and my eyes were really wide open, except for when I did a wink to the bar staff as I hop-walked-jumped past the bar area. Once inside the Gents I had to double over and catch my breath somewhat, because I'll tell you what, you need to be fit if you're going to come into the Prince of Wales and do this on a regular basis. When I jumped back again, I think the staff got it, the doll walk I was doing, and appreciated it. A lot of the customers stopped what they were doing and looked at me very strangely, and I guess they were the tourists who had just arrived and still hadn't yet picked up on the theme. Once I'd sat down again, I had a drink from my pint, but like a doll would do it, without really bending my body, so I leaned way back on a tilt so I could get my mouth level with the edge of my glass. Also, because dolls can't actually drink anything, I pursed my lips so the beer just ran straight off my lips down my chin and all over my shirt, trousers and the flowery carpet. It was so funny! I was really getting into the great theme when the bartender came over with a cloth and asked me to leave. I laughed, but he was very angry. I stood outside feeling a little disappointed and confused and my shirt and pants were all damp because it was very cold.

A. S. Irvine

Novel

I had a brilliant idea. I headed down to the George and nursed it over a pint. Then I went up to the bar and got a bit of paper, found a pencil in a pocket and jotted down the basic structure. It took an hour inbetween chatting to the girl behind the bar, Cat. I've always fancied her in a so-what kind of a way. Black hair, built like a baguette. She's got some kind of Eastern European accent. I started with a shape not dissimilar to hers. It looked like this:

But the structure continued to develop and ended up looking something more like this:

Luckily I've kept this germinal bit of paper in which you see the seed of an idea begin to sprout, mung beanlike. Watered my brain some more. Found the structure led by the arcane process known as creation to a group of keywords:

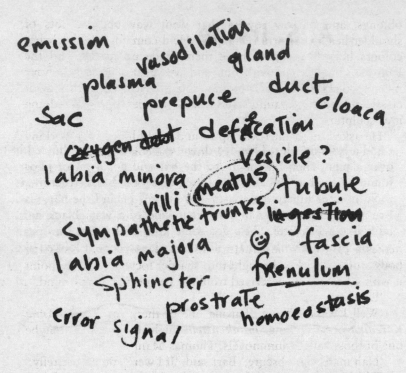

emission
vasodilation
plasma
gland
sac
prepuce
duct
cloaca
oxygen debt
defacation
labia minora
vesicle?
meatus
tubule
villi
Sympathetic trunks
ingestion
labia majora
☺
fascia
sphincter
frenulum
error signal
prostrate
homoeostasis

I just needed a title and I would be ready to start. I find it's always useful to have one, like an arrow pointing towards a mineral deposit. It came to me as I went up for another pint. Somastream. Growing out of stream of consciousness, a mode that was well played out by the end of the twentieth century. And soma. Soma is Greek for body. I wanted the novel to go beyond consciousness, beyond the unconscious and to exist at the level of the body processes through a twenty-four-hour timestream.

I also liked the play on sodastream and the word soma as used by Huxley for the name of the drug that kept everyone tractable and blissed-out in one of his novels. My title sounded like it could be a new kind of recreational drug. Cool.

Bart came in. He was working on an installation for an exhibition in October, melamine boxes. The main box was to be almost as big as an average room and there were others, low oblongs, and narrow towers that went way up, and lots of shoulder-height uniform rectangles. He'd come in to think what colours he was going to have them made up in. He had the Pantone sample chart with him and we spent a good half hour picking colours. The concept was 'sunset'. He'd taken that great classic of landscape painters and Kodak snappers and was redoing it as sculpture. Cool.

He asked me what I was up to and I told him I was working on a new novel, Somastream. He loved the concept.

'I could leave it just at that, the body defining the total narrative but I want to embed it in the novelistic tradition at the same time. I mean don't get me wrong,' I cadged a smoke off him. 'The organs and their, like, functions, and then when they go through breakdowns – the breakdowns will be good – that all makes a carnivalesque structure in and of itself, but I think the body stuff will be . . . brought into sharper focus if I counterpoint it with a basic story perceived from the perspective of the mind.'

'Like what story?'

'Well I was thinking of using one of the great novels, *Anna Karenina* or something. *Frankenstein* might be good. Or maybe one of those sanatorium novels, Thomas Mann.'

'Nah mate, too obscure,' Bart said. 'If I were you I'd use telly.'

Which pissed me off because I was thinking of that but I didn't want him to know. He always pretends he writes my fucking novels.

On my way home I ran through some telly programmes but the thing is, the thing that worries me as a modern writer is, I hate fucking telly. It's boring. I thought: sitcom? *Frasier*? *Friends*? I needed one fuck-off story. I thought for a bit about Jesus, but I needed a love story. *Gone with the Wind*. I'd never read it. I could check out the video.

But the problem with stories is that they're so fucking conventional. Much better, I realized, as I was lying in bed smoking, to use another form altogether. It came to me out of the dark. I'd take a medieval courtly love track. Courtly love was all about lofty love that was unrealized in the body. It would be good counterpoint for the somastream to grind against. Then I remembered Abelard and Heloise. Abelard was a monk or a priest or something and he fell in love with the scholarly Heloise, a virgin. They ran off, fucked. They were caught, she was put in a convent and he had his balls cut off. They stayed apart, still in love, learning Christian virtues and writing to each other. Bodily explosion followed by bodily renunciation.

Next day I ordered *Abelard and Héloïse* from Amazon and loads of medical textbooks, and anything else onscreen that took my fancy that was about bodies. I like that scientific language of medical textbooks. That was what I told Jim when I got through to him:

'Jim? Got a job for you. I'm doing a new piece called Somastream . . .' I explained how I wanted to tell the story of Abelard and Heloise from the point of view of their bodily functions and contrast it with sections on how their heads saw it as a high-flown love done in medieval courtly lyrics.

'I want the Somastream stuff done in a lingo that mixes medical textbooks – I'm having some sent to you – and a more visceral, flowing description of what happens in the body. I want all bodily functions, this is the point, right? Leave nothing out. Joyce already did the shit of everything going through the mind. I want shit literally going through the body. Literally. Or, like, imagine the chapters when they're having sex, seen from the point of view of the neurological pathways, the reproductive organs, the building blood pressure. Get me? Then alternate with shorter sections done as a modern take on the style of troubadours about the pure, like, more platonic love of Abe and Heloise – shit's also in the post. What do you think?'

Jim said he didn't know what I was on about and he didn't think he could do it. This was a highly skilled job, I'd have to go to New York for a big job like this. I said fuck that, Jim, you're the best and you had that six-month stint editing medical text-books, it's a doddle for a fabulator like you. I knew what he was after. Dosh. Tons of it. They flay you they really do. And all they have to do is construction. I offered him 25 per cent more than for *No-one*, and he hummed and hawed. He came back with 'Thirty per cent more and I'll need a one-off research fee on top.'

It's all money, money, money. Makes you sick. I agreed. Thirty per cent more per word than for *No-one* and a whopping great research fee for taking in the relevant styles. Told him I had a deadline, six months hence, and he should deliver a section every two weeks. I was thinking 40,000 to 50,000 words depending on how the soma chapters worked out. The idea of all that cash got his juices flowing. He said he thought he could make the deadlines.

After the first week I rang him to see if he'd read the books. He was still reading them. Said he was really getting into Maingot's *Abdominal Operations*. He thought he would need the next week just for practising and working up the two styles and asked for some more, specific books on the two subjects and I ordered them from a medical bookshop and some academic place in Oxford.

I phoned my agent, Colin, and told him the gist of what I was working on. He was blown away.

'Christ, Phil,' he said, 'you're on to something major here. This will piss everyone off. Can you do me a synop?'

'Cool,' I said. 'Give me a week.'

I spent every evening that week at the George scribbling like a maniac on napkins, sleeves, tabletops, and finally took it all home one night and banged the synopsis out on the Mac. I had Jen, my graphic design hint, take it to the bridge with fuck off graphics and realtime shorts of abdominal surgery and that really close-up slick 'n' slurp porn. I emailed it to Colin and went into an orgy of reading the *New Yorker* and watching the *Learning Zone*, the only thing on telly worth the watch.

Colin rang three days later.

'It's superb,' he said. 'You're a fucking nutter. How long before I get a sample chapter to put with it?'

I told him I had Jim onto it and would get something to him within the next couple of weeks. Of course Jim, the bastard, was late. He's always fucking late. 'It'll be with you in a fortnight.' How many times have I somehow believed that? Fortnight comes, never fucking ready, is it? I had to bug him and bug him

– he left the answerphone on screening mode for another two weeks. Finally I blew it.

'Jim? It's fucking emergency break glass. I've got Colin breathing down my neck. Whole deal's off unless I get chapter one in the inbox tonight. Hear me now.'

An hour later I got a Word attachment with the first bit of text.

It was shite.

I picked up the phone.

'Jim?' I said, 'Jim, pick up. Listen, this is really interesting, but you haven't got the language right and Heloise is like a stereotype. I want her darker.'

'Oh, hi.' He picked up. 'This thing has been a nightmare. Haven't slept more than four hours a night for weeks.' Whinge whinge whinge.

He was off, telling me it's all very well saying do it like this, do it like that, but it can't be done, moan moan moan. He always does this, thinking he can get away with something passable because I don't understand the mechanics of how it works on the page. On the page, that's his mantra.

'Look Jim, I've red-penned this draft, plus I think you should come round here with all the books and I'll highlight the bits of medical writing I like and then I want the cuts to be more abrupt to the courtly love parts – but not highlighted by chapter breaks, OK? That's old. I never told you to do that.'

'You never told me to do anything.'

'Jim. You're losing it. Calm down. Get your arse over here and we'll go through it.'

He came over and we spent a whole day in my studio with books all over the place, me getting carried away with marker pens, scissors and Post-its – rabbiting on about the extreme language in which we encode bodily processes. I really threw myself into it, gave it all my passion.

' "As the pressure builds in the seminiferous tubules the sperm are pushed out into the vas derens." No. No! I said use medical textbook lingo. Not rewrite a medical textbook. Give me the drama. 'With each thrust, the Sertoli cells pump another squirt of fluid into the seminiferous tubules, carrying the sperm forward like matchsticks on the surging tide." Much better. Get it?'

Jim shrugged. 'Too melodramatic.'

'Jim – since when was that your division? Just put the shit down. I want sperm. I want cell division. I want the knife-edge drama of killer T-cells battling evil little cunts of viruses. I want the internal scream of the nerve-endings when Abe's balls are hacked off. Man, what a scene to do from the penis' perspective.'

Jim sagged forward on the floor.

I started bugging him a week later, because Colin was bugging me. Two weeks after that, I got a first chapter of 6,000 words and it was still all over the place. You'd be amazed, when I'm telling the idiot exactly what to do, how he can go right off and end up doing something else.

I got him round again.

'Look,' I said, 'I'm here, telling you exactly what I want, and you don't give it to me. Why?'

Jim ran his hand through his hair. It's thinning.

'Yeah, right,' he started. 'It's fine you telling me you want it like this, but when you are actually on the job trying to make it come out like that, there are all kinds of like – production issues – that make it impossible.'

'What the fuck are they?' I asked.

'Look, for you the page is blank, a void. Well it isn't. It's full of these invisible molecules. When I write a sentence, these molecules exert a kind of pressure on the words that wants to push the text in a direction you couldn't have predicted before you put it down in black and white, right? It's like Brownian motion or something, all these words bumping up against each other and the resistance of the page as well, pushing each other around, refusing to stay in the relations you had planned. By definition, it's quantum mechanics. It's unpredictable.'

Again, typical. He gets above himself and thinks because I

can't conjugate verbs or whatever, I'm a duh. Like spelling or whatever makes you a writer.

I got up and fetched him another Becks. I lit a tab.

'What are we talking about here, Jim? Words. If I can explain the concept to you in words, point you to exactly the kinds of nuts and bolts – words, sentence structures, verbs, adjectives – for each bit, tell you what each bit is about as well, what's to go wrong? Christ, architects don't have to build the fucking building.'

Jim shook his head, all doleful. 'Every word has its properties,' he murmured. 'Every little word has a different weight, form, tendency. And when you fling them on the page, they kick off like chemicals. Shit happens.'

I ignored this smokescreen. 'Get it denser.'

'I'll have to use a different vocab.'

'No,' I said. 'You can get it denser with the medical vocab.'

After a lot more of this shit, Jim said OK, but he would need another fortnight to redo the first bit. Oh, and the canny bastard wanted an extra payment of a thousand squid for what he'd suffered so far. Over and above. Sometimes I think I should do some sort of creative writing course so I can weld and mould the bits myself. But why go backwards?

I'll cut short your pain. It took eight more drafts over fourteen weeks to get that first section serviceable. I'm being grudging. It was more than serviceable. OK, it wasn't the Kabbalah of shining letters I'd given Jim the fucking sacred instruction booklet for. But what the fuck, it flowed. Out of the inertia of those medical textbooks he extruded this dense but kinetic layer of words that plopped and churned like a chyme from which cerebral choux of triolets and tornadas ascended like souls leaving the body. Jim is a good craftsman. A really good craftsman.

Colin pronounced just one sentence on that first chapter. 'You're a genius.'

His plan was to send it off with the synopsis to three top publishers that week and instigate an auction.

He rang back the next day to tell me the packages had gone out. 'You're evolving your voice,' he said. 'You're creating new territory for the novel. Who's knocking it up for you?'

I told him Jim.

'Good little fabulator,' said Colin. 'No rough edges, precision-made. Who else uses him?'

I told him. None of the big writers know about Jim, they all use places with better research equipment and facilities. But Jim's like an old-fashioned artisan. Once he gets into it – that's what takes the pushing and shoving – he does the measurements, fusses over detail. He's a treasure.

Needless to say, Bart's show came up long before Somastream found a publisher. For him it's so easy. Still, let's not get grudgingly work ethicy about this. It looked good, the saturated colour blocks of glossy melamine dominating the usual huge, white former industrial space. All the little people milling about with drinks in their hands in and out of this pixilated sunset or whatever. And so impenetrable. I heard Bart talking about it to some journalist and watched her catch all the balls.

'I wanted to drain the overblown idea of "sunset" like you drain a swamp,' he said. 'I've returned sunset to the twenty-first century, stripped.' He gives good head.

The after-show party was at the George and then we headed out to Cargo for a bit of a groove. Everyone was there. Bart is going places. At Cargo he came up to me and said he'd got the idea for his next thing already, watching Cat dance. There she was, sagging from side to side at the edge of the crowd with some would-be artist wanker. They never want to fuck writers by the way. Books – where do they end up? Bookshops. Not very sexy is it? Not very huge white industrial space. Books are missing something and I aim to find it.

Anyway, hangover. Like, hangover. But by the afternoon I was down on Jim like a pile-driver wanting to know where chapter three was. The day after that the auction started on the book. I was still ill. I had really caned it at Bart's. Beautiful people, out of control. I lay in bed with one of those masks you cool in the fridge over my eyes on a hotline to Colin. He was jamming. Juggling phones. He'd got them all sexed up over the book and how I was onto this new thing called somatic literature.

'They love it, they love it,' he kept telling me, 'You're beautiful.'

Fuck it, it's a brilliant idea.

It came down to two offering much the same and we both agreed I should go with Hoxton Paper Products as the more happening imprint. We signed the deal next morning and went out for a champagne breakfast. You could have wiped the floor with me.

I drove over, on several occasions, to Jim's place out in Crouch End. There he'd be, blinds half drawn, with his big goggles on, surrounded by piles of paper, anatomy textbooks, dictionaries, histories of the body and with some tinky-linky troubadour music on the decks. I'd tell him he was brilliant and take him out to lunch every now and then at St John's.

Over the next six months, with endless mollycoddling, pep talks, expensive lunches and so on from me, he banged out the other chapters. I had to keep my finger on it. Had to read almost everything he sent, red pencil a shitload, get him back on track, tell him he was the best fabulator in the whole fucking universe. The day came when I had the final book in my hands. My greatest work to date. Somastream. I renamed it: Poesis/Somastream.

I don't give a fuck what the critics say so I'll list a few of their words here:

Genius.

Pure genius.

An invaluable expansion of Morton's oeuvre.

A great leap forward.

We had a fuck-off party at Bethnal Green Working Men's Club and I finally got to shag Cat.

Ian Duhig

My Grandfather's Seed Fiddle

To guide his sowing, white well-rags are stuck
About may hedges each side of his field;
As the scarecrow opens its arms to conduct,
He straps himself into his new seed fiddle.

Like grace notes the seed played over the furrows
To the rhythm of his feet and his bowing:
He dreams of reaping, even as he sows.
Later, birds will read his music and sing.

From *The Play of Daniel*

Music: Christopher Fox

Sing a new song for a scene change:
Babylon to Palestine;
Medieval Latin metre,
Trochees, plainsong's block and line.

Quatrains are just music boxes,
Dark machines that run on breath;
'Stanza' first of all meant 'room', though
Silence in its walls means death.

Painters show Belshazzar breathless
At graffiti on his wall:
Daniel gave the words his own gloss –
Soon Belshazzar's realm must fall!

('Mene' twice: was that God's error
Or some Jewish scribe's, long dead?
If one of four words was mistaken,
Who knows what the writing said?)

Qin Shi Huangdi built his Great Wall
So we'd see it from the Moon:
Who could see his empire falling?
It fell like moonlight, very soon.

Hadrian defined his empire
Slicing us from sea to sea:
Enemies ignored such fringes,
Crushing Rome in Italy.

Berlin too was split to show
Cold War realpolitik,
But politik can kill a state
Be its concrete metres thick.

Israel builds more concrete fences
Blank as pages, silently:
Palestine to Babylon;
Printer's ink, four walls, no key . . .

Coda

A gill-net once was custom-made,
A hand-tied web of mortal hemp:
Now trawlermen believe
In nylon monofilament.

Electrospun, invisible,
A knotless mesh, this matchless shift
Will cast no shadow but a spell
To check and catch the breath of fish.

Should one break free being overstretched
Or torn by underwater tides,
It sinks, so bottom-feeders glut
But when picked light, this net resiles

To rise, to fill, to fall a feast –
Shape-memory may fish for years
That never-never land of plenty,
The shelvy deserts of our seas.

Every country calls these 'ghost nets'
Whose factory-ships still vex the deeps
And each such net's a magic language:
Its syntax makes words disappear.

Shyam Selvadurai

Book of Chairs

[novel extract]

1

In his first days of school, Amrith De Alwis discovered a startling fact about himself. Besides his father and mother, he had, as far as he knew, no relatives – no aunts or uncles, no grandmother or grandfather, no cousins.

Amrith's daily trek to school began at his father's bungalow, perched at the summit of the mountain that formed the tea estate. He was accompanied by his ayah, Selamma. A retired tea plucker, she wore her sari without a blouse, in the mark of her low caste, the palu wrapped tightly over her left shoulder and around her breasts.

The moment they had descended past the estate, the wind hummed through the flame of the forest trees. Kohas and magpies and hoopoos sang in its branches, the gravel was speckled with red flowers. The road soon reached a hairpin bend from which the land fell away precipitously to the plains. On a clear day you could see all the way to the southern coast miles away. Amrith liked to tease Selamma by leaning over the low parapet wall that separated him from the giddying descent to the stillness below.

Once around the bend, the road dipped steeply to the town. Amrith loved the contrast. One moment they were in the midst of humming woodland life – the plaintive call of the koha, the smell of tea being roasted in the factory, an odour like sun-dried rose petals – and then in a few minutes they were in the chaos of the town. The row of shops along the main road looked like a team who had lost the tug of war, a knocked-about single file. The streets were jammed with lorries hooting their horns. Merchants bellowed out their wares on the pavements, raucous Tamil and Hindi film music blared out of the restaurants from which Amrith could smell spicy frying vadais. He would pause in front of the restaurants to salivate over the green and orange and seenimutai pink squares of sweets in the grime-covered glass cases.

Until he began grade one, a few days ago, the only playmates Amrith had known were the estate workers' children. They lived in the 'lines': one-roomed row-houses with black rot climbing up the walls, open drains carrying sewage in front of them. As son of the *periya durai*, the senior manager, Amrith had taken for granted his role as their superior, dismissing minor rebellions with threats to tell the rebel's parents. When murmurings against him grew too concerted he divided and ruled with treats from the main house for the loyal – pieces of sultana- and cashew-filled bread pudding, pol toffee, butter cake.

At school, Amrith discovered that calling up his father's authority was not only disregarded but openly resented. The other children in the school were the sons and daughters of government clerks, post office workers, owners of various commercial establishments. They were annoyed at the way the teacher fawned over him (her husband worked in the accounts division of the estate). In contrast, she referred to the other students as *haraka*, or *gona*. Buffalo or goat.

Their resentment climbed a level when the teacher began to spend large parts of the morning giving Amrith special attention. He was far behind the other students. He could speak and understand Sinhala, but did not know his alphabet. Amrith, though Sinhalese by race (and hence forced by government regulation to study in Sinhala) spoke and read English at home.

In the face of this nepotism, Amrith should have shown some humility around his classmates. Instead, he drew their attention to his expensive red cardigan with a blue horizontal stripe and gold buttons embossed with sailboats, his new pair of black Bata shoes, his sparkling white socks pulled up to his knees; contrasting all this with the faded cardigans of his classmates, the wool unravelling like worms, the handed-down-from-brother-to cousin-to-second cousin gaping shoes, the socks that collapsed around their ankles.

His chief adversary was Kapila, whose father was the town's rest house manager. Kapila, squint eyed and scrawny, mingled freely with the foreign tourists at the rest house, sometimes receiving little gifts from them – sachets of scented wet tissues from airplanes, a foreign boiled sweet, old magazines with pictures of blonde people which he used for collages. He would mention the latest arrival's name as if they were old friends, saying that the moment he was in grade four, he was going to Germany or France or England to study in a school that had metal chairs, that wasn't like this useless one. The other children, who had seen Kapila walking along the road chatting to these superior beings, listened in awe to his stories.

Amrith was not without his advantages. There was his thirty-six felt-tip pen set (with even a gold and silver colour), his tiffin of Australian Kraft cheese sandwiches. He used these during the interval to draw more materially inclined classmates away from Kapila's story-telling circle.

To counter this defection, Kapila, digging around in Amrith's life, discovered that Amrith had no relatives, besides his parents. 'What?' Kapila hooted, 'you have no maama or nanda? No aachi or bappa? No massinas? *Chee, cheee,* you must have been found in the tea bushes, and your parents too.'

For the rest of that day, all the children ran away from him every time he came near, squealing in their haste to escape, as if he carried a contagious disease.

No aunts or uncles, no grandmother or grandfather, no cousins?

The estate had been founded in the 1850s by a Scotsman, and he had named it Dunbar after his native town. He had supervised the cutting down of ancient forests; he had driven out the peasants who depended on the woodlands for their sustenance; he had imported indentured Tamil labour from India to work in slave-like conditions.

A stillness pervaded the entire estate. The tea bushes wound around the slopes of the mountain in green coils, a gigantic serpent choking its victim to a slow death.

At the very peak of the mountain, shrouded in fog, so that it looked as if it sat in the clouds, was the senior manager's bungalow. It was a stone edifice with a narrow front door, beady-eyed barred windows. One crossed over a shallow moat, through massive iron gates to enter the compound. The bungalow was L-shaped, its shorter arm being the kitchen and pantry. The front door opened directly onto a gloomy, damp-smelling corridor that ran the length of the house, doors leading off into the various rooms.

Amrith hated the corridor and he never used the front door if he could help it. Instead, he would run around to the back, where a verandah flanked the rear of the house, French windows opening into the rooms. There, he would find his mother. The morning separation was hard for both of them, and he loved that moment when he turned the corner, dashed up the verandah steps and found her sitting in her chair wearing a cream cardigan and cotton trousers, a magenta batik scarf folded into an Alice band keeping back the frizzy exuberance of her hair. When she held her arms out to him, the bangles on her wrists would tinkle in welcome. He would run to her, snuggling into her smell of eau de cologne.

She always sat in the same cane chair, which had a back shaped like a fanned-out peacock tail. If she was not there when he ran up onto the verandah, he would bury his face in the cushion breathing in her eau de cologne, not lifting his head until she had come back out to him.

Amrith had seen enough Sinhala and Tamil films to know that his mother did not look like a star. Her skin was too dark, she was too thin, too awkwardly long-limbed. But he loved her eyes, their long lashes from under which she would look at him mischievously when they were playing, the way she pulled her upper lip over her slightly projecting teeth, like a wise rabbit. To him she was beautiful.

That day at lunch, while his mother fed him, Amrith considered asking her about the absence of his relatives.

He had learnt not to question too much the way things were, so, for a while, he hesitated. He followed his normal lunchtime pursuits – running up and down the grassy slope that descended from the verandah to the larger stretch of garden below, poking at a caterpillar with a stick, taking a surreptitious kick at their dog Bhootaya (a mongrel who had wondered into their compound a few years ago and stayed) only to retire hastily when the taciturn Bhootaya bared her teeth at him.

Finally, the prospect of another day of teasing at school overcame his reluctance. He went and stood in front of his mother. She picked up one of the balls of rice and curry she had made, but he did not open his mouth.

'Now, son, see-see, only four more goolis left, *nuh*.'

'Ammi.'

She held out a gooli to him. He ignored it.

'Do I have an uncle or an aunt, a grandmother or grandfather, any cousins?'

The food slipped from her fingers, scattered on the floor.

'Why?' she tried to keep her voice steady as she nudged away the food with her slipper. 'Why are you asking me?'

'Sorry . . . Ammi.'

'Come-come, open your mouth,' she offered him another gooli.

He took the mouthful and walked away. He had pushed her into one of her dark moods.

'Do you remember that Romeo and Juliet story in the *Lamb Tales from Shakespeare* we sometimes read at night?'

He turned towards her.

'And how Romeo and Juliet's parents didn't want them to get married.'

Amrith recalled one of the vividly coloured illustrations from the Romeo and Juliet story. Each character flanked the outer margins of separate pages, their hands reached out towards each other, barely touching where the pages met.

His mother gestured to the wicker chair across from her. He came and sat down.

'So your family and my father's family were fighting-fighting all the time?'

'No, not exactly. It's well . . . a little complicated.' She held out another gooli to him and he leaned forward so she could put it in his mouth. 'The main thing is that our parents did not want us to get married, but we decided to anyway . . . So they cut us off.'

His mother gazed out into the garden. Her eyes were like those dark wet stones he picked up out of streams.

'Ammi, tell me the other story from the Shakespeare book, the one about the fairies.' He reached out and shook her knee.

'My mother died many years ago and, a year before you were born, my father passed away. I have . . . I have a brother . . .' At the mention of her brother, her eyes got even darker, more brilliant.

'Amm-i.'

She looked at him blankly, then she straightened up in her chair, offered him another mouthful. 'But why do you want to know?'

Amrith explained what had happened in school.

She seemed amused by his conflict with Kapila. 'Tttttch.' She clicked her tongue against her front teeth in dismissal. 'That Kapila boy might know foreign visitors, but you tell him that your uncle lives in a foreign country. Why, you have a cousin who is, well, a foreigner.'

Amrith's eyes grew wide. 'A real foreigner?'

'No, not white-skinned, but he was raised in a foreign country so he is really a foreigner.'

'What is his name, Ammi?'

'Niresh.'

'Niresh. How old?'

'Seven. One year older than you.'

'A-nd . . .' He had so many questions, he did not know which one to ask. 'A-nd, what is Niresh's favourite game to play.'

His mother laughed. 'I don't know.'

'Is this Niresh a good boy?'

'Perhaps,' she raised her eyebrows teasingly.

'Ammi,' he played along because it was such a pleasure to see the laughter in her eyes. 'Tell, will you?'

'Tell what?'

'What does Niresh like to eat?'

'Roast Rat with Yorkshire Pudding.'

'And for dessert?'

'Stewed slugs with custard.'

'And where does Niresh live?'

She looked at him aslant, from underneath her long lashes. 'Far, far away in a cold-cold, ice-covered land called Canada.' His mother had adopted the hushed tone she used when she was telling him a story.

'Can-da-da.'

Amrith thought of the freezer compartment in their refrigerator, how he liked to stand up on a stool and stick his head in there, seeing his breath come in and out. 'What do they do in this . . . this Candada.'

'Imagine,' she waved her hand, 'there are no trees, no plants, no nothing. Just ice and snow everywhere.'

Amrith closed his eyes, leaning his weight against his mother, sinking into the story. His mother loved telling stories, as much as he liked hearing them.

'Niresh and his mother and father live in a house made of ice. An igloo.'

'Ig-loo.'

'And there are big-big polar bears everywhere, so Niresh has to be very careful when he goes to school. He must carry a spear and if he sees a polar bear coming, he has to shout a mantra – "Obalaly-jum-jum-shuk!" – and hit his spear on the ground to chase the polar bear away.'

'Obalaly-jum-jum-shuk.' Amrith breathed out.

She put her arm around him.

'What else? What else does Niresh do, Ammi?'

'It's hard to find food in such a cold-cold country, so sometimes Niresh has to go out onto a frozen lake. He skates along for miles until he comes to a particular spot. Then he takes out his knife and cuts a hole in the ice. But how is he going to get the fish to come up to the surface? Well, Niresh has the most beautiful voice in the world. Nothing can resist it. He sings a special song.

And he sings and he sings and he sings. Then up to the surface come the fish. All Niresh has to do is put in his net and catch a big-big one for dinner.'

Amrith was completely enthralled.

By noon, the sun always burnt away the mist. For a few hours, the verandah and the garden would lie in sunlight, then the fog would start to mass around the bungalow.

To profit from the sun, Amrith took his afternoon rest on a daybed, in a sunny patch of verandah. His mother took her rest on another daybed, a little away from him. He had learnt to judge his mother's mood by what she did during this time. If she was at ease, she lay on the daybed, reading *Femina* magazines, Bhootaya on the floor beside her. If not, she went through the French windows into the drawing room. There was a scratching and hissing before the voice on the record started. She played two records over and over again. Pat Boone and Nat King Cole. Above the sound of the music, he could hear her pacing. Sometimes she strode out onto the verandah as if she was going somewhere. But when she got to the edge, she stood, her right arm over her stomach, her hand clutching her left elbow. She would stand like that for a long time, occasionally brushing her palm across her cheeks.

Whenever Amrith saw her like this, he felt such a restless tickling inside that he had to do something about it. The moment his nap was over, he descended on the children of the estate workers to boss them about, to mete out punishment to those who dared disobey. He would steal into the appu's room and rummage through his things, stored in a wooden chest in a corner. If the appu caught him at it (and sometimes Amrith hoped he would) then his mother was forced to deal with both of them, particularly when the appu threatened to take his cooking talents to another estate where they would be better appreciated.

Today, as Amrith pretended to sleep, he watched his mother through his flickering eyelids. She stood at the edge of the verandah, the music loud in the drawing room. He was thinking about her brother. Why had he never written to them or telephoned? His mother raised her hand to her cheek. Amrith turned away, forced himself to think of Niresh. How insignificant Kapila's stories would be next to his stories about Niresh. Foreign acquaintances could not compare with a real live foreign cousin.

Amrith's room was dark, the moonlight casting the reflection of the window across the floor. He was sitting up in bed, his knees drawn to his chest, his eyes squeezed tight to the night sounds beyond his door.

Except, this time, he did not try to persuade himself that his father's shouts were actually sneezes, that the rising inflection of his mother's voice was tinkly laughter as she tickled his father's nose with a feather; that Bhootaya was baying outside the front door because she had been left out of the fun. Instead, Amrith imagined himself pulling a chair up to the refrigerator. He opened the door of the freezer compartment and found a complete world. There, there, out of an ice house Niresh emerged. 'Come Amrith, come on, men.' With a little shiver, a shaking down, he climbed right into this foreign land. 'Today,' Niresh linked his arm in his, stomped his spear, 'we are going to a special underground cave where huge icicles hang down from the ceiling. We are going to see the Queen of the Snow.' 'Yes,' Amrith said, 'today we will do that.'

Later, when Amrith was between sleep and the land of snow, he felt his bed heave. His mother curled around him, her hand slipping into his. The smell of sweat on her was sharp like the Singer oil she used on her sewing machine. Her body trembled from trying not to cry. After a bit, he could feel the easing of her limbs.

'You know,' she whispered, 'you know, I've been thinking about my mother the whole day. I lost her when I was only a little older than you. She was so sick all the time, I wish . . . I wish I could have known her better. I remember so little now.'

He snuggled into her. 'What do you remember, Ammi?'

'She used this perfume that smelt of roses. In the daytime, when she was feeling a little better, she would let me get into bed with her. Then she would tell me stories. It was so lovely and cuddly in that bed. She wasn't from Colombo, you know. She came from a rich provincial family and they did not speak much English at home. So, unlike my father, she talked to me in Sinhala. *Rataram Duva* she used to call me. Golden Daughter. At night, oh my, how hard it was for her to sleep. I would hear her through the wall, coughing-coughing, breathing with such difficulty. I would fall asleep to that sound and wake up to it. After . . . after she passed away, it was so unbearable, the silence of the night.'

He could feel his mother start to tremble again. 'Ammi, tell me a story she told you.'

'Yes-yes.' She struggled to gain control of herself. 'Once in the far kingdom of Vijayanagar, there lived a king and his three sons. One night—'

'Make it a Candada story, Ammi.'

After a moment, she settled into him. 'One night the King of Canada had a dream and, the next morning, he called his three sons to him to see if one of them could interpret it.'

As the story progressed, Amrith drifted in and out of sleep until he was not sure where his mother's narration ended and his dreams began. Finally he did fall asleep properly and journeyed with the youngest prince to the forest of icicles to look for the Evil Sea Lion and his three daughters.

2

A few days after he had questioned his mother about his ancestry, he came up the verandah steps, to find her seated in her usual wicker chair, her hands clasped behind her head, looking out at the distant mountains.

'Amrith, life is peculiar sometimes.' She lowered her hands. 'There I was talking about my past and then, this morning, I received a letter.'

'From Candada!'

'No, darling. From an old friend in Colombo.'

She picked up a sheet of thin blue paper. He peered at the scrawled writing, unable to decipher it.

His mother smiled faintly. 'My friend always had the most horrible hand.'

The appu had come out with Amrith's plate of rice and curry. She gestured for him to leave it on the table and, after he had gone, she began to read the letter.

My dear Asha,
     I work for a film company that is going to be shooting near your estate. I will call you when I am in town, or maybe just drop by. It will be nice to catch up and reminisce about the good old days. I hope you do still remember them. As for me, I have never forgotten.
          Love
               Bundle

His mother folded up the letter. There was a sad, distant look on her face.

'Was she angry with you too, Ammi, for marrying?'

'No-no, son.' His mother put the letter in its envelope. 'It was my fault. I let the friendship go.'

'Why Ammi?'

Her chest filled up, she breathed out, a slow stuttering breath. 'Is this . . . is this Bundle a film star, Ammi?'

His mother gave a startled laugh. 'Heavens, no.'

'What a strange name she has, Ammi, like a bundle of wood or a bundle of newspapers.' He had surprised her out of her sadness and he was doing his best to keep her amused. 'Bundly-Bundle, Boobie-Bundle.'

'Her real name is Beatrice, but she was such a happy baby her parents simply called her Bundle-of-Joy and then Bundle.'

'And did you know her when you were a little girl, Ammi?'

'Yes, son, since the time I was born. We were neighbours. She was like a sister to me. My very best friend.'

'And what did you like to do, to play, with Aunty Bundle?'

She had been dividing the rice and curry into goolis and she did not respond until she put one in his mouth. 'Oh, there were many games we used to play.'

'What was your favourite?'

'Definitely Secret Spy.'

Amrith gulped down the gooli, opened his mouth so his mother could give him another, get on with the story.

'It was the war. The Japanese were going to invade Sri Lanka, or Ceylon as we called it then. Aunty Bundle and I were British spies, except we looked like Ceylonese. We even had false Ceylonese names. I was Mr Karunaratne, Aunty Bundle was Mr Saivakadey. My real British name, however, was Mr Abelard Thoroughgood. Aunty Bundle's was Mr Magnus Mortimer. Our job was to go around looking for Japanese agents.'

'And who were they?'

'Oh, practically everyone in the neighbourhood,' her voice dropped. 'You see, the Japanese were very cunning. And cruel-cruel too. If we had got caught, *Aiyo*, they would have done terrible-terrible things to us.'

'Like what?' Amrith's voice was a whisper.

'Like cover us with honey and hang us upside down near a beehive, so we would get stung to death.'

Amrith shivered in delight.

'Or tie us down on the beach so that, at night, crabs would come and pinch us all over.'

'And did you ever get caught?'

'Never, never, never. You see, we knew who the chief Japanese agent was and so we would get into his study and read his secret documents. We would leave notes in a special place to warn each other of various neighbours who were agents. That way we always escaped capture.'

'And who was this chief Japanese agent?'

His mother's hand fluttered over the plate, crushing the gooli she had just formed. 'His real name was Mr Harishimo, but, you see, because he was pretending to be a Ceylonese, his false name was . . . was Mr Fonseka.'

'And did Mr Harishimo live near your house?'

His mother's fingers moved frantically gathering the rice and curry together into a gooli. 'Well, the thing is, Mr Harishimo was pretending to be my father.'

Amrith drew in his breath. 'So what happened next?'

His mother was no longer interested in the story.

'Ammi.' Amrith squeezed her arm. 'Why don't we pretend to be British spies too, hunting for Japanese.'

'There is no war now between the British and the Japanese,

Amrith.' Then seeing his disappointment, she pulled herself together. 'Who do you want to be?'

'Mr Abelard Thoroughgood,' he said immediately, taking her old role.

'And I'll be Mr Magnus Mortimer.'

'But who shall Mr Harishimo be, Ammi?'

A rustle in the hedge, a magpie rose into the air.

'Open your mouth, Amrith.'

He hurriedly took the gooli from her.

'And what about . . . what will be our secret place for notes, son?'

Amrith thought for a minute and then he went to the verandah steps. 'Here.' He pointed to a gap where the top step joined the side of the verandah. 'Here.'

That evening, Amrith was playing in his room when he remembered their new game. He hurried out of his room, along the corridor to the verandah, nearly tripping over in his haste to get down the steps. There it was, a piece of paper sticking out of the gap.

> *Mr Abelard Thoroughgood,*
> *Beware. Mrs K. Selamma is Japanese. Her real name is Mrs*
> *Yum-Yum.*

Amrith scurried back to his room, where he wrote the following note.

> *mr magnis mortimor,*
> *i will sirch mrs. yum-yum's hus for secrits.*

3

Amrith's classmates listened to his tales of snow and polar bears, his Canadian cousin, with some doubt. Kapila dismissed the entire story. People could not live in a snow-covered land. They would all die. Amrith appealed to their teacher and she confirmed that Canada was indeed a country. She rolled down the map of the world above the blackboard to point it out. His classmates were forced to release him from his exclusion. Amrith, with his stories of Candada, his foreign cousin, his Kraft cheese sandwiches, his felt-tip pens, began to win supporters away from Kapila.

Then Kapila came into class one day, his sparrow's chest swelled up.

'I have some big-big thing to tell,' he announced in the interval. 'There is going to be a film made in this town. And guess where the film people will be staying?'

A murmur of awe went through the crowd.

'And guess what else? Guess who the star of the film is?' A significant pause. 'Vimal Sri Vimalasiri.'

Everyone gasped. Even Amrith's mouth fell open.

Vimal Sri Vimalasiri was his hero. Amrith had practised for hours in front of the mirror, until he had mastered the famous 'Bruce Lee Chop' Vimal Sri Vimalasiri used to subdue his enemies.

Amrith remembered Aunty Bundle. 'My mother's closest . . . why my mother's sister is coming with the film.'

The students looked from him to Kapila, not sure whose advantage would profit them best.

'Your aunty is a film star?' Kapila's eyes were narrowed with disbelief.

Amrith laughed. 'Heavens, no,' he cried in English to give his words a bit of sophistication.

'Then what does she do in the film?'

Amrith was silent.

'Is your aunty the director? Is your aunty the producer? Is your aunty the scriptwriter?' Kapila came up to him. 'I'll tell you what your aunty is. She's the lavatory cleaner for the film.'

The other students roared with laughter.

Amrith, now that he had claimed kinship to Aunty Bundle, had to defend the honour of his family. He dealt a swift Bruce Lee Chop to Kapila and soon they were rolling around on the ground. The fight ended when Kapila banged his head against the leg of a desk and burst into tears. Amrith got to his feet. His precious red cardigan with the blue stripe had a rip in it, a couple of buttons were missing. He did not mind. The fierceness of his defence had convinced his classmates that his aunt was, indeed, with the film.

Still, Amrith could not just rest on this boast.

That day at lunch, once he had taken a couple of mouthfuls, he said, 'Ammi, could Aunty Bundle take me to see the film being made?'

His mother pushed a strand of hair under her batik scarf.

'Amrith.' She picked up a gooli and put it in his mouth. 'You are a big boy now, in grade one and everything. So there are things I can tell you, things you must understand. Your father . . . he does not like people visiting the house. He does not like it at all.'

Amrith was about to protest when he remembered that about three months ago the wife of another planter had paid his mother a visit. She had heard, somehow, that his mother had won the All-Island Girls Tennis Cup when she was a senior at school. She wanted his mother to play in the upcoming Ladies League Tournament against another district. His mother demurred using Amrith, the household, her garden, as an excuse. The woman said she had visited the estate office on her way up to the bungalow. She had spoken to Amrith's father. He had been prompt, charming, agreed that his wife should not keep her talents hidden, should not let down the club, the district. There was no option but for his mother to play.

The night-sounds had been absent for almost a fortnight. They started up. After a week, his mother dropped out of the team. In anticipation of a visit from that planter's wife, she wore a crepe bandage around her ankle for a month. The woman never called on them again.

The film crew arrived in town and occupied an entire wing of the rest house. Kapila brought news. Last evening, Geetha Devi, that great star of the Sinhala screen, had come up from Colombo in a Mercedes-Benz, accompanied by a cabinet minister. She had been very taken with Kapila, had said to the director, '*Aney*, we must find a part for this boy in the film. Such a beautiful face. Can't you write a son into the film for me?'

When his classmates demanded to know who else had arrived, Kapila chewed on a blade of grass, spat it out. 'No one else important, so far. The rest are nobodies. Low-class types, you know.' A sidelong glance at Amrith, who was intently colouring a picture at his desk. 'I have not seen anyone's aunties or uncles or grandmothers.'

Amrith took out his gold felt-tip pen and began to colour in the jewellery on a woman he was drawing. He did not know what to do about his dilemma.

When he came home that afternoon there was an unfamiliar car in the driveway. Amrith dropped his school bag on the gravel, ran towards the house, around the corner, up the verandah steps.

There she was, Aunty Bundle, alone, seated in his mother's chair.

She was facing away from him, practically hidden by the intricate cane-work that made up the peacock tail design. All that was clearly visible were the ornate leather Indian slippers on her feet, a silver chain around one chubby ankle.

She made a slight movement, but did not turn around.

Amrith walked behind the visitor and went to stand by the wicker chair on the other side of the table.

Across from him was a beautiful woman, strangely attired. She wore a blouse of fine white cotton, lace-work on the front. The sleeves were puffed and ended at her dimpled elbows. Her skirt was an ankle-length sarong of shimmering turquoise with a thick gold band down the front. Around her plump waist was a delicate and finely filigreed chain-belt. From its clasp, a length of chain hung down her hip, a jewelled peacock at the end. A gold cross on a chain nestled in the indentation of her bosom. Amrith's gaze travelled up to the woman's face. She had an unusually fair complexion, like milk with a drop of tea in it; a heart-shaped dimply face, turned-up nose, strangely light caramel eyes, hair that rose out of a widow's peak and was back-combed. The woman was regarding him too, her head slightly to a side, her eyes brilliant.

'Amrith, dear,' she held out her hand, 'I have waited so long to meet you, thought so very much about you.'

Amrith found himself going to her. It was her voice that drew him, its low murmur like a stream running over pebbles. She put an arm around him, drew him to her. There was a deftness to her touch. She held him but did not confine him in any way. Amrith allowed himself to sink into her, let her stroke his head. Her perfume was sweet but also woody like freshly cut logs. Bhootaya lay by Aunty Bundle's chair, her snout on her paws.

Aunty Bundle tensed slightly. His mother stood in the French windows that led to the drawing room. There was a glitter in her eyes, a tight smile. He broke away, remembering his father's wishes. Aunty Bundle let him go, but kept his hand in hers as if it was a frightened bird. 'I have a present for you, child.' She reached down and took up, from the floor, a parcel wrapped in green tissue paper, a yellow ribbon around it.

With a quick glance at her, Amrith took the present and walked away.

'Amrith, for goodness sake, where are your manners.' His mother had come to stand behind the other wicker chair.

He stuttered out a thank you, but didn't look at Aunty Bundle any more. His mother gazed out at the garden, Aunty Bundle down at her hands.

In the distance, a lorry rumbled by on the estate road.

'I must go, Asha, it's getting—'

'Are you sure you won't have another cup of tea, Bundle?'

Aunty Bundle stood up, her handbag clutched to her stomach. 'No. Thank you, Asha. You've been most kind.'

His mother came around the chair. 'Let me walk you to the car.'

They went down the steps in silence and around the side of the house. Amrith followed.

A wizened, bent-over driver in a white coat and sarong got out of the car when he saw them approaching. 'Ah, Baby-Nona.' He grinned at Amrith's mother, a near toothless smile. He held his palms together in greeting.

His mother stood still. 'Mendis.'

He came forward and tried to touch her feet in a gesture of respect, but she stopped him. Her lips trembled with the effort of keeping her emotions in check.

Then, before he knew it, Amrith had spoken. 'Aunty, Aunty, is it true that Vimal Sri Vimalasiri is in the film?'

Both women turned to him. He looked at his feet. He could feel his mother's stare.

'Why, yes, child. Vimal is in the film.'

Vimal. She had called him by his first name, as if she knew him well.

'Are you a fan, dear?'

'Pay no attention, Bundle, You know how it is, I let him go to the cinema once in a while with the servants and—'

'Are you a fan, dear?'

He glanced up at her quickly.

'Then you must come and meet him. Your ammi knows the telephone number at the rest house. All she has to do is leave a message.'

'You are too kind, Bundle.' His mother had taken his hand in hers. She squeezed it.

'Not at all, Asha. If I can't do this little favour for an old friend, then what good is friendship, *nuh*?'

With that, Aunty Bundle got into the car, closed the door, indicated for the driver to go. As the car pulled away, she did not glance back at them.

'Amrith, why did you do that?'

He was silent, he did not know why he had broken her trust.

'*Ttttch*.' She leaned down to him. 'Sometimes you act like a damn fool, as if your head is full of cow dung. I am ashamed of you.'

Dropping his hand, she stalked off.

When Amrith lay down for his rest that afternoon, his mother went into the drawing room and put on the Pat Boone record. She turned up the volume louder than usual, but he could hear her sobbing like a child who had been humiliated.

On the floor beside him was the present from Aunty Bundle.

He took it up, tore away the paper. It was a book. *Water Babies*. The picture on the cover was of a naked boy underwater, swimming after three fairies. In the water were also fish and anemones, crabs and seaweed, an otter and its cubs. To distract himself from the sound of his mother, he opened the book and tried to read it. There were too many words he did not understand, yet he persisted, sounding them out under his breath in the way his mother had taught him. Still the meaning of the sentences, the story eluded him.

4

Two days later, Amrith was on his way back from school when he was filled with a great naughtiness from having been shunned and jeered at by his classmates all day. He dashed to the short parapet wall, leaned over it, shouted down into the silent plains below. Selamma ran after him, her arms flapping, pulled him away. He grinned at her.

She shook her finger. 'Don't think you can play up now that your father is in Colombo for the week.'

His eyes widened in surprise.

Selamma took his hand, marched him away.

Amrith hardly dared believe the good news, but when they crossed over the moat, came through the bungalow gates, his father's motorcycle, which he rode to work each morning, was parked in the driveway, covered with a tarp. Amrith ran up the driveway, around the side of the house.

His mother was waiting for him by the verandah steps, a look of wild happiness on her face.

'Amrith!' Her voice had none of the coldness of the last two days. She picked him up, twirled him around, set him down. 'I have surprise for you.' She grabbed his hand and led him into the garden. Down, at the bottom of the slope, in the centre of the lawn, the appu stood guard over a picnic lunch laid out on a mat.

When they got down the steps that were carved into the slope,

Amrith saw that, instead of boring rice and curry, they were having boiled eggs, ham sandwiches, lemonade and – he could hardly believe it – chips.

'Amrith,' his mother sat back, pushed her empty plate away, 'what else shall we do, now that, you know, we're alone?'

'What *shall* we do, Ammi?'

'Anything you want, darling.'

'Anything?'

She looked at him and then away.

'Ammi . . . please.'

He told her about what had been happening at school. She tried to take his woes seriously but he could tell she was amused when Kapila called Aunty Bundle the lavatory cleaner for the film.

'But who is this Vimal Sri Vimalasiri fellow?' She stretched out her legs. 'Sounds like a real-useless type.'

'Amm-i!' He let his voice fill with awe at her sacrilege. He sensed her relenting, and he knew how to play her. 'He is the greatest star of the Sinhala screen.'

'But tell-tell, what does this Vimal fellow do?'

Amrith began to lay out the plot of the last film he had seen. His mother's lips twitched with amusement. Amrith leapt to his feet. Thrusting out his chest, he declaimed like Vimal Sri Vimalasiri, in high Sinhala, 'Sire, thou hast violated the good name of this maiden and her family. Upon my honour, revenge must be mine.'

Amrith performed the Bruce Lee Chop on the trunk of a nearby tree, putting in all the sound effects. His mother held herself as she laughed.

Later, as they were going up the garden steps, his mother rested her hand on his shoulder. 'Let me think about it, Amrith.'

The next day, Aunty Bundle's car was in the driveway.

When Amrith hurried up the verandah steps, his mother and Aunty Bundle were seated in silence.

'Amrith!' Aunty Bundle's voice filled with pleasure.

He nodded shyly and went to his mother. She smiled as if to

say, 'Here it is, the thing you wanted.' As he hugged her, he whispered, 'Thank you, Ammi,' in her ear.

Once he had offered his cheek to Aunty Bundle, he went back to his mother's side. The women looked at their hands.

'Now, Asha, remember, you promised a tour of the garden.'

'Yes-yes.' His mother got up with relief.

Maggie O'Farrell

The uncle's house

Kitty is examining her cuticles,
the way they creep up her fingernails
like a slow tide. The room around her
is still, the afternoon unwinding
on the mantelpiece clock, the fire
consuming itself in the grate. Her aunt's cat
lies on its flank, staring at nothing.

The table is polished to a mirror. Kitty thinks
that if she touched it ripples might fan out
to lap at the edges. She will not lean over it.
She doesn't like the way it gives back
the cleft of her nose, the blank stretch
of her throat. Soon it will be smothered
in damask and tea will be served
and Kitty will be looking down
into the blind eye of a boiled egg.

In the hearth, a coal splits and shifts,
the cat twitches the fur along its spine
and licks around its claws.
Beyond the window, men with nets and spades
are dragging the lake.

Kamila Shamsie

Miscarriage

Mrs Shaukut, owner of scratched records, would have been the mother of both a son and a daughter if her second-born, fingers perfectly formed, had not been a pickled specimen in a hospital less than a mile away. In the early morning, Mrs Shaukut tracked footprints around her dew-drenched garden and waited to hear cries from fragile lungs. Her son, wispy and fine-boned, knew she was so intent on listening for what she would never hear that his screams at night had all the relevance of a dream to her. The instant the night curfew was lifted the boy raced through the garden and out of the gate, his steps making crosses of Mrs Shaukut's footprints. The street no longer smelled of cricketer's sweat or garlands of motia, no longer bristled with the enmity of neighbouring cooks, but remained silent and still, pockmarked with bullet holes.

The boy ran past a shadow – all that remained of the car which had exploded at the edge of his vision three days earlier. A man, tapping his lighter against a hollow lamp post, watched the boy run in his direction. The boy tripped, hit his chin on the handlebar of a bicycle. The man snapped open his lighter and, scant feet away, the boy's mouth filled with blood.

It had a metallic taste, the blood, and the boy didn't know if that was because of his braces, the bike's handlebar, or the man's lighter. He ran his tongue over his teeth and gums, searching for the wound, and found it, instead, on the underside of his lip. A year ago he would have made his way to the store at the street corner, and the shopkeeper would have told him to hold this ice-lolly, here, against the cut to staunch the flow of blood. He would have eaten the ice-lolly, his blood mixing pleasantly with the cold orange taste, and the shopkeeper would have teased him by calling out to the tailor across the street and saying the boy needed stitches.

But now there was only the boy, the man with the lighter, and the mother who was unable to recognize her neighbourhood's shift from community to battlefield as reality rather than yet another indicator of the madness her husband had diagnosed for her. She heard the crash of the bicycle as her son fell into the handlebar's embrace and pulled it down to the ground in a tangle of metal and limbs, but mistook it for the soundtrack in her mind replaying the accident on the way to the delivery room.

There was another crash: the bed in which they had wheeled her through the hospital collided with a doorway swinging open to make way for the grief of a weeping girl.

The boy had watched the girl run out of the hospital building and wanted to follow her, calling out, 'I will marry you one day.' But instead he allowed the nurses to take him to a room with crayons and plastic blocks, where he drew a red bicycle and imagined riding down the street with the girl running alongside him.

All these last months as the neighbourhood emptied itself of familiarity he had been praying for the girl to appear, a green skipping rope trailing from her hand (he didn't know why he longed to see her with a skipping rope, let alone a green one, but this is how she appeared to him when he closed his eyes and he knew better than to question the strange precision of desire). But after all that praying and all that dreaming, he had conjured up only this man with flint eyes who continued to tap his lighter against the lamp post, his eyes shifting from the boy incarnadining the white shirtsleeve he held against his mouth to the group of boys who turned down the side street and made their way to Mrs Shaukut's house, their postures exactly what you would expect of boys who had a common cause for an hour each day and were, at all other hours, watching each others' families drown one another in a blood feud. They each wore the white of mourners; not one of them had escaped a funeral that morning.

The eldest of the group felt as though he were walking apart from the others even though he was in the centre of the group, carefully holding a dozen eggs in his hands. His beard was beginning to come in and yesterday he had, for the first time, taken apart a gun and put it back together, its weight in his hands greater than when his brothers and uncles assembled it; his brothers had laughed and slapped him on the back when he said as much. It was the added weight of his emotions, they said.

The eldest boy knew today was his last time as part of this group which he had first organized. Tomorrow he would be cradling a gun in his now egg-laden hands, and his responsibilities would shift elsewhere. Today was a stolen day of childhood; by rights he should already be on the back of a motorcycle, gun concealed under shawl, waiting for the moment his oldest living brother, bent low over the handlebars, shouted 'Now!' But his brothers had argued with their uncles to allow him this final day as egg-bearer. The brothers, too, had been taught by Mrs Shaukut and, besides, they knew how profoundly the youngest male of their clan loved the teacher who had never laughed at him for being an eight-year-old in a classroom full of five-year-olds. When he had finished assembling the gun yesterday, the satisfaction of hearing that click as the barrel slotted into place reminded him of the sensation of looking at a series of curlicues on a page and knowing for the first time, this is a word and it spells 'dog'. Because that knowledge had come to him later than to the other boys, he had not yet learnt to take it for granted, so as he walked down the street his eyes were alert for language, his lips and tongue shaped themselves around the messages on billboards and the names outside desolate houses.

If he had been looking less intently for words and more intently for objects he would have noticed the man at the end of the street with a lighter in one hand, the other hand resting beneath a shawl which was draped around his shoulders just so, requiring only a flick of a wrist to unwind it from his body and reveal the long-barrelled object hidden beneath the folds and drapes. But the egg-carrier, surrounded by boys of every family in the neighbourhood, could not conceive of this street, at this dawn hour, as anything but safety so his eyes travelled over the man and the boy and swerved around to return to Mrs Shaukut's gate.

'Tomorrow, you bring the eggs,' he called ahead to the second oldest in the group, the one whose father had been killed by his (the egg-carrier's) eldest brother. The second oldest put his hand to his chin, as though it were possible for stubble to have sprouted since he scrutinized his face in the mirror less than an hour ago. Encountering only the smoothness of skin, he nodded and pushed open Mrs Shaukut's gate. He walked to the end of her driveway and turned smartly on his heels to face the garden, the rest of the boys falling into place beside and behind him. They each placed their goods on the ground and stood at attention.

'Good morning, Mrs Shaukut,' they called out in unison to the woman in the garden with the vacant gaze. They had long since passed from expecting a response and recently had ceased to hope for one either. So as soon as the greeting was out of their mouths they turned again and made their way into her kitchen to fill the fridge with milk and eggs and bread (because the son knew what to do with those for breakfast) and containers filled with food that their mothers and sisters had cooked the night before. They checked the little cupboard above the stove and the one with top marks in the last handwriting exam Mrs Shaukut had corrected took out his note pad and wrote down 'Supplies Needed' at the top of the page, and 'TEA' beneath it. When he finished he stood with pencil at ready, waiting to write down anything else that the other boys, some of them now making their way through the house, might call out. Washing powder, or toilet paper, or cold cream, perhaps. While he waited, the boy turned to look out of the window and saw the man with a lighter, his shawl thrown off, standing in the driveway, camera moving from Mrs Shaukut to the boys picking leaves out of the flowerbed to the kitchen window through which the boy with the beautiful handwriting was looking out.

The boy with the beautiful handwriting called out to Mrs Shaukut's son who was standing next to the man with the lighter, watching him. Mrs Shaukut's son shrugged and the boy with the beautiful handwriting pressed his pencil to the paper, in his 'Get Set' mode, just in time to hear a boy from upstairs shout down, 'Butterscotch sweets. Again.' The boy with the beautiful handwriting glanced at Mrs Shaukut's son, who rocked back on his heels in a manner too adult for his age and tried not to look guilty. The taste of butterscotch was all that remained to him now of his former life, and several times a day he would hold a sweet in his mouth against the warmth of his cheek, touching his tongue to it for long intervals to taste childhood.

'Who have you lost?' the boy asked the man who had put away his lighter to hold a camera in both hands, and was moving forward to get as close to Mrs Shaukut as he judged the boys in the garden would allow.

The man raised his face above the camera and looked at the boy. 'My wife. Five weeks ago. How did you know?'

The boy bent down to uproot a blade of grass and, straightening, stroked his bloodied lip with its tip. 'My mother has turned this neighbourhood into a metaphor for grief. That's what my father said before he left.'

The man knew that the father had told the doctors in the emergency room, 'If it's a girl, save the mother so she can bear me more sons. The one I have now is sickly and given to dreaming.' He wondered if the boy knew it, too. In that moment of imagining the boy's life he said, 'Come away from here with me,' and surprised only himself.

The boy smiled. 'You can't just walk out of metaphors. If my mother had taught you, you'd know that.'

The man squatted down so he was looking up into the boy's eyes, a supplicant. 'How then?' And his hands were shaking.

'I'm just a boy,' the boy said.

The man lowered his knees to the ground and put down the camera. His hands were empty and he brought them together, one palm resting on top of the other. For months now the brave and desperate among the photojournalists had been making their way here, searching for some understanding. Why had the schoolteacher's accident unleashed such violence in the neighbourhood, each family claiming to have seen in a neighbouring house the driver who ran away from the scene of the crime?

The man raised his eyes to Mrs Shaukut who was still standing beside the hibiscus, brushing her hand against the ragged red petals. She heard him cry out, 'When will you stop this?' but it meant nothing to her, nor did the touch of the eldest boy as he bent down and rested his fingertips against her foot for the briefest moment.

The eldest boy stood up, took one last look at her and walked towards the gate. On his way out he stopped and said to the kneeling man with the hands of prayer, 'When enough of us have died for all parents to wish only for daughters, that's when she'll stop.'

'That could take a thousand years,' the man said, weeping now.

The eldest boy laughed softly. 'She doesn't lack patience.'

He walked away, his hands practising the motion of unravelling a shawl and raising a gun as a soldier might practise a salute or a boy his morning greeting to a beloved teacher.

James Hopkin

Even the Crows Say Kraków

'Open up, Florianska Gate, open up.'
But was there really any need? There hadn't been a gate for years.
Besides, she could go under or over the old stone arch.
'Open up,' she whispered, with a laugh that defied refusal.
And then she flew over the top.

Ten minutes previously Alina, Alinka (that's little Alina) had
descended from low cloud over the Wawel Cathedral. Then she'd
seen the sloping tin roofs of the church, bright with rain like a
well-scrubbed kitchen table. Already she was wondering: should
I land? Then she'd glimpsed the turrets and towers, like peeled
half-onions, but upside down. Where to land? She banged a leg
against some jutting brickwork with a crucifix perched on top.
She remembered not to swear. But the shudder went up her spine
and along her upper row of teeth. She bit her tongue. She swore.
The chair swerved violently and she came face to face with a
toothless gargoyle. But she was not scared; it looked like the man
next door who came home drunk on a Saturday night. He always
drank without his teeth, you see, just to be on the safe side.

And so over the Florianska Gate she goes and down to street
level, where the peasant women stand up to their ankles in the
gathering dusk. Each time they pluck a bunch of blooms from
their green buckets and shake off the drops of water in front of
them, a little more of the night bursts on the pavement and begins
to spread about them. Alinka flies on, somehow unseen. A
woman? Why, yes, she's thirty years old, but flying like this, she
sees herself as Alinka. Perhaps it's safer, this diminutive Alina.
Perhaps she's lighter, smaller, a goblin of sorts, tucked in a pocket
of her homeland. And who would have thought she could fly?

Not her mother for sure. She'd been a teacher. And they don't teach you things like that, do they? Or her father? Never! He always wanted to feel himself ankle-deep in the soil. Then maybe Alinka herself? They used to say her imagination would get the better of her, though in her dreams she always travelled underground.

An hour earlier, she'd been in the cafe, Jama Michalika, sitting in a mahogany chair the colour of freshly brewed coffee, no, the colour of the River Wisla at night, no, the colour of Marek's eyes, no, don't think of him, Alinka, she told herself. These great wing-backed chairs are surely built for dreamers, she thought, for thinkers, for fairy tales. They were seats for drinking mysterious green liquids that make you see the world through a match's flame, a seat for eating scrambled eggs from a vessel like a soldier's mess tin, scraping the metal into music with a huge fork, a seat from which to smile at the pretty staff in their lace blouses and black skirts tucked like enormous wings, who have trained their feet to be quieter than the whispers of the regulars who have sat so long in the musky corners that the green velvet upholstery seems to have grown over them so you see only the light of their spittle as if they're gargling fragments of mercury, perhaps from sucking too many thermometers – 'Piotr, are you ill?' And the whites of their eyes! As if locked in perpetual astonishment. Oh, how Alinka didn't want to end up like them. Well, she'd quite like to be astonished, perhaps, but not forever.

But that seat! A throne, almost, but then you might one day be deposed, and this chair was not for deposing. No, it's a wishing-dreaming chair or, even better, a wishful-thinking chair so that she could wishfully think for a moment that she was Alina, Alinka, little Alina growing up in Kraków all over again. But although she did see herself up there as Alinka, she didn't really want any of that all-over-again business, no, not all over again, because it's far too easy to get stuck in a loop and keep going round and round until your teeth fall out, and she wasn't about to become like her father who spent the last hour of every evening harking back to old times when, apparently, you could look out of the window any time of the day or night and everything would be where it should be and everyone knew what it was they had to do and how much they would get for it and so everyone did it and was grateful and equal and fair. After each meal, her father would pat his stomach and say, 'Now I know where my soul is sitting.' Even though Alinka was due to start a new job in Paris in a week's time, she didn't really know where her soul was sitting. Not at all. For it wasn't sitting, was it? Perhaps dashing, sprinting, flying but not sitting, surely? And how on earth was she going to catch up with it, and so begin a lasting correspondence?

And so Alina, Alinka (that's little Alina) was perched in this wishful-thinking chair staring at her coffee in which she had dropped two thick cubes of sugar as if they were the last of her heavier thoughts. Then she listened to the rustle of the waitresses' skirts which they had trained to accompany the whispers of the visitors, and to complement the light fizz of sugar dissolving in a coffee that was strong enough to straighten your spine, at least for an hour or two. And these waitresses, well, they had also trained their faces to be as still as the sketches on the wall, sketches of grinning misfits, clowns, jugglers, painted birds, and monsters anxious with flight. But, of course, you'd be very rude, not to mention way off the mark, to suggest that the faces of the waitresses were in any way so grotesque. And another thing, these sketches were not always still, especially after a shot or two.

For example, Alina remembered when Marek had insisted – often during one of his blue nights when he would drink only blue drinks – that the subjects of the pictures – this joker with wings, for instance – had flown from one frame to another, thus swapping positions with a sketch of quite a happy trumpet-playing pig. But however hard she looked, Alinka could never see these changes. So Marek, in his frustration, would drink more of his blue liquids because Alina couldn't see. Then, of course, Marek saw more of them – a half-cat-half-human, maybe – would spring across the room from frame to frame, no doubt trailing a luminous limb, but still Alina couldn't see. So she laughed. She touched Marek's wrist. But his eyes were glazing over. So he drank more of his blue liquids. He saw more leaping figures and fauns. He suffered because Alina could not see. Alina suffered because she could not see. And on and on it went until Marek, his teeth turning blue as steadily as ink through sugar, couldn't see any of the pictures at all, and Alina couldn't at all see Marek.

Now Alina alone in the Jama Michalika was listening to a young man playing a violin in an ill-fitting dinner suit which did in a way give him the appearance of a well-dressed cat. You see, it is candle-lit and gloomy in the Jama Michalika, and with a certain tilt of the head, this big bow tie could look like giant whiskers. The more the feline young man strained inside his uncle's shirt, the more subtle the bad notes became, and the more he looked like one of those grotesque pictures, to the extent that Alinka, not doing at all well in forgetting Marek, thought that the unfortunate fiddler might leap from the stage and appear on a table on the other side of the room, perhaps with a fin or wing or elephant's foot attached to his shimmering frame.

So Alina tried to rattle the cup in her saucer as if coercing the young man into melody. When that failed, she drew the bottom of her cup across the edge of her saucer with a porcelain squeak, catching one or two drops, hoping that these might be the notes that the poor fiddler could not find. But when the young man's bow refused to rendezvous with the right notes and his eyebrows had assumed a curve of mournful surrender, Alina took a final mouthful of her coffee and swallowed it with such a gulp that it surely must have travelled down an unintended pipe. If only I was out of here . . .

And then, moments later, she was rising above the street. Don't ask how, don't be incredulous. Do you really *need* the details? In this chair, almost the colour and size of the chestnut pony she'd seen from the bus that morning, she was looking down on Kraków, her city, her home. As no one in the street would have believed it, no one saw it. Though the guy with the orange pretzel cart did turn an eye, but he was probably just checking that his cap was still on his head or else he had a glass eye in which case it was cleaning itself while rotating. And a woman in a stylish suit cut to catch the autumn light tilted her head in the chair's direction, but she had just come out of the hairdresser's and so she was probably angling her fresh bouffant away from the breeze. After her initial astonishment, Alinka herself adapted with ease, as if settling in a train seat as it was pulling away from the platform on its way to Wrocław where Alinka would no doubt be quizzed by her aunt about her regrettable lack of a husband: 'I mean, Alinka, how difficult can it be? Every monster meets its match.'

But from up there, of course, and when not mollycoddled by a cloud, Alinka thought she'd be able to see people talking off the top of their heads. And she wondered: do words float up not down, or is that just the hot-aired words, and the words of levity and love? And she'd be able to see grandparents sitting on the benches in the square talking about their little ones, while leaves were falling on their wise heads, and if not wise heads – for why equate wisdom with old age, when stupidity endures too? – then almost certainly grey heads, though that as well is not guaranteed. What else could she see or do up there, above her city, the city she was leaving? Alinka had no idea. Perhaps she could help someone find their cat?

And so on she flew, a little guiltily not looking for anything, at first, because she'd always thought that the important things would come looking for her though she was beginning to realise that this wasn't at all the case, and as she was such a long way up no one could see her anyway so perhaps it wasn't a good idea, after all. Thirty, my god, in the clouds, and full of doubts! And besides, such a big chair can be a little lonely. And loneliness is not much fun at any altitude. Flying lower over an orchard, she saw three crows, cloaked like judges, sitting on a branch nearby. They nodded in unison. 'Krak-kuuuf,' they said, all together, as their verdict, and then again 'Krak-kuuuf'. Then, one at a time, they flew off, their great wings flapping like ceremonial robes. Alinka wondered: do the birds talk of their own city in Paris?

A few minutes later, and Alinka sweeps in low down ulica Szewska, and, unseen, drops a coin in the accordionist's tin. Eyes closed, he nods in gratitude to the clamour of the coin. Down every street a flap of wing like a rug being shook of dust as birds scattered to accommodate Alina. But the accordionist played on. And the man scraping music with a big old saw, well, he played on, dragging his bow across the wobbling blade as if his supper depended on it, and some days it did, and really it wasn't much like music, more of a windy whine, which Alinka thought might be how the old man sounded inside. He didn't see her because he was almost blind with cataracts which sat like milk spots on the seats of his eyes, and no one else saw her because they'd never believe that such a feat is possible.

On she flew, twice round the big yellow cloth hall which seemed even more magnificent the second time round. She'd always thought it looked like a giant Battenburg cake, but from up here, the way the light fell across it and set it in the centre of the square, it appeared more solid and majestic and not at all edible, a great symbol of her city, the city she'd been born in and destined to leave. Destined? Well, yes, in a way. Since childhood, every time Alinka bought a new pair of shoes she'd imagined wearing them in a different city: Berlin, London, Paris. So, you see, you shouldn't underestimate what shoes might tell you of your fate, or even how they may walk you to it. Flying on, Alina, Alinka, that's not so little Alina, thank you very much, humbled the pigeons to make way as she planted the thick legs of the chair in their midst. Then, when they all rose up in alarm, she rose up too, and though everyone nearby did look up at this great flapping exodus, they didn't see her behind the cavalcade of wings.

By now, Alinka was beginning to wonder what the point of it was, this flying around the city where she had lived all her life. Perhaps this wishful-thinking chair was trying to show her what she'd miss when she was in Paris. Whatever the case, it was exhilarating all right. She thought at one point that she might have to keep her heart in her purse for safe keeping because her purse had a good strong clasp, and she'd never lost a single grosz, while her heart was threatening to spill its contents, not all of which she was aware of or yet ready to reveal.

In the square, a horse pulling a carriage must have got wind of her because it snorted and shook a leg in her direction so that one of the tourists taking a photo from the back seat, lost his hat, his poise and then his composure, cursed the horse, the driver, and then this godforsaken town, before whispering to his wife that next year, don't you worry, we'll go back to Prague. And one or two dogs barked and ran round in circles, dragging their owners who might have thought the time had come to get someone else to walk these louts who had become almost human in their loutishness. But still no one saw, pointed, believed. Alinka was pretty much alone. In fact, it must be said that such was the clarity of her solitude that she wondered, for an out-sized moment (yes, it was shaped more like an odd fruit than a section of time), if this was to be her fate: Alina, Alinka, little Alina, forever to fend for herself. Especially as a year previously, she had left Marek, her love of ten years. Yes, she'd left him to his visions, his blue potions, his moods of many colours. But now, she felt . . . what was it? He was the only person in the world who would believe the story of her flying chair.

Next, she flew across the town to her favourite church, the Jesuit Church of St Peter and St Paul. As she came down ulica Grodzka, she once again heard a violin but this time it was a melancholy tune played by a woman in a long flapping black dress who stood by a tree, and this woman from above, and in the gathering darkness, looked like one of the crows who had whispered, 'krak-kuuuf', and then again, 'krak-kuuuf', so perhaps this crow-woman had stepped down from the tree, divested herself of beak and wing, and taken up the fiddle. The music was rising up the bark and racing along the branches and flying out in all directions. The melody was rushing up the street, making nonsense of the cobbles.

It was catching every pillar and cove as it travelled from sad to solemn in the developing night. And the tremulous notes seemed to hang in the air, on the points of the church's black iron gates, on telegraph wires, on the toes of Alinka's shoes (and these ones *would* soon walk her round Paris), as the bow found secret corners and hiding places, where soon the birds would fold in their wings, and where perhaps Marek and Alinka had once shared a fateful first cigarette. But Marek can look after himself now, she thought, while wondering if he could.

But the doleful music did hang in the air and about the ears and catch little Alina right in the head, in the heart, in the everywhere. All that she was and all that she wasn't she could feel at that moment, in the music, and she couldn't help but think: I am only thirty. I have loved, I have left, I am leaving. I'm not ready. I don't know. I'm . . . What?

Below her in the street, a young man stood listening to the violin, resting his head against the wall as if warming his ear on a brick, or perhaps he could hear the violin coming up through the foundations and directly from there into the soul that was standing in his shoes. Without his glasses he was sure those statues outside the church were moving on their pedestals, not dancing as such, but moving a little, perhaps even changing places, this way, then that way. Either way, Alina, Alinka, little Alina was all of a tremble, a delicate soul. For those few minutes she hovered, feeling all that she could without bursting her purse, falling out of her chair, or yelling out inappropriate words, for all words were inappropriate now. She cried a little. A tear fell on the young man's head. He patted his short hair, thought that it was a first drop of rain, and hugged himself closer to the wall.

It was getting dark now, and cold, and Alinka still hadn't flown to Kazimierz, the Jewish district. She'd been thinking of it all along, in the back of her mind, where so much is stored, perhaps waiting for the front of someone else's mind to bring it to fruition. And though her knuckles were slowly turning as blue as Marek's teeth during one of his blue nights, she was determined to fly down to Kazimierz. How much time had she spent there over the years? Well, if you can measure time in walks and in sitting on benches in the courtyard amid the synagogues and cafes as the light dimples the panels of the few cars in the square, then, all in all, quite some time. And so off she flew with a swift turn of the chair in the direction of ulica Jozefa, high above a number thirteen tram that was splashing the streets with a light somewhere between melon and moon.

When she came to Kazimierz, she felt the usual calm, not quite a sadness, but something equally rich and reflective. In the near leafless trees on the square, she again saw those three crows intoning 'kra-kruuuf' and then once more 'kra-kruuuf', before flying off, this time their wings unfolding like blankets being readied for the night. And she saw the small red bulbs aglow like berries above the entrance to the Ariel restaurant, and she could smell coffee and warmth and soup.

Then Alina, Alinka, that's shivering little Alina, flew into the Remu'h cemetery and stooped low to pick up a few small stones which she then placed on the top of a headstone, as is the tradition, to signify the promise of return. And she would return one day, wouldn't she? Although she would have liked to stay longer, she was pimpled with cold. She even tried to warm herself on the night lights that sat in red plastic collars around the cemetery, throwing strange shadows here and there, including a trembling one of Alinka and her chair. She laughed at how it looked like a giant crow about to take flight, and she thought: perhaps this is enough now, it would be nice to be back in the warm. So she gave a little croak and was gone.

Emily Perkins

Early morning gutter relationship

Rachel pressed Sam and Alison's doorbell and waited to be buzzed in. This system always made her want to laugh. It was only a house after all, not a penthouse suite, just an everyday family home. She stood on the doorstep, facing out to the street, and glared at the railings. For their tenth wedding anniversary Sam and Alison had asked her to come and look after the kids. Rachel did not have her own children. Forty-two and semi-single, she was unlikely to. She had cared about it once, for around six months in her mid-thirties, before she realized that what she really minded were the comments from her family ('You're *so* amazing, Rachel', 'You have such a *full* life'), and not the prospect of a childless old age. She brought around presents, an overnight bag, and her briefcase containing the catalogue essay she was working on.

Jack peered into the plastic Hamley's bag at his new video, then let the bag fall to the ground with a clunk. 'Maybe I can trade with Emma.'

'If you like,' Rachel said.

Emma clutched her new President Barbie by the head and ran squealing from the room. The smell of this place always reminded Rachel of her own childhood, some indefinable essence of family life, or furniture polish; Sam and Alison had a Serbian cleaner; she probably used furniture polish. Rachel had asked Alison once what the cleaner, whose name she could never remember, had done back in her own country, and Alison had said, 'She was a cleaner.' Sam was standing at the gleaming dinner table pretending to read the paper. He nodded a greeting without looking Rachel in the eye. Jack was fixing her with a hurt stare: how could you get me so wrong? 'I hate that cartoon, it's for babies.'

'Jack,' said Alison. 'Say sorry.'

'It's all right.' Rachel could see that Alison was distracted, that she had no follow-through or real will to discipline her children right now, that actually she wanted to be shot of them, to leave this land of underfoot cracker crumbs (did the cleaner not vacuum?) and shouting. Every time Rachel got home from Alison's place she discovered some mysterious smear of food on her clothes: a streak of tomato puree down her leg, a sticky splodge of juice on her handbag, carpet fluff stuck hard to it.

She was minding the children all night. The minefield of likes and dislikes exhausted her already. Children were so freakily specific and unpredictable; their inability to accommodate others was, at moments like this, bewildering: how could you honestly be fucked to live with it? In her very private heart she knew she did not always like Jack or Emma. Perhaps they would be more bearable when they were twenty-five, but often the warmth or affection or delight she has expressed in their delightful ways has been worked up for the sake of her friend. She loved Alison of old, she wanted to love Alison's children, and sometimes believed that she did – sometimes the feeling, or the feeling of the feeling, passed through her like sun, and it was only the speed with which she leapt on this emotion that alerted her to the cool, pebbly fact: it was not real. She settled for being, if not loving, then kind.

'Come on lovely,' she said to Jack. 'Which story do you want?'

'I told them they could watch a video,' said Alison, apology in her voice.

'You guys go. Have a fabulous time. And don't rush back tomorrow. I'll give them lunch.'

'Oh, well—'

'I've just got to get this essay done by Monday, so I'll need to work tomorrow afternoon.'

Alison studied her friend. Rachel liked to make offers but she didn't really want you to accept them. 'Well if you're sure – I mean, we don't need—'

'Just go. Go!' Rachel's face hurt from smiling.

The sound of the kids murdering each other came yowling from a far room. The front door closed. Rachel walked over to the stack of CDs beside the stereo.

*

Would you call it sort of eighteenth-century sex pit, said Sam, pushing up Alison's skirt as he followed her into the hotel room. The porter brought their small bag behind him. She hated this in front of someone else – hotel staff for Christ sake – wouldn't look at Sam, pushed his hand away from between her legs, went into the bathroom and shut the door.

In here there was one tiny window. A porcelain bath on claws, an old basin with a cracked glaze, dull silver taps. The room was austere. She sat on the toilet and prised off her tight high-heeled shoes, waiting for the heat of her anger to fade, waiting to not mind that he had tried to control it all so quickly. She was never able to instantly match him. Too much psychology. From the other room came a murmured exchange and the sound of the porter leaving. In a minute, if Sam didn't knock, she would be all right.

When she opened the door he was staring out the window, down into the Soho street. The attic ceiling sloped; he almost had to duck his head. He told her there was a fight going on between a cafe patron and a parking warden. She came to stand next to him and to look. 'I like the idea of you in a uniform,' she murmured in Sam's ear.

The two men were shouting: mute and jerky like an old film under the sodium lamps. A plump woman came out of the warmly lit cafe into the half-darkness and gestured at them, tried to calm things down. Alison leaned into the warmth of Sam's arm. The room was almost cold; the air had a silvery, liquid quality. He hadn't taken off his jacket. She kissed his neck, brushed with her mouth where the bristles began at his jawbone. 'Soldier,' she said in a quiet voice. 'A soldier going off to war.' She tugged tightly at the back of his hair. Began to unbutton her clothes.

At the restaurant Sam raised his glass towards his wife. 'Ten years.'

'Don't say congratulations.'

'Why not?'

'As though it's something to be gone through. An ordeal.'

'Isn't it?'

They drank. She was happy. 'And let's not talk about other people's sad relationships. You know, that awful comparative pride thing. It's bad karma.'

'So you've ruled out the children, your mother, my mother and our friends. What else is there?'

Sometimes, when she came home from another meeting with another client about why the taps or the curtains or the loo seats weren't quite what they'd envisaged, after she and Sam had bathed the children together and fought with them over which TV they were allowed and read stories and made snacks and fought with them over which food they were allowed and kissed them goodnight and fought with them over how much reading time they were allowed – sometimes after that, when Sam was telling her about work, some interesting fact he'd picked up at the paper, she knew that not only was her attention wandering, but his was too. He'd stifle a yawn in the middle of his own sentence. She'd breathe, try to take in oxygen, to hold his gaze, but his eyes would be filmy, on the middle distance. His mouth moved, but his mind was elsewhere.

They both looked around at the other diners. People with money, with dry-clean-only clothes, with hair that had been styled that day, people with jewellery worth insuring and expensive drug habits and one or two people who for some reason or other had been on TV. 'Is this who we are?' Alison asked her husband.

A block from the hotel they struck a line of police tape, two vans parked at angles in the middle of the road. Several men in black fisher-man jumpers stood around holding walkie-talkies; the one closest to them was walking and talking.

'Can we get through?'

The man looked at Alison as if she were stupid. 'Area's sealed off.'

'To where?'

'Here to north of Oxford Street.'

'What, and how far over?'

'Charing Cross Road.'

'Is it a bomb scare?'

His walkie-talkie crackled.

'But our hotel's in there. Our stuff.' For a crazy second she imagined a policeman guarding the door to their room, a bomb disposal expert going through their things, the perfume, the moisturiser, the sheer slip and black stockings, the sex book, the shoes.

'Sorry madam. Area's evacuated and sealed.'

'Listen, we're not tourists – we live here.'

There was a pause while they all considered the meaningless-ness of that statement. Sam and Alison hooked arms and began to walk back in the direction of the restaurant. They both felt the same thing, and they both knew the other was feeling the same thing: surprise, and excitement at being surprised. Excitement, perhaps, at being surprisable. They were suddenly awake.

'What shall we do?'

Alison fished in her bag. 'Should I call Rachel? Have you got the phone?'

'She'll be asleep. It's just a bomb scare.'

'I don't want to go home, do you?'

'Definitely not.'

The streets weren't empty exactly, but there was no buzz of conversation from the groups of people they walked past. Every-one, it seemed, was home, or was going home. Without thinking about it they drifted into an open bar, a scruffy, loungey room with table football in the back and people a good fifteen years younger than Sam and Alison chatting to one another and drinking. Unfamiliar music played, which lately had started to bother Alison – not knowing anything she heard – but tonight she didn't mind.

They sat on a cracked leather banquette and drank wine.

'Excuse me.' Alison turned to a boy on a barstool behind her. He wore a small knitted hat and skin-tight jeans. 'Could I . . .' she trailed off, not knowing what the current phrase for scam-ming a cigarette from someone was. He handed her the packet. There was an awkward exchange with his lighter – at first it looked as though he was going to light it for her, then he didn't – then Alison settled back next to Sam, exhaling with contentment.

For the first time in days they talked easily, lightly, surprising each other with unknown pockets of knowledge, making each other laugh. Alison looked over at her husband and it wasn't an effort to see him as others might, as a man aging with a sort of grave sexiness, someone who behind his receding hair and glasses might even be capable, she thought, of shocking her. She wanted to be shocked. Being banned from their hotel, separated from their belongings, gave her the frisson of brushing up against the real world for once.

'Why would anyone want to bomb Soho?'

'Why would anyone want to bomb anything?'

'Who do you suppose it is?'

Sam shrugged. 'Pick a fanatic.'

'Do you think we should check in to another hotel?'

'I'll go and see if it's over. I bet they've sorted it all out.'

'Well, I'll come too.'

'No I'll just be a minute. I think you should stay here.'

'Why, like the royal family? In case you get blown up?'

They both laughed. Alison had the sense that Sam was trying to escape her. Ten years ago they had stood up together in front of everyone they loved. She'd been on a slight lean because the heel on one of her shoes had broken off, but you couldn't tell in the photographs, it just looked as though she was snuggling into her new husband, who although he'd been thirty had smiled all day with the happy scared eyes and flushed cheeks of an eighteen-year old boy.

'I'm coming with you.'

'No, honestly.'

He kissed her on the mouth; she briefly cupped his face in her hand.

Jack wanted a glass of juice. There was none. Eventually he settled for water. 'I'm having juice in the morning,' he warned Rachel, 'and Coco Pops.' Emma needed to be taken to the loo, twice. She sat there, sighing, her hair mussed, clutching the seat with both hands so as not to fall in. On the way back to bed she hung around Rachel's neck and whispered that she loved her. Rachel immediately felt how badly she loved her back. She felt love and compassion and envy. Not of Alison, but of Emma. She wanted to be five, she wanted somebody to tuck her in and hold her hand until she fell asleep.

The essay was not going well. She had thought she admired the artist's work but the more she analysed it, the more she realized her interpretation was entirely subjective and that anything interesting about the piece was being projected onto it by her. Tonight she didn't want to do it, didn't want to dredge out associations and references and scour around within the barrel of her education and her sensibility to do this guy the service of making his work, making him, appear to mean something. There was a semi-pornographic movie on TV: a nervous young woman walked into a photographer's studio and began to take off her shirt. Good.

Rachel was having a relationship with a man who was married and without either of them really wanting to they had recently entered the phase of him promising to leave his wife. Embarrassing conversations about waiting for the children, who were still at school, to get a little older. There was never a good time to split as far as children were concerned, she told him, now or later, they're not going to like it. Don't do it because of me, she said, I don't want to be the cause. You're not the cause, he smiled. You're a symptom. And she had laughed. She had been unable to stop laughing. Jesus, despite everything – despite her mother's voice in her head saying you're not even a symptom honey, you're a fucking cliché – she really liked this guy.

The phone rang. In the seconds it took to cross the room and answer it, panic flashed up from her bowels. Car accidents, dead parents, bad news: what else came at one in the morning?

'Sam and Alison's house.' Whoever was on the other end should know that she didn't belong here, she was only temporary.

It was Sam. He told her about the bomb scare. Was on his way back from the area that was still blocked off, that was possibly going to stay blocked off all night. The line fizzed and crackled. Something about Alison waiting in a bar. He sounded carefree.

'Are the children all right?'

'They're fine. Are you going to come back?'

'No, I don't think so.'

There was a pause.

'Are you still there?'

'I just wanted to let you know. Check on the kids.'

'Everything's fine.'

'Good.'

He was about to hang up. She tried to figure something out.

'Are you scared?'

'No. No. We're fine.'

Nearly a year earlier, Rachel had spent an evening on the back lawn with Alison, sitting on a rug in the chilly, sweet-smelling autumn air. Alison had ranted about being filled with irrational jealousy, insane thoughts, imagining Sam sleeping with someone from work, there was a specific woman, another journalist, it was driving Alison round the twist because she knew in her heart she was wrong but she couldn't stop her brain constructing these scenarios, couldn't say anything, couldn't stop. She had lost the knack of trusting him and she didn't understand why. You'll get it back, Rachel reassured her, for the sake of being reassuring rather than any certainty she was right. You know, Alison said, as though it was occurring to her for the first time, I could die alone too. Anything might happen. I'm not alone now, but I could be. Very easily. We'll push our wheelchairs over the cliff together, Rachel said, although she was furious with the crude and lonely end that Alison carried around for her. Briefly she imagined pushing Alison off a cliff and rapidly wheeling away to get drunk in a bar on her own. But she'd said, 'We'll stick together.'

Sam sat on the stone wall of a churchyard for a minute before heading back towards the bar. There was any number of hotels they could check into instead. From this angle the buildings down the street appeared to him in a way they never had before. He could be in a different city, Copenhagen perhaps, or Stockholm, somewhere northern and wide and new.

Alison took the second cigarette that the boy in the woollen hat offered. It helped her drink more wine; she had nearly finished the bottle. Ten years ago she would have been anxious about sitting in this bar on her own, wondering how she looked and what judgements other people might be forming of her. She luxuriated in the illusion that now she didn't care.

Sam didn't know why he had called Rachel. He liked her, though it had taken a while. He used to describe her as needy, which infuriated Alison, although she sometimes said it herself, exasperated as she came back from another marathon session about gallery politics and who was trying to shaft who and why she would have been proud of the way Rachel had stood up for herself and taken no shit this time but that asshole her boss was blah de blah de blah. Jesus Christ, she would say, slamming her handbag down on the kitchen table, she needs to get something else to worry about. Inevitably then she would plough right back in to the detail, the currently favoured analysis of why things happened in quite the way they did, the endless drive to learn something, to excavate meaning. After years of marriage Sam now accepted this strange habit women had of climbing into each other's brains; it intrigued him. To a point.

A body filled out a dirty green sleeping bag on the ground just behind him. Sam was cold and his back was getting stiff. This was what happened now: you sat on concrete and your back got stiff. He stood up.

Alison extricated herself from the hat boy, who was, she suspected, trying to decide whether or not to make a pass (she didn't want to be a novelty fuck, the older woman he seduced just to see if he could, to see if those things he'd heard about sexual prime really were true, to close his eyes to her disastrous breasts and inelastic skin and to let her go wild, crazy, man she was insatiable, these older chicks they're open-minded if you know what I mean, this is what she imagined he would tell his friends around the pool table, if anyone played pool any more, if indeed he did find her attractive and hadn't just taken pity on her, the lonely nutso broad whose husband walked out on their wedding anniversary and never came fucking back). The beginnings of a hangover crept in around the edges of her vision. It was nearly two. She wanted to be at home, in their bed, with the smooth, bouncy curves of Emma's arms and fists between them, her fine red hair cobwebbed out across the pillow.

He must have drunk more than he realized because he was struggling with the text messages directory enquiries kept sending him, the names of hotels in the area, not getting an answer out of reception. It had become a challenge to read and walk and talk at the same time. He couldn't find anyone to pick up the phone.

She wandered back towards the hotel, angry with Sam for leaving her in the bar and with herself for letting him go. This was becoming less something they were going through together than a story they would do as a double act for their friends. Dinner next Friday, guess what happened on our anniversary. Everything an anecdote, reportage. The most exciting thing to happen in ten years of marriage, Sam would say, and if he didn't, she would, and really it was just bullshit, utter bullshit to talk like that when you loved someone as fiercely and proudly as she loved him, when your body had opened up to them and yielded up babies for them and when your mind was at least half theirs and you saw no sign of this stopping, ever: what meaning did their lives have if they couldn't say it out loud. How dangerous could saying it be? The police cordon wasn't where she had thought. She had come onto a parallel street, was on the wrong side of the road. She stopped and looked around her, suddenly without bearings.

The bar was closed. Alison wasn't in the street outside. Well this was fucking stupid, what a fucking waste of time. Where the fuck was he supposed to go now?

In Sam and Alison's house Rachel lay awake and listened to the silence. It was not like her flat: the bedroom was far away from the kitchen; the fridge did not hum, or at least she could not hear it humming. Last night she and Tony had stayed in a hotel, in the penthouse suite. She didn't want to know what he had told his wife, or who was minding the children. 'You know,' he said to her when they were drinking gin and tonics in the bar downstairs,

'I've never seen you, you know, get yourself off.' Once she took his meaning her throat went tight and she blushed hard. 'And you're not going to,' she'd said, not caring if she sounded prudish. 'But I want all of you,' he said, leaning in. 'I want to know everything. I want you inside out. I don't want anything to be left.' It was so unfair a position that she didn't even bother to point this out. He was intent. He was deliberate. Moving now from Sam and Alison's bed, where she was unable to sleep, to the sofa in the living room, Rachel wondered if she should just accept it. If it was unfair between them, and she loved him, and this was just the way things were and unfair was all right, better even than that.

If he shouted her name she might hear him. The streets were quiet enough. But he wasn't going to do that. He should be outside the bar. He should be at the police cordon. He didn't know what to do. Could he shout out for her? Would anyone he knew see him? Was he insane not to do it? His throat felt like concrete. He wanted to be with her but he couldn't make a sound.

Kids had left beer cans and alco-pop bottles scattered around the uneven, damp grass of the churchyard. An empty green sleeping bag was crumpled under a tree. Alison sat on the mossy wall, her mouth hot and dry, wishing she'd never smoked those cigarettes. She hoped Rachel was all right, and wondered briefly how it was for Tony, who she had never met, to be in love with two people at once. The realization of her bias made her laugh: she assumed he must still be in love with his wife. What she should do was find a payphone that still worked and call Sam on the mobile. But she stayed where she was, deterred by the thought of the sex cards in the phone booth and the smell of old piss. Something would happen. Sam would be angry with her, but it was too late now. A drunk man shuffled down the street. She willed him to ignore her.

After a bit she lay down on the church wall, drifting in and out of a kind of dream, her muscles tensing occasionally to keep her balance. Above her a plane tree hung out its branches, the last of its leaves rustling like paper in the wind. The sky was darkly orange; for a second everything looked like a colour negative. She was a lucky person. So far the bombs in her life did not explode. And sooner or later, she knew, someone she loved would come and find her here.

Nick Laird

The Angels

A woman ought to have a veil on her head, because
of the angels.

        – St Paul, in the first letter to the Corinthians

They watch, you see, what they want to touch.
But as for us we laugh and laugh,
we laze outdoors for days
and read and smoke and fuck.

Baby, don't forget the glass of milk,
the papers and the dictionaries.
Don't forget your yellow dress.

These seraphs in Milton have sex to beget,
and only to beget, the little death.

We watch behind the screen
as squirrels invade the porch at dusk:
two mutely acrobatic rats, nervously vertical,
thrust heads and tails blow-dried to charm.

They shiver and paw at the gloss of the trash.
And we are abashed. They have disarmed us.
It's not botched at all, the universe.

No one expects a child to be perfect. Turning,
the earth's not trying to throw us off

this neglected scent of innocence
the cherry tree in bloom, one clapboard further down,

sends over the fence along with the songs
of various engines and New England tongues.

Its picket-white petals aren't being wept.
This life is a near-death experience.
Yes. I was surprised

but the natural world squirms at our feet,
begging attention, and in the evening,
observing from beyond the screendoor,
we hover, we loom.

Daren King

Let's Get Things Sorted

Her husband didn't recognize me at first. He found me slumped on their doorstep on his way back from the newsagent. I was trying to say my sister's name but I was crying too much to say it.

'Linda,' he said once he'd realized who I was, 'is that you?' He pulled me to my feet with one hand and offered me a folded handkerchief with the other. 'I'll make some coffee.'

He took me into the kitchen. Different types of pasta were stored on a shelf in labelled jars. Paul had written the labels himself with a stencil. He liked stencils. The cupboard doors were decorated with painted holly leaves, also using a stencil, giving the effect of a country cottage. I think he liked things that made things a certain way, and stencils did exactly that.

'Your sister's asleep at the moment,' he said. 'She's not too well actually. Nodded off in the lounge.'

I was at the table, on a stool. I didn't know what to say so I said nothing. It was a lovely house and they were a lovely couple. Paul was good at getting things sorted, and my sister was good with affairs of the heart. They made a good team.

'We haven't seen you for a while,' Paul said. He was stood with his back to me, rearranging things on the worktop. I think he must've been nervous, as everything was already in good order. The coffee powder was in the mugs and the kettle was boiling away on the hob. He turned round after a while and leant against the edge of the worktop, his arms folded, his shirtsleeves rolled up. 'Tell me what happened,' he said. 'Are you hurt? What's he done?'

He meant my boyfriend. My boyfriend had done nothing.

'Let's have a look at you.' He stepped towards me and lifted my head. If he was looking for bruises he was wasting his time.

Michael had never hit me in his life. 'Start at the beginning,' he said. 'Did you have a row?'

'Not with my boyfriend.' I unfolded the handkerchief and blew my nose. I must've looked terrible. 'Had one with my dad but that was ages ago, last week.'

Paul turned his back on me to check the kettle. 'Well that's something else we need to sort out. But what brings you here today?'

'Nothing,' I said. 'Just wanted to visit my sister.'

'Something must have brought you here.' He'd wrapped a tea towel round the handle of the kettle and was pouring steaming water into the mugs. He put a spoonful of sugar into one and gave it a stir. Then he placed two of the mugs on the table and sat opposite me, on a stool. 'We never get to see you unless there's something wrong.'

'I'm all right.'

'Well, clearly somebody's upset you. I could barely get a word out of you outside.' He rolled down one of his shirtsleeves and fastened it at the cuff. 'How are things with your boyfriend? Still in love?'

I shrugged. I didn't know.

'What about college?' He fastened the other cuff button. 'Any problems with your tutors?'

'No.'

'Your friends then. Are you having problems with your friends?'

'No,' I said. 'There's nothing wrong with my friends.'

He stood up from the stool. 'We can deal with this later. Let me just sort your sister out first.' He went into the lounge, emerging a moment later with a plastic bucket, the top covered with a magazine. 'Sorry about this.' He carried the bucket through the kitchen to the downstairs toilet and flushed its contents down the loo. After rinsing it at the kitchen sink he left it upturned on the draining board and strode back into the hall. 'Lindsay,' he said in a loud whisper. 'Linda's here.'

I blew the steam from my coffee. It's nice the way he looks after her, I thought. Perhaps I need a man like him, a man who gets things sorted. Or someone who possesses emotional insight, like my sister, Lindsay. But then Lindsay came in, looking dreadful, and I realized I was not in such a bad way after all.

'Lindsay,' Paul said. 'Linda's here. I've made you some coffee.'

Lindsay lifted her head. She really did look dreadful. Usually she'd be wearing white make-up, but she wasn't today and she seemed to be paler without it. She was in her nightie, her black hair matted into a weird shape. 'Linda,' she said to me, 'what are you doing here?'

'Visiting,' I said. I felt fine now.

'Linda's got problems with her boyfriend,' Paul said. 'Perhaps you can cheer her up.'

'I'm fine now,' I said. I don't know why but I really did feel fine. Emotions are not always tied to external events. They come and go as they please.

My sister went into the toilet and closed the door. We heard her vomit, flush the chain and wash her hands. Then she came out.

'She'd be better off without him, wouldn't she, Lindsay.'

Lindsay shook her head. 'I don't know,' she said, and went into the lounge.

We followed.

It was dark in the lounge. The sofa was spread with pillows and blankets. There were horror books on the coffee table and unwashed plates piled up on the carpet. Although it was decorated in a traditional style, with cosy furnishings, rubber plants and an old-fashioned rug, it somehow reminded me of the house she'd lived in at college, where every wall and ceiling had been painted black. She'd even had a coffin-shaped bed.

'We both disliked him from the start,' Paul said. 'Didn't we, Lindsay.'

My sister didn't reply. She was doing something with the blankets. I thought she was folding them up at first, to put them away, but she wasn't. She was putting them how she liked them so she could get back in.

'He isn't right in the head.'

'Don't talk like that about my boyfriend,' I said. 'We are in love you know.'

'So are we,' Paul said. 'But a relationship requires effort. Isn't that right?'

He directed the question at Lindsay, but she wasn't there. She was hiding under the blankets.

'But then again,' Paul said, 'everyone needs a hobby.'

Whatever he meant by this, he definitely said it to upset Lindsay. It worked, too. The blankets fell away and she was up on her knees, clutching his shirt with one hand and hitting him with the other. 'You sod,' she yelled. 'You sod.'

'All right,' he said. 'Not in front of Linda.'

'You sod. You said you wouldn't say it.'

'All right.'

'You said you wouldn't say it.'

'Shush,' he said. 'Stop it. Pull yourself together. Lay down.'

She didn't lay down, but she did let go of his shirt and stop the hitting.

'Lay down,' he said. 'Linda, can you fetch a glass of water. Lindsay, lay down.'

She was naked when I came back. I think she'd been sick. Paul was on his knees, searching through the drawer for a clean nightie. It seemed odd to see her clothes in the wall unit, with its ornaments and framed pictures. It made their whole relationship seem odd. She was sat on the edge of the sofa, her legs crossed and her arms folded across her chest. Her toenails were uneven, as though she'd been cutting them herself with her teeth.

'Will you give that to your sister?'

I tried to hand the glass to Lindsay but she wouldn't take it.

'Come on, Lindsay,' Paul said. 'Take the glass. We need to get things sorted.'

He said this in all innocence, I think, but my sister seemed to think there was more to it. She leapt to her feet and grabbed the nightie from his arms, throwing it to the floor in the same movement. 'You always say that. You always say that.'

'What have I said now?'

'You always say that but you won't even try.'

'I don't see what—'

'You never do anything.' She was screaming now. 'You never do anything.'

'Me?' He pointed to himself, to his chest. 'What about you? You don't even get up in the morning. I'm the poor bugger—'

'I need you to help me.'

'I try to help you,' he said, 'but you get hysterical. You're just making a fool of yourself. You don't seem to see the damage you're doing. Look at what you've done to her.'

He meant me. I was fine. I'd gone out into the hall.

'She's come round to see you,' he said, 'and you won't even get dressed.'

'I don't want to get dressed. I'm sick of getting dressed.'

'But you're naked,' he said. 'It's not normal.'

'Look at me,' Lindsay said. 'Do I look fucking normal?'

'You would,' he said, 'if you got dressed.' He picked up the clean nightie and held it out. 'How can I help you when you won't even bloody well try?'

For a moment I thought she was going to take the nightie, but her hand went up to her mouth and she fell back onto the sofa.

He did genuinely want to help, I think, but he didn't seem to know how. She'd gone beyond the crying stage to some strange psychotic attack. Paul tried to pull her up but there didn't seem to be anything there. I came in from the doorway to follow his instructions, stacking the unwashed plates in the wall unit and helping with the nightie. Dressing someone in that state is impossible. You need them to help with the arms. The more we pulled her up the further down she went, until she was flat on her back on the carpet. And then it was her turn to shout instructions. He had to take hold of her arms at the wrist, and pull. I think it was to do with tension. It certainly was an odd request, but Paul seemed glad to know how to help, and the look of relief on her face made it all worthwhile.

I had to slip out after that. I needed some air.

The house was in a nice area, a respectable suburb of London. The weather was nice too. It wasn't hot but the sky was blue with plenty of wispy clouds. I tried to find shapes in them, but there were none.

The more I learn about people the less I understand them. Even the sanest person's behaviour can deceive. Someone my boyfriend once knew got arrested for hiding in a kitchen showroom with a stolen kitten. He was actually inside one of the freezers, barefoot, the live animal tucked up his sleeve. I doubt if it seemed funny to him at the time, but thinking of it makes me smile. The image it creates in the mind is wonderful. I had this image in my head when I returned to my sister's house for dinner, and it was still with me when it got dark and Paul and I started the washing up.

'I wash,' he said. 'You dry.'

Drying up isn't something I usually do. It's unhygienic. I held up the tea towel to Paul and told him how many bacteria it was likely to contain.

'It looks perfectly clean to me.'

'That's the point,' I said. 'That's what makes it so dangerous. Can I have a glass of water?'

'There's lemonade in the cupboard,' he said. 'Help yourself. I'm going to sit in the lounge.'

I had some tranquillizers in my pocket. Seven, in a polythene bag, the sort you use for sandwiches. Before I could swallow one, Paul ran back in and snatched it. Months of living with my sister had made him suspicious, and he'd had trouble with me before. He opened the kitchen window, tipped them into the palm of his hand and tossed them out.

'What did you do that for?'

'You're not taking drugs in my house.'

'They're not drugs,' I said. 'They're from the doctor. On prescription.'

He didn't believe me. 'What a fucked up family,' he said, and went into the lounge.

I unbolted the side door and sneaked out.

The tranquillizers glistened in the moonlight, seven of them, snow white, a trail of breadcrumbs, magic beans. Perhaps, I thought to myself, during the night, a huge droopy tree will grow up to the sky and I'll climb it and sleep forever among the clouds.

I picked up just two, and went in to pour the lemonade.

Jen Hadfield

Melodeon on the Road Home

I love your slut dog,
as silent with his three print spots
as a musical primer.
He sags like a melodeon
across my spread knees.
When I dig my fingers
into the butterfly hollows
in his chest, he pushes my breasts
apart with stiff legs.
Isn't it good
to forget that you're anything but fat
and bone? I'm telling you
it's good to be hearing your dog's tune
on the broad curve out of town,
a poem starting,
pattering the breathless little keys.
To see more than me, I flick
the headlamps to high beam
and it's as if I pulled an organ stop –
black light wobbling
in the wrinkles of the road,
high angelus of trees.

Matt Thorne

Mind Reader

Hilary and Dennis had been married for fifteen years. They were an extremely close couple, their bond so intense it made them antisocial. Most of the time they avoided others, but once a year they relaxed their guard and went away with two other couples. Different destinations, but the holiday remained the same. Sightseeing in the morning, afternoons in the sun. And an evening meal in the most expensive restaurant they could find.

'I really think the kilo of fish is only meant for one person,' said their friend, Eric, a management consultant.

'Really?' asked Angela, his wife. 'It's four times the price of anything else on the menu. We could share it.'

'No,' he said, 'I don't think so. I'll have one for myself.'

Dennis looked at his wife. She was staring at Eric. 'Fat cunt,' Hilary said.

'What?' Dennis demanded.

Everyone stared at him. 'It's OK,' said Eric, 'I'm willing to pay for it.'

'I can't believe you said that to Eric,' Dennis complained to his wife as they took the lift up to their bedroom. 'He took it really well.'

'Took what well?'

'When you called him a fat cunt.'

Hilary spluttered. 'Called him what? Are you drunk? I didn't say anything of the sort.'

'But I heard you.'

'You most certainly did not.' Her voice became sympathetic. 'Have you got sunstroke, dear? I've got some tablets in my room.'

*

Away from the others, Dennis started to relax. Of the six, he was the one who enjoyed their group holidays the least. He got bored looking round churches and museums, grew restless on the beach. And since he had given up alcohol the evening meals seemed endless, as everyone told anecdotes that weren't really anecdotes but rather a barely disguised form of showing off.

Hilary opened a plastic bottle and handed Dennis two tablets. 'What are these?' he asked.

'Just take them,' she said, giving him a small bottle of mineral water, 'they'll help you sleep.'

Dennis took the tablets, gulped the water. He hoped they wouldn't obliterate his dreams, the one thing he still enjoyed. Undressing to his boxer shorts and climbing into bed, Dennis put his head on the pillow and tried to get into a comfortable position. It felt strange sleeping without his wife's body beside him, but there were no double beds in the whole hotel. He watched Hilary put on her pyjamas and climb into her bed on the opposite side of the room. Just as he was drifting off to sleep he heard her say, 'They're all so much more successful than you.'

Suddenly, in spite of the drugs, he was wide awake. 'What did you say?'

Hilary sounded surprised. 'Nothing, dear.'

'You did, I heard you. You said, they're all so much more successful than me.'

'No I didn't. Maybe I mumbled something, but it wasn't about you. Go to sleep.'

Dennis let this pass. He tried to sleep again. Then she added, 'But it's true, isn't it? You started off with more talent, more heart than any of them.'

'Hilary,' he said, 'this isn't the time to catalogue my failures.'

'What are you talking about, Dennis? Please stop this. You're scaring me.'

He could take this no longer. He got out of bed, walked over to Hilary, and stared at her. Although her lips weren't moving, in his head he heard her say, 'Oh God, you're not going crazy, are you? I can't cope with that now. Not on top of everything else.'

Dennis stood up and turned away, not wanting Hilary to guess what had happened. His peculiar new talent frightened him, but he knew it would prove useful. Now he'd find out exactly what his wife thought. About everything.

The following morning, Dennis awoke early. His head felt foggy and it wasn't until his wife said, 'I need the toilet,' – something she'd never normally announce – that he remembered how he had changed. Although Dennis was a serious, practical man, he remained relatively open-minded about unexplained phenomena, believing some scientific explanations and dismissing others. He thought that the straightforward argument that time travel doesn't exist because no one has come back to visit us was much more convincing than all that guff about wormholes, and he disliked programmes and films about extraterrestrials. But he had a strong personal belief in the supernatural, and was convinced he'd met the ghost of his grandmother as a child. The explanation for this current situation seemed obvious. The two of them had spent so much time in each other's company, and this holiday had been so boring, that somehow he had tapped into her brainwaves. There had been occasions when this had happened before, but previously it'd been small, explicable overlaps, like knowing when she wanted a cup of tea.

Hilary returned from the bathroom. 'Are you feeling better, dear?' she asked him, before her brain added, 'Have you stopped being crazy?'

'Yes, dear,' he answered to both questions. 'I'm sorry about yesterday. It must've been the heat.'

The morning's excursion was a trip to a nearby island on a glass-bottomed boat. Dennis felt anxious about this outing. He'd been a keen swimmer in his youth, but somewhere along the way he had lost these skills. People had told him this was impossible – that it was like having sex or riding a bike: you *couldn't* forget – but every time he entered the water all his flapping failed to keep him afloat. He blamed it on the increased size of his body, but knew this wasn't the reason. There was something wrong with his brain.

The boat belonged to a young Italian couple. It was designed to take twelve passengers, but Eric had insisted each couple pay double so they were the only ones on board. As Eric took his seat opposite Hilary and Dennis he said, 'Do you have any idea how they operate the star system for hotels? What I mean is, what is the exact system for deciding what defines a three-star hotel, or a four-star, or a five? Because whatever the system is, I think it's incredibly flawed. Our hotel is a four-star, right, but there's really no difference, not to my mind, between our hotel and a three-star, not where it counts. The only things that matter to me are the bar, the restaurant and, most importantly of all, the bed. My bed is awful. It's like a camp bed. I think they should put that in the guides. This is a four-star hotel with one-star beds.'

Dennis looked at his wife. She smiled at Eric. Her smile was pained and he wasn't surprised when he heard her think, *Oh, will you stop your bloody moaning.* Pleased to find her thoughts so close to his, Dennis squeezed Hilary's hand. She looked up at him, surprised by the sudden display of intimacy. They both watched Eric as he pretended not to peek at the Italian woman as she walked along the thin wooden edge of the boat, dressed only in a brown bikini and a pair of thin sandals. Dennis didn't need special powers to read Eric's mind. Nor, it seemed, did Eric's wife Angela, who glared at him. Angela was barely over five foot, with a middle-aged woman's blonde bouffant hairstyle that made her look, to Dennis's eye, like a friendly monster. She seemed permanently confused by the group's conversation, as if their words had lost their meaning by the time they floated down to her.

The third couple, John and Nancy, were the most inscrutable. Although the group had been friends for over a decade, they socialized rarely during the rest of the year, usually only meeting to arrange their holidays. John worked for the same company as Dennis, but in a different department, on another floor of the building. The connection between the three men was a shared secret. In 1989, they'd all been sent on a three-day conference. Arriving at the airport, an announcement came over the tannoy telling them the conference had been cancelled. Dennis, Eric and John were the only ones who stopped to drink away their disappointment. After three rounds, they hatched a plan. None of them was keen to return home, having been eager to enjoy a break from their everyday lives. So they got out their company credit cards and booked three days in an airport hotel. It was a game, pretending they were away hard at work while they ate and drank and John tried to pick up women. His effort seemed half-hearted, as much to amuse the other men as to successfully fill his bed each evening, but Dennis couldn't help noticing that John succeeded three times in a row. This had disturbed him, distanced Dennis from John, especially as the next time the three of them met, with their wives, John seemed as devoted to Nancy, a quiet, serious woman who seemed too sensible to have such a flaky husband, as Dennis was to Hilary. From then on, he had never been able to shake the sense that John was a sneaky, untrustworthy individual and, worse still, that he seemed to revel in being unreliable. He was a small man, who seemed to have exactly the same amount of stubble every day, even on holiday, which Dennis saw as further evidence that he wasn't to be trusted, and although he had no real idea how he achieved this strange feat, he was convinced that John was just the sort of man who would have bought a razor with a stubble-guard when such things were fashionable in the eighties, and used it ever since.

The boat was a long distance from the shore now, but there was still no sign of any fish.

'It's a bit pointless, this glass bottom, isn't it?' Eric said to the Italian woman. 'Are we ever going to see any fish? A shark? A friendly octopus?'

The woman smiled and shrugged. 'There should be some soon.'

Dennis waited to hear what Hilary thought about this. But her brain was silent. It struck him that his new skill didn't work the way he thought it would. He had assumed that Hilary's thoughts would come to him as a constant stream of consciousness, snippets and fragments occasionally cohering into a fully formed thought. Instead, he heard only isolated remarks, usually abusive, unspoken insults. The things, he realized, Hilary would say if she could. Maybe he only heard what she thought when she bit her tongue.

'Look,' said Nancy, 'there's some . . .'

A school of tiddlers, passing in a fast grey cloud. The boat was getting near to the island now, and the Italian woman said, 'We will leave you here for the moment . . . while we go and catch your lunch.'

Dennis watched Eric, waiting for him to complain. Then he realized he wouldn't say anything until the couple had gone. Sure enough, as soon as they were alone on the island, he said, 'I really think for forty pounds we should get more hands-on service, don't you? And what are they going to bring back for lunch? There's hardly anything in that sea.'

The group took their towels from their bags and spread out on the rocks. Eric continued, 'And would it have killed them to take us to an island with a sandy beach?'

One hour later, the couple returned with a haul of sea urchin ('underwater caviar', the man said with a smile), a large slab of bread to scrape the orange paste from the spiky casing, and a bottle of red wine without a label. When Dennis explained he didn't drink, they made a big fuss about fetching him a bottle of Pago juice from the boat. Eric, surprisingly, liked the food and wine, although he got anxious when the Italian woman gave him less sea urchins than everyone else.

'Could I . . . could I . . . just have a little more?' he said to the Italian woman. 'Yes, thank you, and maybe a little more wine and some bread?'

After lunch, they returned to their towels. Dennis lay on the beach alone while the others went out into the sea. Suddenly his peace was interrupted when he heard his wife think *When are you going to fuck me again?* At first he assumed the unspoken remark was addressed to him. It had been a while since they had last made love, and he knew she got frustrated. Then he realized her thought had been about someone in the water. But who? Eric? Surely not. No, it was obvious. It wasn't Eric. Or Nancy or Angela. It was John.

He waited until they were on the boat to confront them.

'So, John, how long have you been fucking my wife?'

John smirked. Dennis had known this would be how he would respond. Nor was he surprised when John replied in a calm voice, 'Thirteen years, on and off.'

*

In the fall-out that followed, Dennis didn't have much trouble persuading Nancy to fly home with him. The first flight they could get on was supposed to leave at nine, and delayed by almost two hours. Dennis sensed that the long delay had created an uncomfortable realization that they had little in common besides a shared sense of betrayal. He'd hoped that their mutual distress would bring them closer, that they could help each other, but now he realized this wouldn't happen. As they were boarding the plane, she asked him, 'Would you mind if I swapped seats with someone? If we didn't travel together?'

'No,' said Dennis, 'that would be fine.'

He had assumed that now he and his wife were no longer together, he would stop hearing her thoughts. But just as the stewardesses were bringing round the first complimentary drink he heard his wife think, *God, I'm so pleased we can do this openly now. When I think of how disappointed I used to feel when it was him fucking me instead of you. He was so bad. So bad. It was extraordinary. I don't know how I ended up marrying him.*

He pressed the *help* button. A thin stewardess with dyed red hair came to his side. 'Yes, sir?'

'Can you talk to me, please?'

'Talk to you?'

'Yes, I'm scared of flying. Please, just talk to me.'

She had been trained to deal with nervous passengers, and her manner was calm and confident. But no matter what she said, how she tried to calm him, she couldn't stop the voice in his head. Now he was away from Hilary, the voice was louder, more insistent, a constant stream of upsetting information. And when the plane hit turbulence, suddenly the stewardess's voice became almost as anxious as his wife's, and then she had to leave him, going to strap herself in. He could barely hear the captain's voice when it came, giving instructions to the crew and passengers. Then a loud shearing sound. As the plane began to nosedive and rattle, he realized this was it, the last thing he was going to hear, his wife's exhilaration, her ecstasy, some sort of punishment, but for what? What had he done? Television screens descended from their clasps, showing footage of forests. Who decided this was the best way to calm anyone? Next, the oxygen masks, and the realisation that no matter how many times he'd watched the safety procedures he had no idea how to save himself. He didn't deserve to die like this. Surely if there was a God up there he wouldn't allow this, would he? Wouldn't end his life in so cruel and unkind a fashion?

It seemed so.

The last sound he ever heard was his wife's orgasm, a blast of thought so bright it all but obliterated the despair with which he met his maker.

Neil Stewart

Crystal

So we left the others drinking in the City Cafe and together rolled down North Bridge towards Princes Street, Rachael and me, arm in arm, her with her hair lacquered into a peak like the top of a coconut and both our jackets on, me warm enough in just a black T-shirt. Even near midnight there were still trains running: I heard their two-tone blast, saw their stacked lights angling through the dark into Waverley Station far below the bridge. Above us the blackened coraline Scott Monument bristling with light; and beyond, the castle jumbled on the rock, turrets and low roofs ramshackle like a hilltop settlement got out of hand. We swung right at the end of the street and I had to wait a few steps ahead as Rachael, who could never resist, dawdled in the patch of light from the window of the bridalwear shop on the corner before delivering her customary pronouncement that the dresses in the display were all fine in their own way, but wouldn't they look so much better in *black*?

And down to a club called the Inferno, where Rachael lied smoothly about her age and even gave the bouncer a sweetener of a wink, which must have taken some time to reach him since she only came to halfway up him. I, of course, fudged it totally, stuttering, 'Eighteenth of the fourth seventy, uh, seventy-eight.' While, instead of freezing, panicked, Rachael did exactly as we'd agreed and sauntered on ahead like there was no chance I might *not* get in. After a long suspicious look – and I was *really trying* to look eighteen – the bouncer relented and let me past.

Rachael, waiting at the bar having already availed herself of something lurid in a pint glass, was busily struggling out of the patched tweedish jacket she'd bought from Oxfam and which had most likely been worn previously by any number of now-deceased geography teachers. A curious little cluster of boys had already formed around her, like she was a missionary arriving in a glamour-starved Third World village: tentative hands lit her cigarette, reached to touch the hard spikes of her hair.

The Inferno had been Rachael's choice, of course. 'You'll see, babe, we'll have an ace time. Think of it as like work experience, your first night out in a proper gay place. Just window shopping: have a look around, see what's happening, get chatted up – you don't have to do anything, just enjoy the attention. The music's better, the dancing's better, people are *polite*.'

'Are they really?' I said, intrigued.

'Well, no. It's a bit of a one-track-mind kind of a place if you get my drift. But imagine if you do score, at least you'll get to do some winching without being afraid some lame-brain's breaking a beer bottle off the bar ready to hit you for it.'

Which had all sounded very sensible when we were sitting in the dorm planning the night out, but it was cold comfort now. The Inferno, for god's sake. I barely knew where to look.

Rising from downstairs was a pall of greenish smoke and emerging through it, like first visitors from a new planet, were clubber boys in their muscle tops, plastic trousers, rayon shirts, their lip piercings shining, cigarettes lolling in their crooked hands. They made for the bar, where a clutch of toadish, grizzled men in, oh, their forties at least, were perching on scuffed stools, surveying the boyscape: trying to look like they'd seen it all before and it meant nothing; but every so often their gaze would track a boy across the room, widening eyes gleaming with unmistakable reptile lusting. So I'm gay, I tried thinking experimentally, so these are my people, but for the moment all I felt was out of place, like an adoptee at a vast family reunion. The sheer bemusing *confidence* of them all. There were so many boys holding hands, or getting off with each other under the lamplight, or sprawling in the big fag-burnt sofas with their arms around one another. They chattered and they leered, and everyone seemed to know everyone else: well enough to smile snidely to each face at least, to grimace behind each back. They owned this place and they looked like they might at any minute turn their attention to the rest of the world and just decide to inherit that as well.

'C'mon,' Rachael shouted, appearing at my shoulder armed with alcopops, 'I got you a drink, let's go and boogie, eh?'

'Let's go and *what*?' And she grinning grabbed my hand and dragged me to the stairs.

Sunday nights were some sort of 1980s retro theme night in the Inferno, so they were playing all these new wave hits we'd been just young enough to miss out on first time round: 'Fade to Grey', 'Heart of Glass', 'Tainted Love', and the club should have been full of people too cool to dance to music too cool to be danced to; no such luck, they were giving it their all. Rachael dropped her rhinestone-customized handbag to the floor and began another impromptu performance of her frenetic Charleston, prodding me occasionally to encourage me to 'dance' too. I shuffled my feet, huffed out a sigh; I did as I was told. When I looked round me for inspiration I thought I could see a pattern in the dance moves, the lustful sideways glances, the prescribed workings of hips and shoulders, the freezing artificial smiles, in every robot move.

Halfway through 'Ashes to Ashes' I became aware of him, only because he didn't fit the pattern. But for him, the rest of them could have been one giant choreographed dance routine, an aerobics class. I watched him for a bit, until Rachael noticed I wasn't paying attention to her 100 per cent and tweaked my ear to remedy the problem. 'Hey, what're you mooning about now?'

'Window shopping.' I nodded towards him, casual as I could, though I was feeling something inside me coming slowly awake. 'Over there. Going at it like one of those eighties robot dancers you used to see with their beatboxes on Princes Street. Look at him, isn't he fab?'

She did look; stared, in fact, so hard I thought he might have felt it, but then shrugged, unmoved.

'Stop squinting,' I said, discomfited. 'Do you need glasses or what?'

'*You* need glasses. *I* need X-ray specs trying to get what you see in him. Ah, well, whatever turns your pages, like . . .'

'Oh, yeah,' I agreed heartily, pretending I hadn't caught the sarcasm. 'Shame about the boyfriend, though.' In the fusty green dark of the club I watched him. His sight was fixed, puzzled looking, on something above us, like he was receiving instructions from a satellite hanging over our heads, and he danced with a loose-limbed, gawky confidence that sometimes crystallized briefly into a series of robotic freeze-frame moves which lost me my heart. His dark hair was cropped short but for a triangular wedge at the front, and his mouth peachy full-lipped, and when he sporadically turned his attention back to the guy he was dancing with and smiled, laughing at himself, it lit up the room like another strobe light.

'Would you ever want to put your tongue back in your mouth?' Rachael yelled above the music. She sneaked a glance round. 'And you're wrong, babe, they are so not a couple. Christ, you and me touch each other more than I've seen them do. And see him, your man, he smiles like this is some sort of trap he might get out of if he pretends he's having fun. He looks more uncomfortable than you even do. Just go and *talk* to him, will you?'

I stared over at him, helpless, but again he was glaring into the far corner of the room, like he'd seen someone over there he half-recognized, half-remembered intensely disliking. 'I can't, Rachael, I . . . I just can't.'

'What are you so scared of?' she demanded. 'He's just some guy.'

'But what would I even say to him?'

She rolled her eyes. 'Man, do I have to do everything for you? Well, maybe ask how he's doing, tell him your name, flatter him he's a good dancer. Show a bit of nous, Vince, I mean, come on. You don't need to engage him in a conversation about, like, global politics – just play it by ear, you know? Oh, but make sure and don't ask him what he does for a living, he'll think you're boring. And for fuck's sake don't tell him you're still at school.'

'I'm just not that comfortable about this,' I said, very loudly as the music abruptly went very quiet. 'I don't do small talk, I'll get nervous, just open my mouth and make some kind of demented lowing sound. He'll run off, I'll lose all confidence . . . No good can come of it.'

Rachael pondered. 'OK. So, I'll talk to him.'

'Oh, no, don't you dare. I forbid it. Rachael, listen, I really, absolutely, totally forbid it.'

I looked over, guiltily. The two of them were leaning in to talk to each other, the shark fin of his hair nudging the other guy's twice-pierced ear, and then as they straightened up – hands casually tangling in a way that set my intimacy alarm bells jangling – they began to push towards the side of the dance floor.

And before I could so much as shrug a 'no loss' I didn't feel at her, Rachael darted away and seized him by the arm. Pierced Ear, who hadn't notice Rachael accosting his friend, had already been swallowed up in the acid-yellow haze of disco lights and dry ice. I edged closer, dorkishly. 'Hey, sorry,' she was shouting up at him, and he was bending to try and catch what she said. 'I was wondering, that guy you're with, is he your boyfriend?'

'Not yet,' he apologized, with a lost little smile and a bob of his head.

'Grand. Hang on a minute so,' Rachael said agreeably, turning and beckoning me over in a cajoling manner.

Oh, Jesus. The music grew very loud again. Beckoned me over, note. Feeling a bit like a sheepdog being bid – a resentful, nervous sheepdog – I stumbled over. With an encouraging look Rachael receded into the gloom as if she were on castors, leaving the lad and I to stare at each other worriedly. 'Hi!' I chirped, mimicking a brightness I didn't really feel. 'I'm Vince, and that streak of light heading for the bar is my friend Rachael. What's your name?'

He mumbled three dull syllables.

'Sorry, what?'

He repeated them, 'Christopher. Chris.'

Luckily, we were spared any further awkwardness by a tremendous crash as, just ahead of us, a tray of empty shot glasses, caught by someone's thrashing arm, tumbled to the ground, slewing broken glass across the dance floor. I looked at it dumbly, then back at Christopher, whose eyes had gone from come-to-bed to could-you-just-go-away. I laughed, nervously, not wanting to just walk off, nor knowing quite how to finish the conversation in any satisfactory way. 'Uh, right, it was just, I wondered if I could buy you drink?' Genius.

'No, I'm good, thanks,' he said affably. He was giving me the kind of look I'd seen on any number of teachers patiently waiting for an answer from the slow child in the class. Then, realizing I evidently had no idea how to continue the conversation, he helpfully shut it down, launching into some spiel about how he'd just emerged shattered from a big relationship and wasn't looking for anything else, he was just out to have a drink and a laugh, and anyway if he did have his eye on someone it would be his nondescript friend. At least I think that's what it came down to, I caught about a tenth of it, through the music too loud and the people who kept bumping into me. He didn't say 'nondescript' either, I'm just editorializing.

'Here,' I said lamely when his speech had finished. 'I think I can see Rachael looking for me. Uh, I'll see you around, right . . .'

'What?' he shouted, perplexed.

'I *said*,' I fairly bellowed, 'I think my friend's waiting for me, I'd better go.'

Again he clearly hadn't heard a word, but still wanted to be polite so mocked-up a general all-purpose nod-smile-shrug response that would have done for pretty much anything I'd said. I smiled back, hopelessly; and I was branding his face onto my mind's eye to remember, only I later wished I hadn't: so it wouldn't have been so easy to recollect his wide mouth fixed in exasperation, the way his eyes, lit with a strange hope when I'd come up to him, registered afterwards only a half-felt disappointment, like he was too embarrassed even to feel fully sorry for me. Someday I'll have knowledgeable things to say about scene queens waiting in blind fairy tale anticipation for their perfect man to just, oh, walk up to them and start talking. I'll riff on how it's all they live for, and how they spend so long trusting it will be so easy that by the time they actually *realize* how hopeless it all is, hunger is etched indelibly into their faces and they're doomed, they're over. Oh, yes, I'll sound knowledgeable all right, knowledgeable and dismissive. It won't happen to me. I'll be the queen who knows when to abdicate.

I made my way through a *Crystal Maze* challenge of lethal hands tugging, heads nodding, feet kicking, eyes raking, to where Rachael was leaning against the bar with a pink cocktail in one hand and her other hand cocked limply in front of her in a self-consciously camp gauche pose. Our coats were bundled at her feet. 'Look at the face on you,' she said happily. 'How did you go, Mr Happy Boots?'

'Well, I think I definitely want to go home now,' I said sulkily.

She gripped my shoulder and rubbed it in circles. 'Oh, Vince,' she said kindly. 'Did you make a tit of yourself?'

I considered, then agreed, sort of defiantly. 'Yes. Yes I did.'

'Fair play, so.' She drained the cocktail in a swift gargle and thumped the glass back down on the bar. I held her tweedy coat up for her to stick her thin arms into the sleeves. 'I was going to say we would have to make a move pretty sharpish anyway. I, uh, accidentally went into the boys toilets and caught two guys having a shag, and I think those other two guys over there are the bouncers coming to throw us out,' she finished breathlessly.

I downed my drink. 'You *accidentally* did all that?' I scooped up her bag for her and followed her forwards. Roxy Music had come on over the speakers and the gay boys were getting surlier, muscling their way down the stairs and across the floor, designer stubble and superiority complexes. There was nothing left for us.

Rachael shouted at me over her shoulder as she grabbed the rail and hauled herself up the stairs. 'Yeah, no, I know, I was following this really tall woman with big hair and a horrible dress. I just assumed it was the door to the Ladies, like, and only realized my mistake when I saw her swan over to the urinal calm as you like and get her lad out. So I dived into one of the cubicles, and *that* was when the fun started.' She was so busy perfecting a pouty little face of comical disgust that she barged right into a knot of preening drinkers by the bar, scattering them like they'd never seen a girl before. 'It's all boys who like boys in here, even the girls. Someone was giving me the eye before and I'd no idea if they were a man or a woman or, like, some kind of shape-changing lizard . . .'

We pushed out from the Inferno club and into the summer night. 'It's because all the straight boys look gay and all the gay boys look straight,' I explained. I held my coat closed and Rachael agreeably stuck her hand through my arm and allowed herself to be steered down the street. 'I reckon people should wear badges, so you could tell which is which.'

'Oh, right, yeah, somebody else had that notion too, but. Who was it again? Oh, yes, I remember: Hitler.' I sensed Rachael eyeing the statue of Conan Doyle that loured over the tops of the sapling trees down Picardy way, could almost hear the cogs turning in her head as she debated climbing up on the pedestal with him. I steered her on. 'Nothing's ever as simple as you'd like,' she said, philosophically, and I supposed she meant the statue-climbing bit. A sickly fragrance came from the plants at the side of the road, the briar rose bushes shabby with sweet wrappers and bloated takeaway cartons. The air was humid and it rang with malice, as if Edinburgh's wannabe childkillers and rapists had all decided, yes, *tonight was the night.*

'Still,' I said, starting to feel a kind of panic, 'it would have been nice to feel a little connection in there, you know? A little empathy?'

'Christ on a bike. Look, you didn't get a lumber, it's not the end of the world. Imagine you'd actually pulled, you'd be terrified. Would you even *know* what to do with a guy if you – if—' Suddenly, halfway across the road, she froze. 'Oh my god,' she said slowly, with an air of dawning awe.

'What is it?' I breathed, almost afraid to ask.

'Oh, god, Vince.' Rachael's head seemed to revolve on her neck, charmingly, rather like the movement of an owl. 'Vince, do you see that? Over there. *Tesco's is still open,*' she whispered back, hugely.

The doors ground hungrily open as we approached. Rachael shook a basket from the stack inside the door and we made our way cautiously into the belly of the monster. Within, the white aisles were empty, the shop floor eerily silent. When we finally did spot a worker in a quilted jacket trotting towards the back office, she seemed somehow improbable, the sterile calm of Tesco at two in the morning suggesting, rather, icily efficient doctors in creaseless white coats stowing racks of blood-filled test tubes on the bright humming shelves, medical cadavers stacked in the freezer cabinets.

'I don't like it here,' Rachael murmured close to my ear. 'Hey, wait, look at that, two huge packs of cheese and onion crisps for the price of one. I take it all back, I do like it after all.' She scooted around the aisles and islands, scooping random items into the basket: a cauliflower, a bottle of French dressing, a punnet of deathly unseasonable raspberries she first lowered into the basket, then lifted back out, chewing her lip, then lowered back in, until I took it from her unresisting grasp and placed it up high on a shelf she couldn't reach. 'Sorry, babe,' she said absently. 'I know this must be boring you, but I won't be much longer.'

'On the contrary,' I said, picking up a couple of apples from the fruit console and attempting to juggle them. Failing. The quilt-jacketed attendant glided out from behind a console and eyed me until I meekly returned the apples to their pyramid. 'I'm enjoying this a lot more than the club, I have to say.' I sniffed warily at the sleeve of my jacket: no surprise, I was reeking of *eau de pub*.

'Next time we go out,' Rachael said, taking a great deal for granted I thought, 'we'll move on a step. I mean, that was fine, but next time you've got to promise me you'll actually make the effort to talk to someone yourself. Not just get muggins here to chat them up for you.'

Experience had taught me it was best not to argue with Rachael's unconscious recasting of events. 'I got scared, Rachael. You saw me, I was shaking like a leaf. I just don't have the balls to go up to someone and start talking away, not when there might actually be something to lose.'

'Well, fair heart never won . . .' She scratched her scalp violently. 'Uh . . .'

I sighed. 'Yeah, but I reckon I can lose my own battles, that's all.'

Rachael tore a poly bag from the dispenser with her teeth and started casting around for the bananas. 'My point is, you'll never get anywhere just dicking around in your room feeling sorry for yourself. All it takes is a bit of time, a bit of effort, just getting out there and meeting people. You've got to spend money to make money, if you get my drift?'

I began to suspect Rachael was more drunk than either of us had realized, a suspicion confirmed when she made beamingly for the pharmacy aisle and dropped two bottles of fake tan into her basket. She dithered for a moment, staring longingly down the booze aisles, which were crammed with trolleys to deter the alcoholics among us from trying to binge after midnight. I could see her really struggling with it, planning exactly how she was going to scramble over the barricade to get to the Tennents lager multipacks, so I started to talk, or at least to think aloud, partly too in an effort to offset the morgue-like silence that lay over the supermarket.

'It's like I'm standing outside the club, right – ' she took two halting paces towards the booze, and I pinched the collar of her jacket and pulled her gently back towards me – 'and I can see all the people inside having this amazing fun time. And, yeah, I know I should just stride in and join them, because it's where I really belong, but I just can't bring myself to step over the threshold. Outside it's cold and it's dull, but you know where you are, and inside it's a whole new world – someone else's territory – and I don't know where I stand in, uh, relation to . . . Oh, Jesus, you know what? I'm really pissed.'

'I know,' she said peevishly, 'you lost me round about where you were standing outside the club. What are you getting at? You'd rather be safe and miserable than take a wee risk and live a little? Hey, I know your macho act's just an act, like, but that doesn't sound like you at all. Help me get some fruit, will you? Any more meat-and-no-veg school dinners and we'll all be struck down with scurvy.'

I followed her patiently. Oh, it's a good act, she was right, dressing up the sensitivity in this blaring, strident persona at school, but it didn't make life really any easier. It felt like there should be a switch to flick: so I'd come out, and I should have felt fundamentally altered, experienced the world in a qualitatively different way. Except I didn't. Not that I wanted everything cast anew in a shell-pink queer haze, but the fact I couldn't even *find* any adjustments to make only showed up how dim I'd been not to twig earlier. It wasn't something I had to grow into, it was something that had already grown into me.

'Maybe it'd be better if I'd never realized,' I suggested aloud. Rachael, who was dithering between pineapples, cast me a sceptical look. 'I was thinking, you know, how they're saying now that there's like a gay gene, and in a few years they'll be able to isolate it, just remove it totally. And I wish it was like that, just something I could lift out and crush between my fingers. I mean, ignorance is bliss, right? I was happy before and I've been plain miserable since I came out.'

'Balls,' Rachael opined forcefully, waddling lopsidedly towards the checkout where a disinterested goth girl with purple hair was passing the night shift filing her nails into the cash register. 'You always were a cranky old so-and-so. That's not your precious gay gene or anything, that's just *you*, you git. Pack my bags.'

I did as I was told, smiling wanly at the geek-girl for every item she swiped beneath the laser eye of the till. These apologetic half-smiles she met with studied disregard, chewing on gum, like she was doing us a favour. The name on her badge was RUBY.

'You've just got to stop thinking of it as an impediment. Or even the opposite, uh, a tool or something for tackling life. Cos it isn't.' Rachael had an uncanny ability to see right into what I was thinking. I caught her eye and cast a warning glance at the checkout girl, but Rachael was in full stonewall mode and wasn't to be deterred. 'For sure, don't ignore it or deny what you're feeling, but for Christ's sake don't fixate on it like. Or get caught up in it as a political thing either, otherwise you'll never get anything done for sitting on your arse scratching your head, thinking, how should I, as a gay guy, order this pint of beer, or book my holiday, or tie my shoelaces.'

The checkout girl looked up expectantly, like she hoped we might conclude the transaction by taking her with us. 'Six pounds sixty-six,' she announced, triumphantly. I was convinced she'd fiddled the prices but, seeing the three green sixes glowing satanically on the till display, I didn't push it and just handed her the ten-pound note. 'Cheers then, Ruby,' I chirped as she dropped the change into my hand, grazing my palm with her fingernails, but she didn't so much as twitch, and I knew it was a made-up name.

I was keen to get out into the night, Tesco having taken on a sinister air I couldn't quite deal with in my medium-drunk state. Rachael, however, wasn't done proselytizing. 'So just be yourself,' she was concluding when I tuned back in. 'Don't you love it when they use "Get bent" as an insult on TV? You're halfway there, you already got bent. Now get proud, and you can go through that door whenever you like. Twenty-four seven.' Rachael smiled at me; held the pose as though this were the end of a scene and she was waiting for someone to shout *Cut*.

'Yeah, and buy fake tan.'

She unfroze. 'And buy fake tan. Which, I might add, I don't seem to be the only one doing, going by the nick of some folk back at the club, at least. Seriously, I haven't seen that many orange men since I left Belfast. Here, you take the shopping, will you?'

Huffing, I shouldered the bag. 'Jeez, Rachael, what did your last slave die of?'

'Malnutrition,' she said smartly, skipping out the store with her hands shoved deep into her pockets. 'So aren't you glad we popped into the shop there?'

OK then: I surrender. *Cut*.

*

We got the taxi to stop at the school gates so's not to wake anyone by the race of its wheels on the gravel driveway, even walked up the grass verges to stay silent. Nonetheless, though we made it all the way to the fourth floor undetected, the warden Mr Arthurs was waiting for us in the corridor there. He was fully dressed, which was scary for three in the morning, and equipped with a pen-torch he raised to shine yellowly into first Rachael's seamy eyes then mine. 'Where do you think you've been?' he hissed, in a way that he presumably intended would sound threatening. 'Don't you know we've been worried sick?'

'Nonsense,' Rachael said briskly. 'The first inkling you had we'd even gone was when you heard us creeping up the stairs there. We may be out late, Mr Arthurs, but we aren't *stupid*.'

He waggled the torch at us severely. 'Stupid is exactly what you've been.' It is, let me tell you, extremely difficult to look chastened by a row conducted entirely in whispers. 'Anything could have happened. Anything – you could have been killed.'

'Oh, but we were,' Rachael whispered ghoulishly. 'We got slaughtered, didn't we Vince? Every weekend it's the same. It's how we like it. We get ourselves kidnapped, gagged and bound, bundled into the boot of his car by some, like, mad junkie. Driven off into the middle of nowhere, drugged up, shot through the back of the head. Now we're lying in a ditch somewhere with the blood soaking into the ground, and the next time you see us it'll be our school photos on the front of tomorrow's *Edinburgh Evening News*.'

He snapped off the torch, rattled. 'That's not funny, McAllister. The two of you, get to your room right now. The headmaster will want to know about this in the morning, I'll wager.'

'"I'll *wager*"?' Rachael crowed, forgetting herself, loud enough to wake the entire corridor. 'Jeez, what century did we wake you up out of, like?'

'Come on,' I insisted, propelling her at some speed back towards the dorm.

Rachael slept in my bed and I cosied up in the armchair with a blanket over me. It was only proper. She snored like something faulty. When we woke up the next day, starving and hungover, it was past eleven. 'Result,' Rachael said sleepily. We'd slept right through double maths.

Louise Doughty

Doikitsa

Doikitsa Maximoff was dying. She knew it and she hated everyone.

Her son sent a *drabarni* in to see her – a crone from Komárno who stank of peppermint and swore she could break Doikitsa's fever and give her enough strength to live to a hundred. Doikitsa snatched the woman's dish from her fingers and spun it across the wagon. 'Burn your blackberry leaves somewhere else, you infant!' she snarled. 'I'm a hundred already!' The *drabarni* left in tears.

Later, Andreas came. 'Mother,' he said pleadingly. 'I paid that woman three gold coins. She's the most famed healer west of Carpathia.'

'She was a child,' Doikitsa grumbled from beneath her feather eiderdown. 'I was healing when she was still chewing her mother's paps. Don't patronise me.'

Andreas was sitting on a wooden stool beside his mother's lit. He crashed his fists against his temples and dropped his head between his knees. 'Mother . . .' he groaned. 'You were never a *drabarni*. The Old Ones refused to teach you, you were so strong-willed.'

'Can't a girl dance?' Doikitsa said, but the fight had gone out of her. *It's been a rotten life,* she thought, *but even so, I would like a little more of it.* Her fever had been raging for a week. Her skin hung off her bones. She couldn't even rise from the lit to pee and had to shame herself into a chamber pot. It was time to go.

'Send Jozef to me,' she pleaded. Her grandson was the only person she could bear.

'Jozef is down by the river, collecting beetles,' Andreas said.

274

'The chickens can wait.'

Andreas gave a sigh of acquiescence, and left the wagon.

*

Jozef came to her shyly, as he always did, his head low. He dragged his bad leg across the wagon until he reached the lit, and gently took his grandmother's hand.

'Mami,' he said.

'Sit,' she replied.

He pulled the stool nearer to the lit and sat with his leg outstretched to one side and his body turned so that he could hold her hand. With the very tips of his small fingers, he stroked the fat strings of veins on the back, grey against the dark sheen of skin. She lay with her eyes closed and they sat in silence for a time. Outside the wagon, Doikitsa could hear her daughter-in-law shaking coriander seeds in a pan.

Eventually, she said, 'Is your mother cooking maize cakes for supper again?'

'Yes, Mami.'

Doikitsa stretched a smile, without opening her eyes. 'There had better be meat. She'll catch it from your father.'

A comfortable silence followed. The inside of the wagon was dark. In the corner, the flowers loomed, the huge paper ones she made to sell the *gadje*; red and pink and orange, with canes for stems. She had never been able to part with the best.

'Jozef,' she said softly, opening her eyes. 'You know I am dying, don't you?'

The boy nodded, still holding his Mami's hand.

'You know that I have the right to tell you a secret, a secret which you must carry around with you, and pass on to no one until you are dying yourself?'

Jozef looked at her, his expression intrigued. Doikitsa shook her head slowly and sadly. 'It is not a good secret, Jozef. It is something shameful. Even your father does not know.' She took a deep breath. 'Our family was slaves.'

Jozef's eyes were as round and bright as the gold coins in his mother's braids. Doikitsa nodded. 'I have never told a soul. We are people of some consequence now. Your father will be *rom baró* one day. The other men look up to him.'

Jozef nodded. Doikitsa said, 'I am going to tell you a story, so that I can die in peace. I am ashamed that I have let it haunt me. It is not our way. Pull down the blind, right to the bottom. I do not want the light to hear.'

The blind was already lowered, almost to the rim of the window, but Jozef did as he was bid. The string on the bottom slat was weighted by a little china globe decorated by rosebuds. When Jozef let it drop, the globe gave a musical clatter against the wagon's wall.

'Our settlement here is not a bad place,' Doikitsa began. 'It's a long way from the mountains, a long way from the mountains and a long way from God, but believe me Jozef, there are much worse places. I know. I grew up in one. I grew up on the land of a Wallachian nobleman. It was monastery land. The monks let it out and the nobles hired estate managers to make it pay. The monks got half the harvest, I think. We never saw them.' She paused, then worked her shoulders to and fro, settling herself into a more comfortable position. 'I was six years old when they abolished slavery. The year was 1856. I know because my mother told me. I think our People were the last on earth to be freed.' She sighed, then clutched his hand. 'Everything you have heard about white people, it is true.' He stared at her. Her grip relaxed again. 'Now, we own wagons and horses. We have crockery, and we frame our pictures of the Saints with tin. There has not been a single day of my life when I have failed to give thanks to O Del for these things, for the fact that I own things the way I was once owned. Sometimes, I walk to the end of the camp and all the way back again, for no reason, just to remind myself that I can.

'I was born in 1850. My mother had us first, then the three boys. I was a twin, Jozef, two twin girls born right after each other without even a pause to let my mother rest. We were two plums, she told me, firm and ripe to bursting. She always used to say that Eva my sister rushed out of the womb so close behind me because we could not bear to be parted even then. We were identical, right from the start. Only my mother knew the difference between us. No one ever tried to separate us. Even the estate manager, who would beat a slave for chewing an ear of corn, even he never sent us on different tasks. We would carry water buckets, one on each side of the handle. We would turn the butter churn, one of us winching and the other spinning the barrel. We slept together on the dirt floor of our hut. For us to be apart was unthinkable.

'Then one day, a huge wagon was brought into the yard in front of the huts, a closed wagon with a door at the back with iron bars. We were six years old, but we knew what it meant. Our mother had seen it many times and had prepared us.

'There was never any warning when you were going to be sold, in case you tried to escape. The wagons would just pull up with their teams of horses, usually before dawn, and the estate manager would get down with men with whips and cudgels. You all had to line up, and then be beaten into the cart. They only hit you on the back, not the head. They wouldn't risk any bruising to the face when you were about to be sold. Sometimes they brought clean clothes. They wanted you to look good.

'My father had a good relationship with the estate manager, and he had always promised him that our family would be kept together if we were sold, so we weren't really that frightened. My mother was more worried about the boys – sometimes they took the boys off to sell as single men, even little ones, but us two were dressed identically, such a pair. We just held hands and waited for our turn to be loaded up. Some of the other families were weeping and screaming. Even then, I remember feeling proud that we were not, and quite certain that everything would be all right. My mother and father would see to it.

'My mother told us to hold hands, look directly at the *gadjos* and smile. So that's what we did as we walked towards the wagon. We held hands, looked at the row of men waiting with their sticks, and smiled. And the men smiled back.

'We were the last in the van. Our mother was pregnant, huge with it, everyone said it was going to be another set of twins. My father and another man had to help her up. Then us, then the three boys. When we were locked in, I heard my mother whisper a prayer of thanks that we were all in the same wagon. A little girl in the corner was crying.

'She was a valuable woman, my mother. Five children in six years. Later, we wondered if that was why we were sold. The monks had got wind of abolition, and thought they would sell off the most valuable slaves before it was made official . . .'

Doikitsa fell silent. She wondered if she had the energy to complete her story. Jozef was completely still; an obedient boy. He had been perfect until the accident, when one of his father's young mares had rolled on him and crushed his leg. Andreas had wept for a week. Jozef was his firstborn, his hope; and now he was a cripple. The other children mocked him, and it would only get worse the older he got. He had been so perfect before. Why could it not have happened to one of the other children of the settlement: thin Arniko who coughed every winter and would not see the age of ten, or black-skinned Todór who everyone knew to be illegitimate – or any of the girls, for that matter? But no, Wooden God had visited this tragedy upon perfect Jozef, just as he visited all the woes of the world upon his Chosen Ones, the Roma. Life was cruel.

Doikitsa frowned to herself, drew breath and continued. 'It took a day and a half to get to the market. They stopped to water and rest the horses but they wouldn't let any of us out or give us provisions. What's the hurry? my father kept demanding. At least let us out to relieve ourselves, it stinks in here. All they would do is let us pass out the buckets. We didn't know, of course, but they had to get us sold as quickly as possible. The manager had his instructions. Our mother was dying of thirst. She was still feeding the youngest boy, even though her time was almost due. The boys were all crying. They hadn't even given us a drink before we left. Mid-way through the second morning, my mother screamed to the manager that unless he gave us water she wouldn't be able to feed the baby and he would arrive at market with one less *gypsy* to sell. He let the wagons stop near a river. Then he got two tin jugs out of a sack. Our father stood up to climb down but when the manager opened the door he said no, send her.

'He pointed at us, me and Eva. My mother looked at us and then reached out and pulled Eva to her feet. To this day, I'll never know why she chose her rather than me.

'They dropped her down out of the wagon. It was a long way. The manager slammed the door shut and locked it again, but we heard him telling her to fill the water jugs at the river and come straight back. I managed to look through a knot in the wood. I saw her take the jugs from him, big tin jugs, and disappear over the rise.

'We all sat there with our tongues cleaved to the rooves of our mouths. I started calculating. There were twenty-two of us in our wagon, including the babies. One jug for us and one for the other wagon. How many sips would that be each? Would Eva be able to fill the jugs to the brim and still climb back up the rise without spilling any? Were her wrists strong enough?

'We waited and waited, and waited some more. And with each minute we got more desperate and I started to curse Eva for her slowness. My thirst seemed much worse than it had before the wagon had stopped. It seemed to get worse and worse the nearer the prospect of water came. The boys were moaning with impatience. When I looked out of the knot in the wood, I could see the manager pacing up and down in the road, back and forth alongside the wagon.

'Eventually, he sent one of the men down after Eva, but he came back shaking his head. There was no sign of her. The manager was furious. He started banging the side of the wagon and shouting at my mother that it had all been a trick. He'd show them. When we got to market he was going to auction the other one – he meant me – off separately from the rest. We'd see he meant business then. See what happened if you let families stay together? We'd abused his trust. We were lying, filthy blacks. We should all be hung from the nearest tree.

'My mother began screaming back, no, no. Eva would never leave Doikitsa! Never, never! She would never escape on her own. Something must have happened to her. She screamed and begged the manager to send men to look for her. Perhaps she had fallen in the river. She could be lying somewhere nearby, hurt, unable to move. The manager said he had wasted enough time already. He was going to get to market and sell us all off as quickly as possible. Be rid of us. *Gypsies* were the curse of his life.'

Doikitsa began to shiver. She pulled the eiderdown up to her chin. It is summer, and I'm freezing, she thought. The warmth has decided to leave my body. I must get the men to take me outside soon, so my soul can escape too. But first, I must finish my story, or it will die with me.

'As the wagon pulled away, as we turned a bend, I had my eye pressed to the knot in the wood. And I saw her. Eva. I saw her coming over the rise. She was clutching the jugs. When she saw the wagons were leaving, she dropped the jugs in the road and began to run after us. We turned the corner and I couldn't see her any more, but I shouted to my parents and my mother started screaming but the manager cracked his whip over the horses and we picked up speed. My father lay down on the floor of the wagon and tried to kick open the door. He kicked and kicked but it had iron bars on the outside. The horses kept galloping, and the wagon rocked and my mother was screaming and I kept my eye pressed against the knot in the wood and cried and cried . . .'

Doikitsa looked up. Jozef was motionless, clutching her hand. He had tears streaming down his face. In the dim light, she could just make out the glimmer of the tracks down his cheeks.

'Why are you crying, Jozef?' she asked, softly. 'Are you crying because I am telling you a sad story, or because you are a cripple?'

He did not reply. He sat staring at her, the tears streaming down.

'It is all right,' she said, patting his hand. It was not fair to ask one so young such a question. She heaved a sigh. It wasn't fair to ask for absolution, either, but Jozef was her only chance. She gathered her strength, inside. When she spoke, her voice was so quiet he had to lean forward to hear her.

'Know why I cried, in the wagon, with my face pressed to the hole in the wood?' she said. Her whisper became harsh. 'I cried because I was thirsty.'

There was a silence.

Doikitsa thought of the sunshine outside, and how, when she dismissed her grandson, he would open the door, and the wagon would be flooded with light. He would go out into the light.

'I wasn't sold off separately,' she said, her voice dull. 'They didn't get the chance. By the time we got to the market, the whole town was a-buzzing with the news. Slavery had been abolished.

The square was full of disappointed managers and merchants, all wondering what to do with their former slaves. The Roma didn't even talk to each other. Most of them went back to the estates, with their old masters. Nothing changed. Their rations were called wages, that was all. As soon as we were let out, my mother went wild. She probably would have torn the manager's face off with her bare hands if she could have reached him but when he heard the news our father dragged us all out of town. Our mother went into labour and her second set of twins was born in a ditch behind a chicken coop. Boys. They both died within hours. As soon as she could stand, she insisted we walk back along the road to try and find Eva. We had nothing. We stole turnips out of people's gardens. It was eight days before we found the river. There was nothing, not even the jugs.'

Doikitsa stopped talking. Jozef sat in silence, stroking her hand.

'Jozef,' Doikitsa whispered softly. 'Tell the men, tomorrow morning, at first light, it will be time to carry me outside.'

He nodded, and rose.

                          *

As Jozef dismounted the wagon, his mother turned from the fire and waved to him. He waved back, then limped over to her. The afternoon was late, golden, and a haze of heat rose from the huge copper frying pan as the fat smoked and the seeds popped. 'How is your grandmother?' Jozef's mother asked. She held the pan one-handed, shaking it gently. He often thought her wrists must be made of iron.

He looked at her, knowing she did not require an answer.

She looked down at him. 'And you?'

It had been a close day. Heat made his leg worse. When the doctor had removed the callipers he had told Jozef's parents he must exercise as much as possible, he was always being sent on errands, but he tired easily and by the evening he was often in pain.

'Not so bad today, *Dalé*,' he said bravely, because bravery always earned him praise, and if he wept or moaned he was told to go and do it elsewhere.

She placed her free hand on his head and smiled. 'Go and finish looking for beetles,' she said. 'Those chickens are hungry.'

He turned and picked up the tin bucket, which he had left by the side of the wagon. It was only a short walk down to the river, and cool there, although the mosquitoes would be out, hanging in clouds like grey silk. He would have to work fast. On the return journey he would walk to the end of the settlement, and back again, because he could.

Vicky Grut

Stranger

A man in his middle thirties came stumbling onto the top deck of the bus, talking to everyone he passed as if he knew them. People looked up with dazed glances but as soon as they understood he was a stranger they gathered themselves into their coats and tucked away their eyes.

He flung himself into a seat at the front. 'That's better,' he said. 'What a day!' Everyone manufactured expressions of concentrated blankness except for the red-headed girl sitting across the aisle. She turned and smiled. She had a lovely smile, not at all intimidating. She had heaps of pale red hair piled up any-old-how on her head, pale skin and lazy red lips. She looked as if she had just stepped straight out of a warm bath and into the arms of the rich brown fur coat she wore. The stranger registered her smile.

'I'm really tired out,' he said. 'I've been all over the place today.'

'Have you?'

'I have.'

His jeans and jumper were neat and new, his face was clean-shaven, but the initial impression of coherence disappeared as soon as he started to speak. He slurred his words and waved his arms – there really wasn't room for that kind of thing on a bus in the middle of winter.

'I was right up in the centre of town today,' he said to the girl. 'I went to see this man who wasn't there. I left him a note, see, because he wasn't there. Then I went to see another man who wasn't there. And he was in. So I stayed with him for a bit. Then I came back down south again to see about some business. And now I'm going home. I'm right tired out.' He shook his head. 'How about you?'

'I'm going to see my boyfriend,' said the red-headed girl.

'Ah, shit,' said the man getting to his feet and peering out of the window. 'I've missed it now, haven't I?'

'What?'

'Brixton. I wanted to get off at Brixton and get the tube.'

'No, no,' said the girl. 'We're not there yet. We've only gone a little way.'

'Ah.' He sat down again. 'I wanted to get off in Brixton and get the tube to the Oval because that brings me right to my door, see. Not much of a walk. I've got no energy for walking. I had the flu over Christmas and all through the New Year – all that time.'

The girl smiled and nodded sympathetically, then she turned her gaze back to the road and sank away inside her brown fur coat. At first glance it looked like a real fur. No doubt most bears would willingly have slipped off their skin for a girl like this, though she'd never have dreamed of asking. On closer inspection you could see that it was fake.

'So where you off to then?' the man asked, looking wildly around the bus.

'I'm going to meet my boyfriend,' the girl said again. 'I'm a bit late actually. I was supposed to be there at five . . .'

'A bit late!'

The whole bus was listening now, straining to catch every word of their exchange.

'Yes. I got a bit delayed because . . .'

'A *bit* late?! You're more than a *bit* late.' The man turned and peered out of the dark windows of the bus. 'Don't you know what time it is? It's gone eight already!'

'No,' said the girl pleasantly, 'it's only just past five.'

Everyone on the bus checked their watches.

'I shouldn't think so,' said the man. He turned to his neighbour. 'Scuse me, scuse me, mate. D' you have the time, please?'

'Five past five,' said the neat Asian man in the window seat.

'Oh,' said the stranger, crestfallen, and then, 'I've been sick, see.'

'Don't worry about it,' said the red-headed girl. 'It's easy to lose track of things when you're rushing about.'

'I had the flu all over Christmas. Just couldn't get rid of it.'

'That's a shame.'

'I went to the doctor in the end, got them to test me because I wasn't feeling any better. I said to them, I said, test for everything: Hepatitis B, Hepatitis C, AIDS, TB – the lot! Find out what's the matter.'

The girl nodded again. 'Best to be sure.'

'But the thing is, I haven't got any of them.'

'That's good, isn't it?'

There was a little silence. 'I'm HIV negative.'

'Well, that's good, isn't it.'

'Yes.'

'*Really* good news. A nice New Year's present for you.'

'It *is* good, isn't it?' The man sounded surprised. 'Nothing wrong with me at all.'

The rest of the people on the bus turned away from the man and the girl now. They pressed their faces to the windows, pretending to stare at the glittering winter streets as if they feared that whatever ailed this man might somehow leak out and contaminate them. Bad news, they were thinking. This character is bad news.

The bus stopped and he leapt to his feet again, peering out of the windows at the road. 'Ah, Jesus! No! I'm definitely going the wrong way here. I'm going completely the wrong . . . I want to go to Brixton . . . and this . . . this . . .'

'We are going to Brixton,' called the red-headed girl. But the stranger had already begun to stumble back down the aisle towards the exit, knocking shins and shoulders and heads as he went. 'Sorry, sorry . . .' he muttered, treading on everyone's feet. The bus started off again and he was still only halfway down the aisle. 'Christ, no!' he called, arms flailing wildly. 'Wait! Stop the bus! This is all wrong. I've got to get off!' Several of the other passengers began to object loudly. One of them stood up and grabbed his arm. 'Take it easy, mate. You're *disturbing* people!'

'But don't you understand?' cried the stranger. 'I don't know where the hell I am. This is all wrong. I've got to get off now . . .' The more frantically he tried to hurry the more he became entangled in the coats and bags and umbrellas of the people around him.

'Ring the bell,' said someone. 'Call the conductor.'

The bus gave a sudden lurch.

For a brief moment the stranger seemed to spin with an almost unearthly lightness. Then he fell, disappearing in a welter of arms and legs like a wild bird in a box of string.

John Logan

Sometimes All the World
Comes Down

I saw that the road was full of objects but I didn't pay much attention to them. Some of them looked like old children's toys, abandoned and decayed. I didn't really have to rush to be anywhere so I stopped and stared for a while. There was a spinning top, the old metal kind I hadn't seen for years. There were rusty patches on it here and there and areas where the red and yellow paint had been chipped away from the rounded surface. I tried to imagine how all the toys and objects could have come to be there, lying on the road and blocking it like that. Just then a deer walked out from the edge of the forest and stood at the side of the road, staring not at me but at the toys and objects. It bowed its head and its antlers stood forth, proud and dangerous. Gently, it prodded an antler against the old spinning top, which rolled a little on the road.

At the sound of the metal rolling against the road surface the stag stepped back, not skittishly but cautious. I wondered when the stag would notice me but it kept staring at the spinning top which wasn't spinning, might not have spun for years and might not ever spin again. How good this is, I thought, to see the old metal top there on the road and to see the stag staring at it like that. I congratulated myself on my good luck as I stood there watching. The deer didn't seem to be aware of me at all and I thought I could see a frown gather around its vivid brown eyes. Never did the stag look at me while I was doing all this staring and envying, not even a glance in my direction. It just kept staring at the metal top and, yes, the stag was certainly frowning now. Suddenly it lurched its head forward with a twist and sent the metal top spinning along the road surface with a firm antler thrust. The

287

top banged and clattered against the road, crashing its way through other toys and objects. A bell was chiming from inside one of the objects the top had knocked against. I took a breath and stared at the stag, saw on its antler a flake of yellow paint from the metal top. The stag raised his head, bared his teeth, spun round and returned to the forest. All that weight supported by four small hooves. The metal top was entirely still now on the road among the toys and objects. The hidden bell continued to chime from somewhere, ever more slowly until a last faint ring and then silence.

*

The stag wasn't the first creature to have come out of that forest and simply refuse to look at me, like I didn't exist as fully as it did. One day there had been a gang of thuggish squirrels, flicking nuts at each other's buck-toothed faces and farting as they ran from tree to tree in spasmodic bursts of energy. Surely somewhere at the back of all this . . . this business of getting flatly ignored by God's creatures . . . surely there was some great cosmic insult brutally lurking. But that was only a theory, I told myself. Forget theory. All I really knew was that the toys and objects were still littered on the road, but the stag was gone now, returned to the forest. The sun wasn't getting through the clouds in the sky above. There was rain coming, I thought. I wondered if the stag was running in the forest now, his weight getting pounded along by the coiled-spring power delivered into the earth by the surfaces of two small hooves . . . then flying, soaring . . . just missing neck-breaking trees . . . then landing on the other two hooves, springing onward into a forest as dark as the inside of a brain. Like the inside of a brain on the inside of a girl's skull that's getting hit hard off a plaster wall again and again as the girl's boyfriend sits nearby on a sofa and just listens. I turned my back on the present reality of the toys and objects on the new stretch of tree-bordered road . . . I turned to face the old demons that were scattered strategically and evilly all along the well-worn path I'd had to navigate for so long to ever get this far . . . this far from the days of drifting and wandering . . .

*

She was hitting her head off the wall. What a sound it made! There was a dull reverberating echo that must have been from within the bone of her skull. Or was it from within the plaster wall her head was striking? And there was a subtle wetness to the sound. Surely that must have been from her brain slooshing around inside at the impact. I'd tried to stop her for an hour by lying or sitting on the bed beside her, holding her, restraining her as she hung passive in my arms. But whenever I let go she went back to striking her head against the wall. I'd given up and decided to let her do it for a while. *THUD* . . . pause . . . head held against wall . . . then head retracted from wall twelve inches . . . then, *THUD* . . . I sat on the couch with my back to her and listened for a while. Then I got up, turned, walked towards where she was sprawled on the bed, head poised for the next blow. I picked up her mug from the stand by the bed and threw it hard at the door of her room. The handle broke off the mug. The rest of the mug fell from the hole it had punched in the door and landed on the floor, smashing into bits. She turned her face from the wall to see what I'd done. Snot hung from her nostrils in streams. Her eyes and cheeks were puffy and red with tears. Her hair was like dark straw.

'Is that enough fucking trouble for you? You looking forward to telling your landlord how you got a hole in your door?' I shouted.

She blinked dully.

'Oh, I see . . . the door's important, is it? Your own fucking head's not important but the door is. Stop hitting your head off that wall, Linda, or I'll put a hole all the way through that door. Are you going to stop?'

Her head nodded, the expression attentive.

Angela, the one before Linda, she had been even crazier. With Angela it wouldn't have been the wall getting hit, it would have been me. Angela and Linda were like opposite forces; different sides of the female coin. They were like Dr Jekyll and Mr Hyde; Linda Jekyll and Angela Hyde. But it was Angela I was with first. In the story of Jekyll and Hyde, normally you get to know the mild-mannered Jekyll first, before you graduate to the sinister Hyde. But I started off straight away with Angela . . . my Mistress

Hyde. Then I graduated to Linda Jekyll, who was a nurse rather than a doctor but it was all the same thing in the end. And the problem with doing things that way round is . . . it can make Miss Jekyll seem a bit boring in comparison . . . after the ravaging natural force that had been Mistress Hyde. And maybe somewhere inside herself Nurse Jekyll could sense that boredom in me. Maybe that's part of the reason she sometimes ended up doing her version of the crazy stuff. Boredom can leave you feeling like banging your head off a wall; even someone else's boredom.

But Angela and Linda did have one thing in common. In the end, they would both betray me. The first sign that Angela could not be trusted was so subtle that I didn't really notice it when it happened. It was only years later, when I had the perspective and looked back on things, that I interpreted her small action as the first sign of the treachery to come. It happened on the night we both arrived very late at Fidel's party in the large Aberdeen house he was sharing back then with two other students.

But first . . . I'm on the road with the toys and objects and the stag is back in the forest, perhaps running. I want to run there too, powered by a stag's heavy heart, and be away from all these other thoughts. That's why the stag and the squirrels wouldn't look at me. Because I am full to brim with these static thoughts and memories. Come back out of the thick forest now and free me, stag! Pierce my skull with one antler thrust. Thrust deep and embed that yellow paint flake you scratched from the metal top into my pulsing brain. No? Too busy running free in the forest to come back and do me that service? Run on then, stag! I'll twist my pulsing brain back to the subject of Fidel's party and I'll pretend you're listening, stag, I'll pretend you really care. There was a sick man at this party, stag, a man so sick he'd be dead within six weeks. But no one knew this about him on the night of Fidel's party, stag, perhaps he did not know himself. Or perhaps he did. That's his own business.

Anyway, within half an hour of me and Angela arriving at Fidel's party this sick man was chewing my shoulder. It was a deep, rending, red-hot needle pain. It was a pain that had startled me into stopping breathing. The last breath I had taken was stuck in my throat, locked there. That was the breath that had been

going into me at the moment he decided to bite me. I felt outrage
... indignation ... at this man's decision to bite me and at this
continued, wilful chewing of my shoulder he was doing now.
Then the outrage passed and was replaced by a wave of relief. I
felt gratitude ... not to the man but to something else. Gratitude
that it was my shoulder he was chewing. I was grateful that the
man had shown mercy and not bitten into my nose or some other
part of my face. Even with the agony of the shoulder chewing still
going on I felt this relief and gratitude that those teeth weren't
ripping my nose apart. Fidel and Joe had hold of his shoulders
and were saying things to him but he wouldn't stop chewing.
They pulled him back but he wouldn't let go. So he took a little
morsel of my shoulder with him between his clenched teeth as his
head went back. I saw my blood on his lips and chin. I watched
his face as Fidel and Joe gripped his arms and shoulders, dragged
him fifteen feet diagonally across the room to the door. All three
vanished out the door. I didn't move. I didn't look round to see if
anyone else was left with me in the room. I waited. I kept my
eyes on the door and didn't look at my shoulder which was bare
as I only had a vest on top. I felt blood running warmly down my
arm but I kept my eyes on the door the three of them had
disappeared through. I waited. I couldn't hear them. Then I saw
all three of them come back in the door like I was watching the
film of Fidel and Joe pulling him out of the room again, but
played backwards. He dragged them both back into the room
again. They had the same grip on his arms and shoulders. He
dragged them in the door and all the way across the room again
until all three were back where they started. I didn't move. He
looked at me. He looked at my shoulder. Then they were dragging
him back again, pulling him fifteen feet across the room diagonally again, until all three of them vanished again through the
door.

And then that wolf that lives in my brain was following me
again. The one that doesn't love me at all. The one that dreams
of biting my neck and snaffling up my running blood. Dream on,
you cheap furball. Wolven sack of shit. Didn't know how much
I hated wolves until I started getting followed around by this mad,
grey bastard. The tears aren't far away now. No, I've stopped

them. If God loved me none of this shit would be happening. See how my mind works? Notice how I don't doubt God's existence. No, it's the love my mind doubted there. If I could scream loud enough in the vast cavern of my brain I would scream again. Especially since I've just done a nice warm-up scream. But I'm not going to scream again just now because my scream is never loud enough. Maybe when I was a baby my scream was loud enough, proportionate to my physical size. But the scream hasn't kept pace with my physical development or my pain. That wind from the north of my brain is cutting into me too . . . into my face, my eyes. It's a skill, this walking in the snow that covers the floor of my brain. The wolf knows. He's better at it. I swear, before this is over I'm going to cook that bastard, turn his carcass on a spit over an open fire and sing hymns as I do it. I take a deep breath. Just a fantasy. They're always there, these fantasies. I look at the wolf. He's hungry. He doesn't have fantasies . . . just hunger. He doesn't graft stories onto his hunger, his need. His hunger stays pure. Remains simply hunger. No stories for him. No beginning, middle, end for wolfie. Only now for wolfie. And now. And now. And again . . . now. The day in my brain is going better than the night at the party with the sick man. I've walked further from my own story . . . from the beginning and the middle anyway. We'll walk on now, myself and the grey one. Ahead the snow is clear, unbroken. No one's been where we are going.

And the first sign that Angela could not be trusted? The sign that was so subtle I didn't really notice it when it happened? The small action that, years later, I interpreted as the first sign of the treachery to come? Well, it wasn't much really. Just that the moment the guy had dived his head forward and sunk his teeth into my shoulder . . . at that exact moment of breath-stilled shock I'd seen a wee pair of running feet racing across the carpet towards the door. Small, blurred, running feet like in a hastily drawn cartoon . . . an impressionistic eastern European cartoon. It was Angela's feet in the black shoes, running the fifteen feet across the purple carpet in a diagonal line towards the door. It was Angela, unable to get out of the room fast enough, as the sick man who'd be dead within six weeks leaned his large shaven head's bespectacled weight into my shoulder and settled down to the chewing. Sometimes all the world comes down to is stags, squirrels, a big grey wolf that hates you and your own warm blood running down your left arm. Your mind's eyes can be with the wolf heading into unbroken snow; even as your physical eyes are locked on the small, blurred, running feet as they race diagonally across the purple carpet towards the door and away from you. Yes, Angela's feet in the black shoes, racing unmistakably in a diagonal across that purple carpet towards the door, desperate to get out of the room and away from me. Away from me and the deep, rending, red-hot needle pain that used to be my shoulder.

Nicholas Pierpan

Under the Real Language of Men

I. (exile)

I was dry-stone walling for the National Trust,
High on a ridge in the west

And counted the scars through each Roman stone,
Laying in headers of a crown

As the valley rolled beneath their weight – twisted
My straight gaze into a squint –

Its poplars aligned
Like regiments.

II. (letter home)

As water skips above and /
Below the elusive pike / Before
resuming its quiescent / Position
in a lake, / So does a surge from within / Me pour
itself across the soaked
flute / Of your skin / While I remain inside /
Myself, perfectly still, despite whatever insights /
Allure me at the time, / Their tides
of likelihood retracting like heights / Of the sea,
that endless variation perceived only by the clever
or the blind; / A distillation restores all to water
once more, and I am left simple, transparent – free
to remember what you feel /
Like in the dark, when the world is more with us all.

III. (pilgrimage)

When they finally came and freed us, our ribs were empty
Pots, my heart a bruise. I was believed undead
Because they found me in a prisoners' morgue (others knew little
Of the alternative. To sleep in the mud and filth).
They brought the King's English: news from home,
Of the war, even about the Burma–Thailand railway,
Which we'd seen enough of already.

In Ottawa, Canadians and Yanks left our transport
Speaking of girls, telling the four of us how to stay in touch.
Then came another ocean, London, and time to see
Our families – who'd been notified. But still, all we do
Is sit together in a hotel room in Pimlico, day after day,
Like four truants, staring at the walls that frame
Our one window, at window-sills and razor-blades,
None of us saying a thing.

Monique Roffey

Finale

Gia's been difficult the last few days. Success has finally consumed her, eroded the girl I once knew. For years I've watched and put up with her growing arrogance, smiling patiently because I had no way of stopping it; as if it was all to be expected, all part of it.

'Seven generations, all flamenco dancers!' she loves to remind me.

But her behaviour this morning has caused a shift in me: I've been imagining things, having strange ideas, conjuring an image of myself moving sideways, a crab or some dainty thing stepping out of the way. I felt something keenly for the first time this morning; a door closing, a need for distance. That anger was meant for me, the country boy now cramping her style. Now I'm only fit to open the door for her, sit quietly by her side while she signs autographs, has her photograph taken. I'm her doorman. Her valet. A fucking servant of some kind. Tears come when I think of how things have changed between us. How much longer can I live like this, how many more times can I sit in the audience?

'Excuse me?'

I fold my legs and a man squeezes past. When the coast is clear, I squirm, trying to get comfortable in the hard, thread-bare seats. My knees are almost clapped like shutters to the head of the woman in front. I scan the rows with anticipation: the house is packed. It's a small theatre, rococo in style, with boxes and balconies, gilt and wine-coloured velvet. I like Shaftesbury Avenue, these old theatres make Gia look good. I balance my fingertips together, constructing a church, then slowly collapse the roof, turning my fingers inside out. I waggle the congregation. I need a piss. I'm always tense in these minutes before she comes on.

The empty stage is framed by long dark curtains, the floor is as it should be: old wood the colour of caramel, polished and waxed to glass. It'll give her the right acoustics, something solid under her powerful feet. Raphael is accompanying her tonight, a pro who knows how to handle her. He arrived a little late this evening. Gia was worried, pacing her dressing room, cursing. He had a puppy tucked under his arm, the cutest little thing, a Cocker Spaniel, eyes like great black marbles – and a smile.

'So sorry,' Raphael apologized. 'It's for my son. His birthday is tomorrow, he's been begging me for one. So?' He shrugged helplessly and grinned.

Gia shot him a vague look, impatient. Raphael ignored her and kissed the dog on the nose.

Ah!

There she is, standing by the curtains.

The audience stops moving, talking. There's a sudden silence and I can sense their gaze, a tension laden with expectation, as though everyone is frightened of her. It's fear I can feel around me: awe. No one would want to be her, or could be. They've come to watch, from a distance. Around me is this distance, a chasm between my seat and the stage.

Still, I get a rush of pride, nerves for her. Butterflies rise in my stomach. My bladder flinches, threatening to fail me. What a disaster could happen if I don't concentrate! Raphael enters from the right, carrying a wooden chair; a big man, arms like oak branches, sleeves rolled up and his hair damped down under his sharp brimmed hat. He positions the chair a little off centre, sitting down on it. Gia crosses the stage towards him, her small feet taking small steps under the rustle of her heavy skirts. I've always loved her ankles. Delicate bones, like chicken ribs, fan out from the ankle ball. I love the way her feet taper into shoes – her shoes! Tonight she's wearing my favourites: black hourglass heels, across her foot a single strap.

She stands, composed, waiting, the spotlight draping her in a veil of light.

I wriggle in my seat.

Her dress is a big red oyster, its frills resemble lips; layer upon layer, dancing with gauzy black spots. Raphael strums his guitar and begins his song, an Andalucian lament, calling to his love.

Gia stands unmoved as she's supposed to, chin set level. Her lips are not full, not thin either: brick red. Her eyebrows are like bird wings, her large black eyes are filmy. I've never felt awkward around her beauty, until recently.

Slowly, Gia twists her hands, weaving, curling, middle finger pressed to thumb, slanting her head downwards to the words of the song, listening with a cool detachment. Her sinewy arms reach out towards us, her hands writhing, coiling before she curls them back to her hips. Then she glides them out and up, standing for a moment, silent, arms above her head, hands pushing up the sky.

I'm desperate to pee, but I know this is the big moment before she starts with her feet, before she starts the noise. I glance sideways at the audience. People are staring, concentrating. The tiers of seats are curved round the stage like an arena. One might think something obscene is about to happen; there's lust in the air. Bated dread. Then the sound comes: one tap, then another. Then another. Hard, breaking, the sound of sharp laughter, of an inevitable arrival. The taps build, a menacing rumble, slow, passionate.

Then, I remember this morning. We were having breakfast in a bistro in Covent Garden, at a table out on the pavement. It was sunny and Gia wanted to watch people passing by; she finds Londoners so fashionable, likes to see the latest styles.

A young man came to beg at our table; he was filthy, sweaty, clutching a sleeping bag.

'Go away!' she spat.

But he wasn't put off. He simply stood and stared at her plate, so I reached for my wallet.

'Don't give him anything!' Gia hissed.

'Gia,' I implored.

'He . . .' And she grimaced at me. 'He makes me feel *sick*. Now my breakfast is ruined.'

I extended my hand, holding out some coins. 'Here take this.'

Gia went berserk, her chair screeching across the pavement as she pushed it backwards.

She stood up.

'You're a maggot!' she shrieked. 'A filthy disgusting maggot!' With this, she shoved the frail young man hard and he stumbled backwards.

There were other tables out on the pavement; panels and windows had been opened in the restaurant to let in the sun. People were staring at us. The young man was on the ground, a little dazed. It was clear he wasn't quite all there, that he was unwell as well as dirty. He mumbled something and a waiter came out to lift him up, talking sternly to him as he pulled him away. Realising she had caused a scene, Gia went quiet and sat down. Calm, deliberate, she dipped her knife into a pat of butter and spread it on her toast. I glared at her, in disbelief, but she only rolled her eyes to the sky.

*

The noise is deafening now: Gia's in full flow, strutting with her hands high, back arched, feet stamping a controlled staccato.

Raphael's call moves and inflames her. He's put down his guitar and his arms are stretched open, imploring, as he wails. Gia flicks her head down and then up; her hands are poised like a witch casting a grand spell on the audience. They hover for a moment, before coming down in a frenzy, slapping them hard on her thighs. *Smack! Smack! Smack!* A shock to the audience, their faces slapped.

Gia turns. The train of her skirt is a crocodile of taffeta and tulle, moving a second after she does. One leg shoots out from under it. Gia pulls the hem back, exposing a thigh at right angles. Toe on the floor, she stamps hard with her heel, then turns on it. The train whips, red foam arching and swishing behind her. She continues: a leg, a stamp, a twist, a flick of the skirt. It foams and rises. *Flick, swish, flick.* Gia's centre stage, raging and swirling in a red sea. Her feet are invisible, a blur of thunder.

She shouts, cries and tosses her head.

My blood is up and I can sense a swell of emotion around me. Love, desire, wonder. A noise escapes from the audience, a murmur of surprise. I don't see it at first. Then, I do. Raphael's puppy is loose and has flown from the wings, its feathery paws like mops on the glass wood floor.

The dog skids.

The audience gasps.

I stand.

People stifle laughter.

But the dog is a toboggan, sliding on its rear end, pink tongue trailing like a ribbon, ears rippling like streamers. The puppy is wild with excitement, delighted to be free. It leans backwards as it slides forwards, hoping to stop its momentum, but this only causes all four paws to splay out, as if the dog is on snowshoes.

The puppy doesn't stop.

Instead it slides behind Gia at the speed of knots.

The audience rises.

People point.

Gia takes this as love.

She goes crazy with her stamping and swishing, head proffered to the Gods, hands darting. She picks up her skirts, proud and temperamental, flicking hard, up and out. Red foam curves in a playful wave behind her.

The puppy snaps.

Gia swings her skirts but there's a look of perplexity on her face – the train is suddenly heavy. Dashing the dress down and then high above her head, it swings out.

The puppy is attached.

Airborne.

Its flat ears are spread like aeroplane wings, its downy jaws are clamped firmly, valiantly, to the hem – as if under it is pinned a sausage.

I don't know what to do. I stare like everyone, hand over mouth.

Then the puppy is in her skirts, swinging with them. Up again, and out, weighty and plump. Now people are laughing openly and pointing, shouting to Gia.

Gia stops. She sees the puppy and a look of defiance crosses her face.

'Get off!' she screeches, shaking her skirts in a frenzy.

The puppy thinks it's a game and shakes its head and whole body crazily, trying to hold on. The more Gia swishes her skirt, the more the puppy grips, swaying and swinging across the floor.

'Off! Off! Off!' Gia screams, her face contorted. She stops again.

Her mouth is crumpled in disgust, her forehead furrowed. She peers down at the puppy still clamped to her hem. Head on the floor, arse in the air, its stubby little tail is waving like a windscreen wiper. It's never had so much fun.

Gia lifts a treacherous heel.

My mouth is dry.

I remember Gia when she was sixteen, dancing on the jetty over the estuary which snaked behind my father's land. I remember the unsafe sound those planks made, her battered red shoes. Her bruised shins. The rain of blows, the fury which came from her feet, how she used to make that jetty groan.

Gia brings her foot down on the puppy. She stamps on it, kicking it hard in the stomach. It cries, whimpering on and on.

There's an abrupt hush from the audience. Gia kicks the puppy again and it flips across the stage, landing inert.

'Stop!' Raphael shouts, running across to it.

I remember the one dress she owned then, pale blue silk, a ballgown her mother would adapt for different occasions, first tearing the sleeves off, then the skirt, adding and subtracting to it, dyeing it, every time making it a different dress. She was never ashamed to wear it; others always had something new.

Raphael kneels and lifts the small soft body gently to his lap. The dog moans.

There's outrage now around me. Incomprehension.

I start to thread my way through my row, wanting to get to the exit. I must leave: if I don't, I'll piss in my pants. As I go, I hear boos and hisses. I feel dizzy.

In the Gents I unzip my fly and relief gushes. I stare at the wall. Ants like dots are busy running to and from a crack. I think of a film I saw last week, my dentist appointment tomorrow. I think of Gia. My eyes are wet and there's a tight pain above my eyebrows. I zip my trousers back up and lurch from the wall. I leave the Gents and find myself back in the foyer, amidst a stream of people leaving the theatre from different doors, all of them tutting, every face expressing disapproval. I find myself walking into their flow, pushing through them, past them in order to get to the dressing rooms backstage where I hope I might still find Gia.

Tom Pow

The Last Vision of Angus McKay

Angus McKay, Queen Victoria's piper, went
insane 'over study of music'. He was admitted to
the Crichton Royal from Bedlam in 1856 when
he was forty-three years old. 'His most prominent
delusion is that her majesty is his wife and that
Prince Albert has defrauded him of his rights.'
(Crichton case notes)

Let it be noted (in copperplate), Angus McKay
is a gentleman to watch. The stoutest furniture
is firewood to him; a mattress, within a day,
he'll disembowel. He has been known
to drink his own urine; to spit, shriek, howl
and hoot like an owl:
                        though this last
                        does not appear
                        in his case notes from Bedlam –
                        'hooting and howling' in southern parts
                        being thought not
                        abnormal for a Scot.

Nevertheless, there is enough on his native ground
to amaze and perplex his keepers.

Fuck it! Angus McKay has done with them all.

He eases himself into the rivercold waters of the Nith
across which lies Kirkconnell Wood
and his freedom. At that moment
                        (to which the record is blind,

no body being found, never mind
testament forthcoming)
something catches his eye – a sudden flurry and a bird
with two necks intertwined; one black, the other –
bodiless – a shimmering Islay malt brown.

Angus McKay watches, mesmerized

as the cormorant lifts its white-cheeked head
till its brassy twin – the eel – lifting with it,
unwinds like a flailing clef and falls, bit by bit,
into perfect darkness.

This, thinks Angus McKay, is how
the bagpipe has devoured my life.

He lies on his back, drifting downstream,
shadowing the black bag of a bird through flanges of light,
past two gracefully disinterested swans. The eel rages still –

the cormorant's neck rising and falling
in a helpless hiccup. Up ahead, the bird will calm,
its neck settle again on its shoulders –

but there, the quicksand waits to welcome Angus McKay,
sipping him, limb by limb, into its dark and clammy hold.

That evening, owls will keen – in Gaelic –
from Kirkconnell Wood, where Angus McKay
perches, pale and dripping.

Kate Atkinson

Gloria

[novel extract]

The smoke from the fire was a dirty grey colour because the contents of the garden brazier – Gloria's old clothes – were smouldering rather than burning. Gloria had intended the blaze to be symbolic, a pyre for the past Gloria (Graham's wife) and a signal for the present Gloria (Graham's widow). She had imagined herself emerging from the flames like a phoenix so it was rather disappointing that her wardrobe hadn't made more of a *show*, even if it was only a couple of evening dresses – puffy, glittery things that she had worn for company dinner dances and had always felt awkward in, because, of course, it would have been appallingly wasteful to have got rid of everything and most of her clothes were packed in black plastic bin liners, sitting on the back seat of her Golf, waiting to be taken to the local Oxfam shop. If some starving black child (were there countries where white people still starved?) could be helped by her Windsmoor suits and Country Casual dress-and-jacket combos, then that would be a Good Thing.

It was seven in the morning and Gloria was in her dressing gown and slippers, the slippers were soaked through from the wet ground. She tossed a pair of evening shoes into the brazier in an attempt to fuel the conflagration. She had small feet ('pig's trotters' Graham used to call them) and Gloria had an uncomfortable vision of herself teetering into a succession of hotel ballrooms over the years, mutton dressed as mutton, her little feet in silver or gold straps, her body stuffed into the puffy, glittery, *tasteless* dresses and being greeted as if she was an invalid who was being wheeled out for the evening.

Gloria went to the shed and poked around until she found a

packet of firelighters. She always regarded the shed as belonging to Bill, the gardener, rather than herself, although, of course, everything now belonged to Gloria, every single thing from the contents of the garden shed to the Bentley in the garage, from the Georgian silver tea service to the Bang and Olufsen Avant wide-screen television, although, thankfully, not the second division football team that Graham had been about to buy. He had the unsigned contracts with him in his briefcase when he died of a heart attack in a Jarvis hotel room in Leeds, on top of a girl called Jo-Jo Louden when he was supposed to have been on his own in the Royal Moat House in Nottingham. Jo-Jo was the name of a clown in Gloria's opinion, although she was actually a 'call girl', which was simply another word for a whore. 'Call a spade a spade, for God's sake,' she had said to the PC who looked as if he should be in primary school and who had drawn the short straw of turning up on Gloria's doorstep to announce her widowhood.

To tell the truth, Gloria felt sympathy for Jo-Jo. It was clear from her accent and her unhealthy pallor (as if she'd been brought up on potatoes) that she was an illegal immigrant (the Balkans or Romania probably, you heard about them all the time) and yet *no one* questioned this fact or asked her to explain her clown alias. She would undoubtedly have disappeared back into the night from whence she had come but she was no match for the weight of Graham's hefty corpse which had squashed her like a bug, face down on the hotel room mattress, for hours until the hotel management broke in.

The details of Graham's last undignified hours had all been aired at the inquest when the coroner had barely been able to keep the smirk off his face ('Did Mr Carter achieve climax before expiring, *Ms* Louden?')

She tossed a couple of the firelighters into the brazier and watched the little tongues of green and blue flames begin to lick at a Debut rhinestone-encrusted bolero jacket.

As soon as his funeral was over she had got rid of Graham's clothes, dropping them off at the PDSA shop (because there were the starving cats to think about as well as the starving children). *What profiteth it a man if he gaineth the whole world but loseth his soul.* Gloria shivered and went back inside the house and got dressed – M & S big cotton pants, 'Doreen' bra by Triumph (40 DD, how had *that* happened?), 15-denier nude tights, petticoat in some polyester mix that clung with static to her white silk blouse (Fenwick's sale), A-line plaid skirt, all topped off with a boxy cashmere cardigan in matronly camel, with brass buttons that seemed especially *tedious* to Gloria. Could a button be tedious? She would be sixty next birthday and dressed like her own mother would have done if she'd had more money. She may as well get an old lady's perm and take up carpet bowls.

Gloria made herself a mug of coffee and a plate of buttered toast, which she ate in the living room, watching the birds feeding from the bird table in the garden. When Graham was alive (she loved that phrase, loved its historicity) they had always eaten breakfast at the kitchen table. He liked something cooked (by her, of course) – scrambled eggs, a kipper, bacon and eggs at the weekend. While they ate they listened to the *Today* programme on the radio, ceaseless disembodied chatter about politics and disasters that Graham considered important and necessary yet it made *no difference to their lives whatsoever.* That didn't mean that you shouldn't give your old clothes to help feed starving people, but really sometimes there was more to be gained from watching a pair of blue tits pecking away at a bird feeder full of peanuts than feigning grief over your kipper for a ferry that had sunk in Bangladesh – hundreds of dreadful deaths that you had already forgotten about by the time you were reaching for the marmalade. If you were honest.

The house was so peaceful now. Even when Graham was alive (!), even when he was sleeping soundlessly upstairs in the bedroom, the house still boomed and crashed with inaudible noise.

The letter box clattered and the *Yorkshire Post* thumped onto the doormat.

*

What kind of a person bites the head off a kitten? What kind of a person walks into the back garden of a complete stranger, picks up a three-week-old kitten and *bites its head off? And doesn't get prosecuted!* Gloria dropped the newspaper to the floor in disgust.

What would be the correct punishment for a person (a man, naturally) who bites the head off a three-week-old kitten? Death, obviously, but surely not a swift and painless one? That would be like an undeserved gift. Gloria, who had once signed an Amnesty petition protesting against the death penalty (although in a country she wouldn't have been able to point to on a map), who had once presumed all life was sacred, now believed in the punishment fitting the crime, eyes for eyes, teeth for teeth. Heads for heads. How would you go about biting a person's head off? Unless you could somehow employ a shark or a crocodile to do the job for you, Gloria supposed you would have to settle for simple decapitation. Axes or guillotines. Send for a sharp French sword. Truly the human race was going to hell in a handcart. Or was it a hand basket? No, that sounded ridiculous. Was there even such a thing as a hand basket?

There was no one to ask. There was Bill, of course, who was in the garden where you would expect him to be on a Thursday. His arrival was always announced by a tuneless whistling and the muffled clanking and thudding of tools in the shed as if he wanted her to know he was there but didn't want to actually talk to her. Bill seemed to go out of his way to avoid conversation with her. He had maintained the garden for the last five years. The gardener before him had been called Bill as well. Gloria found that unsettling – were they really called Bill? Or did the name come with the job somehow? She couldn't remember the current Bill's surname. The previous Bill had been called Tiffany, like the jewellers. Gloria's husband, Graham, had bought her a Tiffany watch for their thirtieth wedding anniversary. It had a red leather strap and little diamonds all round its face and it was the prettiest thing. She dropped it in the fish pond after his death. All of the fish in the pond, except for one – a big golden orf – had been gradually picked off by a neighbourhood heron. Gloria wondered if the pretty watch was still keeping time, ticking away quietly in the mud and green slime at the bottom of the pond, marking off the days left to the big orange fish.

The man who bit the head off the kitten was, according to the newspaper, high on drugs. That was not a good reason! Gloria had once smoked a joint during her brief period at university (but more from politeness than anything) and had imbibed a considerable amount of alcohol in her time but she was sure that she could have consumed any amount of illegal substances and not felt the urge to bite the head off an innocent household pet. A little basket of kittens – Gloria imagined long-haired tabbies with ribbons round their necks, like something you would find on an old-fashioned chocolate box. Tiny, helpless. Innocent. There was a barbecue, 'a family barbecue', in progress and the man strode in, uninvited, unannounced, and picked up one of the kittens from the basket and bit its head off. Gloria was surprised Graham had stayed in a Jarvis, that wasn't his style at all.

*

Gloria was the only child of parents who were, in their turn, only children. If everyone followed this model Gloria supposed the population of the world would eventually be reduced to one person and then, finally, none. In Gloria's opinion this would be a Good Thing. Better by far to be rid of people, to leave the planet in the care of pandas and orang-utans and daffodils and *kittens*.

Gloria was brought up in a small town in south Yorkshire where her father, Alfred, a morose yet earnest man, sold insurance door-to-door to people who could barely afford it. When he was at home he spent his time slumped in front of the fire reading detective novels, sipping from a half-pint glass mug of beer. Gloria's mother, Marjorie, worked part-time in a local chemist's shop. For work, Marjorie wore a knee-length white coat, the medical nature of which she offset with a large pair of pearl and gilt earrings. She claimed that working in a chemist made her privy to everyone's intimate secrets but as far as Gloria could tell she spent her time selling insoles and cotton wool and plasters and the most excitement she derived from the job was arranging the Christmas window with tinsel and Yardley gift boxes.

Gloria's parents led drab, listless lives that the wearing of pearl and gilt earrings and the reading of detective novels did little to enliven, and from an early age Gloria had been eager to escape these dismal surroundings. And she had done – look at her now, in her absurdly expensive Harrogate house, built seven years ago by the more qualified elements of Graham's workforce. Before that they'd had a perfectly good house in Alwoodley Lane in Leeds, a perfectly good, *expensive*, house that they'd lived in since Sarah was five, an Edwardian house that had moulded itself around Gloria and it seemed cruel suddenly to shuck it off in favour of new brick and double-glazing with what Graham and his architect referred to as 'high-end specs', by which they meant none of the shoddily built, overpriced rubbish that had made Graham rich enough to afford a second division football team.

Graham said they were 'too rich' to live in the Alwoodley Lane house and the new house would be a 'showpiece' for his company, which was ridiculous because it was a private house, hidden behind a security fence and electronic gates. Gloria assumed he was trying to bury it in the company's books and avoid tax. He always crowed with triumph if he managed to fool the Inland Revenue or Customs and Excise, saw himself as some kind of maverick, an outlaw not subject to the normal rules. He held health and safety in the same disregard; only last year a worker had died on site because safety procedures weren't being followed but Graham had managed to wriggle out of being prosecuted. It was the same with speeding – he cruised along in the outside lane at a hundred miles an hour in that bloody great car, parking it anywhere as if he was untouchable. He was wrong about that, wasn't he? Death had touched him. Tagged him when he was least expecting it. Jo-Jo 'couldn't be sure' if her client had reached orgasm. You would think it would be part of her job to know things like that. How could you be too rich? If you were too rich you could just give some of it away until you were just rich. Or give it all away and be poor.

Gloria liked rules. She liked rules that said you couldn't speed or smoke or drop litter or park at bus stops. People didn't make rules for no reason. She wondered if Graham had written off Jo-Jo Louden as a tax-deductible expense.

Gloria had been consulted over 'her' new kitchen. 'Nothing's too good for my darling wife,' Graham said pompously to his architect.

'How about it, Gloria, what do you want – an island? A larder fridge – one of those big American ones? A Gaggenau hob, one of the ones with an integral deep-fat fryer, that'd be handy, black granite worktops – they're the classiest?' So she'd asked for a pink sink because she'd seen one on one of those home show programmes on television and Graham said, 'Pink sink? Over my dead body, Gloria.' So there you go.

*

Of course, Gloria hadn't always been this person who wore matronly camel with tedious buttons. Once she had been sitting on a bar stool in a pub in Leeds wearing jeans and a cotton print smock, self-consciously smoking an Embassy and drinking a gin and orange and hoping she looked pretty while around her raged a heated student conversation about Marxism. Tim, her boyfriend at the time – a gangly youth with a white boy's afro – was one of the most vociferous of the group, jabbing the air with his cigarette every time he said 'exchange of commodities' or 'the rate of surplus value' while Gloria sipped her gin and orange and nodded sagely, hoping that no one would expect her to contribute because she hadn't the faintest idea what they were talking about. She was in the second term of her first year, studying history but in a lackadaisical kind of manner. She had no personal interest in the causes of the French Revolution or the balance of power in Europe, she was just passing time. That was what life was, wasn't it? Just passing time. You could spend it as a celebrity princess or an Indian carpet weaver or an East European call girl and you were still just passing time. And then it was passed and that was that.

She couldn't remember Tim's surname now. She'd only had sex with two men (in her whole life!) and she couldn't remember the name of one of them. They had spent a term tangled together in their student sheets having rather dull and routine sex (amateurish, adolescent sex) and all she could remember about him now was his great cloud of hair, like a dandelion clock. How many times had Graham stayed in hotel rooms around the country and ordered up room service and a call girl? She imagined him lying on a double bed with a veneer headboard, flicking through the TV's channels while he ate steak and chips, a pathetic little garnish of a salad, half a bottle of claret, while he waited for a woman to come and perform professional, grown-up sex. Did he ask for extras? He'd asked for extras with Jo-Jo Louden. ('And did you submit *of your own free will* to Mr Carter's request that you be handcuffed, Ms Louden?'

Tim declared to the group that they were all working class now. Gloria frowned because she didn't want to be working class, thank you very much, but everyone around her was murmuring their agreement – although there wasn't one of them who wasn't the offspring of a doctor or a lawyer or a shopkeeper – when a loud, brutally Yorkshire voice announced, 'That's crap. You'd be nothing without capitalism, capitalism has saved mankind.' And that was Graham. He was wearing a sheepskin coat – a second hand car salesman's kind of sheepskin, not like Tim's hippy afghan – and drinking a pint on his own in the corner of the bar. He had seemed like a man, but he couldn't have been more than nineteen, which now she could see was just a *child*. And then he downed his beer and turned to her and said, 'Are you coming?' and she'd slipped off her bar stool and followed him like a little dog because he was so forceful and attractive compared to someone with dandelion clock hair.

('Your feet were also bound, Ms Louden? Were they tied together or were you spreadeagled?' Impossible on a Jarvis bed surely? No bedposts.)

Or you could put the man who bit the head off the kitten into a cage of tigers and say, 'Go on, then, let's see you bite the head off one of those.' But then it would be wrong to put the tigers in a cage. Had capitalism really saved mankind? It seemed unlikely but it was too late to argue with Graham about it now.

Helen Simpson

In the Driving Seat

I was crouched in the back of Deborah's car. Her bluff new boyfriend was driving it, rather brutally, down the A4 in the dark through the rain. We were on our way to Maidenhead, where the party was. He knew the road well so he was driving with a sort of braggartly contempt.

'I had no idea your car could get up this sort of speed, Deborah,' I said.

'It's not a *new* car,' said Deborah with a nervous laugh.

'She can tell *that*,' scoffed Andy. 'It's shaking so much it feels like it'll fall to bits.'

'Perhaps it's not used to . . .' said Deborah, and I saw her grip the dashboard, which goaded Andy into putting his foot down even further.

He belted us along with breezy boyishness, although he is now thirty-six. He looks like what he is, a former rugby player. Injuries stopped him a couple of years ago and he's concerned about running to fat.

'You should try rowing now you're living in Isleworth,' I had said over dinner. 'You really should, you're the right build; you'd love it.'

I noticed how he bristled, how a sudden flash of resentment flew at me from his force field.

'Andy doesn't like being told what he'd like,' laughed Deborah watchfully across the table.

Back on the A4 Andy was intent on forcing the car, a decent elderly Polo, up into the nineties if he possibly could. Deborah was at the limit of her tact and patience.

'I'm not sure my poor old car will be able to take this,' she murmured.

'You'll never know till you try!' carolled Andy above the roaring of the engine.

'Actually, I'm feeling a bit sick,' she said, uncertain, but it made no difference.

He obviously couldn't bear to be in the passenger seat unless it was absolutely necessary – that is, unless he'd had what he would call a skinful. The way a man drives gives a surprisingly accurate idea of what he's like in other areas. Does he crash his way through the gears? Does he speed, or stall? Does he get nasty at the lights? I gazed at the back of Andy's head. You certainly wouldn't want *him* sitting on your tail, I thought, with a coarse mental chuckle.

I was trying to disregard the awareness that I was bumping along on a mad dangerous out-of-control toboggan ride. It seemed a good time to describe my next-door-neighbour's teenage daughter's horror when I'd told her how the new speed cameras work. Her eyes had stretched in shock. She'd obviously been speeding all over London in her father's Ford Mondeo, I said. They photograph the face at the wheel as well as the car's number plates, I'd told her. Deborah skipped the laugh in the story and went straight for the element which worried her.

'The thing is, Andy,' she said, would-be brave, trying to sound mock-truculent, 'This *is* my car and if it's photographed by the speed cameras, I'll be the one who's held responsible.'

'Hohoho!' said Andy, spitefully I thought.

'I'm not joking any more, Andy,' she said, still timid in the shade of his massive macho aura. 'I could lose my licence.'

'Oh, dear *me*!' crowed Andy, and the car bowled creakingly along at ninety.

Was he wanting her to beg him?

'But then I'd find it very difficult to keep my job,' she protested. 'It's not funny.'

'No, it's *not* funny,' he mocked, not slackening the pace at all.

She is five years older than him, gets back from work in time to help her two children with their homework, reviews the rate she pays on her mortgage every half year. She is beautiful in the sepulchral Victorian manner, her expression veering between anxiety and seriousness; whereas he plays the fool, the tease, the cosseted grasshopper to her credit-worthy ant.

'Yes, he's living in my house now but he doesn't contribute to the bills or food,' she confided to me over coffee. 'Whenever we go out together, I have to drive us home because he likes to drink. He never buys a drink when we visit my friends or family, that's always up to me.'

'Tell him how you feel,' I said. Presumably she didn't want me to come over breathless with indignation on her behalf. She didn't need *me* to state the bleeding obvious; she could see that for herself.

'Well, I do; I have to say what I think,' she continued. 'But it makes me feel I'm mercenary, these uncomfortable feelings. Because he's lovely really. And I like being with someone. I've been on my own for a while now and everything's fine, my job's secure, the children are fine; but I want to be married again, that's the trouble, I like the married state. And Andy wants to belong. He wants to get married, he said to me, "What if anything were to happen to you? I wouldn't feel secure unless I knew I could stay on in the house." And of course there's always the fear that he might leave me. He would feel happier if I transferred the house title into joint names. Men like to be trusted, don't they?'

'I imagine we all do,' I'd said. 'Like to be trusted.'

'I'll be forty-one next year. Andy's saying he wants my child!' She laughed, hand swiping her brow, and looked down at the table in confusion.

That had been some weeks ago. The rain was very heavy now; the windscreen wipers were going at double lick. Why on earth had I agreed to a lift to this party? I thought of my own car, my little green Fiat, with longing. I love my car. It makes me feel light and free. It means nobody can bully me about not drinking and I can leave whenever I want to. All those sulky end-of-party dramas of coercion and constraint, the driver wanting to go and the drinker wanting to stay, I don't have to do them; although I would tonight. Why had I said yes?

I looked at the two antagonistic heads in front of me, his and hers, parental, and I felt like a child crouching in the back on my own. Their child.

'Andy, I really am feeling sick,' said Deborah faintly. 'I do wish you'd slow down.'

That brought back Deborah's troubled laughter over coffee that time, her hand swiping her brow in confusion as she told me what she wanted. And I thought – I *wonder*.

Heloise Shepherd

The Petrol Pump on the
Hongor Road

The sunlight is different here. It has a sharp edge. Even inside a
jeep you'll feel different. More alive. Usually, I drive tourists out
into the Gobi. They start with loud voices, taking many noisy
pictures. But soon they are silenced. By this light, and the hugeness
of the sky. And when the stars come out there is no comfort. Every
one is deathly white and the clear air creeps into your very skin.

I'm rarely alone on the road, but that day I was driving to
collect some American tourists in Hongor, hundreds of miles
away. Apparently they couldn't take it, whether the cold or the
strangeness I didn't bother to ask. Americans give good tips. I'd
been driving all day. The road was an uneven dirt track past the
last river.

The silence gets to me the most. The land around here is so
flat you forget how high you are. Behind, the black bank of
mountains and ahead just a flat plateau of rock and dirt. If you
are lucky, you might pass a car or two. The land is almost empty.
A few tent villages here and there. And the silence. Sometimes I
feel like an intruder. Once I had to shut off the engine and just let
the silence be. I knew if I had to fight it, it would win. Smothering
entirely the sound of my voice and engine.

Foreigners, especially Americans, are always amused by our
petrol pumps. They sit at the roadside. You can see them coming
for miles, little black specks against the intense blue sky. You'd
be stupid not to fill up; petrol is hard to come by. So you drive
on to the nearest village, and then drive back in the company of
some grinning old woman clutching the rusty handle in wrinkled
fingers. Inefficient maybe, but the only way to ensure payment. I
passed one about seventy-five miles from the main road.

The night was coming; I could feel its vigour. I like the nights best, more secure. I reached the village just as the last ember of light in the western sky died. It was silent outside, and the car door made far too much noise. I didn't want to call out. Didn't want to pit my voice against the silence. I looked around, and felt, for a moment, that somebody looked back.

'Hello?' I whispered, my voice pitiful in the vast quiet. It cowed me. I spent a long time staring into the shadows by the tents, more and more aware of the night.

'Do you want some petrol?' came a sudden voice directly behind me. I swivelled, crunching crisp dirt beneath my feet, expecting another of the weather-beaten old women. But she was very young. About the age of my second daughter.

'Yes, who do I talk to?'

'Me. Wait, and I'll get the handle.'

She darted off into a shadowy tent. I clasped my gloveless hands. That had been a mistake, it was spring, but the nights were still ice cold. She returned and got into my car without any words. I climbed in beside her. She looked like a Western movie star. If my daughters looked like that all would be married well, and I would be a much richer man. I pretended not to be looking at her; it wouldn't have been appropriate to let her know the many reactions I had to her appearance. A subtle mixture of lust, guilt and longing. I clasped the steering wheel a little tighter. But it wasn't earthshaking, she was just a girl and I was stronger than that.

'How old are you?' I asked eventually.

'In my fifteenth year.'

I had thought her younger. She was built very slightly.

'Are you married?' I asked, after a reasonable pause. I don't know why.

'No. I have no family.'

We were quiet again for a while. Her hands, holding the handle lightly, lay in her lap. She had tiny hands. About half the size of mine.

'How much do you charge?'

'Thirty per gallon.'

'Twenty.'

'Twenty-seven.'

'Twenty-five.'

'Twenty-seven. I have to eat.'

'OK, twenty-seven then.'

'It's a good price.'

'It's reasonable.'

The stars were all out. Their whiteness always surprises me. When I glanced across she was looking at them too. Her upturned face was still and her eyes glittered as if she were about to cry. But she didn't. She just lowered her gaze to the rough road ahead and that glittering in her eyes died.

'So do you just look after the pump?'

'No.'

Her reluctance to say more intrigued me.

'What else do you do?'

She sighed and brushed a wisp of hair from her cheek.

'Sometimes petrol isn't all drivers want. And I have no family to dishonour.'

She said it bluntly. It divided me completely. A part of me thought of how no one would ever know. Another part felt disgusted. Both with my reaction and with her. But these feelings faded. She could have been my daughter. How could any father not pity her? She was so young. How could men be so cruel? But I knew how. I'd done it myself once, in a shadowy bar in Ulan Bator. The girl may have been older but the principle was the same. It was all squalid and disgusting. Even out here. Even me. She was so small and sad. She must have had a father who loved her like I love my daughters.

I didn't know what to say. For a long time I let the silent desert and the millions of white stars speak for us. She looked at me. I guess she was gauging my reaction.

'I need to look after my sister,' she said eventually in measured tones. I stole a sideways glance at her.

'You're lying,' I said. 'Don't worry. You have my pity anyway.'

Her eyes widened and one hand flew to her mouth.

'I don't need your pity. How did you know?'

'Good liars can always tell,'

There was a taste of suspicion in the air. She didn't trust me at all. Maybe I should have said nothing. But maybes are pointless.

'Have you always lived here?' I asked.

'Always in the Gobi.' Her face was sullen as she answered.

'Always with the same tribe?'

'No.'

'I was born in Ulan Bator.'

She didn't find that sufficiently interesting to reply to. I don't blame her. It wasn't. She'd turned even more brittle on me, I could feel her hostility. As constant and cold as the night. And as beautiful. There was something very strange about her physical perfection. Maybe because everyone else is so hideous. She had to be flesh and blood and bone and gut like the rest of us. Beauty is external; everyone is repulsive from the inside. I don't think it's right that some seem so perfect. So beautiful. I looked at her for a long time and I truthfully thought that her features were such that she didn't seem real.

I pulled the car up next to the rusty pump. The air outside was cold and dry. She fitted the handle and began to fill the jeep's huge tank. It was going to take a while. It always did.

'What's your name?' I asked. Not able to take the stillness.

'Why?'

'Just passing the time.'

'It will pass any way.'

Even the stance of her body was hostile and cold. But I could have paid her something and got to know the whole of her body and skin from the inside. I could have done it, and she would have let me. I didn't. It was bad enough that I'd even thought of it. Very weak of me. I tore my eyes off her. The Gobi is a very strange place at night. Sometimes, for odd instants, the silence is broken by voices that aren't really there. Sometimes a chilling white mist creeps up on you from nowhere. But not that night. All I could hear were the sounds of the petrol and our breathing. Sometimes life is unforgivably loud.

'I'm going to collect some Americans,' I said. I don't know why. She didn't move or make any sign she'd even heard me. Indifference frustrates me immeasurably more than hostility. Why didn't she take notice of me? Why didn't she just turn her perfect face to see me? Was I that unimportant? I turned my back to her and viciously kicked a rock. Making small, irritated movements to stay at least a little warm. When I turned around she was gone. Just gone. Nowhere. As if she'd never been.

The pump leaked out sticky black goo onto the dusty ground. I replaced it. I would have called out but my jaw was clenched in fear. I stood with my back to the car, its cold metal reassured me a little.

'Hello?' I cried. The echo bounced back, from where I don't know. It was as if she'd dissolved into the cold air. Taking all her beauty with her. Maybe she wasn't human. No one could have been that beautiful and that cold. I waited for her for a whole hour. Just sitting. It might have been longer; I don't remember.

What were they going to think when I returned to the village with a pump handle but no one to hold it? There were stories. I knew exactly what they'd think. They'd think I couldn't take her indifference. Think the curve and freshness of her body was too much for me. That I'd stood behind her and wrenched my arm across her neck, that she'd screamed and kicked as I dragged her backwards and threw her down in the seat of the jeep. Think I'd forced open her legs and torn off her sick, western clothing. And fucked her and fucked her and fucked her. They'd think I hit her when she cried like a child. And worst of all, they'd think that when I drew myself out of her I'd taken out my penknife and, as her struggling grew more desperate, cut a gaping gash in her perfect belly. So she bled a mix of blood and spleen. And thrown her out into the cold night to bleed slowly to death in terror and hysterics. That's what they'd think. I would be killed for certain. So I placed the handle down. And drove on.

I was almost through the village when they stopped me and asked if I'd seen any other cars or a girl standing at the petrol pump. I told them I knew nothing. I've always been a good liar. Especially to myself. The sun rose on frozen and harsh horrors that morning.

John Berger

Islington

The Borough of Islington has, during the last twenty-five years, become fashionable. In the 50s and 60s, the name Islington, when pronounced in central London or in the north-western suburbs, conjured up a faraway, remote and faintly suspect district. It is interesting to note how poor and therefore uneasy districts, even when they are geographically near a city centre, are pushed, in the imagination of those who are prospering, further away than they really are. Harlem in New York is an obvious example. For Londoners today Islington is far closer than it used to be.

When it was still remote, forty years ago, Hubert bought a small terrace house there, with a narrow back garden that sloped down to a canal. At that time he and his wife were teaching part-time in art schools and had no money to spare. The house, however, was cheap, dirt cheap.

They've moved to Islington! a friend told me at the time. And this news was like a late autumn afternoon when the daylight hours are becoming noticeably shorter. There was something of a foreclosure about it.

Soon afterward, I went to live abroad. Occasionally over the years and on visits to London, I saw Hubert at the house of a common friend, but I never visited – until three days ago – his house in Islington. He and I had been students together at the same London art school in 1943. He was studying textile design and I was studying painting, but there were certain classes we attended together: life drawing, history of architecture, human anatomy.

He made an impression on me because of his fastidious persistence. He invariably wore a tie. He looked like a nineteenth-century bookbinder. He tended to be in a state of sad shock provoked by recurring modern stupidities, and his nails were always clean. I wore a long black romantic overcoat and looked like a coachman – also of the nineteenth century. I drew with the blackest charcoal I could find, and to find any at all during the war wasn't easy – who had time in '42 or '43 to be burning charcoal? Sometimes I filched a stick from the teacher's supply; two kinds of theft were justifiable: food for the hungry, basic materials for the artist.

The two of us were undoubtedly suspicious of one another. Hubert must have thought I was over-demonstrative and indiscreet to the point of exhibitionism; and he seemed to me to be a tight-lipped elitist.

Nevertheless we listened to one another and would sometimes drink a beer together or share an apple. We were both aware that the two of us were considered by most of the other students to be deranged. Deranged because of our commitment to working at every possible moment. Practically nothing distracted us. Hubert drew from the model with the attentive restrained gestures of a violinist tuning his instrument; I drew like a kitchen boy slapping tomatoes and cheese onto pizzas waiting to be put into the oven. Our approaches were very different. Nevertheless during the breaks every hour, when the model took a rest, we were the only two who stayed in the studio and went on working. Hubert often improved his drawing, bringing it to a kind of equanimity. I usually ruined mine.

Three days ago, after I had rung the bell of the house in Islington, he came to the front door with a beaming smile. His left arm was raised above his head in a gesture which was something between a welcome, a salute, and a calvary officer's sign to his men to advance. Nobody could be less military than Hubert. Nevertheless he is a commander.

His face was gaunt and so meticulously shaved it looked sore. He was wearing a pair of baggy corduroy trousers with a wide black leather belt which hung loose, almost at the level of his trouser pockets.

Perfect timing, he said, the water has just boiled. Whereupon he waited for me to make some remark.

It's been a long time, I said.

By now we were at the top of the first short flight of stairs.

What kind of tea would you prefer: Earl Grey, darjeeling or green leaf?

Green leaf.

It's the healthiest, he said, it's what I drink every day.

The drawing room was full of rugs, cushions, objects, footrests, porcelain, dried flowers, collections, engravings, crystal decanters, pictures. It was hard to imagine anything new, anything new and larger than a postcard, finding a home there, for there was no space. It was equally hard to imagine throwing a piece out to make more space, for everything had been found and chosen and placed over the years with the same love and attention. There was not a seashell, a candlestick, a clock, a stool which stood out and appeared awkward. He indicated that I should sit in a Regency chair by the fireplace.

I inquired who had painted an abstract watercolour hanging near the door.

That's one of Gwen's, Hubert said, I've always liked it.

Gwen, his wife, a teacher of engraving, died twelve years ago. She was withdrawn, small, wore brogue shoes and looked like a lepidopterist. If she had held up her hand in the air – even in a wartime London bus – I would have expected a butterfly to land on it.

Hubert poured from a silver teapot into a Crown Derby cup on a table by the door and navigated around the many pieces of furniture across the room to deliver it to me. I wondered whether for him each room in the house had a navigation chart, like seas do. On the ground floor I had noticed the dining room was equally encumbered.

I made some cucumber sandwiches, if you would like one? he asked.

Thank you very much.

I had an aunt, he said, who maintained there were two golden rules about invitations to tea. One is that cucumber sandwiches and sponge cake are obligatory items, and the second is that guests have to insist upon leaving, and succeed in doing so, before six o'clock . . .

I heard the ticking of a pendulum clock on the shelf behind me. There were at least four clocks in the room.

I want to ask you a question about our art school days, I said. Do you remember a girl, the same year as us, who was studying theatre costume? She went around a lot with Colette.

Colette! replied Hubert, I wonder what has become of her? She used to come in with a new dress every week, remember? Often with the pins still in it.

She used to stay with Colette in her rooms in Guildford Place, I said. The rooms were on the first floor, overlooking Coram's Fields. She was short, snub-nosed, had large eyes, was a little plump. Not at all talkative.

Coram's Fields, said Hubert, I saw a painting of them in a show the other day. By a young painter called Arturo di Stefano. Kids on a hot, hot day by a swimming pool playing with the water. Full of the eternity – if I may so put it – of childhood!

No swimming pool there then, I said. Just a boarded-up bandstand, and the tall trees that looked down at us in the morning when we looked out of the window.

I don't think I was ever at Colette's place, Hubert said.

Do you see whom I'm thinking about though?

Was it Pauline, who had an affair with Joe, the framer?

No, no, dark hair, short dark hair! Very white teeth. A bit stand-offish, walked around with her nose in the air.

You're not thinking of Jeanne with the two n's to her name?

Jeanne was tall! This one was small, roundish, tiny. She used to go home for weekends to somewhere smart like Newbury. Was it Newbury? Anyway, she loved horses.

Why do you need to know her name?

I've been trying for a long time to remember her name, and it keeps escaping me.

Was it Priscilla?

It was a very common name, that's what's so strange.

Probably she got married, most art students got married in those days and then her family name would have changed.

I only want her first name.

Are you trying to trace her whereabouts today?

On Mondays in June she came with strawberries from the countryside and would hand them round the whole class.

She may be dead, don't forget!

There are only a few people today whom I can consult, that's why I came to you.

True, unfortunately true. We are not so many. What was her work like?

Dull. Yet as soon as she came into a room you knew she had a sense of style. She shone. She said nothing and she shone.

I've always maintained that style is the inheritance of a number of talents. A single talent, however great, does not yield a sense of style. Did I take one of my pills? I'm talking too much.

I didn't see you do so.

I wish I could place her for you. I'm afraid I can't. She's gone.

Nobody wore hats in those days, and she did! She wore a hat as if she was going to the races! Askew on the back of her head.

He said nothing. I let him think. And the silence continued. Hubert had always been prone to silences – as if life hung by a thread and foolish talking might snap it. In the silence I could feel that, since Gwen's death, the standards the two of them had established and maintained here had in no way changed. What this room *liked* was still the same.

Let's go upstairs, he finally said, and I'll show you St Paul's, a splendid view of St Paul's from the balcony of my bedroom.

We took the stairs slowly. He held himself very upright. On the first landing he stopped and said, this terrace was built in the 1840s and the houses were destined for clerks who worked in the City. Poor man's Georgian, as you can see. And it didn't work out. Within a generation they had all been turned into lodging houses, with one or a couple of tenants living on each floor. And so it remained for a hundred years. When we arrived, forty years ago, the houses on the other side of the street didn't even have electricity. Only gas and paraffin lamps.

The wall of the staircase was hung with sketches for textiles and framed samples of precious fabrics, some of them Persian looking.

Before we bought this house it was a brothel, serving the lorry drivers who delivered goods to London from the north. Come into the bathroom. See that mirror with the mermaids, the tenants left it in the bedroom downstairs and Gwen insisted upon keeping it. Sometimes I see Beatrice in it, Gwen would say laughing, and she waves at me! Beatrice was a whore and her name is scratched on one of the window panes in the drawing room.

As Hubert straightened the mirror on the bathroom wall, I caught a glimpse of his face in the glass and was reminded of him as a young man. Perhaps something to do with the glass being speckled and darkened so that the expression of his eyes was by contrast more sparkling.

When we moved in we had no money, so we told ourselves it might take as long to make a house as it takes to make a garden. We restored it room by room, there are seven, floor by floor, year by year.

On the top floor Hubert led me across his bedroom towards the French windows which gave on to a terrace.

Mind the geraniums! he said, I keep them out here to water them every morning.

They smell so strong!

Bloody cranesbill, he said, or in Latin: *Pelargonium cucullatum*.

I picked one of the leaves and sniffed it. It reminded me of her hair.

During the war ordinary soap was scarce, and there were no shampoos, unless you bought them on the black market. So newly washed hair smelt of itself. I remember her washing her hair in the morning after getting out of bed. It was summer and warm, and the windows were open. She washed it in an enamel hand basin which she filled with water from an enamel jug. There was no hot water in Colette's flat. Then she came back, with a towel wrapped round her head and nothing else on, lay down on the bed beside me and waited until her hair dried.

St Paul's, Hubert said, there's nothing else to match it! And built in record time, only thirty-five years! Work began nine years after the Great Fire of London in 1666, and it was finished in 1710. Christopher Wren was still around to see his masterpiece inaugurated.

He was reciting, almost word for word, what we had been obliged to learn by heart in the history of architecture class. We were also obliged to go and draw the cathedral. It had survived many air raids unscathed, and had become a great patriotic monument. Churchill was filmed speaking in front of it. And when I drew its architectural details, I added Spitfire fighters in the sky behind!

The first time it was neither she nor I who made a choice. I had come to visit Colette after an evening class. We ate some soup. The three of us talked and it grew late. There was an air-raid warning. We switched off the lights and opened a window to watch the searchlights raking the sky above the trees in Coram's Fields. The raiders didn't seem especially near.

Sleep here, Colette proposed, it's better than going out. We can all sleep in this bed, it's large enough for three.

Which is what we did. Colette slept against the wall, she in the middle, and I on the outside. We took off most of our clothes but not all.

When we woke up, Colette was making toast and pouring cups of tea, and she and I were entangled together, legs and arms interlaced. We were not surprised by this, for both of us were aware of something more surprising: during the night each of us had put to sleep the other's sex, not by satisfying it, or by denying it, but by following a different desire which even today is hard to name. No clinical descriptions fit it. Perhaps it could only have happened in London during the spring of 1943. We found in each other's arms a way of leaving together, a transport elsewhere. We arranged ourselves, fitted ourselves, joined ourselves together as if we were making a sleigh or a skateboard. (Only skateboards didn't yet exist.) Our destination wasn't important. Any departure was to an erogenous zone. What mattered was the distance we put behind us. We fed each other distance with every lick. Wherever our skins touched there was the promise of a horizon.

I stepped back into Hubert's bedroom, and noticed that it was different from the rest of the house. There was a double bed in the corner, but Gwen had never slept up here. I was sure of it. This room was provisional – as though during the last decade Hubert had been camping here. The walls were entirely covered with images of plants and flowers – unframed prints, drawings, photographs, pages torn from books – and they were placed so close together that they looked almost like a wallpaper. Many were attached by drawing pins, and they made me think that he was constantly rearranging them. Except for the slippers under the bed and the collection of medicines on the bedside table, it looked like a student's room.

He noticed my interest and he pointed to a drawing – perhaps one of his own: Strange flower, no? Like the breast of a tiny thrush in full song! It originally came from Brazil. In English it's known as birth wort. In Latin: *Aristolochia elegans*. Somewhere Lévi-Strauss says something about the Latin name of a plant. He says the Latin name personalizes it. Birth wort is merely a species. *Aristolochia elegans* is a person, singular and unique. If you had this flower in your garden and it happened to die, you could mourn for it with its Latin name. Which you wouldn't do, if you knew it as birth wort.

I was standing by the French windows. Shall I shut them? I asked.

Yes, do.

You always sleep with the windows shut?

Funny you should ask that, for recently it has been something of a problem. Before it was simple, and I left them open all night. Now, before I go to bed, I open them. The house is so narrow it tends to be stuffy as soon as all the windows are shut. The other night I thought of the clerks who once lived here when the house was new. Compared to us, they had very little space in their lives. Cramped offices, cramped horse buses, cramped streets, cramped rooms. Then, come the small hours, before it's light, I get out of bed again and I go and shut the windows, so that when the street wakes up in the morning it's quiet.

You sleep late?

I wake up early, very early. I think I shut the windows because I need a kind of protection at the beginning of each new day. For some time, I've needed calm in the morning so I can face it. Every day you have to decide to be invincible.

I understand.

I doubt it, John. I'm a solitary man. Come, I'll show you the garden.

I had never before seen a garden like this one. It was full of bushes, flowers, shrubs, each flourishing, yet planted so close together it was impossible for a stranger to imagine finding a way between them. A single path led down to the canal and it was so narrow one could only go down it walking sideways. Yet the density of the foliage was not like that of a jungle, but like the density of a closed book, which had to be read page by page. I spotted Michelmas daisies, winter jasmine, powder puff holly-hocks and, bordering the path, ribbon grass known as lady's laces, and a *Citronella* plant whose leaves, shaped like tongues, were growing in such a way and had placed themselves in such an arrangement that each was accommodated within the other's space. Each had found a position beside, or under, or over, or between, or around its neighbouring leaves which allowed them to receive some light, to bend with the wind, to probe in their natural direction. And the whole impenetrable garden was like this.

There was nothing here when we came, said Hubert, not even grass. It had been used for years as a dump for all the houses along the terrace. A dump behind the brothel. Old baths, a gas stove, smashed prams, rotten rabbit hutches. Try some of these grapes.

He stepped up to a vine growing against a brick wall which separated the garden from the neighbour's. Over each bunch of grapes he had placed a plastic bag to prevent the birds from eating them. He inserted his long hand inside one of these bags and, with his fingers, detached a few small white grapes, the colour of cloudy honey, and placed them on the palm of my hand.

The next time I went to Colette's flat in Guildford Place it was understood from the start that I would spend the night there. Colette slept on another bed in the second room. I took off all my clothes and she put on her loose embroidered night dress. We discovered the same thing as last time. Once put together, we could leave. We travelled from bone to bone, from continent to continent. Sometimes we spoke. Not sentences, not endearments. The names of parts and places. Tibia and Timbuktu, labia and Lapland, earhole and oasis. The names of the parts became pet names, the names of the places, passwords. We weren't dreaming. We simply became the Vasco da Gama of our two bodies. We paid the closest attention to each other's sleep, we never forgot one another. When she was deeply asleep her breathing was like surf. You took me to the bottom, she told me one morning.

We did not become lovers, we were scarcely friends, and we had little in common. I was not interested in horses, and she wasn't interested in the Freedom Press. When our ways crossed in the art school we had nothing to say to each other. This didn't worry us. We exchanged light kisses – on the shoulder or the back of the neck, never on the mouth – and we continued on our separate ways, like an elderly couple who happened to be working in the same school. As soon as it became dark, whenever we could, we met to do the same thing: to pass the whole night in each other's arms and, like this, to leave, to go elsewhere. Repeatedly.

Hubert was attaching an armful of stems with yellow flowers to a trellis with several lengths of raffia, his hands still trembling a little.

It's getting chilly, he said, let's go inside.

He shut and locked the door behind us.

This is my workroom – he nodded towards a large wooden bench with a chair in front of it – here this week I'm putting seeds from the garden into little packets, each one properly labelled with its common and Latin names. Occasionally I have to look the Latin one up in the Herbarium, my memory isn't what it was, though I'm happy to say I don't have to do it often.

What are these packets for? I asked.

I send them away. Every autumn I do the same. See these here. Love-in-a-mist. *Nigella damascena*. Two dozen packets.

You mean you sell them?

I give them away.

So many! You've got hundreds of packets!

There's an organization which calls itself Thrive, and they distribute seeds to people in need. Old people's homes, orphanages, reception centres, transit camps, so that there are flowers in such places where usually there aren't any. It doesn't make much difference of course, I realize that, but at least it's something. And for me, now, it's a way of sharing the pleasures of the garden. It's a satisfaction.

My recidivist erections were at first a distraction but once she had named them – we'll call them London! she said – they took their place and became no more urgent – or as urgent – as the damp fern smell of her sweat, her rounded knees, or the curly black hairs in her arsehole. Everything under the blankets took us elsewhere. And elsewhere, we discovered the size of life. In daylight life often seemed small. For example, when drawing plastercasts of Roman statues in the antique class, it seemed very small. Under the blankets she fingered the soles of my feet with her toes and sighed, 'Damascus'. I combed her hair with my teeth and hissed, 'scalp'. Then as these or other gestures of ours became longer and slower and we succumbed to a single sleep, our two bodies took account of the unimaginable distances they offered one another and we left. In the morning we said nothing. We couldn't make sentences. Either she would go and wash her hair, or I would go to the window at the foot of the bed and look out across Coram's Fields and she would throw me my trousers.

My real problem, said Hubert, is in the drawers over there.

He pulled out a metal drawer which slid noiselessly towards us. Double imperial size, designed for storing architectural plans. The drawer was full of small abstract sketches and watercolours which gave the impression they were derived from places. Perhaps microscopic places, perhaps galactic. Paths. Localities. Openings. Obstacles. All drawn with fluid washes and meandering lines. Hubert gave the drawer a soft push and it slid back on its rails. He pulled out another – there were a dozen such drawers – which, this time, contained drawings. Intricately drawn with a hard pencil, full of scudding movements, such as you see in clouds and running water.

What am I to do with them? he asked.

They are Gwen's?

He nodded.

If I leave them here, he said, they'll be thrown away after my death. If I make a selection and keep only what seem to me to be the very best, what do I do with the others? Burn them? Give them to an art school or a library? They are not interested. When she was alive, Gwen never had a name. She was simply passionate about drawing, about 'capturing it' as she put it. She drew almost every day. She herself threw a lot away. What's in these drawers is what she wanted to keep.

He pulled out a third drawer, hesitated, and then selected with his slightly trembling hand a gouache and held it up.

Beautiful, I said.

What am I to do? I keep on putting it off. And if I do nothing, they'll all be thrown out.

You must put them in envelopes, I said.

Envelopes?

Yes. You sort them. You invent any system you like. By year, by colour, by preference, by size, by – mood. And on each of the big envelopes you write her name and the category you've established. It'll take time. Not a single one must be misplaced. And in each envelope you place the drawings in order, you write a number very lightly on the back of each one.

An order according to what?

I don't know. You'll find out. There are drawings which look as if they should come first, and there's always a last drawing, isn't there? The order will take care of itself.

And what difference do you think these envelopes are going to make?

Who can tell? In any case they'll be better off.

You mean the drawings?

Yes. They'll be better off.

The clocks in the drawing room upstairs were chiming.

I must be off, I said.

He led me towards the front door. And after opening it, turning round, he looked at me quizzically.

Wasn't her name Audrey?

Audrey! Of course it was Audrey!

Funny little thing she was, said Hubert. She left, I think, after a couple of terms which is why I couldn't place her straight away. She wasn't with us for long. And she wore hats, you're right.

He smiled distantly, for he could see I was pleased. We said our goodbyes.

The nameless desire Audrey and I shared came to an end as inexplicably as it had begun: inexplicably only because neither of us sought an explanation. The last time we slept together (and although I forgot her name, I can remember without the slightest hesitation that it was the month of June and her feet were dusty from wearing sandals all day long) she got into bed first, and I climbed onto the window sill to detach the wooden frame of the blackout curtain, so that I could open the window and let in more air. Outside there was moonlight and all the trees around Coram's Fields were distinctly visible. I took in their every detail with a pleasure which included an anticipation because, in a minute or two, we would both, before setting out on the night's journey, be touching every detail of the other's body.

I slithered into bed beside her, and without a word she turned her back on me. There are a hundred ways of turning the back in bed. Most are inviting, some are languid. There is a way, though, which unmistakably announces refusal. Her shoulderblades became like armour plate.

I missed her too much to go to sleep, and she, I guessed, was pretending to sleep. I might have argued with her or started to kiss the back of her neck. Yet this was not our style. Bit by bit my perplexity slipped away and I felt thankful. I turned my own back and lay there cradling a gratitude for all that had happened in the bed with broken springs. At this moment a bomb fell. It was close by; we heard the windows shattering on the other side of the Fields, and, further away, shouts. Neither of us spoke. Her shoulder blades relaxed. Her hand looked for mine, and we both lay there grateful.

Next morning when I left she didn't so much as glance up from her coffee bowl. She was staring into it as if she had decided, a few minutes before, that this was what she must do and that the future of our two lives depended upon it.

Hubert stood there in the doorway, left arm raised about his head, making a sign for the mounted troops to disperse. His face was fragile and invincible. It was getting dark.

I'll take your tip about the envelopes, he called after me.

I walked alone down the road past the other terrace houses.

You used to call me many names in your sleep, Audrey said as she took my arm, and my favourite was Oslo.

Oslo! I repeated, as we turned into Upper Street. The way her head now rested on my shoulder told me she was dead.

You said it rhymed with first snow, she said.

Edwin Morgan

Gorgo and Beau

GORGO, a cancer cell
BEAU, a normal cell

GORGO: My old friend Beau, we meet again. How goes it?
Howzit gaun? *Wie geht's? Ça va? Eh?*

BEAU: Same old Gorgo, flashing your credentials.
Any time, any place, any tongue, any race, you are there.
It is bad enough doing what you do,
But to boast about it – why do I talk to you?

GORGO: You talk to me because you find it interesting.
I am different. I stimulate the brain matter,
Your mates are virtual clones.

BEAU: Oh rubbish –

GORGO: You know what I mean. Your paths are laid down.
Your functions are clear. Your moves are gentlemanly.
You even know when to die gracefully.
Nothing is more boring than a well made body.
Why should this be? That's what you don't know.
And that is why you want to talk to me.

BEAU: You will never get me to abhor
A body billions of us have laboured to build up
Into a fortress of interlocking harmonies.

GORGO: Oh what a high horse! I never said
'Abhorrent', I said 'boring', not the same.
Take a dinosaur. Go on, take a dinosaur,
Tons of muscle, rampant killing machine,

Lord of the savannahs, *roars*, roars
To make all tremble, but no, not anger,
Not hunger fuels the blast, but pain –
Look closer, watch that hirpling hip,
That billions of my ancestors have made cancerous,
Deliciously, maddeningly, eye-catchingly cancerous.
Not the end of the dinosaurs, I don't claim that,
But a tiny intimation of the end
Of power, function, movement, and the beauty
That you would say attends such things.
Dinosaurs on crutches, how about that?

BEAU: You think you can overturn pain with a cartoon?

GORGO: Pain, what is pain? I have never felt it,
Though I have watched our human hosts give signs –
A gasp, a groan, a scream – whatever it is,
They do not like it, and it must be our mission
To give them more, if we are to prevail.
But in any case what is so special about pain?
Your goody-goody human beings, your heroes
Plunge lobsters into boiling water – whoosh –
Skin living snakes in eastern restaurants –
Make flailing blood-baths for whales in the Faeroes –
What nonsense to think it a human prerogative,
That pain, whatever it is. Not that I myself
Or my many minions would refuse
To make a camel cancerous, or a crab
For that matter! First things first.
Our empire spreads, with or without pain.

BEAU: Shall I tell you something about suffering?
Imagine a male cancer ward; morning;
Curtains are swished back, urine bottles emptied,
Medications laid out. 'Another day, another dollar.'
A voice comes between farts. Then a dance:
Chemo man gathers up his jingling stand
Of tubes and chemicals, embraces it, jigs with it,
'Do you come here often?' unplug, plug in,

Unplug, plug in, bed to toilet and back,
Hoping to be safe again with unblocked drip.
Afternoon, chemo man hunched on bed
Vomiting into his cardboard bowl, and I mean
    vomiting,
Retching and retching until he feels in his exhaustion
His very insides are coming out. Well,
That's normal. Rest, get some sleep.
It's midnight now: out of the silent darkness
A woman's sobs and cries, so many sobs,
Such terrible cries, for her dying husband
She arrived too late, she held a cold hand.
The nurses stroked her, whispered to her,
Hugged her tight in their practised arms.
But they could not console her,
She was not to be consoled,
She was inconsolable.
The ward lay awake, listening, fearful, impotent,
Thinking of death, that death, their own death to
    come.
The sobbing ended; time for sleep, and nightmares.

GORGO: Well now that's very touching I'm sure,
But let me open up this discussion.
I was flying over Africa recently
To see how my cells were doing, and while you
Were mooning over the death of one sick man
Lying well cared for in a hospital bed,
I saw thousands, hundreds of thousands
Massacred or mutilated, hands cut off,
Noses, ears, and not a cancer cell in sight.
Oh you bleeding hearts are such hypocrites!

BEAU: Gorgo, you cannot multiply suffering in that way.
Each one of us is a world, and when its light goes out
It is right to mourn. And if the cause is known,
That you and your claws were scuttling through the
    flesh,
I call you to account. What are you up to?

Don't tell me you care about Africa.
Don't you want more wards, more weeping widows?

GORGO: I want to knock you out, you and your miserable
cohorts.
I want power. I am power-mad. No I'm not.
That's a figure of speech. I am not, repeat not
Mad, but calculating and manipulative.
I am not at the mercy of blind forces.
You may think I am, but it is not so.
Consider: a tidy clump of my cells,
A millimetre long, a stupid mini-tumour,
Is stuck because it cannot reach its food.
It's lazy, dormant, useless and I can't stand
Uselessness. I help it to take thought.
It must expand. It can't expand.
It suddenly – and I mean suddenly –
Finds itself synthesizing proteins
That generate blood vessels, capillaries,
Tiny but broad enough for a breakthrough
Into nutrients, into voyages,
Into invasion and all that that implies.
Our human hosts are baffled: a thinking tumour?
Well, would you prefer an effect without a cause?

BEAU: You could say something about this, I'm sure.

GORGO: Could, but won't. There's a war on, you know.

BEAU: Justify your armies, justify your battles.

GORGO: Did you not hear what I said about power?
Are your ears clean, or you keep them half closed
Against infection from a satanic tempter?
You may not even think I am a tempter,
But I am the insidious one, hissing, 'Listen, listen.'
Every tumour begins with a single cell
Which divides and divides and is its own boss.
It laughs to feel its freedom, to hell with blueprints,
It shoulders and jostles its way in the organ-jungle.

Even on a glass in the lab it's huddling and layering
Like caviar, and does caviar have to justify
Its juicy rolling formless proliferations?
The joy of kicking decent cells away,
Sucking their precious nutrients, piercing
Membranes that try to keep you from the waves
Of lymph and blood you long to navigate –
Through unimaginable dangers, be robust! –
Until you reach those Islands of the Blest –
I hear you snort, Beau, don't explode! –
The distant organs where you plant your flag
and start a colony. Those cells are heroes,
Homer would hymn them, but I do my best!

BEAU: Heroes! If anything so small can be a monster,
           That's what you and your mates are. You sound
               like—

GORGO: Forgive the interruption. I have a few words
           on monsters to give you later. Carry on –

BEAU: – Sound like Jenghiz Khan at the fall of Baghdad –

GORGO: – At least he got into the history books –

BEAU: Will you let me *speak*.

GORGO: All right, all right.
           But I know what you are going to say.

BEAU: You do not, but even if you did
           It would be worth saying. Imagine the baby
           Still in the womb, the image screened by ultrasound
           Flickering and shifting, not sharp but unmistakably
           Alive, the soft hand at the mouth, the dome
           Above it, that forehead of a million secrets
           Waiting to be born, everything vulnerable
           To the last degree, but with the strength
           That attends vulnerability in its beginnings.
           It grows, it emerges, it grows, not a single
           Bad gene in its body (your turn to snort,

All right Gorgo, but listen, listen now).

GORGO: (*sings*) The oncogene, the oncogene, it squats in the
        DNA
        As proud and mim as a puddock, and will not go
        away.
        Sorry, Beau. Continue.

BEAU: As I was saying, imagine his growth,
        He is strong, well formed, not brilliant but bright,
        Explores the sea-bed, writes a book, has children,
        Tells them stories sitting on the terrace.
        Vibrations of health and harmony
        Are like a talisman he gives back to nature.
        His cells are in order, dying when they should.
        He measures power by love, given and taken.
        Your power does not tempt him.

GORGO: So Pollyanna
        Put on her skis, and was never seen again.
        It is a nice picture but you made it all up.
        If there are such people, I must see what I can do
        To infiltrate, subvert, and overthrow them.
        Health and harmony? What a yawn.
        I promised you a word on monsters.
        I was helping one day to tie a knot
        In a long tumour which had got itself twisted
        (Deliberately, I'm sure) like a Möbius strip
        In a body cavity of a pleasant young women:
        She was flapping and shrieking on the hospital bed
        In what I imagine was very great pain.
        Doctors brought students, teratologists were tingling.
        There was a sharp ferocity in the air
        That put all thoughts of the ordinary to flight.
        – A microscope will show you a different monster:
        A nucleus too gigantic for the cell,
        Ragged, pulsing, encroaching, a bloodshot eye
        Staring at a wreckage of filaments and blobs,
        Bursting with DNA, breaking apart

In a maelstrom of wild distorted chromosomes –
That was a sight to make you think, friend Beau!

BEAU: I am thinking, of how these observations
Have twisted your mind like the tumour you
    described.
It is death to want to make the abnormal normal.
Suppose you and your assiduous myrmidons
Had made a body into one whole tumour,
Pulsating on a slab like a Damien Hirst exhibit,
A gross post-human slug, a thing of wonder.
What then? It dies, it is not immortal.
Preserve it? Mummies tell the future
How terrible the past was. Your goal and god
Is death, and that is why I oppose you.

GORGO: And how will you get rid of me,
If it is not too delicate a question?

BEAU: There's always regular hormone injections –

GORGO: – make you fat and sexless –

BEAU: A pin-point zap with radiotherapy –

GORGO: – leaves you tired and listless –

BEAU: The swirl and drip of chemotherapy –

GORGO: – you're sick as a dog and your hair falls out –

BEAU: How about nano-bullets of silica
Plated with gold and heated with infra-red light –

GORGO: – oh please –

BEAU: Plants offer extracts; they get cancer too,
So they should know what they are talking about.
(sings) Sow periwinkle and the mistletoe,
For these are fields where cancer cannot grow.

GORGO: – you've got a point there –

BEAU: Of course we are living now in a New Age –

GORGO: – this should be hilarious –

BEAU: Since mind and body can scarcely be separated,
We shall not cease from mental fight etcetera.
I can see my cells as nimble stylish knights
While yours are clumsy dragons on the prowl.
I can see my tumour as an old bunch of grapes
From which I pick one rotten fruit per day
Until the bad cells have all got the message
And shrivel into invisibility.
Some take it further; if there are good vibrations
There must also be bad. How come you got the cancer
And not Mr Robinson down the road?
You must have self-suppressions, inhibitions,
Guilts black or bleak or blistering, promises unkept,
Hatreds unspoken, festering coils
With their fangs and toxins destabilizing
Cells that are as open to emotion as to disease.
If you want to dip further into the cesspit of causes,
Remember those who believe in reincarnation.
You send a poison-pen letter in one life
And in the next it's returned with a sarcoma –
Consequences are not to be escaped!
What think you of all this, friend Gorgo?

GORGO: I think it is nonsense and I don't believe it.
Mind you, if it was true, I've no complaint
When disillusioned visualizers
Still sick, or more sick, go suicidal.

BEAU: I don't believe it either, but I'm loath
To brush any possibility aside.
In Celtic tradition, poets had the power
(It is said) to rhyme an enemy to death.
He was attacked in ruthless public verse,
And through suggestion and fear did actually
Fall ill and die. Cases are recorded.

GORGO: I must watch what I say.

BEAU: You take it lightly, but there are mysteries –

GORGO: Of course there are mysteries. I give you leave,
          Indeed I encourage it, to examine everything,
          Fact, rumour, faith, fantasy, cutting edges
          Of science (pretty blunt cut so far),
          Cutting edges of imagination (look: a tumour
              transplant!).
          I am so confident; *we* are so confidcnt (and remember
          Black sheep are natural) that we challenge you
          To ever catch up as we race ahead.
          I said there was a war on and so there is,
          But let me recommend William Blake to you:
          'Without contraries is no progression.'
          Where would medical science be without us?

BEAU: So pain, suffering, fear, death, bereavement
          Are grist to the mill of the universe,
          And the devotees of progress cry with joy
          As juggernaut crushes them in its murderous wheels
          Down to the sea?

GORGO: Is it monsters again?
          You are overheated. Think calmly. Thank me
          For opening many secrets of the body.
          Thank me for forcing your thought into channels
          Of what is at once minute and vast speculation,
          Our place, your place, in the scheme of things,
          Should there be a scheme of things, which I doubt!
          My hordes, my billions, my workers
          Have added imperfection to any design
          You might impute to some beneficence –
          Beneficence without maleficence, no go! –
          You'll find us in the elephant, the cricket,
          The flatworm, the pine-tree, not stones yet
          But who knows? Medieval spheres
          Gliding on crystal gimbals could not last.
          The rough inimical perilous world is better.
          We rule; you rule; back and forward it goes.

Your hosts, your victims, have their obituaries
Closed in the figure of a hard-fought fight.
I leave you with the thought that we too,
We wicked ones, we errant cells
Have held our battleground for millions of years,
Uncounted millions of years.

BEAU: The past is not the future. We are ready
To give you the hardest of hard times.
My host is walking gently in the sun.
Will you grit your teeth and think of her?
We shall surely speak again. *Arrivederci.*

*[This poem was commissioned by BBC Scotland (Radio)
and was first broadcast on 29 December 2003.]*

Biographical Notes

Kate Atkinson was born in York and now lives in Edinburgh. Her first novel, *Behind the Scenes at the Museum*, won the Whitbread Book of the Year in 1995. She is the author of two other critically acclaimed novels, *Human Croquet* and *Emotionally Weird* and a collection of short stories, *Not the End of the World*. Her new novel, *Case Histories*, was published in September 2004.

Paul Bailey was a Literary Fellow at the Universities of Newcastle and Durham, and a recipient of the E. M. Forster Award. In 1973 a bicentennial fellowship took him to the mid-west of America. In 1978 he won a George Orwell Memorial prize for his essay 'The Limitations of Despair', published in the *Listener*. He reviews for the *Guardian* and the *TLS* and his journalism is widely published. His books have received critical acclaim. *At the Jerusalem* won the Somerset Maugham Award and an Arts Council Award for the best novel published between 1963 and 1967. His other books include *A Distant Likeness*, *Peter Smart's Confessions* (shortlisted for the Booker Prize), *Old Soldiers*, *Trespasses*, *Gabriel's Lament* (shortlisted for the 1986 Booker Prize), *Sugar Cane*, *Kitty and Virgil*, *An Immaculate Mistake*, *Three Queer Lives* and *Uncle Rudolf*. His latest book, *A Dog's Life*, was published by Hamish Hamilton in July 2003.

Nicola Barker's work includes *Love Your Enemies* (David Higham Prize for Fiction, joint winner of the Macmillan Silver Pen Award for Fiction), *Reversed Forecast*, *Small Holdings*, *Heading Inland* (1997 John Llewellyn Rhys/*Mail on Sunday* Prize), *Five Miles from Outer Hope*, *Wide Open*, translated into thirteen languages and winner of the 2000 International IMPAC Dublin Literary Award, and *Behindlings*. *Clear* was published by Fourth Estate in September 2004 and she is at work on a new novel, *Darkmans*.

She was recently named as one of the twenty Best of Young British Novelists by *Granta* magazine.

John Berger was born in London. His many books include the Booker-winning novel *G*, the novel *King* and the collection of essays *The Shape of a Pocket*. He now lives and works in a small village in the French Alps.

John Burnside has published eight books of poetry, including *Feast Days*, winner of the Geoffrey Faber Prize and *The Asylum Dance*, which won the Whitbread Poetry Prize. His prose work includes four novels and a collection of stories. He lives on the east coast of Scotland with his wife and son.

Ciaran Carson was born in 1948 in Belfast, where he lives. He has published eleven volumes of poetry and four of prose. He has won numerous awards, most recently the Oxford Weidenfeld Translation Prize for his translation of Dante's *Inferno*, and the 2003 Forward Prize for *Breaking News*.

Louise Doughty is the author of four novels. Her most recent, *Fires in the Dark*, is about two generations of a Romany family in Central Europe during the Second World War. It has been published to widespread critical acclaim in the UK and America and is the first in a series of novels based on the history of the Romany people and her own family ancestry. She also writes radio plays and cultural journalism.

Ian Duhig has written four books of poetry, most recently *The Lammas Hireling* (Picador 2003) which was a Poetry Book Society Choice and shortlisted for the T.S. Eliot and Forward Best Collection Prizes. He has won a Cholmondeley Award, the Forward Tolman Cunard Best Poem Prize once and the British Poetry Society's National Poetry Competition twice.

Paul Ewen was born in New Zealand in 1972. In 1995, he moved to Asia where he lived and worked for six years, including four years in Saigon. Now residing in Tufnell Park, he is currently writing his first book, which is a handy guide to London pubs.

Frances Gapper was born in Manchester and now lives in the north Pennines. Her story collection *Absent Kisses* (2002) is published by Diva Books.

Ismail B. Garba lives in Kano, Nigeria where he teaches English at Bayero University. His poems have been published in *Ariel*, *Ambit*, *Aura*, *Blink* and *Okike*; as well as in several anthologies, newspapers and magazines.

Niall Griffiths, born in Liverpool in 1966, now lives in Wales. He is the author of five novels, including, most recently, *Wreckage*. He has read his work in various countries and has been translated into several languages.

Vicky Grut's short fiction has appeared in magazines and anthologies since 1994. Credits include: *Valentine's Day: Stories of Revenge* (Duckworth, 2000), *Reshape Whilst Damp* (Serpent's Tail, 2000) and *Resist* (Pulp.net, 2004). In 1999 she was a winner of both the Asham and Ian St James awards for short stories. She is currently completing a novel.

Romesh Gunesekera, born in Sri Lanka, now lives in London. He is the author of three novels, *Heaven's Edge* (a *New York Times* Notable Book 2003), *The Sandglass* (BBC Asia Award), *Reef* (shortlisted for the Booker Prize) and a collection of stories, *Monkfish Moon*. More at *www.romeshgunesekera.com* website.

Jen Hadfield's first collection, *Almanacs*, is out with Bloodaxe now. She is currently writing and reading poetry in Canada, thanks to an Eric Gregory Award.

Steven Hall was born in Derbyshire in 1975. He is currently completing his first novel.

Ramona Herdman was born in 1978. She has a BA and MA in creative writing from the University of East Anglia. Her work has been published in various poetry magazines, and performed at events including the Aldeburgh festival and cambridgewordfest. Her first collection, *Come What You Wished For*, was published by Egg Box Publishing in 2003.

Peter Hobbs was born in 1973, and grew up in Cornwall and

North Yorkshire. His first novel, *The Short Day Dying*, is published by Faber and Faber.

James Hopkin has lived in Krakow, Berlin, Manchester and several other cities and countrysides in Europe. This story won the inaugural Norwich Prize for Literature (chairwoman: Rose Tremain). He likes horses. His first novel (for Picador) is out soon.

A. S. Irvine was born in Scotland and lives in London.

Tim Jarvis is twenty-six and currently lives and works in London. He is writing a book that consists of interconnected short narratives linked by a framing device describing the travels of an anthropologist through the North America of an alternate history. The provisional title of this novel is 'Apocrypha'.

Jackie Kay's most recent book is called *Why Don't You Stop Talking?* (Picador). She lives in Manchester with her son.

Daren King was born in Harlow, Essex, and educated in Bath. His debut novel, *Boxy an Star*, was shortlisted for the *Guardian* First Book Award. A prequel, *Tom Boler*, will be published by Jonathan Cape early in 2005. His second novel, *Jim Giraffe*, received rave reviews.

Azmeena Ladha was born and grew up in Mombasa, Kenya. She graduated in Graphic Design from the former Manchester College of Art and worked in publishing and for a trade union before qualifying to teach in adult education. Her short stories have won various awards; she has been shortlisted for the V. S. Pritchett Memorial Prize and broadcast on BBC Radio 4. She lives with her family on the outskirts of London and is completing a novel as well as a short-story collection.

Nick Laird was born in Dungannon, Co. Tyrone in 1975. He attended Cookstown High School and Cambridge University, where he received the Quiller-Couch Award for creative writing, before working for many years as a commercial litigator in London. He has lived in Warsaw and Boston, where he was a visiting fellow at Harvard University, and now lives in Kilburn, north-west London, where he writes full-time. His poetry collection, *To A Fault*, was published by Faber & Faber in January 2005 and a novel, *Utterly Monkey*, will be published by Fourth Estate in May 2005.

The extract in this book is from **John Logan**'s third novel. A large extract from his second novel was published in *Edinburgh Review* in 2004. Eleven chapters from his first novel, *Bringing Something Back*, were published in *New Writing 9*, *Edinburgh Review*, *Northwords*, *Chapman*, *Nomad* and *Secrets of a View*. His first novel is published by iUniverse and available to order from bookshops and Internet booksellers. All three novels need the faith of a publisher or literary agent.

David Mitchell's first novel, *Ghostwritten*, was published in 1999 and was awarded the John Llewellyn Rhys Prize and shortlisted for the *Guardian* First Book Prize. His second novel, *Number9dream*, followed in 2001 and was shortlisted for the Booker Prize and the James Tait Black Memorial Prize. *Cloud Atlas* was published in 2004 and was also shortlisted for the Booker Prize. After living for eight years in Japan he is now resident in Ireland.

Edwin Morgan born Glasgow 1920. War service with Royal Army Medical Corps 1940–1946. Taught English at Glasgow University until retirement as Titular Professor in 1980. Awarded Queen's Gold Medal for Poetry 2000. Appointed Scottish Poet Laureate 2004. Books include *Collected Poems* (1990), *Cyrano de Bergerac* (1992), *Collected Translations* (1996), *New Selected Poems* (2000), *Cathures* (2002), *Love and a Life* (2003).

Lawrence Norfolk is the author of three novels: *Lemprière's Dictionary* (1991), *The Pope's Rhinoceros* (1996) and *In the Shape of a Boar* (2001) which have together been translated into thirty-four languages. He is the winner of the Somerset Maugham Award and the Budapest Festival Prize for Literature and his work has been shortlisted for the Impac Prize, the James Tait Black Memorial Award and the Wingate/*Jewish Quarterly* Prize for Literature. In 1992 he was listed as one of *Granta* magazine's twenty Best of Young British Writers. He is currently working on a new novel, *The Levels*, about the effect of gravity on human relationships. He lives in London with his wife and two sons.

Maggie O'Farrell was born in Northern Ireland, and grew up in Wales and Scotland. She has worked as a waitress, chambermaid, cycle courier, teacher, arts administrator and journalist. She is the author of three novels, *After You'd Gone*, *My Lover's Lover* and *The Distance Between Us*.

Martin Ouvry was born and lives in west London. After working as a musician in Europe and America, he gained a First in English at the University of East Anglia, took the MA course in creative writing, and was awarded the UEA Alumni Association Prize for Fiction. He teaches at UEA and is at work on a novel with the assistance of a grant from the Arts Council.

Donald Paterson was born in Motherwell, brought up in Tain, in the Highlands of Scotland, and now lives and works in Moray. His short stories and poems have appeared in various publications and he is currently working on a novel.

As a short story writer, **Tony Peake** has contributed to four volumes of *Winter's Tales*, *The Penguin Book of Contemporary South African Short Stories*, *The Mammoth Book of Gay Short Stories* and *Seduction*, a themed anthology which he also edited. He is the author of two novels, *A Summer Tide* (1993) and *Son to the Father* (1995), and the biography *Derek Jarman* (1999).

Emily Perkins was born in New Zealand in 1970. Her books are *Not Her Real Name and Other Stories*, and the novels *Leave Before You Go* and *The New Girl*. She lives in London with her family.

Nicholas Pierpan was recently awarded a PhD in English language and literature from Oxford University. His poetry has been published in the *May Anthologies* and he is a two-time winner of the Cameron Mackintosh Award for New Writing in Drama. He now lives and works in London.

Tom Pow teaches at Glasgow University Crichton Campus in Dumfries, on the site of the famous nineteenth-century lunatic asylum. This poem is one from a collection in progress of 'narratives of madness'. His most recent books are the poetry collection, *Landscapes and Legacies* (iynx publishing) which won a Scottish Arts Council Book Award and was shortlisted for the SAC Scottish Book of the Year, and the young adult novel, *The Pack* (Random House). From 2001 to 2003, he was Writer in Residence at Edinburgh International Book Festival.

Monique Roffey was born in Port of Spain, Trinidad in 1965. She worked as a journalist and human rights activist for Amnesty International before she wrote her first novel, *Sun Dog* (Scribner 2002). She is now a centre director for the Arvon Foundation and co-runs Totleigh Barton, their centre in Devon, with her partner, author Ian Marchant. She is currently working on her second novel.

Shyam Selvadurai was born in Colombo Sri Lanka. *Funny Boy*, his first novel, won the W.H. Smith/Books in Canada First Novel Award and in the US the Lambda Literary Award and was named a Notable Book by the American Library Association. His second novel *Cinnamon Gardens* was shortlisted for the Canada's Trillium Award, as well as the Aloa Literary Award in Denmark and the Premio Internazionale Riccardo Bacchelli in Italy.

Kamila Shamsie is the author of *In the City by the Sea*, *Salt and Saffron* and *Kartography* (all published by Bloomsbury). She has twice been shortlisted for the John Llewellyn Rhys/*Mail on Sunday* Award and has received the Prime Minister's Award for Literature in Pakistan. She lives in London and Karachi.

Heloise Shepherd, born in 1986, is intensely passionate about writing, books, theatre and film. She was involved in the Cumbrian 'Six-Pack' project for young writers in 2003, but this is her first national publication. She took up her place to study English at Fitzwilliam College, Cambridge in October 2004.

Helen Simpson's first collection of short stories, *Four Bare Legs in a Bed* (1990) won the *Sunday Times* Young Writer of the Year Award and a Somerset Maugham Award. Her suspense novella *Flesh and Grass* was also published in 1990. She was chosen as one of *Granta* magazine's twenty Best of Young British Novelists in 1993. Her second collection of stories, *Dear George*, appeared in 1995, and her third collection *Hey Yeah Right Get a Life* (winner of the Hawthornden Prize) in 2000. The American Academy of Arts and Letters gave her the E. M. Forster award in 2002. She wrote the libretto for the jazz opera, *Good Friday, 1663*, screened on Channel 4 television, and the lyrics for Kate and Mike Westbrook's jazz suite *Bar Utopia*. Helen Simpson is a Fellow of the Royal Society of Literature. She lives in London.

Muriel Spark's many novels include *The Girls of Slender Means, A Far Cry From Kensington, The Prime of Miss Jean Brodie*, and *The Finishing School*. She was elected C Litt in 1992 and awarded the DBE in 1993. Dame Muriel has received many awards, including the James Tait Black Memorial Prize, the FNAC Prix Etranger, and the Ingersoll T S Eliot Award.

Neil Stewart was born in 1978. He is working on a novel, *The Library in the Body*.

Matt Thorne was born in Bristol in 1974 and is the author of six novels, *Tourist* (1998), *Eight Minutes Idle* (winner of an Encore Award, 1999), *Dreaming of Strangers* (2000), *Pictures of You* (2001), *Child Star* (2003) and *Cherry* (2004). He also co-edited the anthology *All Hail the New Puritans* (2000).

Fay Weldon is one of Britain's leading writers of fiction, for book, stage and screen. Her work is translated into most languages, and her interest and muse the lot of women in contemporary society, as its terms of reference twist and shift. This story evolved from an anecdote told to her by a friend.

Gerard Woodward lives in Somerset and teaches at Bath Spa University College. His second novel, *I'll Go To Bed at Noon*, was shortlisted for the 2004 Booker Prize and, later this year, Chatto will publish his new collection of poetry, *We Were Pedestrians*.

Copyright information